The critics on Erica James

'There is humour and warmth in this engaging story of love's triumphs and disappointments, with two well-realised and intriguing subplots' *Woman & Home*

'Joanna Trollope fans, dismayed by the high gloom factor and complete absence of Agas in her latest books, will turn with relief to James' . . . delightful novel about English village life . . . a blend of emotion and wry social observation'
Daily Mail

'Scandal, fury, accusations and revenge are all included in Erica James' compelling novel . . . this story of village life in Cheshire is told with wit and humour' *Stirling Observer*

'An entertaining read with some wickedly well-painted cameo characters. It's a perfect read if you're in the mood for romance' *Prima*

'A bubbling, delightful comedy which is laced with a bitter-sweet tang . . . a good story, always well observed, and full of wit' *Publishing News*

'This is a really sparkling novel, full of drama and laughter'
Bookcase

'This book draws you into the lives of these characters, and often wants to make you scream at them to try and make them see reason. Funny, sad and frustrating, but an excellent, compulsive read' *Woman's Realm*

'Erica James' sensitive story . . . is as sparklingly fresh as dew on the village's surrounding meadows . . . thoroughly enjoyable and fully deserving of a place in the crowded market of women's fiction' *Sunday Express*

'Wry humour and romance . . . Erica James is a breath of fresh air' *Daily Mail*

Born in 1960, Erica James grew up in Hampshire. Since then she has lived in Oxford, Cheshire, Yorkshire and Belgium. After a series of diverse administrative jobs, during which she worked in an Oxford college and for a supplier of mining explosives, Erica decided that the best employer would be herself. There then followed several burning-the-midnight-oil years of cottage industry before she turned to the even harder life of toiling at the fictional coal-face of novel writing. She now lives in Cheshire with her two sons, Edward and Samuel. Her short stories have won prizes in various competitions and her first novel, *A Breath of Fresh Air*, was selected for the W. H. Smith's Fresh Talent promotion. She has been short-listed three times for the Parker Romantic Novel of the Year Award, for *Airs & Graces*, *Act of Faith* and *Precious Time*.

By Erica James

A Breath of Fresh Air
Time for a Change
Airs & Graces
A Sense of Belonging
Act of Faith
The Holiday
Precious Time
Hidden Talents

A Breath of Fresh Air
Time for a Change

ERICA JAMES
Two Great Novels

ORION

An Orion paperback

A Breath of Fresh Air
First published in Great Britain in 1996 by Orion
First published in Phoenix paperback in 1996

Time for a Change
First published in Great Britain in 1997 by Orion
First published in Orion paperback in 1997

This paperback edition published in 2003
by Orion Books Ltd,
Orion House, 5 Upper St Martin's Lane,
London WC2H 9EA

ISBN 0 75284 248 X

Printed and bound in Great Britain by
Clays Ltd, St Ives plc

A Breath of Fresh Air

*To Edward and Samuel who handled their
mother's tantrums with such patience.
Thanks to Big G. and all my friends who helped
and bullied me through the darkness,
especially Helena, Maureen and Rosemary.*

'Man cannot discover new oceans until he has courage to lose sight of the shore.'

Unknown

I

Charlotte had never seen a man cry before, so she wasn't sure how to react to her husband's unexpected display of emotion. Not once had she ever imagined Peter capable of crying; it went against all she had ever known about him.

At a quarter to eight in the morning and while tapping open her boiled egg in their Brussels apartment, Charlotte Lawrence had finally plucked up the courage to ask her husband for a divorce and to put an end, once and for all, to his assumption that because he was fulfilled, so was she. She had told him that life under the corporate umbrella was not sufficient to satisfy both their needs. And then he had cried.

Charlotte passed him the box of tissues and tried to assimilate her own feelings. To her surprise, she felt indifference towards Peter, tinged with a hint of embarrassment. True, a man of the nineteen nineties was allowed to cry – men were now allowed the full gamut of emotions, it was no holds barred, cards on the kitchen table; like women, men had emotions, too. But when it was in their kitchen and over their table, it felt all wrong.

'I'm sorry,' she said, knowing how hollow and inadequate her words sounded. She watched Peter scour his eyes with a tissue, then blow his nose. She looked away, down on to the street below, and wished, as she did every morning she looked out of the window, that she was back in England.

She knew it was pathetic, but she couldn't help it. She was homesick. Oh yes, she'd been given lots of helpful advice, mostly from Peter's father. 'I was a prisoner of war for two and half years and managed to enjoy myself, don't see why you can't just knuckle down to it, girl.' Then of course there was his old favourite: 'Stop feeling so sorry for yourself.'

And in simple justification of their nomadic lifestyle, that in eight years of marriage had taken them from London to Singapore, back to London and then on to Brussels, Peter would say, 'Other wives are happy here.'

'But I'm not other wives!' she would say in desperate retaliation, knowing that Peter had no comprehension of her basic need for the simple things in life: stability, security and a suburban high street of familiar chain stores, not the sophisticated expatriate regime of uncertainty, cocktail parties, language classes and flower arranging.

In a moment of cynicism and real rock-bottom boredom, she too had joined the ranks of the flower arrangers, and then Peter had tried getting her pregnant, believing this to be the answer. But this was one area in Peter's life where he had to admit failure. A genius in the mergers and acquisitions department he was, but with a low sperm count there was little he could do in the baby-making department.

Looking out of the window, Charlotte watched the softly falling snow. She felt as though they were characters acting out their parts in a well-rehearsed performance; a scene which she had produced and directed in her own mind for nearly a year now – except Peter was ad-libbing, he wasn't supposed to cry.

'Why?' he said, bringing her back to the script.

She turned round. 'Because I don't like what you're doing to me.'

He sniffed loudly and she could see he was willing his body to act according to the rules of his straitjacketed upbringing – boys didn't blub at boarding school. 'This is absurd,' he said, at last, and in a firm loud voice that had the effect of disciplining those dark, unexplored territories of his inner self. He picked up his briefcase, once more in control. 'I'll be back late. I'm in Luxembourg all day.'

'But the snow, it's far too dangerous, you can't possibly go all that way . . . and anyway, we need to talk.'

'There's nothing to discuss. The answer is no.'

Lying back in the bath, Charlotte waited for the warmth of the water to ease away the strain of not just the past hour, but the past eight years. It took only a few moments before she realised that she wasn't in need of a soothing balm. She was all right. After nearly a year of waiting for this point in her life, she was actually all right. The truth of her feelings hit her quite forcibly and she let out a sudden laugh. It echoed horribly in the bathroom with its high tiled ceiling. She chewed her lip guiltily.

But what next?

And now the second act in her well-rehearsed perform-ance ran through her mind. This was when she stopped dancing attendance to someone else's tune, this was when she whistled the melody of her own life.

She would go back to England, to Hulme Welford, and move in with her parents until she got herself sorted; it would be hell living with her mother again, but Dad would be sweet.

And work. What about work?

Before she had been moulded into a corporate wife she had run her own business: an upmarket sweater shop. But then Peter had come home one evening with that silly grin on his face and told her his boss had asked him 'to consider Singapore'. Within three months the shop had gone, along with her identity, and she had found herself living a twelve-hour flight away from all that was comforting and familiar.

She knew it would be hard starting over again, finding work was never easy. Wherever they had lived she had tried to find her own niche – even if it had always been taken away from her. After seven months of trying to find work in Singapore, she had eventually managed to get a job within the personnel department of an international chemical company, then when Peter's contract had come to an end they had moved back to London. She had just found herself work there, when Peter announced they were going to Brussels. For the first six months she struggled to learn some basic French and was then offered a temporary part-time job working as a volunteer for a helpline service for the English-speaking community. When this had come to an end though, there had been no more work available, not until she had met Christina.

At half past eleven, Charlotte decided to call round to see her neighbour, Christina. She wanted to share this moment with someone – wanted somebody to tell her how brave she was, that leaving her husband was the right thing to do.

Christina Castelli had moved into the apartment next door and had become Charlotte's only real friend.

'A high-class tart!' Peter had announced, calling in for his clean shirts *en route* for the airport, just as the last of Christina's expensive-looking furniture had been brought up to the sixth floor. 'Perfectly obvious what she is,' he had gone on to say. 'The lift stinks of erotic perfume.'

Charlotte had questioned him on this point; how did he know what erotic perfume smelt like? He had fumbled for an answer and then reaching for his suit-carrier had simply said, 'Be back day after tomorrow, any duty free you want?'

'Yes,' she had told him, 'some erotic perfume would be nice.'

He hadn't laughed, but then he'd forgotten how. His life had become too serious; too full of live or die mergers and acquisitions. He was constantly living on his ability to judge whether a thing was a profit or a loss; it was either black or it was white to Peter. The only grey area in his life was her.

Within a few days of Christina moving in, Charlotte had been forced to admit that Peter may have been right. The *femme fatale* fragrance in the downstairs hall, lift and sixth floor landing seemed now to be accompanied by a steady

4

stream of German eau-de-Cologne. Charlotte never actually saw her neighbour's callers, apart from one man, who by accident got the wrong apartment, and when Charlotte tried to point him in the right direction he shot back into the lift, his face hidden behind a copy of *Le Soir*.

One morning Christina knocked on Charlotte's door and invited her in for a drink.

'You must call me Christina,' she told Charlotte in perfect English, beckoning her towards a cream leather sofa, that had more than a hint of Milan to it. 'We have no need to be formal, for I do not think we shall be conducting any business between ourselves. And I may call you . . .?'

'Charlotte, very plain I'm afraid;' Charlotte said, feeling incredibly plain as she sat next to this catwalk beauty.

Christina laughed, a light tinkling laugh, that Charlotte knew would have the ability to whip the boxer shorts off any man in seconds. 'In that case I shall call you Carlotta — that is your name in Rome, where I come from.'

Charlotte never told Peter about her visits next door, not even when Christina came up with a job for her.

'Carlotta, you and I are alike in many ways,' Christina said one day. 'We both need to be kept busy and I know that behind that beautiful smile of yours you are perfectly miserable, so I have found you work, just two mornings a week for a friend of mine.'

Charlotte looked doubtfully at her. 'What kind of work?'

Christina laughed. 'Do not worry, Carlotta, I am not about to turn you into a . . . now what was the expression I heard Mr Carlotta use, the day I moved in . . . ah yes, a high-class tart. No, I would not suggest such a thing.'

Charlotte's cheeks flushed. 'How did you hear that?'

Christina shrugged her silk-clad shoulders. 'It was a warm day, every window in Brussels was open. Mr Carlotta's voice carried well that afternoon.'

In Christina's company, Peter was never referred to as Peter, instead he had simply become the anonymous Mr

5

Carlotta. Christina had told Charlotte on their first meeting that she never wanted to meet or even know the name of Charlotte's husband. 'After all,' she had said, her full lips turned gently upwards in the most seductive of smiles, 'it might be awkward for us both if it turned out that I already knew your husband.'

'No, Carlotta, you are not to work as a high-class tart, but as a receptionist. There now, I think that would suit you so much more, don't you?'

'But I can't speak French very well, never mind Flemish,' Charlotte said hopelessly, and then added, 'I have tried, I just don't seem to be very good at it.'

'Then I will teach you, I am a good teacher.'

Charlotte suddenly smiled.

'Such a beautiful smile you have, Carlotta, but I am wondering why you are smiling. What is it you think I am good at teaching?'

Looking at the reflection of herself in the hall mirror, Charlotte smiled at the memory of that conversation. She would miss her friendship with Christina when she moved back to England; it would be the only thing from Brussels that she would miss. Just as she was about to pick up her keys and go and see Christina, the door bell rang.

She pulled the door open and saw two Belgian policemen standing in front of her. They started speaking in French and even with her limited knowledge of the language, she was able to understand what they were saying.

Monsieur Peter Lawrence was dead.

Shrilling with all the urgency of a telephone, a child's voice invaded the quiet, Edwardian sitting-room of The Gables in Hulme Welford.

'MUMMY!'

Charlotte's younger sister Hilary, who was quite used to her daughter's demanding cry, carried on pouring out cups of tea. Similarly, the Reverend Malcolm Jackson, a robust forty-five-year-old Meatloaf fan and father of three, barely flinched, but not so Iris Braithwaite, a woman who claimed to live on nothing but the remains of her shredded nerves; she jolted vigorously, as though in response to a proffered red hot poker.

A six-year-old girl, dressed in an assortment of jumble sale goods, appeared at the sitting-room door. With cheap yellow beads bouncing on her chest and over-sized, red slingbacks slapping at her heels, she trotted towards her mother.

'Becky,' Hilary said, 'I did tell you not to play with the clothes from the boxes in the hall. Go and take them off, especially those ridiculous shoes, you'll have an accident.'

'Do I have to?'

'Yes you do. Now say hello to Mrs Braithwaite and Malcolm.'

Six-year-old shyness appearing from nowhere rendered the little girl speechless. She played with the biggest of the yellow beads, turning one of her feet inwards. She then remembered what she had wanted her mother for. 'What does bonking mean, Mummy?'

Flanked by an uneasy rattle of china from one side of her and a stifled laugh from the other, Hilary grappled to save the teapot in her hands and to think of a suitable answer. All she could think of was the terrible unfairness of it all.

She had worked so hard today, had tried to make everything just right. It had all fallen apart though, the moment she had opened the fridge door that morning and realised she hadn't got any eggs. The shop in the village had run out of her usual free-range variety and she had been forced to make do with those battery-farmed eggs instead. The sponge, of course, had turned out a disaster and was it any wonder? She had then had to make a back-up batch of scones for her monthly meeting with Malcolm Jackson and Iris Braithwaite – Chairlady of the St John's Replacement Stained Glass Window Committee. Then, just as she'd got the kitchen cleared up, school had telephoned to say there had been a gas leak and all children were being sent home. And on top of all this her sister Charlotte was arriving in a few hours' time, which meant there had been Ivy Cottage to get ready for her, along with the welcome home dinner to prepare for that evening. No, life just wasn't being fair with her today.

Then with shame she thought of Charlotte. Life hadn't exactly been fair to her recently.

It was now two and a half months since Peter had died; the funny thing was, it felt longer.

It had been a sad little funeral, on a cold wet day in Aldershot, with their own family far out-numbering Peter's. She had been so sure that Peter's funeral would have been a rather grand affair, had even bought a hat, which thankfully, just at the last minute, she had left behind in the car. In fact there had been few friends present, hardly anyone to mourn comfortingly alongside Charlotte, just a few duty-bound work colleagues; not even Peter's own brother had turned up. She had felt sorry for Peter's parents; sorry, too, that nobody cried, not even Charlotte.

Afterwards they had all tried to talk Charlotte out of returning to Brussels, had tried to get her to leave everything to the company. 'I must go back,' she had said. 'There are things I need to sort out.' She had been adamant. Just as she had been adamant about buying a house in the village. 'I want to be where I grew up,' she had told them on the telephone. 'Hulme Welford is the only place I know as home. It's got to be there.'

Secretly Hilary was looking forward to having her sister to look after, living as she would be, quite literally on the doorstep. She smiled to herself at the thought of one day taking the credit for getting Charlotte back on her feet. She could almost feel that rosy glow of praise and gratitude, which she knew would be hers within a few months. Yes, she had great plans for her elder sister.

Looking up from the teapot Hilary realised that both Iris Braithwaite and Malcolm Jackson were staring at her, Becky, too. Uncharacteristically she chose to ignore her daughter. 'More tea?' she said.

Taking his cue, Malcolm Jackson held out his cup. 'Just a top-up, please.'

Becky was not to be put off. 'But Mummy . . .'

'Have a chocolate biscuit, dear.'

Wide eyed with delight, Becky took one, thought better, and took another, but then doggedly continued with her line of questioning. 'Philip says he won't give me back my Barbie doll until Ken's finished bonking her. How long do you think that will take, Mummy?'

At the commotion which followed, Becky left her jumble sale heels behind her and took to her own, whilst Hilary did her best to deal with Iris Braithwaite's tea-soaked tweed skirt and the slice of lemon that had ended up sitting perkily, like a Frenchman's beret, on one of her sensible brown lace-up shoes.

Another cup and saucer was fetched from the kitchen and

quickly filled, but conversation, like the tea, was strained, until Iris Braithwaite warmed to her subject: that of the rising sense of apathy in the village. 'It seems to me that people today have lost their sense of generosity,' she said, taking a sip of tea and wincing as she scalded her thin lips. 'Why, I remember a time when we thought nothing of a jumble sale every two months.'

'I think that people are less inclined to throw things away these days,' suggested Malcolm Jackson. 'After all, everyone, in some way, has been affected by . . .'

'It's greed, pure greed,' interrupted Iris. 'People are hoarding things. Greed is such a terrible sin and one to be avoided at all costs.' She punctuated this by reaching for another scone. 'And as the good book says, "Let the wicked fall into their own nets, whilst I pass in safety."'

Malcolm Jackson couldn't resist it and touchéd with 'Ah, but let's not forget "If any one of you is without sin, let him be the first to throw a stone."' His tone was cynical rather than pious and he received a withering look for his trouble.

'We really could do with one more pair of hands for the jumble sale next Saturday,' Hilary said in an effort to steer the conversation back to where it had been before Becky had interrupted. 'We had seven last time, and to be honest we were a bit stretched.'

'What about Charlotte, your sister?' Iris Braithwaite said. 'She could help, she won't have any commitments so soon, will she? Do her good, get her fully integrated into the village again.'

'Oh, I don't think that would be a good idea. Do you?' Hilary asked, turning to the vicar.

'Nonsense,' Iris Braithwaite carried on, ignoring Malcolm's opened mouth. 'She'll need to be busy. When my Sydney died fifteen years ago, the first thing I did was to spring clean the house and organise the summer fête.' She paused as though reflecting on those halcyon days, then said, 'I don't suppose Charlotte will be bringing any of her deceased husband's clothing back with her, will she? We could make good use of that at the jumble sale.' And casting a meaningful glance over Malcolm Jackson's faded sweat-shirt and jeans, she said, 'Perhaps there might even be something suitable for the vicar.'

'I really couldn't say,' Hilary said helplessly, conscious of the sudden sirocco-style exhalation of breath at her side.

It was always the same. Every month, whenever they had to meet to discuss various fund-raising events for St John's, Iris Braithwaite rendered poor Malcolm speechless. Trouble was, Malcolm, being a clergyman, was like the Queen – not allowed to answer back – and she herself, like so many in the village, was just plain terrified of Iris Braithwaite.

'Well,' said Iris, putting her cup down on the tray and then dabbing the corners of her mouth with her napkin, 'I think we've covered everything quite adequately. So, come along, Vicar, it's time we were going. I'm sure Mrs Parker doesn't want us cluttering up her sitting-room a moment longer.'

Dutifully getting his bulky frame to his feet, Malcolm Jackson smiled at Hilary and thanked her for the tea. 'Will you be in church on Sunday?' he added as they moved towards the hall.

'Yes, it's my turn on Sunday School rota – which reminds me, we really could do with a new trainer seat for the toilet. Poor Joel had an accident with the last one.'

'Really, Mrs Parker!' spluttered Iris Braithwaite. 'I'm sure the vicar doesn't want to hear about such trifling matters.'

Oh dear, thought Hilary, another faux pas.

'I doubt whether it seemed a trifling matter to young Joel at the time,' Malcolm said, a smile on his lips. 'No serious damage, I hope?'

'He hurt his bum!' came a loud voice. It was Becky bumping her way down the stairs on her bottom. She was now wearing a pink leotard with grass-stained ballet tights and carrying her treasured Barbie doll in her hands. 'He hurt his willy wobbler as well,' she added for good measure, when she finally bumped to a stop at the foot of the stairs, 'He was such a cry-baby, he cried all during the story of David and Goliath.'

'Thank you, Becky, that's enough,' said Hilary in a tired voice. She pulled open the front door, anxious for the afternoon to come to an end. But Iris was not finished.

'We're a pair of hands short on the church flower rota. Ask Charlotte, it'll give her something to do. Lovely tea by the way, shame about that sponge, though.'

'Have they gone?' It was Philip, a dark-haired ten-year-old boy, calling from the top of the stairs. Satisfied that the coast was clear he raced downstairs and shot into the sitting-room, to gain possession of the remote control of the television before his sister got it.

'What about your homework, Philip?' Hilary asked, fulfilling her son's expectations of her, as she began clearing the wreckage of tea.

'I've done it,' he replied glibly, thereby fulfilling his mother's expectations of him, at the same time waving the remote control device high in the air, just out of his sister's reach.

Out in the kitchen, Hilary fed the dishwasher, cake crumbs and all, mentally going over that evening's meal, and her plan – supper with a few of the neighbours, just to get her sister acclimatised, and, of course, to introduce her to Alex.

If there was one thing Hilary could never be accused of, it was suffering from an over indulgence of sentimentality, and whilst it was all very sad and tragic that her sister's husband had died so suddenly, she knew that one simply had to carry on. Charlotte would now have to build up her life again, with a little help. She would need company, and preferably the company of a man, and Hilary had just the man in mind.

Alex Hamilton had been in the village for just two weeks now, renting the granny annexe of Charlotte's new house, Ivy Cottage. He was, in Hilary's opinion, quite the most attractive man to have hit Hulme Welford since a few years ago, when a rather notorious snooker player moved into the village, only to move out again rather rapidly when he lost his potting technique, along with his fortune.

There was no doubt in her mind that Alex Hamilton was the tonic Charlotte needed in order to get herself back on her feet again.

Hilary looked up at the clock above the Aga. Charlotte's plane would be arriving within the hour and Hilary knew the traffic would slow her down.

'I can always get a taxi,' her sister had said.

'Nonsense!' had been Hilary's reply.

Now there was a part of her that was regretting this rash offer; she had more than enough to do without getting caught up in Friday night's rush hour traffic.

Living 'conveniently placed for Manchester airport', as her husband David so liked to describe the village in his estate agency brochures, was the only tangible disadvantage to living in Hulme Welford, as far as Hilary could see. They were situated directly beneath the main flight path and David had to work hard at playing down the noise to prospective purchasers who came into his attractive black and white half-timbered estate agency office in the centre of the village.

In recent years house sales in the area had sky-rocketed, when Hulme Welford, with all its chocolate-box charm, had steadily increased in popularity with the more adventurous members of the Manchester commuter belt set. When the older and quite dilapidated cottages in the village had been snapped up, small exclusive developments, such as Orchard Way and Pippin Rise, had sprung up like weeds on the perimeter of the village. They provided trouble-free houses for the upwardly mobile; fully centrally heated, double garaged and two bathroomed, gold taps and all. The houses had increased the population of the village, and brought to it an excess of BMWs tearing about the lanes, as well as a universally agreed improvement to the shops. The local infant and junior school had responded in equal expansion and now with its increased numbers and pulsating PTA, could boast not only good academic results, but a swimming pool as well.

Most of these changes Hilary approved of, especially the pulsating PTA, of which she was currently Secretary. Next year she hoped to be Chairwoman. Just recently though, the idea of joining the Board of Governors for the school had taken root, and the more Hilary thought about it, the more the idea appealed to her. She could even buy one of those smart executive-looking suits to wear for the meetings.

Taking a tray of wine glasses through to the dining-room, Hilary's thoughts of whether to buy a navy blue or grey suit were interrupted by a pump-action ring at the doorbell. 'Get that, will you, Philip? It'll be Tiffany.'

'Oh Mum, *Grange Hill*'s on.'

'Oh, all right, I'll go.' She put the glasses down on the oak table in the hall. 'And Becky, you come out of there, you're too young for *Grange Hill*.'

A shrill wail started up from Becky, followed by a full scale riot, as Philip began thumping his sister to make her be quiet. Unperturbed Hilary opened the front door.

'Muffin 'ell, what's going on?'

Hearing their babysitter's familiar voice, Becky leapt off her brother and ran out into the hall. Tiffany fascinated her. When she grew up, she wanted to be just like her – black leggings, huge boots, black-rimmed eyes just like a panda and long, long black hair.

'Can I count your rings, Tiffany?'

'Say please.'

'*Please*.'

''Course you can. Let's see how good your maths is today.'

With tongue-poking-out-of-the-mouth concentration, Becky started to count. First on Tiffany's left hand then on her right. 'Four and three, that makes . . . seven,' she announced after careful consideration.

'Who's a clever little madam then. And what *was* you doing to your brother when I came in?'

'*Were*,' corrected Becky.

Hilary smiled. Tiffany's subversive teaching methods with Becky never failed. She and David could shout until they were blue in the face about the correct use of speech and Becky would just throw it back at them.

'Okay if I dash off straight away, Tiffany?' Hilary said. 'I'd like to try and get there early.'

'Yeah sure, no problem.'

'I'll be a couple of hours at most. David might even be back before me, though I doubt it.' She reached for her keys hanging up on the hook by the telephone. 'Oh Lord!' she suddenly cried out. 'I've forgotten to give the children any tea, I've been so busy thinking about tonight and what with Mrs Braithwaite and Reverend Jackson, I've . . .'

'Got any fish fingers in the freezer?'

'Yes, and there's some cake left over from this afternoon. Oh Tiffany, you are wonderful. What would I do without you?'

Tiffany smiled. If only her mother thought the same.

Pushing her trolley of luggage, Charlotte's eyes searched the crowded arrivals hall for her sister's welcoming face, but all she could see were rows of bored-looking men holding drooping placards bearing the names of their charges. There was no sign of Hilary.

Charlotte felt anxious. She wanted to get this bit of the day over with. Knowing her sister's intense desire to do and say all the right things, Charlotte viewed the drive home with a mixture of uneasiness and hostility.

She paused for a moment with her trolley, letting her fellow passengers push ahead of her. She suddenly felt overwhelmed by the juxtaposition of this large bustling, uncaring crowd around her and the thought of Hilary, lavishing well-intended sisterly love on her. Frightened she was about to cry, she reached into her jacket pocket for a tissue. Instead of a tissue, she found the envelope Christina had given to her at the airport in Brussels. She had kept it in her pocket until she was soaring over the Belgian coast with a glass of champagne in her hand. Then she had opened it and read the card with Christina's beautiful words.

'Leave your sadness behind, Carlotta; leave it in Brussels where it can no longer harm you. Take only your beautiful smile with you and offer it to everyone you meet; it will bring you and them such happiness.'

It was the loveliest thing anyone had ever said to her.

And then as if by magic there was Hilary rushing towards her. To Charlotte's surprise, relief flooded through her.

3

'I'm doing a little supper party for you tonight,' Hilary said, stretching her hand out of the car window to insert the parking ticket in the required slit.

'Oh Hilary, not tonight, I can't.'

'Nonsense, you'll be fine,' Hilary said firmly. She hoped to goodness her sister wasn't going to play the grieving widow round the dinner table that night. Moussaka, mirth and a little matchmaking was what she had in mind, not moussaka and misery. 'You know,' she said, choosing her words carefully, 'you know how desperately sad we all are about Peter, but at some stage you have to pick up the pieces of your life again, so it might as well be tonight.' Especially after all the trouble I've gone to, she thought. 'And anyway,' she added with forced brightness, 'it will be a nice way for you to meet Alex.'

The initial flood of relief Charlotte had experienced on seeing her sister's capable face in the crowd had completely flowed out of her. The familiar twinges of irritation that went hand in hand with the sisters' affection for one another were now beginning to surface.

And Charlotte also knew what Hilary was up to. Ever since the contract for Ivy Cottage had been signed and David had found a tenant to live in the granny annexe, Hilary had never stopped mentioning this Alex Hamilton on the telephone: 'Such a nice man . . . very pleasant . . . he'll be no bother to you . . . quite handy really, you know, should you run out of coffee, or anything like that.'

Well, tonight she would meet him, would make up her own mind. In her opinion, Hilary had been watching too many Gold Blend adverts.

She decided to move on to firmer ground. 'How are the children?'

'As wonderful as ever.'

Charlotte grimaced. Wonderful was not the description that instantly sprang to her mind when she thought of her nephew and niece – seismic savages more like it.

'They're really looking forward to seeing you. You'll be a real aunt to them now, living so close.'

'I hadn't thought of it quite like that,' Charlotte said, horrified at the thought. Living opposite her sister had been the only fly in the ointment of her plan to move back to Hulme Welford.

'Philip's just been awarded his thousand-metre swimming badge and Becky has cracked breast stroke. She's a real natural, Mrs Pulman says.'

Charlotte knew it was always best to let her sister ramble on with motherly pride, and over the years she had mastered the art of half listening and oohing and aahing in the appropriate pauses. 'So, who's coming tonight?' she asked, when at last Hilary had run out of glowing reports of her offspring. 'Will it be smart? I haven't brought everything, the rest is following on in the removal van.'

'No, of course it's not posh,' Hilary said, thinking of all the luggage they had just loaded into the back of David's Volvo: 'It's only family and a few neighbours. There'll be you, me, David, Mum and Dad, and Derek and Cindy. Remember I told you about them moving into Rose Cottage just before Peter . . .'

Hilary's unfinished sentence hung stiffly in the air and an awkward silence filled the car.

'Go on,' Charlotte said at last. 'Say it, Hilary, don't be afraid of using the word. *Died*. Peter died. Okay? His car skidded on ice and hit a barrier at a hundred and twenty kilometres an hour. He was killed instantly. Peter's dead. There, I've said it, you try it.'

Hilary found herself unable to respond to what, in her mind, was an appalling outburst of bad taste. Surely even in grief one had to employ a certain amount of dignity? Looking after Charlotte was going to be more difficult than she had supposed. Her eyes firmly fixed on the road ahead, she decided to return to the subject of supper that evening. 'And the only other guest who'll be there is Alex, of course.'

'Of course,' repeated Charlotte, looking out of the window, not trusting herself to look at her sister.

Adopting a cheery voice, Hilary said, 'Have you thought any more about my offer for you to stop the night with us? I just can't bear the idea of you being all alone. You'll be so lonely.'

It was difficult for Charlotte not to laugh out loud. She had spent the last few years of her marriage feeling alone and isolated.

'Stay with us, Charlotte. Come on, why don't you? Just your first night.'

Charlotte considered The Gables for a moment: the noise, the constant bickering, the fighting – and that was just Hilary and David. She smiled to herself, thinking of the calmness and tranquillity she hoped to have at Ivy Cottage. 'It's kind of you to offer,' she said, 'but I'd rather like to get settled in straight away, there's so much to do. I'm quite looking forward to it really.'

'Yes of course, I understand.' She didn't understand at all. How could Charlotte be looking forward to moving into that house all alone?

They entered the village, and as they passed the prettily painted sign that had helped Hulme Welford win the North-West's 'Best Kept Village' title last year, Charlotte began to feel uneasy. Supposing she had made a mistake in coming back? It was a fact of life, one of those clichéd phrases, trotted out with diligent reverence to the worldly wisdom of those unfortunate enough to have tried it for themselves – *you can't go back*.

Only her mother had actually had the courage to say this to her. 'Charlotte, are you sure you're doing the right thing? After all, everyone knows, only a fool tries to turn back the clock.'

'Thank you, Mother,' she had said. 'I can always rely on you for support, can't I?'

'No point in me lying to you, Charlotte, never lied to you before, why should I start now?'

'Because my husband's just died?' Charlotte had replied, knowing how pathetic she was sounding, whining like a small child. 'And it might be nice to be . . .'

'What?' Louise had said, frowning. 'Mollycoddled? You want me to mollycoddle you? You of all people must know I'm not that kind of a mother.'

It was true. Louise Archer had never been the kind of mother to rush to a bleeding knee-cap with a box of plasters, nor soothe an exhausted child with a bedtime story. She had always been busy at some auction or other, or working in her antique shop, buffing up and restoring her 'finds'. From an early age, both Charlotte and Hilary had learnt where the Germoline and aspirins were kept.

They drove along the main street with its plentiful supply of shops; their mother's antique shop, the baker's, butcher's, grocer's, paper shop and Post Office next door, and then the more upmarket chic clothes shop and the kitchen and bathroom shop. It was just after six-thirty and, apart from the paper shop, everything was shut. She spotted David's office. Charlotte could see a light still on. She thought for one awful moment her sister might want to stop the car and take her in to see David. But to her relief Hilary turned left at the church, drove down Daisy Bank and then turned again into Acacia Lane, a leafy cul-de-sac made up of a handful of small terraced cottages and four large houses set well back from the road.

On the right-hand side was The White Cottage. The house was exactly what its name suggested, a neat cottage with a perfect covering of unadorned white rendering. The garden was equally neat with well-dug, weedless flower beds. Daffodils, now well past their best, had been neatly folded with rubber-bands thwarting any untidiness. This was where Iris Braithwaite lived.

Beyond The White Cottage was Rose Cottage. This came as a complete surprise to Charlotte. Not so long ago Rose Cottage had been a pretty, pale-coloured house. Now it was painted shocking pink, and at the end of the drive was a large sign informing Charlotte it was called 'In The Pink'.

'Derek and Cindy,' Hilary said to Charlotte's look of horror. 'They have a chain of hair salons right across Cheshire and they've turned the house into a sort of health and beauty centre, in record time too. They seem to be doing very well out of it.'

'But it's ghastly. However did they get away with painting it that disgusting colour?'

'Don't ask me. And please, don't ask them. Derek thinks it's quite the thing. By the way, watch out for Derek.'

'Why?'

'Don't be naïve, Charlotte.'

Dropping down into second gear, Hilary turned off the road and carefully drove between two peeling white gates and up a narrow driveway to Ivy Cottage.

Since she'd grown up in Hulme Welford and had made regular visits home throughout her marriage, Charlotte was familiar with every house in the village, except those on the new developments, Orchard Way and Pippin Rise. Ivy Cottage had always been one of her favourites. As a child, she had been fascinated by the house and its occupant, a woman who had been something of a celebrity as a writer of romantic fiction. Blanche Blair had drifted about the village with the glamour one might have expected of a woman of her profession, and she had managed to create an air of mystery around her large Edwardian cottage and beautiful garden. The last years of Blanche Blair's life were spent in a nursing home and the cottage had stood empty. On her death, Ivy Cottage had been snapped up by the Cliffords from Doncaster, who, bringing an elderly mother with them, had the house redesigned to provide an independent granny flat at one end of the house. But the elderly occupant of the granny flat rather ungratefully died and the Cliffords had felt the pull of Doncaster. The house still looked to be one from the outside, but there were two driveways, an original of gravel and one of tarmac.

An abundance of ivy and peeling paint gave the impression that the house and garden were badly in need of work. Yet Charlotte thought it was wonderful. A little sad and drab perhaps, but compared to the elegant, sterile apartment she had left behind in Brussels, with its marble and fake neoclassical gilt work, it was real, and it was hers.

Between them, they took the luggage out of the Volvo and into the house.

'There now,' said Hilary, 'everything's in. Shall I show you round?'

'Haven't you got a meal to prepare?' Charlotte wanted more than anything to be left alone.

Hilary looked at her watch. 'Oh Lord, you're right, I must fly, but are you sure you've got everything you need?'

'I'm fine, really. I'll unpack a few things, have a bath, then be right over.'

'Good idea. I put the immersion heater on for you earlier.'

Charlotte knew she should be grateful to Hilary for thinking of having hot water ready for her, but she felt childishly possessive; it was her house, her immersion heater.

She watched her sister reverse down the drive and turn into her own drive to The Gables. Closing the door behind her, for the second time that day Charlotte felt an over-whelming sense of relief; she had made it this far.

Then for no good reason she could think of, she started to cry.

4

Pound coins chinking in her jacket pocket – the financial rewards of babysitting – Tiffany Rogers sauntered across the road towards 'In The Pink'. She was in no hurry to get home, had even offered to stay on a bit longer to help Mrs Parker set the dining-room table. She was nice, Mrs Parker, though she could do with slowing down a bit; she'd been like a headless chicken just now in the kitchen.

As she walked up the drive, her heavy Doc Martens clomping on the tarmac, Tiffany paused to look at the damage her parents had done to what had once been an ordinary-looking house.

When they had bought Rose Cottage, her parents had taken it in hand, treating it like a client. Only this time they worked in reverse, stretching it to twice its original size by adding two enormous extensions, providing room for a complex of saunas, Jacuzzis, gymnasiums, massage rooms and a hair salon. Now Rose Cottage was beyond recognition, smelling permanently of a combination of hospitals, public swimming baths and hairspray.

The walls, which had once been a delicate pastel shade of pink, were now the colour of a vivid Mediterranean geranium. Tiffany knew they stuck out in the village as flagrantly as she herself did.

Coming to Hulme Welford had not been as bad as it might have been; at least she and her brother could stay at the same school, so had kept all their old friends who were now a short bus ride away. Since she was eight years old they had lived in Wilmslow, but then last year Dad had got this idea that the big money lay in buying a large old house and converting it into a health and beauty centre. Tiffany viewed it more as a temple of indulgence for the privileged few and said as much to her parents at every possible opportunity.

Alone in the salon, Cindy Rogers turned off the lights and, carrying her expensive Italian shoes in her hands, made her way along the corridor that separated the work area from the living area of the house. On her feet all day, Cindy knew she should wear flatter shoes, but she also knew that her slim tanned legs looked even better in a pair of high heels.

She was tired and not looking forward to going out for dinner to the Parkers'. She would have much preferred a good long soak in a lavender-oil-scented bath. Instead she would have to face the ordeal of coping with the excessive amount of food which Hilary would present her with. Eating out always filled Cindy with dread.

She found Tiffany in the kitchen, frying some bacon and making a cup of tea, and at once, Cindy felt the familiar surge of disappointment as she looked at her daughter.

She had so badly wanted a daughter. The birth of her first child, Barry, had been a bad enough blow, but nothing had prepared her for Tiffany. The black patent shoes and smocked dresses she had longed to dress her daughter in had been denied her by this wayward, headstrong child. The shopping trips she had envisaged, the shared girl-talk and mutual understanding of all things feminine had been snatched away, right from the moment Tiffany, at the age of four, had stood in the middle of her bedroom and pulled off the beautiful little dress Cindy had just bought for her in Manchester. 'Don't like it,' Tiffany had shouted defiantly, stamping all over the expensive fabric, 'won't wear it, want to be like Barry.' And she had followed this to the letter, fastidiously copying the way her older brother dressed, until she had started menstruating. At that point, she decided to grow her hair. And then, a year ago, on her fourteenth birthday, she had emerged from the bathroom with her long sandy hair completely jet black. From then on, it seemed to Cindy, Tiffany grew each day more and more like Morticia from the Addams family.

Cindy frowned, then immediately relaxed her facial muscles, knowing how damaging it was for the skin. But the strains of her morning argument with Tiffany were still there, hanging in the air of her bleached ash kitchen. Nothing was going to change her mind; Tiffany and her friends were too young to go off for a weekend in the Lake District on their own. Surely her stubborn fifteen-year-old daughter could see that?

It was Tiffany who spoke first. 'Want some tea?'

'No, thanks. Where have you been?' It came out all wrong and she felt her daughter bristle.

'Muffin 'ell, I've been over at Mrs Parker's baby-sitting. I told you this morning I'd be going there straight after school. You obviously weren't listening.'

They were off again, their mood to one another cold, combative.

'Where's Barry?' Cindy asked, trying to sound conciliatory.

'Up in his room studying.'

'What, already?'

'You should be proud of him. After all, if he does become a surgeon he'll be able to give you the facelift you'll need after all that rubbish you pile on your face.'

Cindy gave up. 'I'm going to have a bath, seeing as you've nothing civil to say to me.'

Tiffany watched her mother go. She hadn't meant to be rude, but her mother's complete misunderstanding of Barry really got to her. Didn't she know how important it was to Barry to get not just good grades in his A levels, but brilliant grades? Their mother and their father just had no idea of the strain Barry was under.

Derek Rogers was having a sauna. He liked a good sweat before going out. At forty-five, when most of his contemporaries were beginning to look their age and were quite prepared to forget about their bodies, Derek Rogers was obsessed with his.

Physically he was in great shape, but mentally he was not. He was bored, bored to death.

The five salons he and Cindy owned throughout Cheshire practically ran themselves and now that In The Pink was up and running and gaining more clients every day, he felt the need for something more challenging. He was bored with the women of Hulme Welford too. They were no challenge to him. They were all so bored themselves that they leapt at the chance of an added drop of excitement in their lives.

Since the age of sixteen when Derek had discovered he was irresistible to women of any age, and discovered at the same time that he was driven by a compulsive need for a variety of women in his life, he had embarked upon countless affairs, leading up to and during his twenty-two-year-old marriage to Cindy. Affairs to him had never been an added bonus; he needed them like a gambler needs the next roll of the dice. He viewed Cindy as his morning cup of coffee: strong and bitter and always there. He never considered whether he loved her or not, that was irrelevant. She was just there, a part of his life.

Out of the sauna, he rubbed himself down with a towel, pulled on a pair of Paisley boxer shorts then walked through to the gym. A quick ten-minute work-out on the exercise bike and then he would shower and get ready. He was looking forward to this evening. It held the promise of something new. He knew Hilary and David of course, living so close, and he and Cindy had been introduced to Louise and Neville Archer some weeks ago. The two guests he didn't know at all were Alex Hamilton and Charlotte Lawrence. He had noticed that chap Hamilton moving into to the granny flat of Ivy Cottage two weeks ago and had seen a lot of books and computer stuff coming out of the back of the removal van, which meant they would have nothing at all in common.

But Charlotte Lawrence, Hilary's sister – now she was a different matter, she intrigued him. He had seen a photograph of her when they had been invited over to the Parkers' for drinks one Sunday lunchtime. Defiant eyes had stared back at him from the framed photograph on the mantel- piece. He had noticed that there was a strong similarity between the two sisters; noticed, too, that while Hilary was a pleasant enough looking woman, Charlotte was the more attractive, more complete somehow – as though the two women had been painted by an artist who had started work enthusiastically on the elder sister, only to run out of paint and motivation by the time he reached the younger woman. Poor Hilary looked a watered-down version of her sister, Derek thought.

All Derek actually knew about this sister of Hilary's was that her husband had recently died and she was coming to live in Ivy Cottage. He slowed the pedals down on the bike, began to think seriously of the evening ahead and the potential it offered. Should he wear casual – navy chinos and cream polo shirt – or one of his new Italian suits? He favoured casual; the cream shirt would set off his tan better. Looking at his paper-thin wristwatch, he considered a quick five-minute session on the sunbed.

5

Thank heavens for Tiffany, Hilary said to herself for the umpteenth time, as she stepped out of the bath and started rubbing her legs with a towel. During the time in which she had collected Charlotte from the airport, Tiffany had not only cooked the children's tea, cleared up afterwards and then coaxed them up to bed, but she had also found time to read a few chapters of *George's Marvellous Medicine* for them. Tiffany really did have the most fantastic effect on both Becky and Philip.

Hilary bent down and tugged at the bath plug, allowing herself a small smile. There'd be no shower for David when he eventually made it home – she had used up all the hot water and there would be no more until half past six tomorrow morning, which was all down to David's excessive desire to economise. It was one of his most infuriating habits, that and being a lousy host. No doubt he would excel himself tonight, drink too much and forget all about their guests. Well, blast David's economising. As soon as she was dressed she would go downstairs and light a fire in the sitting-room. It was the coldest room in the house with its north-facing position, and even at this time of year it could feel miserably damp.

She went over to the chest of drawers by her side of the bed. Hunting at the back of the drawer, she pulled out a brand new pair of ivory-coloured silk pants and a matching bra. One of her few luxuries in life was buying and hoarding new underwear and saving it for just the right occasion.

Just as she was cutting off the price tags in the bathroom, Hilary heard the familiar noise of her own car coming up the drive. Hurriedly she hid the evidence of her indulgence at the bottom of the bin, pulled on the pants and wriggled into the bra. She was disappointed, though, not to be able to savour the moment alone.

Downstairs the front door banged. This was followed by the sound of David's exploratory footsteps pacing through the hall to the kitchen, the sitting-room, the dining-room, until eventually they could be heard coming up the stairs.

'There you are,' David said, coming into the bedroom, pulling off his silk tie and tossing it on to the bed. 'Mm . . . you look nice.' He eyed her more closely. 'Been shopping?'

She laughed and parried his question. 'You look pleased with yourself.'

'I've every right to be pleased. I've sold three houses today, including that architect-designed monstrosity I thought I'd be stuck with for ever. Could be a sign the recession really is letting up at last.'

'That's wonderful, darling,' Hilary said, opening the wardrobe door and trying to sound more pleased than she was. Ordinarily she would have been delighted for David, but not today, not tonight. For David would be feeling in need of some reward, which would involve an effort on her part – and to be honest she just didn't have the energy this evening after the day she'd had. He would also feel the need to celebrate by drinking too much over dinner, which would mean he'd be as good as useless at helping her with the meal.

'I'll just have a quick shower before the mob turns up,' David said.

'There's no hot water left, sorry.'

'Well in that case,' he came towards her, 'I'll have to do something else to fill in the time. 'Are you sure these knickers aren't new?'

Irritation flickered through Hilary as David stroked her

silky bottom. She felt cheated; the pleasure was supposed to have been all hers, not David's.

Half an hour later, opening the front door to the first arrivals, David found himself poleaxed by a mouthful of Miss Dior and an equal measure of Paco Rabanne. He stood back for air as he let Cindy and Derek in, taking from them a bottle of wine and a box of chocolates.

'Go through,' he said, grimacing behind their backs. 'You know the way.'

In the sitting-room the curtains were already pulled across and a fire was blazing furiously. Minutes earlier, in an effort to save wood, David had flung most of the contents of the kitchen bin on to the gently smouldering logs, and now there was a distinct aroma of burning plastic accompanied by an occasional high-pitched whistling noise. Hilary would give him hell later.

'Do sit down.' David gestured to the chintz-covered sofas. Cindy did as she was told, perching birdlike on the edge of the sofa. Derek made himself at home, taking up pole position by the fire, feet a statutory twelve inches apart, hands pushed down into trouser pockets. After a couple of seconds he started to sniff and looked behind him.

'Think your chimney needs sweeping, David. Bit of a whiff coming from it, isn't there?'

That's rich coming from you, thought David, turning to Cindy. 'So Cindy, what can I get you to drink? No, don't tell me, let me see if I can remember. Gin and tonic?' She shook her head. 'Of course not, glass of white wine, that's got to be it.'

Derek laughed, taking his hands out of his pockets, gold bracelet chinking. 'Must be your other girlfriend. Cindy's practically a tee total merchant, always has been, always will be, isn't that right, love?'

Cindy laughed politely, but her perfectly made-up lips remained tightly shut.

David laughed too, it was easier that way. He never knew quite what to say to Derek. After all, what sort of man was a hairdresser? But what really went against the grain with him was that Derek had legitimate access to every woman in the village and surrounding area – he was like a doctor, but without the background or ethical code of practice.

'What's that smell?' It was Hilary, her Royal Horticultural Society apron still on, a *hydrangea petiolaris* working its way up her front. Her eyes were trained on the fireplace.

'That's a fine way to greet our guests, darling.' David knew he was on thin ice, so why not go down with the *Titanic*?

'Hello Cindy and Derek,' she said pleasantly. She gave David one of her slightly stern looks, and said, 'Haven't you got the drinks going yet?'

'All in hand, dear, all in hand. Cindy, what would you like?'

'Perrier please.'

'Mine's a gin and tonic,' said Derek.

It would be, David thought, bustling off to the drinks cabinet.

'Hilary, I hope you haven't gone to a lot of trouble,' Cindy said, hoping against all the odds that it might be just a light supper. 'After all, it's only friends and neighbours, like you said.'

'And family,' called out David, trying to decide whether Cindy and Derek came under friends or neighbours, at the same time trying to conceal the bottle of gin which was Sainsbury's and not Gordon's.

'So Hilary,' Derek said, picking up the framed photograph of Charlotte from the mantelpiece, 'tell us what your sister is like.'

Cindy, her perfectly manicured nails digging into the palms of her hands, closed her eyes. Surely he wouldn't? Not with a woman whose husband had so recently died.

6

Charlotte was late. She had spent longer than she intended in the bath, with a large gin and tonic, and when the bath water had gone cold for the second time, she had wrapped her bathrobe around her, topped up her glass and wandered aimlessly about her echoing, unfurnished new home. The removal van from Brussels wasn't due to arrive until Monday morning, so until then all she had was a put-you-up-bed and a couple of chairs which Hilary had loaned her.

Despite this, and despite the dusty wooden floorboards, the naked walls with their ghostly marks where once there had been pictures, Charlotte was delighted with each room she went into; especially the shambling, wooden-constructed conservatory at the back of the house. It was not a neat modern conservatory sold by an aggressive young man on the doorstep, but one built many years ago that recently had fallen into disrepair. Certainly it looked as though the Cliffords had not made it as far as this part of the house in terms of adding their personal touch.

Opening the stiff door, which creaked and groaned for a good rubbing down and some oil and led out on to the garden, Charlotte let in the cool evening air. The air inside was warm and as thick as syrup with flies buzzing wearily against the smeared glass. In this hothouse warmth, Charlotte began to feel lightheaded. Suddenly she had a very real image in her mind of Blanche Blair sitting at her typewriter in the almost tropical atmosphere, conjuring up one of her torrid romances, hearts beating and aflame with desire.

Laughing, she went back into the house. Buoyed up by three large gins, she felt convinced that she had made the right decision in moving back to Hulme Welford. Ivy Cottage, she decided, was going to be the best thing to have happened to her in a long while.

Peter's idea of a home had been an impersonal base that was neat and tidy, without any added complications such as flower beds, leaking gutters and windowsills that needed painting. Each time they had moved, Charlotte had requested they live in a house, but each time Peter had over-ridden her wishes and insisted they rent an apartment. Admittedly, the apartments they had lived in had not been mean and cramped, far from it. The one in Singapore had been ridiculously palatial, even bigger than Brussels, but it had still felt like a prison cell to Charlotte. 'A prison cell!' Peter had shouted indignantly, when Charlotte complained about their latest home. 'Are you mad, Charlotte? Look about you and see how some of the locals live, ask them whether they think we're living in a cell.'

Perhaps, though, it had not been the physical walls of their various homes that had made her feel a captive. It was the mental confines of a marriage going disastrously wrong that had caused her to feel such a prisoner.

Upstairs, in what was to be her bedroom, Charlotte opened a suitcase and pulled out the first dress that came to hand. She tried to gear herself up for the evening ahead. Trouble was, she had no idea how to play her part. Was she to be doleful, demure or stiff upper lippish, displaying shoulders back and best foot forward? It should, of course, all come naturally, but it didn't, because she herself did not know exactly how she felt. With each day that passed she was conscious only of a deepening sense of guilt which most people around her mistook for grief. She had convinced herself that because of her Peter had tried to drive to Luxembourg when he was no longer in control of his emotions and had died as a result. She had told no one of this, not even Christina, and nobody knew what she had told Peter over breakfast. So there was no one to suggest that perhaps her husband – his mind already on his business meeting – had quite simply hit a patch of ice? And why had she told no one? Because then no one would be able to blame her for Peter's death.

Other than this growing, self-imposed culpability, Charlotte had not experienced any great trauma. After all, she had already experienced every level of emotion during the months leading up to that point of no return when she knew that she could not go on pretending. She had cried gulping great tears alone, night after night, lying in a half empty bed. She had cried in the bath, streams of tearful loneliness. She had even wept in the local supermarket, angry tears of frustration over the *pain de blé* when she had finally come to realise that she would never be the wife Peter needed; the kind of wife who didn't mind her husband having an all-consuming mistress – his work.

She shut the front door behind her, and locking it with the unfamiliar key Hilary had given her earlier, Charlotte started to walk down the driveway. But with each step she took away from her new home, her recently gin-induced confidence began to ebb away, until by the time she had reached the gate, she wasn't at all sure she had made the right decision in coming back to live in Hulme Welford; searching, as she was, for the familiar security of what she'd known P.P. – pre-Peter.

She stood on the pavement and looked across to The Gables. She felt like a small child who has just been given its comfort blanket, only to find the silky edging has come away.

*

Her mother, Louise Archer, opened the door to her. 'Charlotte!' she cried out, as though her elder daughter was the last person on earth she had been expecting to see that evening.

'Mother,' Charlotte replied, finding it difficult to respond in any other way. They almost made contact as they leaned towards each other for a perfunctory kiss.

'Hilary's on the telephone, she won't be long. You look tired.'

'You always say that.'

'Well, isn't that the kind of thing mothers are supposed to say?'

They walked through to the sitting-room, Charlotte following behind her mother.

'Look, everybody, look who's here,' Louise said, in a loud voice. It came out like an over-rehearsed line from a play.

'Charlotte!' Neville Archer said with obvious delight. He levered himself out of a florid armchair and came towards her, spilling a few drops of whisky as he did so. 'How about a hug for your old dad, then? Sorry we weren't there to meet you at the airport – your mother had an auction over at Chester and needed the car.'

Charlotte hugged him warmly. She was always pleased to see her father, with his familiar Toby jug appearance – stout and highly coloured.

'Don't worry,' she said. 'Hilary was there in full control.' Stepping back from him, she said in a voice deliberately aimed at her mother, 'You're looking great, Dad. The new diet's going well, then?'

He smiled at her and at the same time, with great effort, he pulled in his stomach, causing his buttoned cardigan to collapse like a balloon. Lowering his voice so as to exclude everyone else from their conversation, he asked, 'You okay?'

She nodded, grateful for his quiet concern, and said, 'How are the gooseberries?'

He looked worried. 'Not sure, they don't seem as good as last year's.'

Like a number of men and women in the village, Neville Archer spent months preparing for the annual gooseberry-growing contest, but as yet her father's gooseberries had never got anywhere near the weights required to be in the running for a prize. But each year Charlotte hoped that he might be lucky.

She rested a hand on his arm. 'They'll be fine. You'll win something this year, I'm sure of it.'

'Don't, Charlotte, for goodness' sake, just don't start him off about those wretched gooseberries,' Louise said vehemently, shaking her head. 'You know how unbearable he gets on the subject.'

'Talk to you later,' Charlotte whispered to him. Noticing that there were others in the room whom she did not know, Charlotte looked for her sister or David to make the necessary introductions. There was no sign of either. Staring straight at her was an overly tanned, slim woman with a perfect bob of blonde hair, looking for all the world like a candidate for *Come Dancing*. Cindy, Charlotte decided. And over by the hi-fi, it had to be Derek, a dead ringer for Phil Collins if ever there was one.

'Charlotte, you're here at last.' It was Hilary, coming in with a tray of nibbles, and her choice of words did not go unnoticed by Charlotte. 'Have you been properly introduced? I can't think where David's got to, I only asked him to fetch some logs. That was Alex on the telephone, by the way. Poor man, he just called to say he had been stuck in traffic in Manchester, but would be with us as soon as he'd changed. Cindy, let me introduce my sister.'

Cindy stood up, met Charlotte eye to eye, and was convinced she could smell gin.

There were very few women in the village whom Cindy liked: most of them she considered a threat, with the exception of Hilary. Cindy had decided her neighbour was far too busy coping with her own marriage to stray beyond it and so wouldn't recognise a come-on from Derek, even if he handed her a condom with her name on it. On the other hand, she knew instinctively that this woman, standing in front of her, *was* a threat. Those huge, dusky violet eyes and all that luscious raven-coloured hair would be like a gift from heaven to Derek. And she was free and vulnerable. It certainly didn't take too much effort on Cindy's part to see how Derek could make up his mind to take this woman out of herself; to get her over the death of her husband.

Charlotte sensed Cindy's reluctant hand slip in and out of her own and the brittle smile that went with it. She was aware, too, how simply but effectively Cindy was dressed, unlike herself she now realised. The expensive linen suit she had slung on only minutes earlier should have been ironed, but she had been in too much of a hurry and too lazy to bother.

'You must come and pamper yourself some time,' Cindy was saying. 'Grief can have such a devastating effect on the skin.'

'Yes,' Charlotte said awkwardly, wanting suddenly to step away from Cindy, who with her perfect complexion was probably already sizing up Charlotte's skin as pumice stone texture.

Almost as though Cindy had been pushed to one side, there was the Phil Collins lookalike standing before Charlotte, cool as you like, a strategically unbuttoned cream polo shirt revealing a sprinkling of fair hairs on a tanned chest. 'Don't be naïve,' Hilary had said earlier in the car. Charlotte smiled to herself, thinking how she might have fun being exactly that.

'Now you do remember, don't you?' said Hilary. 'I told you about Cindy and Derek and In The Pink.

Charlotte felt the hackles rising. Of course she remembered — she had lost her husband, not her mind. 'No,' she lied for the sheer hell of it, 'no, I don't recall you mentioning 'a Cindy or a Derek.' She heard her sister's sharp intake of breath.

'Continentals don't go in for much handshaking, do they?' Derek said, moving closer to Charlotte. 'They kiss a lot instead.' Which he promptly did, kissing Charlotte on both cheeks.

'How wonderfully flamboyant,' Louise said, raising her eyebrows.

'Well,' gasped Hilary, slightly flustered, 'that's one way of breaking the ice. Now come on, everyone, sit down, make yourselves at home. Anyone for chicken tikka flavoured nuts?'

'Somebody mention food? I'm starving.' It was David with a large basket of logs, which he dropped with a crash beside the fireplace. 'Charlotte, you've arrived. Good to see you. Everything all right over the road?'

'Yes thanks, David, just as Hilary said it would be.'

Shaking his hands clean of log dust, he came over and kissed her. 'This isn't on,' he said. 'You're the only one without a drink. Let me get you something.'

'Only a quick one,' Hilary chipped in, who, like Cindy, was sure Charlotte smelled of gin. In answer to the query written on her husband's face, she said, 'We'll be eating soon.'

The door bell rang.

'I'll get that.' Hilary almost barged past David in her hurry to get to the front door. 'It'll be Alex.'

The rest of the guests sat in awkward silence, listening to the front door being pulled open and the sound of Hilary's voice carrying from the hall. 'Oh Alex, how kind, but you shouldn't have. Really I don't deserve them.'

You're right, thought Charlotte, you don't deserve them, whatever they are, you scheming little monkey.

The sound of Hilary's voice grew louder until she stood in the doorway, a sparkling smile on her face, a bouquet of gypsophila and pink carnations in one hand and a bottle of wine in the other.

'Sorry I'm late, everybody,' said a voice from behind
Hilary. Alex Hamilton made his appearance. 'I hope I
haven't kept you all waiting.'

Smooth, thought Charlotte.

'No, no, of course you haven't,' fawned Hilary. 'Think
nothing of it. We're just delighted you're here.'

Oh, for goodness' sake, Hilary, stop larding it on, cringed
Charlotte, you'll be bobbing and curtsying next. It was
quite obvious to Charlotte that this party had very little to
do with welcoming her home; this was all about Hilary's
honoured guest, Alex Hamilton, and making the right
impression on him. While her sister carried on making a
fool of herself, Charlotte weighed up the recipient of all this
red carpet treatment: about six foot, she reckoned, with fair
hair that was showing signs of greying. He was casually
dressed in an understated kind of way: striped shirt beneath
a pale blue cashmere sweater, jeans and a pair of well-worn
Reeboks. He was probably about her age, she decided, mid
thirties.

'Now let me introduce you to everyone.' Hilary was off
again and beginning to steer Alex round the room, as
though he were a prize bull at an auction. 'And this is my
sister, Charlotte,' she said at last.

'Hello,' he said, taking her hand. 'Welcome home to
England. What time did you arrive?'

'Er . . .' Charlotte was nonplussed. She wasn't expecting
such an ordinary question. For the past two and a half
months nearly everyone who talked to her spoke in clichés –
oh it must be so hard, oh poor you, we're thinking of you.
People spent all their time telling her how she must be
feeling, or how they felt; nobody actually asked her
anything. It seemed as if nothing was expected of her, as
though her role as a widow was to be passive. 'Oh, a couple
of hours ago,' she answered vaguely, at the same time
withdrawing her hand.

'I hope I prove to be a good tenant,' he responded, then smiling, he placed a hand on his heart and said, 'I promise not to hold any all-night parties or to hang out washing on a Sunday.'

'What a shame,' she said, offering him a small smile. 'I like a good party and it's surprising what you can learn about a person from looking at their washing.'

'Especially their underwear,' cracked Derek.

'Well, yes, I suppose so,' said Hilary, thinking of all hers upstairs. 'Now if you could all go through I'll just put these lovely flowers in water and then follow on in a moment.'

They made their way slowly into the dining-room which, after the warmth of the fire in the sitting-room, felt a little cool. They found themselves confronted with a table laid with rigid military precision: glasses standing to attention, cutlery lined up in ranks, napkins with knife-edge creases and flowery name plates pushed to the front of each place setting . . . and just as Charlotte suspected, she had been positioned next to Alex.

'What an interesting painting, David,' she said. 'Is it new?' And while everyone predictably turned to admire a rather nondescript watercolour above the sideboard, Charlotte switched Alex's name for Derek's.

At the head of the table, Hilary was doing her level best to steer the conversation on a straight course, but somehow it kept slipping away from her. And who, she wanted to know, had ruined her seating plan? Secretly she suspected Derek, all that kissing at the start of the evening. And what did Charlotte think she was doing, whispering and tittering like a schoolgirl, down there with Derek at the other end of the table. Lord knows what Cindy must think. A sideways look told Hilary that Cindy was obviously bored and by the way she was poking at her chocolate mousse, she was not going to finish it. Hilary felt slighted. Cindy had barely opened her mouth all evening, had only said anything when she was spoken to. Alex, bless him, had tried several times to talk to her, but Mother was making that exceptionally difficult, monopolising the poor man with all her talk of antiques. And Dad, of course, was just being Dad, and for all his scintillating talk, he might have stayed at home. David was predictably drunk now and telling another of his Rotary Club jokes.

'What's the difference between a Skoda and Prince Charles?'

'Not now, David,' she said warningly, knowing the punchline only too well. She got to her feet and started to gather up the dishes. 'Bring these out for me, will you?'

'Right you are, my little sweetie-pie,' he said jumping smartly to his feet and managing to pull part of the tablecloth with him. Glasses crashed against plates and red wine bled on to the white damask cloth.

'Don't worry, everyone,' shrieked Hilary, who seemed to be the only one who was worried, 'a bit of salt rubbed in and a cold soak overnight will do the trick.'

'And that's just for David,' giggled Charlotte.

Everyone laughed and started to clear up the mess, dabbing the table with their napkins, while Hilary disappeared to the kitchen.

'Bit of a boob that, old mate,' said Derek, the only one not bothering to help. 'Though personally, I'm not a boob man.'

Again everyone laughed, except Cindy.

Derek looked up round the table. 'Nothing wrong in that, is there?'

David shook his head and poured himself another glass of wine. Taking the bottle from him, Derek filled his own glass and then Charlotte's. 'Anyone else?' he said holding up the bottle. 'What about you, Alex?'

'No thanks.'

Derek laughed. 'No, not the wine. Are you a boob man?'

'Stop it, Derek,' hissed Cindy.

'No, let the man speak.'

'I prefer the whole body.'

Smooth all right, thought Charlotte.

'Cheese and biscuits,' said Hilary, reappearing with a large plate. 'Cindy, dip in first before it all disappears.'

'No, really I couldn't, that was all quite delicious.'

Liar, thought Hilary, looking disappointed.

'Mother, how about you?'

'Sorry, that moussaka really finished me off.'

David roared with laughter. 'Has that effect on most people.'

'Is that a piece of Cheshire Blue?'

Hilary smiled gratefully at Alex and passed him the plate.

'*Very* smooth,' muttered Charlotte.

'What did you say, Charlotte?' asked her mother.

'I was just saying how smooth this red wine is.'

Hilary looked warily at her sister. She had the most awful feeling that this moment was the lull before the storm. Something terrible was about to happen. 'David,' she said, in an effort to keep the evening on track, 'what about some port?'

Getting slowly and very cautiously to his feet, David reached for a near-empty bottle of port on the sideboard, along with a tray of glasses, and for those who wanted port, he poured it out as sparingly as Communion wine.

Separate conversations began springing up around the table. Charlotte eavesdropped on what was being said.

'. . . you know, Cindy, Tiffany is such a godsend to me,' Hilary was saying. 'I don't know how I ever managed without her. She's wonderful with the children, nothing's too much trouble for her.'

'Really, I find that difficult to believe. At home she's quite difficult.'

'. . . So Alex, you're in computers, are you? I would think that would be extremely tedious. Can you prove to me it isn't?'

'I'm not sure I can, Louise, not right here and now, but I can see why you might think that.'

Alex turned away from Louise and looked down the length of the table and stared Charlotte straight in the eye. 'What plans have you got, Charlotte, now that you're back in England?'

'Plans?' she repeated. He smiled, a smile, she realised to her horror, that was duplicated, as was the cheese in front of her. Hell, she was drunk!

'I just wondered what you might want to do next?' he said, his elbows resting on the table and leaning towards her.

He wasn't going to give up, was he? 'Get a job of course,' she answered brightly.

Her mother laughed derisively. 'It won't be easy, Charlotte,' she said. 'Haven't you heard, there's a recession on and you're not exactly overly qualified, are you, apart from now having a little French under your belt, of course?'

'Thanks,' Charlotte said, picking up her wine glass and tossing back the last mouthful.

'I'm only being realistic,' Louise persisted. 'Firms have been closing down at a terrifying rate all over the country.'

'But not the antiques trade, that right, Mother?'

An uncomfortable hush fell round the table. It was Derek who broke it.

'I'm sure someone like Charlotte won't find any difficulty in getting a job,' he said, leaning into her and refilling her glass. 'Bet you sound dead sexy speaking French.'

Charlotte giggled and Hilary looked up sharply. 'David!' she snapped. 'Coffee!'

Hauling himself out of his chair once more, David looked pie-eyed round the table. 'Coffee for how many?'

'For eight of course,' came Hilary's swift reply, and then remembering her manners, she looked round the table. 'Unless there are any takers for tea.'

44

'Better make it for seven,' Louise said tartly. 'Your father's fallen asleep again.'

And looking at her father, Hilary stifled a low groan. What must Alex think of them all?

'So, what kind of job?'

Charlotte silently screamed to herself. Why couldn't that smoothie just shut up and leave her alone? How on earth did she know what sort of work she could get? 'Oh, I don't know, something will turn up,' she murmured, 'and anyway, there's no need for me to get a job immediately. Peter has left me very . . .' Her voice faltered and trailed away.

'A job would keep you busy though, wouldn't it?' said Hilary. 'Keep your mind off things.'

'Why don't you come and work for us?' Derek said, winking at her. 'Classy French-speaking masseuse, that would open up the business, eh Cindy?'

'Shut up, Derek,' Cindy said quietly.

Underneath the tablecloth, Derek placed his hand firmly on Charlotte's left thigh.

Charlotte slowly pushed back her chair and rose unsteadily to her feet. She picked up her glass of wine and brandished it in the air, and in a wavering voice said, 'To Hilary, that was a wonderful lasagne . . . I mean moussaka . . . I'd just like to thank you all for a lovely evening, I haven't had so much fun since . . . well not since I told Peter I didn't . . . Oh I'm sorry, I think I'd better go home.' She banged her glass down on the table and, spilling some of its contents, she slumped slowly down into her chair and started to cry.

A stunned silence followed, then a crescendo of activity with Derek offering to take Charlotte home and Cindy hissing like a swan, saying he'd do nothing of the kind. Hilary told David to get Charlotte out of the dining-room and upstairs before she was sick all over their antique Chinese rug. But Louise surprised them all by saying, 'No, don't be silly, Alex can take her home. He lives nearest, after all.'

'Mother!' cried Hilary, a look of horror on her face. 'Alex can't possibly . . . she must stay here with us.'

'No,' wailed Charlotte. 'Not here. I want to go home.'

'No problem,' Alex said. 'I'll take her back to Ivy Cottage. Could someone find her bag for me, please?' And before Hilary could protest any more, Alex led the snivelling Charlotte towards the hall. 'Goodnight, everyone,' he said. 'Don't worry, she'll feel better after a breath of fresh air.'

7

A cup of coffee in his hand, Alex pushed open the door of his office, or what had once been Mrs Clifford Senior's small dining-room. He could feel the warmth of the early morning sun streaming through the window, even though it was only a quarter past eight. He reached up above his desk and opened one of the windows, looking out at the garden as he did so.

High up in the silver birch tree at the far end he could see two magpies building a new nest. Only yesterday morning these same magpies had been forced to defend their old nest from the onslaught of a large black crow. The noise had been incredible, quite unlike anything Alex had ever heard before, as the birds attempted to protect their home, screeching and squawking, their wings beating furiously, while the crow relentlessly swooped and dived, its wings flapping as menacingly as a vampire's cape. Looking at the two determined birds this morning, Alex wished them well, admiring them for their resilience. He watched them for a while and then sat down at his desk. He took a sip of his coffee, leant back in his chair and wondered how Charlotte was feeling.

After they had crossed the road to Ivy Cottage last night he had walked Charlotte round and round the moonlit garden. At one stage she had even recited the words 'round and round the garden like a teddy bear'. With each circuit completed Charlotte began to lean on him less, until finally she reached the stage when she was completely upright. At that point, coming to a halt in the front garden, Alex took her key from her bag and let them both into the house.

They stumbled around in the dark for a while, because neither of them knew where any of the light switches were. As they crashed about, Charlotte started telling Alex to be quiet. 'Ssh,' she whispered, a finger against her lips. 'You'll wake Peter and he won't like that and then he'll be cross.'

'I'll try to be quiet,' he said in a hushed voice, attempting to placate her.

They found the kitchen and the light switch. But Charlotte immediately turned the light off. 'Look!' she said, smiling and pointing up at the sky through the kitchen window, her eyes wide like those of a small delighted child. 'Isn't it lovely? The moon's shining on us, we don't need a light at all.'

On the draining board stood a kettle, along with a glass, a half empty bottle of gin and two empty tonic bottles. He filled the kettle, plugged it in and then turned round to ask Charlotte where the coffee was. But she was gone.

He went out into the hall and found her coming down the stairs. Her smile, which in the kitchen just now he had decided was quite beautiful, had vanished. 'He's not there,' she said in a small, angry voice.

'Who's not there, Charlotte?'

'Peter.'

This confused discovery on Charlotte's part had the effect of instantly sobering her up. She went into the kitchen, flicked on the light switch and rummaged through the cupboards until she found a small jar of Nescafé. He had left her twenty minutes later.

Alex switched on his computer and prepared himself for a few hours' work, even though it was Saturday. Just this week he had been taken on by a small manufacturing company over in Congleton to install and set up a system encompassing accounting, planning, production and stock

48

control. It was going to be a big job, at least five months' work.

Computers had been Alex's 'thing' since leaving university and it had been generally acknowledged, within his field of expertise, that he was brilliant. Henderson & Wyatt PLC, the huge insurance organisation with a head office in London, had known this only too well, which was why the board of directors were so shocked when Alex, their most experienced IT Project Manager, handed in his notice. Large amounts of money, followed by even larger amounts were offered to keep him. But Alex was adamant. He gave the company six months' notice, and when that was up, he relinquished his company car, sold his flat and put his furniture into store. He then acquired the necessary visas, filled a large backpack and headed east – to Poland, Latvia and Estonia, and for no other reason than that he fancied going there.

Friends and especially family were horrified, and after much exchanging of anxious telephone calls, they decided quite simply that Alex was at 'that age' – Alex Hamilton, they came to the conclusion, was having his mid-life crisis early and was best left alone to get on with it.

His return to Britain coincided exactly with his thirty-sixth birthday. Arriving at Heathrow airport a stone lighter, he had a very firm idea as to just what he was going to do next. He wanted to start up his own consultancy, to be his own boss, to do with his life as he chose. What he wasn't so sure about was just where to do it. He had no desire to live in London again, did not want to pick up his life where he had ceremoniously dumped it eight months previously. From now on he wanted his life to be full of spontaneity, decisions to be made by the hazardous toss of a coin. While still in the confines of the airport, he bought a map of the British Isles, laid it out – Scotland balanced on his backpack and the Home Counties covering the bottom of a sleeping girl – and asked another traveller to point out on the map where he had spent his last British holiday. The man said he had spent a very agreeable few days in Cheshire in the New Year. With a pencil poised over the county of Cheshire, Alex closed his eyes. He brought the pencil down on the village of Hulme Welford – this was to be his new home.

A week later, staying in a smart little bed and breakfast on the outskirts of the village, Alex made his first recce of Hulme Welford. His initial impression, on seeing the black and white half-timbered cottages – some even with thatch – was that he liked what he saw. Strolling into the estate agency in the centre of the village, he was soon on his way to take a look at 1a Ivy Cottage, with a view to renting it.

'As you can see, all the alterations are of a high standard, so you'll have no trouble with the property,' David Parker told him, as they stood in the small empty bedroom looking out over the garden and the open field beyond. A tractor was slowly ploughing ridges with a storm cloud of crows following behind. 'Not a bad view either,' David Parker said, smiling, piling it on a bit more, obviously hoping to clinch the deal there and then in the bedroom.

But Alex didn't need any convincing, his mind was made up. Before stepping foot in the estate agent's office he had already tossed a coin – heads, and he would take the first rented property he saw. It had turned up heads.

They went down the stairs and out through the kitchen door into the garden. Alex stood on the lawn and looked up at the house. 'I'd like to take it, please,' he said. 'But, just as a matter of interest, who will be my landlord?'

'Your landlady actually. My sister-in-law.' Locking up the property and walking back into the village, David Parker explained, briefly, Mrs Lawrence's reasons for moving back to Hulme Welford. 'She needs her family round her,' he added.

Alex hoped that this was indeed the case. Sometimes families were the last thing one needed.

Back in David's office, Alex filled out the necessary forms, giving names and addresses of people whom he hoped would supply him with 'a good character reference'.

'And your line of work, Mr Hamilton?'

'Management Consultant, specialising in Information Technology,' Alex answered, deliberately making himself sound like a contestant on *Mastermind*.

'Right. That sounds . . .'

'Respectable enough?'

The two men smiled, understanding each other perfectly.

'I'll have to check these references – that will take about a week – then I'll have to ask for two months' rent in advance and a deposit of four hundred pounds. Is that all right?'

'No problem. When do you think I can move in?'

David Parker looked at the calender on his desk. 'Shall we say in two weeks' time, would that suit?'

It had suited very well. For the past fortnight Alex had begun to establish himself in the village. He was made to feel adequately welcome, in a gentle probing kind of way.

He set out the spreadsheets that he had been working on yesterday morning, flicked a few keys on the PC keyboard and set to. His concentration didn't last long. He looked up and wondered at the sound he'd just heard, a little like a muffled cry, or was it the magpies being assaulted again? He peered out of the window. All was well high up in the silver birch tree. Then followed a sound that was more audible and clearly more recognisable. His landlady was awake and obviously suffering. He got up from his desk and went quickly upstairs to the bathroom, before going next door to see if he could help.

Moussaka second time around was disgusting, especially when it got stuck in the nose. If she lived, Charlotte thought she would never forgive her sister. Clutching her head and stomach both at the same time, she looked down at the kitchen floor. It was not a pretty sight. She had only crawled downstairs to get herself a drink and now she had this awful mess to clear up.

The unfamiliar sound of the door bell made her jump and was enough to set off a second bout of vomiting. This time she made it to the toilet.

When she staggered back into the kitchen, she thought she must be hallucinating. Alex Hamilton was standing at the kitchen sink, filling a washing-up bowl from the hot tap. She stood open mouthed, not knowing what to do. She was still dressed in the clothes she had worn last night, and she felt like a pair of old tights just pulled out of the washing machine.

'Ah, there you are,' he said, turning off the hot tap and lifting the bowl out of the sink. 'I thought you might need some help. I did ring the bell but there was no answer, so I came round the back and found your door open. You must be feeling pretty wretched.'

Charlotte's mouth opened even further. Sympathy was the last thing she had expected: mocking contempt, yes; concern, no. She tried to speak but couldn't and instead rushed to the toilet again.

When she reappeared Alex was down on his hands and knees wearing a pair of pink Marigold gloves. She somehow found the energy to laugh.

He looked up. 'What's so funny?'

'I'm sorry, it's just that you look ridiculous in those gloves. I suppose Hilary bought them, she's tried so hard to organise everything for me . . . she means well . . . and I was a perfect cow last night.'

He got to his feet. 'I'm sure she'll forgive you.'

'You know, it would be a lot easier if you could be a complete jerk.'

'Maybe I am,' he said. 'Have you got any disinfectant?'

She felt too weak and too stunned by what was happening to be of any real use. 'Have a look under the sink,' she said, 'Hilary's bound to have put some there.' Thinking about what Alex had said earlier, that he had found the back door open, she wondered how that could have been. Then she remembered. Last night, before going out, she had opened up the conservatory . . . and had forgotten to relock it. But that wasn't all she had forgotten, was it?

'I've never had to admit this before,' Charlotte said nervously, watching Alex turning out the cupboard under the sink, 'but I have no idea how I got back here last night. I suppose Hilary saw me home.'

Alex twisted off the safety top of a plastic bottle of disinfectant and poured some of the liquid on to the kitchen floor. He turned to face her. 'Don't you remember anything about last night?'

Recoiling from the smell, she said, raising her voice, 'Well, of course I do!' She regretted this, as her head began to pound with the resonance of a kettle drum. 'I just don't remember coming home, that's all.'

'Actually, it wasn't Hilary, it was me.'

'You!'

'For some reason, known only to your mother I think, she suggested I did, not that I minded.'

Charlotte was speechless. What the hell was her mother playing at?

Alex peeled off the rubber gloves and pointed to a glass of murky brown liquid on the table. 'You'd better drink that.'

'What is it?'

'A patented morning-after-the-night-before cure, never fails. I was given it in Poland where they have more than their fair share of hangovers.'

Charlotte picked up the glass reluctantly and sniffed it. 'Smells disgusting,' she said, pulling a face.

'Tastes disgusting as well. But trust me, it works.'

Too weak to argue, Charlotte put the glass to her lips, deciding that if it made her sick, she would at least have the pleasure of making Alex clean up the mess. The thick liquid slipped down her throat, reminding her of the only time she had ever eaten oysters. She shuddered violently and felt

53

ready to pass out.

'I suggest you have a bath now, then go back to bed.'

Charlotte, strangely obedient, did as she was told, until she reached the landing and found herself watching a comparatively unknown man go into the bathroom and start running her a bath. At the sight of Alex bending over the taps and rummaging through her newly placed toiletries, she felt an overpowering sense of intrusion. Peevishly she said, 'I can manage on my own, thank you. You're my tenant, not my husband.'

He looked neither hurt nor offended. Turning off the taps and wiping his hands on his trousers in the absence of a towel, he said, 'Okay, but I'll be next door if you need me.'

8

Iris Braithwaite, armed with a pooper-scooper in one hand and a dog lead in the other, was standing at the end of Charlotte's driveway when she saw Alex Hamilton coming out of the front door of Ivy Cottage.

Hidden by an unruly forsythia bush, and being a founder member of Hulme Welford's Neighbourhood Watch scheme, she had no difficulty in watching Alex unnoticed, as he made his way from one side of the house to the other. She also had little difficulty in piecing together her version of the events of the previous night.

Sin, and sin with a capital S, put all thought of what was on the other end of the dog lead completely out of her mind, until she took a step backwards and found herself slipping on what her eleven-year-old King Charles spaniel Henry had just evacuated. Grasping at a branch of forsythia, Iris Braithwaite managed to remain vertical, thereby keeping intact her highly prized dignity, though not her silk scarf. It floated slowly to the ground and, like part of a magician's act, covered perfectly Henry's squelched offering.

Saturday was Derek and Cindy's busiest day of the week at In The Pink. From the moment they had opened at eight forty-five the salon and gym had been packed. In the back salon, above the sound of the local radio station, Derek could hear Dawn, their beautician, telling a horizontal Mrs Carlton the best way to close up her pores each night before going to bed. Earlier it had been a lesson on the perils of dehydrating the Stratum Corneum by using a defatting something or other. It all sounded pretty convincing stuff, and even if he didn't believe a word of it, the punters did, and that was what counted.

Trying to ignore Dawn's constant stream of prattle, he carried on winding clingfilm around the head of Mrs Jeffs, an attractive bottle blonde from the Orchard Way executive development. She was married to *the* Darren Jeffs, the highly paid key goal scorer for Manchester United – though it was rumoured that Darren was scoring more than goals these days. Until yesterday evening Derek had reckoned Mrs Jeffs was worthy of extra special attention, had thought her to be the most desirable woman in the village.

Now, as Derek looked in the mirror at the sleek face bent over the latest bestseller from Jackie Collins, he viewed her as second rate – he noticed too that she had been reading the same racy page for the past ten minutes. Overnight he had relegated Mrs Jeffs to the second division, for every bit of him wanted Charlotte Lawrence.

He would have to go carefully with Charlotte, he knew: a grieving widow was a harder prospect than a bored housewife. Last night in bed, after making love to Cindy, he had lain awake thinking of Charlotte: of running his hands through her lovely hair with its natural dark colour; of taking her to that secret place, down in the woods near the mere – where he had intended taking Mrs Jeffs.

'*Derek!*' It was Cindy standing next to him, a hot brush in one hand and an aerosol of styling mousse in the other. 'I don't know what you're thinking of, but that's quite enough clingfilm for Mrs Jeffs.'

He looked down at the now unwanted Mrs Jeffs, almost hidden beneath a sombrero of transparent plastic. Frankly though, he didn't give a damn. He decided that from now on, if he was going to get anywhere with Charlotte, he would have to be subtle.

*

Charlotte woke up just after two in the afternoon. She was amazed how well she felt, so well in fact that she wondered whether the hangover, and what had caused it, had all been a terrible dream. But looking at her pile of discarded clothes at the end of the put-you-up, and recognising them by their creases, it hit Charlotte that she had a certain amount of music to face. Earlier, she'd had only a patchy memory of the events of the previous night; now she could remember *everything*. Oh, what a fool she had made of herself, especially all that wandering around the garden with Alex.

Drunk. She closed her eyes and shuddered. She had never been drunk before. Tiddly yes, but not so drunk that she had been sick afterwards.

The most memorable occasion when she'd had too much to drink was when Peter had taken her to meet his parents for the first time. 'I think you should meet my parents,' he had said one night on the phone.

'Why? Am I in for a shock?' she had replied.

Ann and Godfrey were a shock with their puritanical mores. Grace had been barked out at the start of dinner, just as Charlotte had reached for her knife and fork. The first social gaffe of the evening committed she gulped at her wine, saying 'This is lovely.'

'We never touch it ourselves,' Godfrey stated, as upright as a guardsman in his chair.

She tried appealing to Ann. 'Hasn't Peter done well at work this year?'

'We never wanted him to be an accountant.'

Charlotte looked to Peter for his reaction. His face was expressionless, which made him seem so vulnerable. It was then that Charlotte first thought she loved Peter.

At the end of the meal, and having drunk more wine than was good for her, Charlotte committed the final *faux pas*. She reached out for her cup of coffee over the top of a flickering candle and let out a sudden undignified yelp. She dropped the cup, spilling coffee everywhere and saw with horror a flame at the end of her finger – her false nail had caught light. 'I'm so terribly sorry,' she squealed, dousing her finger in the remains of her wine. The hiss was short lived but not the memory of that evening.

In the car driving back to London, she apologised to Peter. 'I'm sorry. I spoiled everything.'

'Rubbish,' he said, smiling for the first time all night. 'You gave them a good shaking up.'

'I don't think they approved of me.'

'Good. Will you marry me?'

That was the impulsive Peter she had loved, and married three months later.

Charlotte pushed back the duvet and got up. She pulled some clothes out of a suitcase, got dressed and went downstairs to get something to eat. She was starving.

There was a strong smell of disinfectant in the kitchen. She opened every window and door and set about making herself a sandwich and tidying away last night's bottles of gin and tonic. As she leaned against the worktop and bit into the bread and cheese, she began to realise just how much her sister had done for her. The refrigerator and cupboards all seemed to be full of basic food and household requirements. She hadn't noticed any of these things yesterday. How ungrateful she must have seemed.

From now on, she decided, there would be no more wallowing in self pity, no more blaming herself and then being bloody to everyone else who helped. It was time to move on. What had happened, had happened. She hadn't killed Peter, the weather had – all that snow and ice. 'I am not responsible for Peter's death,' she said out loud.

It was time to be strong, to be positive and decisive, but most of all, to be nice. Cynicism had played too great a part in her life recently, so much so that it was possible that she had forgotten what being nice was all about. It certainly wasn't humiliating one's sister at her dinner party; nice wasn't throwing up all over the kitchen floor as a result and then being rude to someone who was trying to help. Even so, that drink had smelt awful. She wouldn't apologise for saying that.

After this self-imposed lecture, Charlotte made herself a cup of tea, stood at one end of the empty kitchen and stared hard at the room. Oblong in shape and bordered with good quality pine cupboards with innocuous cream and blue wall tiles, it offered no obvious horrors. Her pine table and chairs, arriving from Brussels on Monday, would finish it off well, together with a fresh lick of paint and some pretty curtain fabric. Then it would feel like her kitchen. This was what she had wanted for so long – to live in a house that was hers, not an apartment that was rented and had no sense of 'home' or permanence.

She began to feel more cheerful and, rushing upstairs to her bedroom, she unearthed a notepad and pen. She returned to the kitchen, where she started to write out a list. At the top of the list and underlined were the words, 'Apologise to everyone'; next was 'Buy paint', followed by 'Check out curtain fabric', and then, after a moment's pause, she wrote 'Buy a dog'. For years she had wanted a dog, but Peter had always said, 'No, how can we?' Given the circumstances, he was right of course.

She was just wondering how she would go about buying a dog when the door bell rang.

Opening the front door, she was surprised to see a large bouquet of red roses proffered by a tanned arm. She couldn't smell the roses but she could smell aftershave and so had a pretty good idea who it was hiding behind one of the brick posts of the porch with his arm extended.

'They're lovely,' she said. 'A shame they're not for me.'

'Oh, but they are,' Derek Rogers said, stepping out from his hiding place. 'They most certainly are for you.' And with one hand placed firmly on her shoulder, he took her inside the house, shutting the door behind them. 'You know, Charlotte, I made myself a promise this morning.'

'That's funny,' Charlotte said, 'so did I.'

'I made a promise to be kind to widows and orphans.'

Charlotte laughed, feeling that perhaps she shouldn't. 'And I've just promised myself to be strong, positive, decisive and nice,' she said.

He smiled. 'Sounds interesting. I hope you're going to be nice to me. You'll need to put those in water.' He handed her the roses. 'This way to the kitchen, is it?'

Why, thought Charlotte, does everyone else seem to think they have a perfect right to gate-crash their way into *my* house? She followed behind, and placing the bouquet in the sink, she put the plug in and turned on the cold tap.

'I think I ought to apologise for last night,' she said above the noise of gushing water. 'I don't normally get drunk.'

'No need to apologise,' he said, stepping towards her. 'I like a woman who can let herself go.'

Turning the tap off, Charlotte took a step back. 'It's just that I wouldn't want you to get the wrong idea about me.'

'And what idea would that be?'

'Well, you know, that I always behave badly.'

He laughed, and moved slightly closer. 'I'd say you behaved beautifully.'

'That's all right then,' she said brightly, remembering last night how she had thought it could be fun to flirt with Derek. She wasn't so sure now. She walked over to the other side of the kitchen.

'So beautifully, in fact, that I spent the entire evening wanting to make love to you, there and then.'

She tried to laugh, to sound blasé, as though she was completely *au fait* with this kind of conversation. 'What, in front of everyone?'

Again, he was moving towards her. 'I think we'd both prefer to do it in private, wouldn't we?'

He's joking, she told herself. He's just trying me out, trying to see whether I'll fall about shocked. She tried another laugh. He came and stood next to her.

At first she was totally passive when he kissed her, too surprised to know how to react. Then, because she was really rather enjoying it, she responded. It only lasted a split second but it was enough to convince Derek that he was a welcome guest to the rest of her body. 'No,' she said firmly, when his hands strayed from her shoulders and towards her neck.

'No such word,' he whispered.

'How about this?' Charlotte said, coming to her senses. 'Cindy!'

'Cindy doesn't mind.'

'Bloody hell!' Charlotte shouted, pushing him away from her. 'So you think you can add my name to your long list of ego boosts, do you?' She moved back to the sink and, picking up the roses, she thrust their dripping stems at his chest. 'I want to keep my promise, Derek,' she said calmly, 'so will you get out of my house now . . . please?'

Iris Braithwaite was doing the rounds distributing the parish magazine. She was just on her way up Charlotte's drive when she heard the sound of the front door being opened and saw Derek Rogers coming out. Iris paused for a moment and turned on her heels, marching off down Acacia Lane to the safety of The White Cottage. 'She's past shame, that Charlotte Lawrence! Her husband's barely cold.' She muttered all the way home in a frenzy of outrage. '*Two* men in one day! I must warn Reverend Jackson, no man is safe. Why the poor man himself might even be in danger.'

9

'Well, you do surprise me,' Louise told Hilary on the telephone. 'I thought you would have raced over the road at the crack of dawn to see how your sister was.'

'Not after her appalling behaviour,' Hilary said emphatically, unaware of her mother's pithy sarcasm.

'Oh don't be such an old woman, Hilary. Charlotte only got drunk. You sound as though she committed mass homicide round the table last night, though to be honest, I can think of one person I would gladly let her murder.'

Finding herself in agreement with her mother for once, Hilary said, 'You're absolutely right, of course – that Derek Rogers is entirely to blame. I did warn Charlotte about him, but you know what she's like, thinks she knows . . .'

'Rubbish! Derek's a dear,' responded Louise, who secretly thought that if Derek hadn't been there last night, they would have all died of boredom. 'I was referring to your father. Dear God, ever since he retired, there's been no keeping him awake. He did the same thing when we were over at the Macmillans' for Easter Sunday.'

Annoyed, Hilary sensed her telephone call being hijacked as she listened to her mother setting off down the familiar track of Dr Neville Archer retired.

For thirty-six years their father had been a GP in Hulme Welford, until last year when he could no longer put off his retirement. Ever since then Louise had complained constantly that their father was at a loose end, permanently moping about and getting under her feet. Hilary could sympathise. She had often thought the same thing about David while on holiday.

Well, that was one thing her sister would be spared. At least Charlotte wouldn't have to put up with Peter getting in the way. Thinking of Charlotte made Hilary remember what she had called her mother for.

'Mother,' she interrupted, 'never mind Dad for the moment. Don't you think you should go and check on Charlotte?'

'Why ever should I?'

'Because, well, she might have thrown up and –'

'What, and choked to death? Goodness, Hilary, you do have a vivid imagination, don't you? Look, it's Saturday afternoon and I've got a shop full of customers. If you're so worried about Charlotte lying in a pool of her own vomit, go and do something about it.'

Hilary put down the receiver with a look of shock on her face. She had forgotten her mother had moved the telephone from her little back office to her desk in the main part of the shop. She cringed at the thought of those customers listening to her mother's one-sided conversation. What must they have thought?

As for going over to see Charlotte, that was quite out of the question. She had no intention of calling on Charlotte, not until her sister had apologised for ruining her dinner party.

In the end, it was Neville – his gooseberries tended to and with time on his hands – who called on Charlotte.

He couldn't be bothered walking to Ivy Cottage even though it was only ten minutes away. He supposed that was what retirement did to you, and he got the car out instead. Turning into Acacia Lane, he hoped that Hilary wouldn't catch sight of him. She would be bound to tell Louise and then he'd never hear the last of it and be restricted to even fewer calories. 'If you're going to lead a completely sedentary life, you must expect to eat less,' Louise had told him the last time he had got the car out for what she called an unnecessary journey. She, of course, cycled energetically everywhere and was the same weight now – as she so liked to tell him – as when she fell pregnant with Charlotte.

'Hello Dad,' Charlotte said, opening the door. 'Come in.'

He stepped inside. 'You look better than I thought you might,' he said.

'Let the side down a bit last night, didn't I?'

He smiled. 'Me too. What a pair we are.'

In the kitchen, Neville couldn't help but notice the opened copy of *Yellow Pages* on the worktop. 'Anything I can help you with?' he said warily. These days he was so used to being told there was nothing for him to do, he hardly dared ask the question.

'There is, as a matter of fact,' she said. 'Have you got a spare hour or so?'

'Yes,' he said, brightening. 'I've got a spare twenty-four, if that's any good to you.'

'Right then,' she said, picking up her bag, 'drive me over to Lower Peover and help me choose a dog.'

Neville followed his daughter out of the house.

He suddenly felt happy. He was going to enjoy having Charlotte around again.

10

Charlotte looked at her watch. It was half past six on Sunday morning. She groaned and tried to ignore the noise coming from downstairs. Surely dogs slept for longer than this? She lay there, listening to the persistent whining for a few moments more, before she gave in, got out of bed and padded downstairs to the kitchen.

Opening the kitchen door, she was all set to be firm, but seeing the small face looking up at her – head slightly tilted – all her strong resolve vanished, and she bent down and scooped the little dog up in her arms.

The dog had looked at her like that yesterday afternoon at the kennels. Mrs Ingram-Walker, whom Charlotte had spoken to on the telephone earlier, had greeted Charlotte and her father at the gate, shouting loudly above the noise of the yapping West Highland White Terrier puppies. 'Found us all right, then? Bit off the beaten track really. Still, you managed it, that's the main thing.'

They walked round the kennels, Mrs Ingram-Walker determined to give them an official guided tour, and enthusing every step of the way. The place was certainly impressive, spotlessly clean and festooned with certificates and rosettes for Best Dog and Best Bitch.

'You know what this is all about, don't you, Charlotte?' her father said as they were shown yet another certificate, this time for hygiene. 'This is the sales pitch to justify the huge price she's going to quote you any minute now.'

'That's just the kind of thing Peter would have said,'

Charlotte replied tersely.

As they were coming to the end of the tour of puppy pens, Charlotte saw a slightly older-looking Westie on its own. 'Why's that one all alone?' she asked.

'Kept her back from an earlier litter, thought perhaps she might be good enough to run on for breeding. Turned out she's not. Always a problem, that. You get stuck with them then – people want puppies, not a dog at seven months. Still, there we are, she's not a bad bitch though.'

'May I see her?' Charlotte asked, bending down to have a closer look at the shy face, tilted to one side and staring up at her from the back of the pen. Charlotte's mind was already made up. It was this dog or nothing.

Holding the little dog to her, Charlotte looked down at the sheets of newspaper she had laid out on the kitchen floor the night before. Mrs Ingram-Walker had said there would be no need, that the dog was completely toilet trained, but Charlotte hadn't wanted to take any chances. 'So you really are a good girl then', she said, seeing that all was dry.

She put the dog on the floor and began tidying up the newspapers. As she did so, *Deaths and Funerals*' caught her eye. All the recently deceased were women and in their seventies or eighties: Mrs Mary Robinson, Mrs Edith Byron, Miss Alice Hayes, Mrs Annie Tompkins and lastly Miss Mabel Unwin. Charlotte looked up from this last entry and turned to the white dog beside her, who responded with another tilt of its head. 'Yes,' Charlotte smiled. 'I think I've found the perfect name for you – Mabel.'

Breakfast was interrupted by the sound of the door bell. Mabel, her head down inside a small china bowl of Weetabix, didn't even look up.

'Fine guard dog you're going to be,' Charlotte said, putting her own bowl of cereal down on the worktop. 'You'll be back to Mrs Ingram-Walker if you don't pull your weight round here,' she called over her shoulder as she went out into the hall.

Charlotte opened the door. 'Talking to yourself now,' Louise said, then gave her daughter a hard stare and added, 'or have you got someone here?'

'What, at half past seven in the morning, Mother?'

'Anything's possible.' Louise tucked a thick wad of newspaper under her arm and looked up the stairs to the landing above.

Charlotte stared at her mother, shut the door and then wandered back to the kitchen, shaking her head. 'Is there anything you wanted in particular? I mean, it's lovely to see you, but it is fairly early to be paying social calls, especially for you.'

'Don't worry, I shan't stop for long. Any tea in the pot? Oh, what's that?' She stared down at Mabel.

'She's a breeder's reject,' Charlotte said. 'Can't you tell?'

'It's too early in the morning to play games with me, Charlotte. Who does it belong to?'

'*She*,' Charlotte said with emphasis, 'is mine. I bought her yesterday from a Mrs Ingram-Walker.'

'Are you out of your mind? How are you going to look after it, I mean her, while you're out working?'

'Oh, so suddenly I'm capable of getting a job, am I?'

'Well, that remains to be seen, of course.'

'Don't spoil it for me, Mother,' Charlotte said, handing her a mug of tea. 'I've always wanted a dog, and besides, I need the company.'

Louise put the *Sunday Times* on the worktop behind her and cradled the mug in her hand. 'But you've got Hilary right opposite you, and there's us, no more than a ten-minute walk away.'

'Yes, and you've all got your own lives to lead.' Charlotte thought that right now she'd rather have Mabel than any member of her family, except her father. 'Look,' she said, 'I can't expect you all to revolve around me suddenly. It wouldn't be fair.'

'Well, I suppose you're right.'

'And while we're on the subject of things being right and fair, what on earth were you doing suggesting Alex see me home on Friday night?'

Louise laughed. 'Just a bit of fun, playing Hilary at her own game. You should have seen the look on her face.'

'I can imagine it,' Charlotte said, almost enjoying the thought. 'So what did you come round here for, apart from a cup of tea?'

'Oh yes. To tell you that you must come to church this morning.'

'Why, is there something special on today?'

'No, but I just think you ought to show your face.'

'You've never forced anyone to church before. Why now, and more importantly, why me?'

'Well, Charlotte,' Louise said, putting down her empty mug, 'thing is, you've been found out. I was in the paper shop a few moments ago,' she nodded towards her copy of the *Sunday Times*, by way of supportive evidence, 'and I overheard Iris Braithwaite talking to Mrs Haslip. Apparently it's common knowledge.'

'What is?'

Louise smiled. 'I have to take my hat off to you, Charlotte, you don't do things by halves, do you?'

'Now who's playing games?'

'You are, by the sounds of things. But I'm not sure Hulme Welford is the right place to be playing them. Too small, too parochial – especially for a woman.'

'For heaven's sake, Mother, what are you talking about?'

'Not just me, what everyone's talking about, that not only have you lured your tenant into bed within twenty-four hours of moving into Ivy Cottage, but Derek Rogers as well.'

68

II

At first Charlotte laughed out loud at her mother's revelation, hot from the lips of Iris Braithwaite. 'But *surely* no one is taking these absurd claims seriously?'

'I think you'll find that most people will be only too keen to believe it, Charlotte.'

'But why?'

'Because it's exciting, it's forbidden, and a woman, at that, is doing it here in Hulme Welford, right under their noses. They want to be shocked.'

'So Derek Rogers could go around seducing everyone and everything, left, right and centre, and that wouldn't be newsworthy, you mean?' Charlotte's voice was beginning to rise.

'Not in the same way. Everyone expects a man like Derek to behave badly, that's entirely within the rules of the game. But you're a widow and expected to behave as such and because you're a woman, you can only play the role of victim. Play it any other way and you're wide open to tabloid sensationalism.'

Charlotte was finding the situation less amusing now. 'But that's ridiculous.'

'I'm sorry, Charlotte,' her mother went on, 'but you've broken the rules and you've been found out.'

'You mean, you actually believe all this nonsense?'

Louise shrugged her shoulders. 'It really doesn't matter what I think, does it?'

'Of course it does.'

'Goodness, I don't understand why you're getting so worked up, you've never been bothered by what anyone thought of you before. Conforming has never been your forte, has it?' She laughed. 'I know you'll hate me for saying this, but there's more of me in you than you'd like to believe.'

Charlotte tried to ignore this last unnerving comment from her mother. 'So, just why are you asking me to go to church this morning?'

'What you get up to in your own home has nothing to do with Iris. She shouldn't be allowed to get away with invading your privacy, or anyone else's for that matter. You've got to fight her.'

Charlotte sighed. Fighting was the last thing she felt like doing at the moment. 'But there's nothing to fight about, none of it's true,' she said in an exasperated voice.

'None of it?' Louise asked, eyeing her daughter speculatively.

'None of it,' Charlotte repeated, looking out of the kitchen window and evading her mother's gaze. Well, there was no need to mention Derek kissing her, was there? And she hadn't kept the roses, she'd given those straight back.

Her mother picked up her *Sunday Times*. 'I must be off. But like I say, just go to church, brazen this out and make sure that as many people as possible, especially Iris, see you there, preferably on your knees. If there's one thing the righteous really like, it's a sinner praying for forgiveness.'

Crashing the breakfast dishes into the sink, Charlotte turned on the hot tap. Water gushed directly on to a cereal spoon, sending up a fountain of water in her face. She wiped herself dry and considered the no-win alternatives: do nothing and everyone would assume her guilty; fight back and everyone would think that the lady doth protest too much.

In front of the altar, a smartly dressed Mrs Haslip was

reading out the week's notices. The rest of the congregation was so absorbed in working out how best to avoid being roped in for the jumble sale and the fork supper, that nobody noticed Charlotte slipping quietly in at the back and settling herself in an unoccupied pew. So far so good, she told herself, wishing that the real purpose of her visit to St John's was to remain discreet to the point of invisibility, instead of being there to clear her name.

She had made up her mind not to come and to hell with everyone thinking she was man crazy. But then she had thought about Cindy and her children, and the terrible unfairness of the situation had hit her and propelled her out of Ivy Cottage and down Acacia Lane to St John's. She would sort this out, not for her own reputation, or Derek's for that matter, but for that of his family. And of course, there was Alex to think of.

The service was under way now. Charlotte stared at the needlepoint design on the hassock in front of her, and thought of the last time she had been in church. Peter's funeral.

Throughout the funeral service Peter's mother and father had sat motionless, their grief kept well in check until the church service was behind them and the funeral party had moved on to the nearby crematorium, where Ann finally allowed herself a restrained display of emotion, the comfort of her husband's angular shoulder supporting her own. It was as though she was responding to the heat of the flames about to consume her son, letting it thaw her customary coldness to give way, perhaps, to a sense of regret.

When Charlotte looked up she found she was no longer alone in the pew. Malcolm Jackson was well into his stride on the theme of spiritual gifts and he was holding up a small pink wallpaper-covered bin as a visual aid.

Sitting on her right was an earnest-looking tall young man of about eighteen, with a strong athletic build. He was wearing a pair of fashionable tortoise shell-framed glasses, half obscured by an asymmetrical fringe dangling down on one side of his forehead. Covering the rest of him was a well-worn jogging suit. Charlotte guessed, from his slightly flushed and glistening face, that he had recently been wearing the jogging suit for its originally designed purpose. There was an aroma about him too that corroborated this. She could feel his body heat radiating towards her and she also thought she sensed some hostility. But no. She was just being paranoid. He turned and looked at her. She smiled, but he jerked his head away and gave his attention back to the sermon.

'Gifts come in varying shapes and sizes,' announced Malcolm Jackson. 'This was once a discarded tin of coffee, thrown away from somebody's kitchen cupboard, but with the gift of creativity we now have a wastepaper bin. I want to challenge each and everyone of you. Go home . . .' a slight pause, a smile . . . 'No, not now, but later, and search through your spiritual cupboards and see what God has given you. What has God given you, that you have been ignoring all these years?'

Not daring to think what might lie in her spiritual cupboards, Charlotte surveyed the congregation and the choir. Iris Braithwaite was wearing a wide-brimmed, brown felt hat which managed to ensure that she was the focal point of the choir. Taller than the other ladies, now all on their feet ready to sing, Iris stood at least five inches higher than anyone else. As Mr Phelps from the Post Office pulled out all the stops on the organ and the congregation rose to its feet, Iris, with both her hands crossed in front of her as though guarding her virginity, closed her eyes, opened her mouth and prepared to give everyone the benefit of her deep contralto voice. Within a few words of the opening line of 'Give Me Joy' – far too modern a hymn for Iris's taste, as everyone knew – her eyes shot open at the sound of the happy clappers three rows from the front. She stared hard at the offending couple, but they carried on courageously right to the end of the hymn.

The singing came to an end and the service continued with 'the Peace'. Anarchy seemed to be breaking out in the pews, with people greeting each other as though they were long-lost friends. No one greeted Iris. Charlotte, balking at the idea of being confronted by anyone she knew, turned to her lone companion, hoping to engage him in dull, safe conversation. She was in for a shock.

'You look like you've just been jogging,' she said. How ridiculous she sounded.

Looking down at his clothes, the young man said a little sullenly, 'Do you mind?'

'Of course not, but you'll probably find there'll be those who do mind, and they won't be happy until they see you in a boring grey suit.'

He almost smiled, almost looked her in the eye. 'It's just the only way I can come,' he said nudging his glasses on to the bridge of his nose.

Charlotte was wondering what he meant by this, when he asked her, 'You're Charlotte Lawrence, aren't you?'

'Yes.'

'Do you know who I am?'

'No.'

And looking her in the eye, he said, 'Have you really been to bed with Derek Rogers?'

'No!' she answered, in a shocked voice. She hadn't been at all prepared for this kind of blatant interrogation, especially from one so young.

Vaguely aware that order had once again been restored, Charlotte turned away from this inquisitive lad and tried to pick up the threads of the service.

'. . . *I believe in one God, the Father Almighty . . .*'

'Believe me, I haven't,' Charlotte said to the young man, wanting suddenly to defend herself. She slipped down on to her hassock.

'. . . *Maker of heaven and earth . . .*'

'Do you intend to?'

'. . . *And of all things visible and invisible . . .*'

'No, certainly not.'

'. . . *And in one Lord Jesus Christ . . .*'

'Good,' said her companion.

A few minutes after the service had come to an end a sizeable crush had developed in the porch. Charlotte decided to remain in her seat until the worst was over. She was alone again, her strange companion having left. He had made his exit just as silently as he had arrived, leaving seconds before the end of the service. Whilst she hadn't particularly liked his line of questioning, there had been something about him she had liked – his straightforwardness.

She caught sight of her sister hovering by the font, holding what looked like a miniature toilet seat. Charlotte smiled at her, remembering she had yet to apologise. Was it her imagination, or had her sister just ignored her? Confused, she got to her feet and joined the queue for the escape route out, thankful that those around her were completely taken up in their own conversations and didn't seem to be at all worried by what she may, or may not have been up to.

From behind her came a voice. 'Charlotte, there you are.' It was her mother, making one of her absurd statements, with her father bringing up the rear. To Charlotte's surprise her mother kissed her. She knew why and was, for once in her life, grateful to her.

The three of them were now level with Malcolm Jackson in the porch and Charlotte began to feel nervous. Had Malcolm heard the gossip? Heavens, he might have been thinking she had been propositioning the young man who sat next to her.

'So good to see you, Charlotte. How are you?' she heard Malcolm say. She nodded mutely, but instead of looking him full in the face, she found her eyes rooted to a small red wine stain on the left cuff of his otherwise immaculate white robe. She wondered if Iris Braithwaite had spotted this during the service and was even now planning a campaign to clean up the vicar of Hulme Welford.

'She's fine,' her mother answered for her. 'We're all rallying round, aren't we, dear, easing your suffering?'

Charlotte looked on bewildered. She had never heard her mother speak like this before. Suddenly, drawn like a magnet to the word suffering, everything seemed wrong. Yesterday she had been happy. This morning, before her mother called in, she had been happy. But it was wrong, very wrong. She had no right to feel anything other than the burden of Peter's death. All that had just passed inside the church, all those words she had listened to and repeated about love and deliverance from evil – she had no right to be there. Not after what she had done to Peter. Panic began to well up inside her. She fought it back, tried to control the monster of guilt within and edged towards the open door and the sunshine waiting outside.

'I shan't pester you, Charlotte,' pursued Malcolm, 'because I'm sure you'll have plenty of offers of help and advice, but if there really is anything I can do for you, you know where I am, though Mrs Braithwaite says I'm the most elusive person she knows. Apparently she was looking for me all yesterday afternoon, had something important to tell me.'

Charlotte forced a smile, wanting more than anything for the conversation to reach its conclusion. At the mention of Iris Braithwaite's name, she changed her mind. 'There is something you can help me with.'

'Yes?' Malcolm looked eagerly sympathetic.

'I just wanted to ask who that young man was, the one sitting next to me at the back of the church?'

'That was Barry. Nice lad, seems to carry the weight of the world on his young shoulders though. He's Derek Rogers' eldest.'

*

Outside in the sunshine and reeling from the shock of what she had just been told, Charlotte leaned against a large ornate tomb, about the size of a Mini, and tried to take in the fact that she had just been confronted by Barry Rogers. *Have you really been to bed with Derek Rogers?*

'Well,' said her mother, 'that wasn't so bad, was it? We would offer you Sunday lunch, but we're off to a car boot sale which starts in an hour, and I need to get there for the pick of the best pieces before the crowds turn up.'

'Don't worry about me,' Charlotte said in a distracted voice, watching her mother walk away. 'I've got plenty to do.'

'Are you okay, Charlotte?' her father said, walking along side her. 'Only you look a bit strange.'

'I'm fine,' she lied.

'No, you're not,' he said. 'I can tell, I was a doctor once, you know.'

'Oh Dad, don't be nice to me, not now, you'll make me feel sorry for myself and that would never do. Peter's father always used to say I was full of self pity.'

'Never mind Peter's father, do you want me to speak to Iris? She's no right spreading lies about the village.'

Charlotte looked up into her father's face and smiled. 'No,' she said, shaking her head, 'but thanks anyway.'

He looked puzzled. 'What for?'

'For believing in me and not what Iris Braithwaite's been saying.'

'Neville, do hurry up,' Louise called out. She was already down at the bottom of the gravel path and pulling open the lych-gate.

For a moment Neville Archer hesitated between his wife and daughter.

'Go on, Dad,' Charlotte said. 'I'm fine, really.'

Alone for no more than a few seconds, Charlotte felt herself the focus of someone's gaze. She looked up and met the icy glare of Iris Braithwaite, who, together with her cronies Mrs Haslip and Mrs Bradley, was encircling Malcolm Jackson in a well-practised pincer movement. A combination of fear and confused guilt told Charlotte to run, but something greater, her anger and her sense of justice, told her that this was the moment to shoot from the hip.

'Hello, Mrs Braithwaite,' she called out, as she made her way back towards the church porch.

In response, the older woman clutched her handbag tightly to her.

'You're just the woman I needed to see,' Charlotte said brightly, now standing directly in front of Iris. Post-service hangers-on, pricking up their ears, turned to watch. They sensed that something cataclysmically more interesting than discussing the vicar's handling of the service was about to happen. Charlotte pushed on. 'I think you have some-thing to say to me, haven't you, Mrs Braithwaite?'

'I certainly have not.'

'Oh, but you have, and not only to me.'

The pearls on Iris's silk-clad chest began to wobble. 'Mrs Lawrence, I assure you, I have absolutely nothing what-soever to say to you.'

This haughty righteousness was too much for Charlotte. 'Do you really think,' she said in a dangerously menacing voice, 'that I am capable of taking two men, whom I hardly know, into my bed one after the other?'

'I know what I saw,' Iris Braithwaite said, holding her ground and looking for back-up from the two women either side of her, who were beginning ever so slightly to distance themselves from Iris.

'You saw two men leave my house, nothing more, nothing less,' Charlotte asserted. 'I suggest you go and undo all the harm you've done with your vile gossip, and you can start by apologising to Mr and Mrs Rogers and their children.'

Leaving Iris Braithwaite looking like a paralysed rabbit

caught in the beam of a car headlight, Charlotte turned and walked away, unaware of the silent applause from those around her who had just witnessed the first ever public dressing-down of Iris Braithwaite.

12

Charlotte felt wretched. Scoring a public victory over Iris Braithwaite should have had her skipping home, happy as a lamb. Instead she was shocked and saddened by what had just happened.

All her life, like so many others in the village, she had viewed Iris Braithwaite as some kind of personal *bête noire*. Iris had ruled the roost of Hulme Welford for as long as Charlotte could remember, her authority never once having been publicly questioned until today. Yet all Charlotte could remember from the short exchange was the terrible look on the older woman's face.

She had noticed that very same look on Peter's face the last time she saw him. She could recall now that look of hurt he was trying so hard to hide from her. So vivid was the picture in her mind that she was back there, in their Brussels apartment, in the kitchen, the smell of coffee, toast, boiled eggs . . . and then her words, words that had stabbed at Peter across the breakfast table: *I want a divorce Peter*. She thought at first that he had not heard her. Then slowly he put his knife down on the plate in front of him – a blob of butter, half melted, clinging to the serrated edge – and he looked up at her, his lips clamped tightly shut, his eyes never leaving her own. He sat like that for what seemed an age; petrified by his emotionally starved upbringing. Nothing had prepared him for this devastating moment in his life.

Oh God, thought Charlotte, crossing the road, what was

happening to her that she could go round hurting people so badly?

Not wanting, just yet, to go back to Ivy Cottage, not with the possibility of being confronted by Hilary, or even Iris Braithwaite, Charlotte turned left and walked down to the main street of the village until she came to Ted Cooper's paper shop.

Behind his back Ted Cooper had always been known as Sleazy Ted. But three years ago, after a lifetime of battling to keep what little greasy hair he had, he'd given up on it and covered the remaining strands with a well-upholstered wig. Then he had become Ted the Toup. Now, after three years of accumulated grime and nicotine, his famous false hair gave the appearance of being fused together into one solid piece.

Charlotte pushed open the door. She saw Ted sitting behind his till. He was leaning back in his chair reading a copy of the *People*. The face of a recently disgraced cricketer stared back at Charlotte. His eyes, beneath his cricket cap, watched her as she approached the counter.

'Hello, love,' Ted said, raising his own eyes over the top of the paper. 'Settling in okay, are you? Making new friends?'

'Not too badly,' Charlotte said, registering the ambiguity of Ted's last question.

''Course, nothing's really changed, has it, from when you left?'

'No, nothing's changed,' she agreed, noticing that Ted's tobacco-stained hands with their effeminately long nails were still the same, as were his cracked and blackened teeth.

She scanned the selection of Sundays on offer. The tabloids seemed to have either a 'distressed' or an 'outraged' Royal on the front page, with the exception of the *People*, who had gone it alone, informing its readership of the lurid sex life of a Northamptonshire top-spinner. The heavy brigade all carried more or less the same photograph of a tired-looking John Major. Having no particular loyalty to any one newspaper, Charlotte picked out the *Independent*, which was the nearest one to her. As she handed over her money she reflected that it seemed a very fitting choice.

Leaving Ted to get back to his reading, she opened the shop door to find herself confronted by a blue anorak and a pink hand-knitted cardigan. Although Charlotte didn't know the couple, she had seen them earlier in church and knew that they had witnessed the exchange between Iris Braithwaite and herself. They smiled at her – a full-blown, obsequious, Cheshire Cat grin. Politely she smiled back, hoping to slide past them and out of the shop. But they were having none of it.

'We'd just like to congratulate you,' the anorak said.

'We certainly would,' the pink cardigan echoed.

'It's about time somebody stood up to her,' the anorak said.

'It certainly is,' the cardigan agreed.

There was a rustle from behind the counter as Ted once again lowered his paper, his attention aroused by something other than bums and boobs. He looked over at them and slithered his way into the conversation with consummate ease. 'Afternoon, Reg, Joan. Congratulations in order, did I hear you say?'

'Didn't she tell you all about it, Ted?' said the anorak, who had now been identified as Reg. Charlotte folded the *Independent* in her hands and looked at the floor.

Reg and Joan closed the door behind them and surged past the displays of greetings cards and racks of magazines in their haste to impart their news to Ted.

'She was very brave,' said Reg.

'Oh, she was, you know,' agreed Joan.

'I really must be going.' Charlotte backed away towards the door. She felt bad enough as it was, without having this misplaced hero-worship to further fuel her considerable guilt.

'She certainly put Iris Braithwaite right on all that nonsense about that hairdresser fellow and her tenant. Of course we didn't believe any of it, not for one moment, did we, Joan?' Turning to reassure their heroine of this fact, Reg and Joan found themselves facing an empty space. They looked about the shop, hoping to unearth Charlotte from behind the rotating rack of thrillers and bodice rippers. They were disappointed.

Hurrying away from the shop, Charlotte was already turning left in to Daisy Bank and making for Acacia Lane. She wanted very much to scream. Coming back to Hulme Welford was supposed to have had a calming influence on her life. It was to have been a return to all that was comfortingly familiar, like the sisterly irritation between herself and Hilary, and the lack of understanding on her mother's part; even the interfering Iris Braithwaite was supposed to have been a necessary part of her rehabilitation. But in less than forty-eight hours she had somehow destroyed the steady equilibrium she had deliberately chosen to return to.

On her first night at Ivy Cottage she had experienced the sensation of having the silky edging torn away from her comfort blanket – now, she had practically unravelled the entire thing.

'And I certainly didn't speak to her, David, not after what she's done,' Hilary said, slamming the dishwasher shut as though underscoring the seriousness of her words, but all it did was make her wince at the sound of crashing crockery within.

'Why are you so cross, Mummy?' said Becky, her head bent over a colouring book on the kitchen table. 'I hope you haven't smashed my Peter Rabbit plate.'

Philip, who was sitting on the back door step scraping the mud from yesterday's match off his football boots, laughed and said, 'Serves you right if Mum has, after you deliberately smashed my Manchester City mug.'

Becky threw a yellow crayon at her brother through the open door. In return she got a wedge of dried mud flicked back at her. She set up a high-pitched wail.

'Stop it, you two,' said Hilary, ramming the remains of breakfast down the waste disposal unit. Turning on the tap, she set off the loud chomping and churning. Above the noise she shouted at David, who was leaning back against the Aga reading the colour supplement. 'I don't know how she had the cheek to even be there.'

'What?' David said without looking up.

'I said . . . Oh, what's the use?' Turning the waste disposal unit off, Hilary said, her voice still raised, 'If we had the next model up, we wouldn't have this trouble. They're much quieter, the more expensive ones.'

David was lost. 'What on earth are you talking about?' He gathered up the papers and headed off to the sitting-room for some peace and quiet. He knew from experience that it wasn't wise to hang about when Hilary was in one of these moods. Quite frankly, he didn't believe a word of what was being said about Charlotte. He wondered though whether this was because he didn't want to believe it, didn't like to imagine Charlotte capable of such a thing.

Hilary pursed her lips, got hold of a wooden spoon and started to push yet more discarded crusts and congealed cornflakes down the disposal unit.

'Mummy?'

'*Yes*, Becky,' Hilary snapped, before reminding herself that it wasn't her daughter's fault that Charlotte was bringing such shame on the family. 'What is it, dear?'

'Mummy, you know Auntie Charlotte?'

'Yes.' Well, I thought I did, she said to herself.

'Why doesn't Auntie Charlotte wear jim-jams like me?'

'What a strange question. Why do you ask?'

Becky looked up from her colouring book. 'I heard

someone at church saying that Auntie Charlotte needs two men in bed with her to keep her warm.'

When Charlotte got home she rushed upstairs and screamed, long and loud, her head inside the airing cupboard where she hoped the sound would be confined. As a form of therapy it fell way short of working. She shut the door and went downstairs to the kitchen where she found Mabel chewing on a squeaky toy bought by Charlotte and her father yesterday, along with tins of food and a lead. Seeing Charlotte, the little dog scuttled over to her. Charlotte smiled and instantly felt better.

She fed Mabel and walked her about the garden wondering what she should do for the rest of the day. She ought to go over and apologise to Hilary but she really couldn't face her sister at the moment. And there was nothing in the house for her to do, not until tomorrow when the removal van would be arriving, and besides it was far too nice a day to be stuck inside.

Seeing the potting shed, with its duck-egg-blue painted door, Charlotte remembered there was supposed to be some garden furniture stored in there. She went back into the house and found the large, clearly labelled, rusty key.

While she fiddled with the key in the lock to make it work, Charlotte could feel the warmth of the sun on her back. It was quite a suntrap, this corner of the garden, with its overgrown flower beds of London Pride, forget-me-nots and tiny, wild purple pansies spilling over on to the path and along the bottom of the brick wall of the potting shed, which was mostly hidden beneath a flourishing wisteria. Against this wall was an assortment of cracked and chipped terracotta pots, some lying haphazardly on their sides. Charlotte thought they looked sad, as if they were still waiting for the Cliffords to come back for them.

Charlotte finally got the key to work. Without any resistance the door swung open. David's particulars of the property had informed Charlotte that not only did Ivy Cottage 'offer a surprisingly capacious potting shed' but that a 'selection of charming, rustic garden furniture could be found within'.

At first glance, this did not seem to be the case. All that Charlotte could discern in the suffused light and cobwebs was that the Cliffords must have forgotten to look in here before they moved. There was an old lawnmower, a collection of brooms in varying degrees of fatigue, a pair of mud-caked gardening gloves, adopting a chilling posture on the floor – as though waiting to pounce on their next victim – along with some shears and a trug full of dead-headed roses. It was stiflingly warm, with an oppressive smell of baked soil and fertilizer.

Charlotte stepped inside and realised that the potting shed was much larger than she had at first thought. Beyond the lawnmower she could see a wheelbarrow and what looked like a selection of old garden furniture.

With Mabel trotting behind her, Charlotte carried two white-painted, rickety folding chairs across the lawn one to sit on and one for her feet. Placing them beside the sprawling fig tree on the left-hand side of the garden, she carefully prised the chairs open. They were filthy, covered with dead insects and patches of flaking paint. She went back into the house and reappeared with a bowl of water and a cloth. A window cracked open behind her and the sound of Bach's Mass in B Minor flooded out, followed by the unmistakable smell of somebody else's lunch being cooked, along with the accompanying clatter of crockery. This reminded Charlotte that not only had she not given a thought to what she was going to eat that day, but that here, clearly, was one of the disadvantages of sharing her house and garden. Should she turn and acknowledge Alex Hamilton, who doubtless was standing in his kitchen watching her, or should she be circumspect and pretend she hadn't heard the window?

She remembered how nice Alex had been to her and that she owed him an apology, so she turned around, ready to give a signal of a peace offering. But there was no sign of him.

She went back to the chairs and started cleaning them. Eventually satisfied that she had done all that she could, she sat down cautiously. The flimsy chair creaked a little, but as it gave no other indication that it was about to collapse, she relaxed into it, clasped her hands at the back of her head, stretched her feet in front of her on the other chair, and turned her attention to the garden.

It was lovely, in need of some work admittedly, but lovely all the same. The lawn was covered with a sprinkling of daisies and dandelions and swept down some hundred feet or so towards a wind break of high conifers, spruces and silver birches and a variety of rhododendrons on the point of bursting into flower. To her right was a deep, neglected border, and behind this, screening her from In The Pink, was a tall copper beech hedge.

Charlotte couldn't help but think she was going to need something more effective than a beech hedge to keep Derek Rogers out.

To her left, on the other side of the fig tree, was more copper beech hedging, but there was nothing beyond it, only a dense thicket.

She closed her eyes, listening to the tranquil cooing of doves in the trees around her, accompanied by the more fortissimo passages of the Bach that managed to reach this far down the garden. With this peace around her, together with the warmth of the sun, Charlotte soon found herself slipping into sleep.

She started, and sat bolt upright at the sound of barking. Mabel. She had forgotten about Mabel. Where was she? Looking towards the house, she saw the little dog lying on the grass in front of the conservatory being stroked by Alex, who was crouched down beside her.

'Hello,' he said, looking up at Charlotte.

She nodded, got up from her chair and walked over to him.

'I just came out to ask if you'd like to join me for lunch.'

'Oh,' she said, surprised. 'I've just eaten,' she lied.

He looked disappointed, squinting his eyes a little against the sun. 'I thought I'd eat out here. Seemed a good idea, on such a lovely day.'

He was right, Charlotte thought, it was a good idea, and she was starving. Why had she just lied to him?

'Roast beef and Yorkshire pudding,' he said. 'Are you sure you won't join me?'

She pushed her hands down into her trouser pockets. 'Oh, go on then, why not?'

Between them they fished out the cast-iron table from the potting shed and whilst Charlotte cleaned it up, Alex brought out two trays of food, along with a couple of glasses and a bottle of red wine. Mabel danced attendance, getting in their way.

'You knew I was lying, didn't you?' Charlotte said, when at last they sat down.

'Let's call it intuition.' He handed her a knife and a fork. 'I bet you haven't eaten a proper meal since Friday night.'

'Have you been spying on me?' Her voice sounded slightly accusing.

'It's hard not to, living so close.' He passed her a glass of wine and raising his own in the air, said, 'Here's to . . .' he paused, smiled and said decisively, 'here's to a good summer.'

'Yes, a good summer,' Charlotte repeated unconvincingly. She took a sip of her wine.

'Bulgarian, cheap and cheerful,' he said, watching her. 'I'm afraid I don't believe in expensive wines.'

'So what do you believe in, then?' The cynicism in her voice was undisguised.

He placed his glass carefully down on the table. 'Good question, that.'

'I'm sorry, that was uncalled for. I promised myself yesterday I'd stop doing that – being cynical, that is.' She put a piece of fluffy Yorkshire pudding in her mouth and then looked away, down to the silver birches, where she could see a pair of magpies building a nest.

Taking the opportunity to look at Charlotte unobserved, Alex decided that the first thing anyone would notice about Charlotte was her shoulder-length hair; it was so dark and without a hint of grey. She was wearing it, as she had on Friday night, loosely round her face, and it framed a mouth that could be described as large, but for his taste was perfect – full and sensuous – and when she smiled, two dimples appeared. He had noticed this the other night, along with the colour of her eyes that he now realised seemed to change colour depending on the light. At dinner they had seemed dusky, almost violet; here, sitting in the sun, he was struck by the dazzling gentian-blue colour they had become. He was also aware that she looked worn out. More than this, she looked uncomfortable with herself, there was an awkwardness about her. Was that suppressed anger, he wondered, anger with life for having dealt her such a rough hand? She certainly deserved to feel that way . . . hadn't he himself once?

'Some magpies are building a nest up there in the tallest birch,' he said, 'can you see? Their first nest was in one of the conifers but it got raided by a crow.' He smiled as Charlotte looked at him. 'Life's hard all round, isn't it?' he said softly.

'This is wonderful,' she said, a piece of beef poised on her fork. 'When did you learn to cook like this?'

'A legacy of my student days,' he said, noting the ground on which she wasn't prepared to walk, 'when I lodged with the redoubtable Mrs Holroyd, sadly no longer with us, but out there,' he cast his arm about him as though presenting the world to Charlotte, 'there's a multitude who carry her memory with them. Actually, she was a formidable land-lady who taught generations of scruffy students the stuff of life – how to cook, wash and iron.'

Charlotte smiled. 'So where did all this take place, which university? No, don't tell me, let me guess. I'd say you were a Cambridge man.'

He laughed, then took a sip of his wine. 'My parents wanted me to go there, to follow in my father's footsteps and my older brother's. I was even offered a place.'

'So why didn't you go?'

'Lots of eighteen-year-old reasons: I didn't want to conform and I didn't want the hassle and all the pressure, so I opted for Leeds instead.'

'Then what, what did you do next, start a commune out on the Yorkshire moors?'

'Guess what? I conformed. As soon as I graduated, I joined up with Henderson and Wyatt and before I knew where I was, I was a fully paid up member of everything I had always despised. Disappointing end to an encouraging beginning, wouldn't you say?'

'If it had stopped at that, maybe, but you're here in Hulme Welford, why?'

Alex told Charlotte how he had ended his career with Henderson & Wyatt, how he had simply sold up and done as he pleased. 'It suddenly became important to me to prove to myself that in the big scheme of things it all meant nothing, all that status, all that supposed power and wealth, it was all a nonsense. I knew perfectly well that me leaving the company meant no real difference in the long term to those individuals concerned. In the short term they were all tripping over themselves to find the right replacement for the dynamic Alex Hamilton, but I bet you, now they'll all be saying Alex who? And that's fine, because that's what they would have been saying in the end when I retired with my slippers by the fireside.'

Charlotte frowned. 'It's strange that, isn't it? Most people like to feel that they're important, indispensable even. It's what gives them their sense of identity, their name tag, if you like.'

'It takes courage to be yourself and to know that you're a significant person in your own right, with something worthwhile to offer, without having to acquire all those labels of self-justification.'

Charlotte thought about this for moment. 'How about marriage,' she said. 'Is that a label you don't need either?'

He looked at her and then, placing his knife and fork together on his now empty plate. 'I was very nearly married,' he answered. *Very nearly married* – how glib he sounded, almost as though his time with Lucy hadn't meant anything. Not so long ago he wouldn't have thought it possible to refer to that period in his life without experiencing some degree of pain. Now here he was, living proof of what his friends and family had told him: *Time is the great healer*. It had taken a while, but eventually they had been proved right. 'More wine?' he said.

'Not for me, thank you. After my behaviour at Hilary's I think I'd better be careful. What does "very nearly" mean?'

A blackbird above their heads in the branches of the fig tree began to chirp. Mabel, in response, got to her feet and barked loudly at it. The bird squawked indignantly and flew off.

'She didn't fall for my understated charm and kept turning me down,' Alex said with a light laugh, and changed the subject. 'So tell me, what's St John's like?'

'Better than when I grew up here,' Charlotte replied, acknowledging that, like most people, Alex Hamilton had his own Achilles' heel. 'It's a bit Low Church for Iris Braithwaite's taste though.' Suddenly she was back in the churchyard, seeing the terrible look on Iris's face.

Sitting here in the garden having lunch with Alex, she had managed to forget what had happened earlier that morning. Thinking of it now, she felt the colour drain from her face, wondered whether Alex himself had heard the gossip that must have touched all corners of the village. But if he had, surely he would have mentioned it?

'What's wrong?' he asked.

'I . . .' This was awful. How was she supposed to tell him? She cleared her throat. 'I probably ought to tell you something before you find out from someone else.'

Alex raised his eyebrows. 'What have I missed?'

Charlotte sighed and told Alex what she was supposed to have been up to with him and Derek.

She watched Alex cross one leg over the other and then pull his foot up towards himself. He was trying hard not to smile, she could tell, but she pressed on, telling him about her mother's visit, Derek's son Barry cross-examining her in church, her exchange with Iris Braithwaite and finally the scene at Ted the Toup's.

'So surely that's an end to it,' Alex said, when she had finished. 'Iris Braithwaite apologises and everyone forgets all about it. You've been exonerated.'

She shook her head. 'No I haven't, and I never will be. Don't you see, they all believed I was capable?'

'Well, to a certain extent, we're all capable.'

'And Hilary ignored me in church this morning, snubbed me. There she was standing by the font with some ridiculous toilet seat in her hands and she turned away when I smiled at her. So much for Christian forgiveness!' She lowered her head, her hair cascading over her face, hiding the tears welling up in her eyes.

Alex leaned back in his chair. He looked thoughtfully across at Charlotte. After a moment's quiet, he placed a hand on her shoulder. She jerked her head up, looked at him and then got to her feet.

'I'd better be going. I'm not very good company at the moment, I'm too busy feeling sorry for myself.' She shook her head. 'And do you know, I was feeling sorry for Iris earlier.'

'Now you've really thrown me,' he said, confused. 'Come on, stay a bit longer and explain that one to me.'

She sat down again, surprising herself that she did so, and willingly. 'You know, I challenged Iris this morning because I truly believed it was the right thing to do, like I thought it was the right thing to come back here to Hulme Welford. Now none of it makes sense any more.'

'Tell me,' Alex said, slowly. 'Tell me about your life in Brussels with Peter, what was it like?'

She kicked off her trainers and played her bare feet lightly over the grass. She thought about Alex's question. Nobody had ever really asked her what *her* life had been like. Assumptions had been made – she had been the wife of a 'bright young thing', they had always been going places, geographically as well as figuratively. They had been well off, comfortably placed, a good future ahead of them and she had tried hard to make a life for herself, always adjusting it to suit Peter, until she had realised she could not cope with knowing that her husband loved his work more than her; that she had become an unwelcome interruption to what really excited him. She then saw herself as just another acquisition, picked up by Peter along the way. She was a necessary part of his portrayal of the perfect corporate man, so long as she was prepared to remain a bit player, with hardly any lines to speak.

Waiting in the wings of her mind now was her programmed response to Alex's question – *it was fun, lots to do and see, all that food and culture* – but she found herself looking Alex in the eye and saying, 'It was empty and cold and I hated it.'

13

'Hello, not interrupting, am I?'

David's arrival, crashing into the garden of Ivy Cottage so unexpectedly, blasted away the tableau effect that Charlotte's words had just created in the soft dappled sunlight beneath the fig tree. His entrance was marked by a confusion of noise and activity, with Mabel barking and the blackbird – who had been frightened away earlier and had since returned – flying off once again to the safety of the beech hedge, squawking noisily as it went.

'Of course you're not interrupting,' Charlotte said, grateful to her brother-in-law that he had saved her from any further revealing disclosures. What had made her say such a thing? She would have to be careful in future, to ensure no further slip-ups like that, for it would only open up the floodgates of confession. *Why did you hate Brussels so much?* would be the next logical question. *Because my husband stopped needing anything in his life, other than work; because my husband made it impossible for me to love him in the way I wanted to.* Oh no, that line of conversation could only lead in one direction, to that dreaded, final denouement – that she was to blame for Peter's death on that icy road to Luxembourg.

'I'll go and get another chair,' she said.

As he watched his sister-in-law walk away from him, David was reminded of the first time he had seen Charlotte. He had met Hilary in his first year at Oxford Polytechnic and during the Christmas vacation he was invited to stay a few days with Hilary and her family. On New Year's Eve Charlotte had turned up from London in a smart little racing-green MG with a boyfriend called Clive. It had snowed for the best part of the evening, and late that night, coming back from the village after a festive drink to Louise and Neville's half-timbered cottage, Charlotte had started laughing, saying she felt like dancing barefoot in the snow. They thought she was joking, but snatching off her thick overcoat and shoes, she had done just that, cavorting like a nymph in the moonlight. Hilary had, of course, disapproved. 'Oh for goodness' sake, Charlotte, stop showing off.' But he and Clive had watched, mesmerised. As the church bells chimed the passing of another year, they had cheered loudly and kissed one another. He remembered wanting to give Charlotte a long, wet, open-mouthed kiss, but had made do with an impetuous collision of their lips.

Three years later he and Hilary were married. By then he had become like a brother to Charlotte, when kisses were a mere respectable brush of the cheek.

Watching Charlotte now as she walked barefoot across the grass, David wondered whether she had ever, since that night, danced barefoot in the snow again.

Alex looked at Charlotte's retreating figure and wondered at what she had just told him – *It was empty and cold and I hated it*. It was a stark and disturbing image she had given and only a fool would think she was referring to Belgium's low population and inclement weather. But something else was disturbing him.

How about marriage, or is that a label you don't need either? Lucy. Twice now in one day he had been forced to unwrap and touch the memory of her. Sat here in the sun listening to Charlotte he had tried to dismiss Lucy from his mind, to relocate this dislodged memory to the back of his brain where for so long it had been treasured and, like so many treasures, rarely touched. She had been a lively forceful girl, and so was her memory, even after seven years.

'Alex, if I've told you once, I've told you a hundred times. I'm not going to throw myself away on you, not when there's the hope of marrying someone who doesn't spend his every waking moment in front of a computer.'

'I don't really want to marry you,' he had laughed, catching her hand in his as they walked along the footpath towards the waterfall at Haworth. 'I just want to get you in bed every night, that's all.'

'Well, you do that often enough anyway.'

Kissing her, he had pulled her down amongst the heather and ripening bilberries despite the presence of a coach party of Japanese tourists, their sunhats bobbing, their cameras swinging.

'You're a lout, Alex Hamilton, and I love you!' she had shouted at the top of her voice, just as the last of the tourists had tried to scuttle discreetly by.

There had been other women in his life since Lucy, but without really trying he had succeeded in keeping any subsequent relationship on a purely superficial level.

'Anything to drink, David?' he said abruptly, getting to his feet.

David looked at the bottle of wine on the table. 'A glass of that would be nice, thanks.'

As Alex went into his side of Ivy Cottage to fetch a glass, Charlotte returned with a chair.

'I see you found the garden furniture. It's old, could almost be antique,' David said.

'Very old, I should think,' Charlotte said, giving the chair a rub with the cloth. 'Back to Noah's cruising days I shouldn't wonder.'

Reappearing with another glass, Alex poured the wine. Charlotte refused any more. 'So David, why aren't you over at The Gables, hard at whatever it is fathers do on a Sunday?'

'If you must know, I've had it up to here.' He pointed to his unshaven chin. 'Hilary's got one on her today. I think it's

95

got to do with . . .' He paused and took a fortifying sip of his wine. 'Well, you know, about . . .' Again he paused and nodded his head in the direction of In The Pink and then back at Alex.

Alex smiled. 'But you don't believe any of it, do you, David?'

'Good heavens, no!' David said, stretching his legs out in front of him and resting his glass on his slightly domed stomach.

'Liar,' said Charlotte suddenly. 'You're just as bad as the rest of them.'

'No, really, I don't. It's just, well, you know what it's like, you can't help but fall back on the old maxim, no smoke without fire and all that.'

'So,' Charlotte said, her eyes narrowing slightly, 'Hilary's mad as hell, is she?'

'Tell me about it,' David said, puffing out his cheeks. 'She's in a right lather.'

'Well, the day's not been a complete waste then, has it?'

'Oh that's great, just great,' David said loudly, tossing back a large mouthful of wine. 'This is what I've got to look forward to from now on, is it? You two sisters winding one another up the whole time and yours truly caught in the crossfire?'

'You know who's really caught in the crossfire, don't you?' said Alex, leaning forward in his chair.

Both Charlotte and David looked at him. 'Who?' they said together.

'Cindy, of course. Has anyone been round to see her and tell her the truth?'

Charlotte pulled a face. 'I'm afraid I haven't had the nerve. Do you think I ought to?'

'How about we go together?' Alex said. 'From what I understand of Derek's reputation, she's going to need some pretty good convincing that nothing did actually happen between you two.'

'I'll think about it,' Charlotte said, avoiding Alex's eyes. She had no desire to rush headlong into Cindy.

Apart from Barry, Cindy was alone in the house. She could hear music coming from his room: monks singing the same thing, over and over again. Uplifting, Barry had called it the other day, on one of his rare excursions out of his room.

Every day was the same. As soon as Barry got in from school he went straight up to his room, music on, head in a book. And today, Sunday, was no exception. He had been in his room since he got back from jogging this morning, only coming out briefly for his lunch and hardly saying a word at the table, just forking food into his mouth absentmindedly, keeping his eyes firmly on the book he was reading. Boys she had known at eighteen had never been like Barry. They had been more like Derek, she thought with a rueful smile. But Barry was a strange boy, so quiet, so preoccupied, and recently even more so. She had tried searching his room while he was at school one day, but had come up with nothing. She had hated doing it, but those leaflets from school had told you what to do if you noticed a change in your child's behaviour. She couldn't imagine Barry getting mixed up in anything like that, not drugs. Tiffany, yes. Like a shot. She winced at this unfortunate pun and put the thought of her children aside. She went through to the *en suite* bathroom and looked in the large illuminated mirror above the his and hers basins.

She stared critically at her face, then gently smoothed the skin under her right eye with a perfectly manicured forefinger. The shaded hue of the slightly loosening skin beneath her lashes was warning enough that her favourite lemon and apricot eye care pack was needed. *Grief can have a devastating effect on your skin* – the irony of her words to Charlotte on Friday night was not lost on her. But she didn't feel in the mood for an eye care pack, and anyway, it was Sunday. Surely even her skin was allowed a day off?

No, she told herself emphatically, don't let yourself go, don't let it get to you. You've survived countless meaningless affairs before, this is just one more. Let it blow over, let him get her out of his system and then that will be that.

She was very calm, really. She had taught herself to be that. Even when she had heard the juniors in the salon, Tracy and Lorraine, tidying up the linen cupboard late yesterday afternoon, she had stayed calm.

'He's at it again,' Lorraine had sniggered.

'But he's got competition this time, hasn't he?' Tracy had replied. 'That good-looking bloke, just moved in.'

Cindy scraped her hair back into a tight ponytail and secured it with a scrunch band. First she cleansed and toned her skin, then carefully applied the sweet-smelling, creamy paste around her eyes.

With ten minutes to wait for the eye pack to do its work, she walked through to the bedroom to get a magazine. Passing the full-length mirror at the other end of the pale peach room, she caught sight of herself, and for a split second she saw a gaunt, white face that looked nothing like her, but like a hideously deformed old woman. Derek would never love a woman like that, a voice inside her head whispered. She stood looking at this terrifying image and then, slowly, it passed, became the face she was accustomed to seeing and the face she hoped Derek loved . . . in his own way.

She went back into the bathroom with the magazine, sat down on the small cane settee by the bath and started to flick through the pages of life-enhancing recipes for sex and filo pastry, trying desperately not to think of Derek and what he was doing to her.

She didn't hate him for what he did, he couldn't help himself half the time – it was habitual. And for reasons she couldn't make sense of, she loved him, always had, and she knew that this would always be there between them . . . but then, so would all the affairs.

By most people's standards she felt that she was still an attractive woman. Her skin was smooth and firm, her bust hadn't drooped, nor had her buttocks. She worked out, ate the right things, rarely drank alcohol and always kept herself well dressed. And she had never once, in all their years together, refused Derek in bed. So why wasn't that enough for him, what more did he need?

And why did that wretched Charlotte Lawrence have to come and live next door?

14

'I know it's my fault,' Hilary said down the telephone. 'It was stupid of me not to put it on the calendar, but Tiffany can't manage it tonight – apparently it's Barry's birthday – and David's got one of his tedious Rotary evenings, and would you believe it, Mum and Dad are out as well? So I just thought, Charlotte, that maybe, and I do appreciate what a busy day you must have had, but do you think you could babysit for me, tonight?'

Babysit! Charlotte looked at the mayhem all around her in the hall and wondered whether her sister had any idea just how busy a day it had been for her.

At eight-thirty that morning rowdy voices, English and French, had added to the noise of the Belgian removal van as it tried to position itself to reverse up the drive of Ivy Cottage. Having already got the huge pantechnicon tangled up in Hilary's terracotta pots at the end of The Gables' driveway, the driver had then endeavoured to squeeze his load through the metaphorical eye of a needle, bringing with it the lower overhanging branches of a rowan together with a good deal of forsythia.

Charlotte had viewed the approaching removal van with apprehension, knowing that coming towards her, with reversing siren wailing, was the past eight years of her life – approximately thirty-two cubic metres of marital souvenirs. Up until this point, Ivy Cottage had been neutral territory, had been devoid of anything to do with Peter. Now it was about to open its doors and embrace eight years of the man, and Charlotte wasn't sure how she was going to feel about this.

'Any chance of a brew before we get started?' the foreman had said, giving her no further time to be squeamish about what was to be spilled out of the lorry.

Five hours later the team of tea- and coffee-swilling men had filled Ivy Cottage and departed, leaving behind them a house full of randomly emptied boxes. With no one to help sort out the chaos, Charlotte had worked on alone until her father arrived.

'Hello,' he called from the open front door.

'In here,' she called back.

He came hesitantly into the cardboard box havoc of the sitting-room. 'Need any help?'

Charlotte bobbed up from behind the sofa. 'Does a fish need water?'

Together they pushed, lifted, emptied and filled until eventually, exhausted, they retired to the crockery-splattered kitchen for a respite.

'I had no idea you'd be all alone. I thought Hilary would have been here to help you,' Neville said, accepting a mug of tea from Charlotte.

Charlotte slumped down into a chair. 'No, she's off on a school trip with Becky's class. Chester Zoo, I think, back about five.'

'I'm surprised no one else offered to help,' Neville said quietly.

She noticed the inclination of her father's head. 'I heard his car leaving just before eight this morning, Dad, unless of course you were thinking that Derek and Cindy might have liked to help.'

Neville looked deep into his mug of tea. 'Well, I wasn't being specific, I just meant . . .'

'Come on, Dad,' she laughed, 'finish your tea and get off home. I need to take Mabel for a walk.'

Charlotte had just said goodbye to her father, closed the

front door and was stepping over boxes of books and piles of unwrapped pictures when Hilary had telephoned.

'I shan't be long, it's a PTA meeting,' Hilary was saying. 'Patricia Longton's away, so I'll be stepping out of my role as Secretary and be acting as Chairwoman for the evening. And anyway, seeing as you've not even seen the children since you moved in, I thought it might be nice for you to have them all to yourself for a while. What do you say?'

Hilary held her breath. She was conscious of the silence at the other end of the telephone. She knew that she was pushing her luck, that she had, since Friday, acted a little harshly towards her sister, as David had gone to great lengths to inform her yesterday when he got back from Ivy Cottage. She had been taking a batch of cup cakes out of the Aga for the school trip when David had breezed in and said, 'Hilary, you're a bloody fool and you're going to have to apologise to Charlotte.'

Concentrating on mixing pink icing in a bowl and searching for the hoard of Hundreds and Thousands that she kept hidden from Becky, Hilary had let David have his say.

'How you could have thought your own sister capable of such a thing! Hasn't she got enough on her plate without you and all the other old biddies in the village making her out to be some kind of insatiable . . .' She had listened to the silence while he seemingly searched his mind for a suitable word. '. . . Slut!' he said at last.

She had looked up at him at this point. 'David, that's not a nice word.'

'Too bloody right, it isn't.'

'What's a slut, Daddy?'

Together they had spun round to see Becky standing in the doorway, practising a few wobbly demi-pliés. 'Don't stick your bottom out,' Hilary had said quickly, bustling about the kitchen and giving David one of her see-what-you've-done-now looks.

'So what do you say, Charlotte?' Hilary repeated. 'It'll only be a few hours.' She wondered whether she ought to mention anything about letting bygones be bygones: after all, this telephone call was by way of an apology, surely her stubborn sister could see that? Then she heard what she thought sounded like suppressed crying at the other end of the telephone. 'Charlotte,' she said anxiously, 'do you want me to come over?'

'No.'

'But you're upset, you're crying. I'll come over and put the kettle on. I'll make us a nice cup of tea.'

'I wasn't crying.'

'Charlotte, it's all right, really it is, tears are all part of the grieving process, you must . . .'

'I wasn't crying, I was laughing, Hilary.'

'Laughing!' What on earth did her sister have to laugh about, for goodness' sake?

'I had forgotten what a persistent pain you are.'

Hilary sighed with relief. 'So you'll do it. See you in about an hour then.'

Still laughing to herself, Charlotte put down the receiver, located Mabel's lead and then found Mabel, curled up inside a knocked-over packing box.

She locked the front door behind her and set off along the drive. Halfway down she noticed a red Citroën come up the parallel driveway. She saw Alex and because the sunroof was open she could hear the sound of Mozart's Requiem. He waved across the front lawn to her and parked the car.

'How did the unpacking go?' he called out.

'Ongoing,' she said, pulling a face.

He came over. 'Sorry I wasn't around to help. Is there anything I can do now?'

'I've stopped for the day, too exhausted to do any more. But thanks for the offer.'

Bending down to Mabel, who was straining on her lead to reach him, Alex said, 'Have you seen Cindy yet?'

'No,' Charlotte said awkwardly, glad at least to have the perfect excuse. 'I haven't had time today.'

He stood up and looked at her. 'How about now? I could come with you. We ought to put her mind at rest . . . and yours.'

Charlotte looked away, wondered why this man was so concerned about everyone else's feelings.

'What's the problem? Are you worried she's not going to believe us?'

'No, it's not that exactly, it's more . . . oh, I don't know, it's sounds silly really, only I don't think Cindy and I are ever going to be the best of friends. I've a feeling she's already condemned me as one of Derek's trophies. Even if I'm found innocent this time, in her eyes it's only a matter of time before I really am guilty.'

Alex shook his head. 'You're right,' he said, 'it does sound silly. Come on, let's just go next door, say what we've got to say and let the poor woman make up her own mind.'

'Do you always bully people like this?'

He smiled. 'Yes, all the time, never stop.'

'Is it possible to see Mrs Rogers please?' Charlotte asked the young receptionist, who immediately pouted her lips in irritation at being delayed at getting off home.

'Have you got an appointment?' she said pulling on her jacket.

'No, but . . .'

'Well, I'm very sorry but we're just about to close and Mrs Rogers is in a hurry. She needs to get off on time tonight, it's her son's eighteenth . . .'

'Thank you, Tracy, I'm sure I can spare my neighbours a few minutes.' It was Cindy, elegantly poised on cerise high heels and wearing a white uniform which gave her slim arms and legs the appearance of being even more tanned. Her hair, unlike last Friday night, was pinned back and showed off a flawless complexion. She was a walking advertisement for In The Pink, what Charlotte suspected all their customers aspired to.

'We don't actually allow dogs on the premises,' Cindy said looking down at Mabel, 'but Tracy will look after it for you.' Ignoring Tracy's look of annoyance at being delayed even longer, she carried on, 'We'll go through to the office where we won't be disturbed.' She turned and started clicking her way down a corridor. As Charlotte and Alex followed behind, Cindy turned and said, 'Derek's busy with Mrs Jeffs at the moment. She's one of his regulars. She comes in three times a week.'

'Really,' said Charlotte, not missing the point of the statement.

Cindy opened a door. 'Mrs Jeffs' husband plays for Manchester United. Maybe you're a fan of football? I'm not.'

Or of Mrs Jeffs, thought Charlotte looking about her and being surprised by the austerity of the room in which they were standing. What they had seen so far of In The Pink was a frothy concoction of pink frilly blinds and flowery wallpaper; here the walls were a cool grey and the office furniture was uncompromisingly black, modern, angular, and shouted no-nonsense business acumen. Charlotte thought Cindy looked more at home hovering by the large desk than she had in the reception area.

'Please, sit down,' Cindy said. 'Would you like a cup of coffee?'

Nobody sat down. Alex spoke first. 'No thank you, Cindy. We shan't keep you long. Your receptionist told us you were in a rush to get away. All we've come to say is that, well, to try and explain that what . . .'

Cindy smiled for the first time.

Charlotte took over. 'Nothing happened, Cindy. Iris

Braithwaite got some silly idea into her head, and went round making a fool of herself and us.'

'I know,' Cindy said softly, though there was little warmth to her voice. This was a new experience for her – one of Derek's women actually protesting her innocence. 'Mrs Braithwaite came to see me last night. She did manage to apologise in the end.'

'I'm so glad it's all been sorted out,' Charlotte said, visibly relaxing.

'Yes,' agreed Cindy, picking up a paperclip from the desk. She turned it over in her hands as though examining it for any possible defects. She looked at Charlotte. 'Except for one thing of course.'

'What's that?' Charlotte said nervously.

'Well, it's only a small thing, but what exactly was my husband doing at your house with a bouquet of roses?'

*

'I knew it, I just knew it!' Charlotte said, as they walked away from In The Pink. 'I knew this would happen. You see what you've done?'

'Cindy would probably have said that to you anyway. Better it was done there in private. At least nobody else was there to hear her.'

'But what was I supposed to say? How could I have answered her question? Oh yes, Cindy, your husband came to see me with the biggest bunch of red roses I've ever seen and kissed me up against the kitchen sink.'

'She didn't expect an answer. She knows perfectly well what Derek had in mind when he turned up on your doorstep. It was a warning shot she was firing, that was all. She needs to convince herself that she's doing all she can to prevent Derek from hurting her any more.' Alex pushed his hands down inside his trouser pockets. 'So . . . he kissed you, did he?'

Charlotte groaned. 'It was just some stupid kind of grope

thing,' she said, exasperated. 'I didn't take much notice of it at the time.'

Alex looked at her and then started to laugh. Charlotte smiled and then she too laughed as she realised how implausible her words had sounded.

Opening Philip's bedroom window, Hilary heard the sound of laughter. She looked across the road and saw Charlotte and Alex walking towards Ivy Cottage. Things were going very nicely.

15

Barry walked blindly behind his sister, allowing her to guide him through the house and out on to the driveway.

'Now stand there,' Tiffany told him, 'and keep your eyes closed, until I tell you to open them.' He felt her hands fumbling at the back of his head, undoing the knot she had tied in the bandana and then he felt the material slip away. 'Open your eyes, now – *surprise*!'

He blinked in the low evening sunlight and then stared unbelievably at a brand new Peugeot 205.

'Well, what do you reckon to that then, Bas?' his father said, leaning against the car. 'Bit of all right I'd say. The most I had at your age was a pushbike.'

'It's great, Dad,' Barry said, still staring at the metallic-grey car. 'I never expected anything like this, I don't know what to say . . . thanks.'

'Nothing like a flash motor to help you pull. You'll have no worries on that score now.'

Barry turned to his mother. 'Thanks,' he said. 'It's a great present.'

'Just make sure you drive carefully,' she said.

'Now all you've got to do is pass your test next week,' said Tiffany, 'and then we can hit the road, just you and me, kid.'

Barry frowned and ran a hand through his hair. 'I might not pass.'

'Muffin 'ell, 'course you will. It's not as if Dad's been teaching you.'

'Less of that,' said Derek. 'Anyway, I don't know about you lot, but my stomach feels like it's been cut off from my throat.' He tossed a key over to Barry. 'Come on, Bas, you can get the feel of it by driving us to the restaurant.'

'We can't possibly go yet,' said Cindy.

'Why ever not?'

'Tiffany can't go looking like that, look at the state of her. They won't let her in the restaurant in those disgusting clothes.'

'Give up, Mum!' shouted Tiffany.

'Don't you dare shout at me for all the neighbours to hear. Just get back in the house and change into something decent.'

Glaring at her mother, Tiffany stood her ground and didn't move.

Barry sensed his mother's anger giving way to bitter disappointment. He felt sorry for her, felt he knew the sense of frustration and disillusionment that filled her life – firstly his father, then himself, and to top it all, Tiffany. It was quite simple really: all his mother had ever wanted in life was a faithful husband and a real daughter.

'Look, Mum,' he said, 'I know it's a pain, but that's how she likes to dress. She's not doing anyone any harm.'

'If you could just quit with all the philosophy crap,' Derek said impatiently, 'we could get a move on.' He shook his head. 'Families, I ask you, who the bloody hell needs them?'

We do, thought Barry, as he walked over to unlock his birthday present.

'I think they must have given me the wrong cassette in the shop,' Derek said, jabbing a finger at the cassette player on the dashboard and ejecting a tape. 'I thought I'd got you the Four Seasons.'

'You have, Dad, it's great, thanks,' Barry said, keeping his eyes firmly on the road.

Derek made a play of reading the label. 'Yep, I knew

they'd made a mistake, this isn't Frankie Valley at all. It's that Nigel Kennedy bloke.'

'Muffin 'ell, Dad,' shouted Tiffany from the back of the car, 'you're a plonker, you really are.'

Derek turned round and grinned at Tiffany. 'I can still fool you though, can't I?'

'Idiot!'

'Don't speak to your father like that,' Cindy said.

'Yes,' agreed Derek, smirking, 'it would be nice to see some respect in this family for a change.'

Barry looked in the mirror and caught his sister's expression of explosive retaliation.

'Good evening, sir,' said the *maître d'* at the White Swan. 'I'm sorry but there are no tables free, perhaps you'd care to wait in the bar, I'm sure . . .'

'That's all right, pal, you're new here, aren't you? Rogers is the name. We've got a booking.'

They watched the *maître d'* move off with his air of grandiose superiority to check the list of reservations.

'If you'd like to come this way, Mr Rogers,' the *maître d'* said, sliding back to them, 'your table is over here. You ordered a bottle of champagne on the telephone. Shall I open it right away for you, sir?'

They sat at a fussy blue and white trimmed table and were handed four over-sized menus. Barry watched his father make a great show of tasting the champagne and declaring it adequate. They raised their glasses and set about playing happy families for the evening – an evening which for Barry stretched ominously ahead.

As a family they rarely spent any time together, and on occasions like this when they were forced to act out the part, it was usually a strain. Barry could already see the strain showing on his mother's face. Ever since he could remember, he had sensed a detachment, almost an estrangement, between himself and his mother. For years he hadn't understood what was going on, but more recently he had come to know that no matter what he did, he could not please his mother, could not make her happy. Tiffany had managed it effortlessly when she was small, but then she had grown up, and almost overnight had destroyed the illusion their mother had so carefully created.

'Happy birthday, Bas,' his father said, chinking his fluted glass against Barry's own. 'Now get this down you, and don't worry about driving home, I'll drive.'

'Cheers,' Barry said, taking a small sip. He had no intention of getting drunk. He had far too much work to get through with his exams only a few days away.

'I still don't get it though, Bas. Why the hell didn't you want a night out with your own mates? You could have gone into Manchester, picked up a few girls, had a party? We'd have paid for it, you know.'

Barry shook his head. 'Wasn't what I wanted.'

'And this was?' Tiffany said, looking about her.

'We don't often sit round a table together and talk, do we?' Barry started to say.

'Just as well,' Tiffany interrupted.

'Maybe Barry's right.'

Barry looked at his mother, searching her face for signs of cynicism. He found none. Perhaps tonight he would be able to broach the subject after all.

'Hey, this is all getting a bit serious, isn't it?' Derek said, draining his glass. 'Come on, another glass of champagne.' He reached for the bottle behind him in the wine cooler. At once, a young waiter, about the same age as Barry, appeared at his side and took over. 'Don't worry, pal,' Derek said. 'I wasn't about to get you kicked out of a job.'

'No worries there, mate. They're understaffed as it is. Even if I gobbed in your soup, they couldn't afford to sack me.'

Derek roared. In response, a few heads bobbed up from their plates around the White Swan.

The waiter was just his father's kind of man, Barry thought, someone as brazen as himself with a-take-me-as-you-find-me attitude. If he were more like that, Barry knew he would get on better with his father.

'Nice bloke,' Derek said, when they'd ordered their meal. 'Will probably do well in life.'

Tiffany sniffed loudly. 'Hope it's your soup he gobs in, then.'

When they had finished their desserts and coffee and Cindy had gone off to the ladies' room, Barry knew he had lost his opportunity. His father was now regaling the young waiter with his life history – his rags to riches saga. 'You see, lad, your life's all before you. What are you, seventeen?'

'Eighteen,' the waiter replied, stifling a yawn.

'So's my lad, look, the one there sitting like a stuffed Henry. Wouldn't think it was his eighteenth birthday today, would you? He should be out celebrating with his mates, shouldn't he, not stuck here with us? I bet you celebrated.' He poked the young waiter in the ribs and gave him a wink.

The waiter looked at Tiffany. 'Too right I did.'

'I've paid the bill, Derek, it's time we were going.' It was Cindy coming back to the table, looking far from pleased.

Outside in the poorly lit car park Cindy and Barry guided Derek towards the car. 'Now you'd better let me drive, Bas,' Derek said. 'Don't want you losing your licence before you've even got it, do we?'

'He's pathetic, he really is,' Tiffany said with disgust, dragging behind.

'Shut up, Tiffany,' hissed Cindy, 'just remember, he's your father.'

'Oh please, how can I ever forget?'

They drove home, listening to Derek singing 'Ooh What a Night' to Vivaldi's 'L'Autonno'. For Barry, the evening had turned out just as he'd known it would. He had been a fool to think that anyone in his family would be interested in what he had to say. After all, to his father he was nothing more than a 'stuffed Henry' – not a very pleasant revelation that, on his eighteenth birthday. But he was used to it, like he was used to all the jokes and innuendoes. Well, he would just have to wait until the right time presented itself.

16

Hilary had come deliberately early, before Iris Braithwaite and the others arrived to help set up the St John's spring jumble sale. At least this way it gave her a chance to get things done the way she liked, and not the way Iris wanted. It seemed a dreadful shame to Hilary that one woman could so easily put a blight on the community. She knew for a fact that more people would volunteer to help out in the village if Iris Braithwaite wasn't already there on practically every committee. 'Sorry,' people would whisper when asked to help, 'no can do, not with *her* to answer to.'

Hilary hadn't seen or heard from Iris in the past week, which was unusual in the run-up to an event such as today's, but Iris's low profile probably had a lot to do with what Charlotte had said to her last Sunday. Even though Hilary couldn't help but admire her sister, she still felt a pang of jealousy that Charlotte had had the courage to stand up to Iris, and she did not. She wished that she had been there to witness it, instead of rushing off home to clear up the breakfast things and get the Sunday roast in the oven. A shame no one had told her at the time what had taken place; it would have saved an awful lot of misunderstanding between her and Charlotte. Luckily though, Kate Hampton, the PTA Treasurer, had told her about it at their Monday evening meeting. 'Your sister was quite magnificent. There was more drama in that church porch than in a week's worth of *Eastenders*. Perhaps we'll see a few changes round here from now on. Belgium's loss is certainly Hulme

Welford's gain. She's become quite the local hero.'

Hilary had tried to clamp down on her disappointment at her sister suddenly getting all the attention. It wasn't quite how she had envisaged things. True she didn't want Charlotte to be miserable, but on the other hand, she didn't want her to come striding back into the village and take over – grieving widows weren't supposed to behave like that. Demure, quietly tearful and in need of a friendly shoulder to lean against was more the mark, surely?

She started setting up the tables, which Brown Owl and her pack of Brownies were supposed to have organised last night, and then she moved on to the boxes of clothes, sorting things out by gender and then by size. She was just holding up a red, lacy G-string – the kind of thing she would never contemplate wearing – and wondering who on earth in the village had donated it, when in walked Iris Braithwaite, followed by Mrs Haslip and Mrs Bradley, each weighed down with several large Tupperware boxes.

'Mrs Parker! I trust you have no intention of offering *that* for sale?'

Hilary flushed. 'Of course not, Mrs Braithwaite. I was just wondering . . .'

'Well don't. Put them, I mean it, in the bin and let's get on, we've lots to do. Mrs Haslip, you get to work in the kitchen, and for heaven's sake make sure the kettles are clean and the coffee urn doesn't have anything untoward inside. I know what those ghastly Cubs are like.'

Philip was a Cub and Hilary wanted very much to rush to his defence. But instead she bent down to the next box of jumble and started sorting through it. It wasn't fair: it was *she* who had done most of the work; it was *her* house that had been used as a collecting point; *their* computer that had prepared all the posters to advertise the event – it was all her time and effort and now, at the very last minute, in came Iris Braithwaite and took command.

It hadn't always been like this. Before she had had the

children she had been a teacher, and quite a good one, in her opinion. She knew when it had all changed – it was having the children and being at home. She had read once that each time the afterbirth was ejected from a woman's body, so was a piece of her self-confidence, taking away her sense of freedom and her courage. Hilary didn't normally believe such fanciful theories, but since having the children she had indeed grown afraid of more and more things: heights, flying, deep water – and Iris Braithwaite.

'Now Mrs Parker, I suggest Mrs Bradley helps you so that we ensure no other unsavoury items end up on the tables. Good gracious, just look at the state of this floor. Mrs Haslip, is there a broom in the kitchen? If so, fetch it here this minute.'

As they worked away under Iris's tyrannical directives, Hilary couldn't help but begin to feel a perverse sense of satisfaction. It looked as though Charlotte's brave words after church last week had had no great effect on Iris after all. So much for being the local hero.

At a quarter to eleven Malcolm Jackson, Charlotte, and the other press-ganged helpers turned up, and under Iris's baleful eye stood ready to receive the flood of bargain hunters.

Jumble sales in Hulme Welford were always well attended, and due to the eagerness of the queue outside, the doors were generally opened early. Today was no exception.

'Right, ladies,' announced Iris Braithwaite, 'are you ready?' She stood poised between the locked door and a small table, which had on it an embroidered tablecloth and a battered Quality Street tin ready to receive the twenty pence entrance fee. She turned the key and addressed the crowd. 'Ladies and gentlemen . . .' But her voice was lost as a loud cheer went up and she very sensibly moved back to her Quality Street tin.

Charlotte and Hilary stood together behind the ladies' clothes stall, ready for the onslaught. Charlotte's initial reaction, when her sister had asked her if she would like to help out, had been to say no, but then, why not, she had asked herself, what else had she to do?

It had been a quiet, pleasant week at Ivy Cottage, apart from Hilary popping over every few hours 'just to see how she was getting on'. She had continued with the unpacking and made rather an expensive purchase – a new car. With Peter's words ringing in her ears, she had tried to convince herself that she need not feel guilty about this: '*It's a false economy to buy second hand,*' he had always said. And as the smartly dressed, Polo-scented salesman in the show-room had said, there was always her own personal safety to consider; statistically she was less likely to break down in a new car than an old one. It still hadn't felt right though, picking out a car with money she believed did not rightfully belong to her.

The subject of Peter's money was one she tried hard not to think about. If she had gone ahead and divorced him, she would have expected nothing. As it was, he was dead, and because of his well-planned insurance policies, she was now reasonably well off.

'How much is this?'

Charlotte looked at the sharp-faced woman in front of her and at the Marks & Spencer blouse in her hand. 'Forty pence,' she replied.

'Forty pence, luv, you've got to be joking. This is a jumble sale, not bleeding 'arrods!'

Hilary had warned her about the hard-nosed profession-als of the jumble sale circuit. She stuck to her guns. 'It's definitely forty pence. It's in very good condition. Look, you can see, it's barely been worn.'

'How do you know that? And anyway, it's only polyester. I mean, it's not silk or anything, is it?'

Charlotte was beginning to enjoy herself. It was good to be arguing on this irrational basis, and over something as trivial as a secondhand blouse. Too much of her married life she had been unable to argue with Peter, who had never liked confrontations. He had always walked away from her whenever she had tried to argue a point.

'Come back and fight with me!' she would shout at him.

'Fight?' he replied once. 'But I'm your husband,' or another time, 'Charlotte, you really do say the strangest of things.' His logic had been irrefutable which had had the effect of suppressing her anger, and in turn had made her angrier still.

'You know how polyester can sometimes bobble up after it's been worn a few times?'

'Yes,' said the woman, screwing her eyes up to look at the cuff Charlotte was showing her.

'Well, look, there's not a bobble in sight.'

'Mm . . .' said the woman, 'perhaps you're right, maybe it's never been worn, but the first time I wear it, it'll probably bobble up something rotten. I'll give you twenty pence.'

'Sorry, it's forty,' Charlotte said firmly, 'and the money does go for a good cause, a replacement stained-glass window in the church.'

'Go on, then, give it here, there's your money, and I'll want a plaque by the side of the bleeding window with my name on it.'

With a triumphant toss of her hand, Charlotte threw the coins into the tin. This was going to be more fun than she had thought.

'However did you manage that?' whispered Hilary at her side. 'I've never been able to hold my ground with that wretched Mrs Barret. Oh look, Malcolm's getting into his stride now.'

Over by the kitchen counter the Reverend Jackson was drumming up interest in the refreshments. 'Teas and coffees now being served, everyone,' he shouted above the din of eager bargain hunters, 'and don't forget the delicious home-made cakes.'

'Hello, you two.'

'Alex!' said Hilary. 'How nice of you to come and support us.'

Charlotte noticed the extra width to Hilary's smile and the hand raised to pat her hair in place.

'How much is this, luv?' It was Mrs Barret again with a navy-blue cardigan in her hand. Charlotte leaned forward, but the old woman said, 'No, I'm not asking you, I'm asking her.' And she thrust the cardigan towards Hilary.

'I see you've already snapped up a few purchases,' Charlotte said, looking at the pile of detective novels in Alex's hands.

'Too good an opportunity to pass by,' he said. 'Five murders for a pound and a book on trees, though I think my ribs have suffered into the bargain.'

'You'll have to get some serious training in before the next jumble sale and wear protective clothing.' Charlotte lowered her voice. 'It's the old women you have to look out for. They're the worst, elbows like skewers.'

'They show no mercy, that's for sure.'

'Come on now, Mrs Lawrence, no shirking. There are customers waiting to be served.' Iris Braithwaite was on the prowl. 'Good to see you participating, Mr Hamilton,' she said. 'May I suggest you try men's clothing just a little further along. There are some rather nice pullovers in your size I think.'

Alex winked at Charlotte and moved off, not to the gentleman's outfitters, but to the miscellaneous junk department.

Charlotte watched him go, at the same time trying to stop the twisted pile of cardigans, blouses and dresses – which seemed to have a life of their own – from falling off the table. She could hear her sister faltering at her side with the indomitable Mrs Barret, who was still haggling.

Smiling to herself, Charlotte observed Alex pick up a revoltingly garish picture of a little boy with a tear trickling down his cheek. To her amazement, he bought it. He started to walk away, but turned back to the table. Something else had caught his eye. Fascinated to see what other rubbish he was about to waste his money on, Charlotte watched him pick up a small spoon. He turned it over in his hands, examined the back of it closely, and then working his fingers down to the bowl he caressed it gently. Charlotte shivered.

'How long do I have to stand here before I'm served?'

'I'm sorry?'

'I want these two skirts, how much?'

'A spoon.'

'I beg your pardon?'

Charlotte flushed deep crimson. 'I mean, a pound. They're fifty pence each.'

The customer handed over her money and moved away. Her place at the table was immediately filled by another. 'Hello Charlotte, heard any good gossip recently?' It was Derek.

'Wouldn't have thought there'd be anything to interest you here,' she said. Looking at Derek's tight faded jeans, pink polo shirt, gold bracelet and cream jacket tossed casually over his shoulder, she added, 'Don't suppose there's anything flash enough.'

He grinned suggestively. 'You'll do for starters.'

Charlotte knew she shouldn't laugh. Men like Derek Rogers needed no encouragement. She tried to sound as businesslike as she could. 'Well, seeing as you've come, you might as well buy something.'

'What a good idea. I could try buying Cindy a present. I hear you came to see her. Did she give you a hard time? She's a real Satan in slingbacks, isn't she?' He put his jacket down on the edge of the adjoining table and started poking around amongst the clothes. 'Oh, what's this I've found?' From the bottom of the pile he pulled out the red lacy G-string. 'Now this is more like it.'

'Oh, go on then, tell me you recognise it,' Charlotte said derisively.

'Now you come to mention it, it does look familiar.' He twanged the garment playfully at her.

At that moment Hilary joined them at the table. 'For goodness' sake!' she said. 'Give that to me, Derek.'

'Certainly not. I want to buy it.'

'Don't be silly. Just give it to me before Iris catches sight of it.'

'Why, is it hers?'

Charlotte burst out laughing. Hilary still looked serious. 'I was supposed to get rid of it, but I forgot. She'll go mad if she sees it.'

'Go on, Derek, hand it over,' Charlotte said, seeing the discomfort on her sister's face. Poor Hilary, she could never see the funny side of things.

'Hand what over?' It was Alex, half hidden behind his ghastly picture.

Derek waved the lacy item in front of him. Alex raised an eyebrow. 'What exotic jumble sales you have in these parts.'

'Hilary won't let me buy it.'

'Perhaps she wants to see the colour of your money first.'

'Well in that case, let me get my wallet.' Derek reached for his jacket and then looked about him. 'It's gone!'

Seeing the G-string abandoned on top of all the jumble, Charlotte made a surreptitious grab for it and passed it to Hilary.

'Come on,' Derek said, his voice beginning to rise, 'a joke's a joke.'

Hilary and Charlotte exchanged worried looks. Rule number one of any jumble sale – *never* put anything down.

'Look. I put my jacket just here. It's cream, it's Armani and it's bloody well gone!'

'Hi Dad, what's all the commotion?'

Derek turned round at the sound of Tiffany's voice, and

then fell back against the table, both hands clasped over his gaping mouth. 'Bloody hell, Tiffany!'

Tiffany's hair was immaculately coiffured into an amazing one-foot-high beehive, and it was shocking pink.

'The trouble with you lot is that you can't take a joke!' Tiffany screamed at her parents in their kitchen.

'Some joke,' Cindy said faintly, her face and lips almost as white as her uniform.

'Right now, girl, you can start by telling us what kind of product it was they used, then we can think how to change it.'

'How the hell should I know, Dad? I just asked for it to be pink. Anyway, I've had enough of this, I'm going out.'

'Oh no you're not, young lady,' shouted Derek. 'I don't want people seeing you like that.'

'Not you as well, Dad.'

She slammed the door after her and stamped off down the drive without a clue or care where she was going. Willing back hot angry tears, she muttered to herself, 'Fifteen-year-old girls don't cry.'

'Thirty-six-year-old women do though,' said a voice.

Hilary Parker's sister was standing in front of her.

'Are you okay?'

Tiffany sniffed. 'Don't know,' she said sulkily.

'Your parents giving you a hard time?'

Tiffany sniffed again.

'Why don't you come and have a boring old cup of tea with me. I'm exhausted after all that sales pitch talk down at the hall.'

'You're not going to tell me I've been stupid as well, are you?'

Charlotte laughed. 'Come on, come and tell me what it's like to be a teenager again. I've nearly forgotten what a miserable time it was.'

*

At Ivy Cottage they were greeted noisily by Mabel at the back door.

'Let her out, will you?' Charlotte said. 'She must be desperate by now. What do you want, tea or coffee or something cold?'

'Coffee please, lots of milk and two sugars.'

'I remember those days.'

Tiffany frowned. 'Why do you make yourself sound older than you really are?'

'Probably because that's the way I feel at the moment. Where do you want to sit, inside or out?'

'The garden would be nice. It looks lovely from my bedroom window.'

They sat on the dry grass beneath the fig tree. With Mabel on her lap, Charlotte kicked off her shoes and looked at Tiffany's heavily clad feet. 'Are those boots as uncomfortable as they look?'

'No, though you have to break them in.' She set to work undoing one of the laces, giving the boot all her concentration. Suddenly she looked up. 'Aren't you going to ask me why I did it?'

Charlotte took a sip of her tea. She looked thoughtfully at this model-thin, fifteen-year-old girl in front of her, with her pale skin, black eyes, dangling earrings and incredible candyfloss hair. 'That depends,' she said at last.

'Depends on what?'

'Depends on whether you really want me to ask you why you did it.'

'I suppose that's it. Mum and Dad didn't even bother to ask me. I really wanted them to ask so that . . .'

'So that you could have a good go at them?'

Tiffany smiled. 'You see, you do remember what it's like to be a teenager.'

Charlotte lay back on the grass. 'Go on then, tell me all about it.'

With both boots off now, Tiffany rubbed her sweaty

white feet, then she too stretched out on the lawn. 'Two reasons really,' she said, looking up at the leaves on the tree above them. 'Firstly I thought it would be a laugh to turn up the same disgusting colour as our house. After all, if they can do it to our home, I can do it to my hair.'

Charlotte smiled, recognising the logic she might well have employed with Peter had he done something so outlandish. 'Go on,' she said. 'What's the other reason?'

'I just wanted to shock the hell out of them!'

Honesty. How refreshing, thought Charlotte. 'Good for you,' she said. 'Though don't quote me on that, will you?'

'Dad's face was good, wasn't it?' Tiffany said, placing a tentative hand on her rigid hair.

'I don't know who was more shocked, Iris or your father.'

'Ma Braithwaite looked great, didn't she?'

'She looked something all right.' Charlotte sat up to finish her tea. 'I don't know your dad well, but I should think that's one of the rare times in his life when he's been left speechless.'

'You're right there. By the way, what happened to his jacket, did you find it?'

'Alex tracked it down. Ted the Toup had bought it from Mrs Bradley and Alex had to barter to get it back again. Ted said he'd paid two pounds for it and that he wouldn't let it go for anything less than three. So tell your father that he owes Alex three pounds.'

Tiffany smirked. 'Dad'll be furious – he paid nearly four hundred for it.'

17

She allowed Alex to lead her upstairs. At the foot of the bed he kissed her, slowly, tentatively, like a faint summer breeze blowing over her. He stood back, held her arms outstretched towards him and entwined his slender fingers through hers. Loving it and loving him, she closed her eyes, capturing the moment for ever, never wanting it to end. She heard a rustle of movement and opening her eyes she found herself staring into the carnal gaze of Derek. His hands reached out for her and pushed her down on to the bed. She turned away and closed her eyes again. She wanted Alex. She called out to him and opened her eyes once more, expectantly. This time, coming towards her was Peter. He lay on top of her and moaned, then she felt his body, hot and wet against her own. He started to scream, violent screams of agonising pain as his body started to open, revealing a shattered ribcage and a pulsating heart. She pushed him away and cried out as she felt herself covered in the wetness of his blood.

Charlotte pushed back the twisted duvet and stumbled to the bathroom. She leaned against the cold sink and stared into the mirror. Covered in sweat, her heart pounding, she ripped off the cotton T-shirt she was wearing and went and stood under the shower, letting the powerful jets of water stab and prick at her. When at last she had stopped shaking, she turned off the water and dried herself roughly with a towel.

In the darkness of the bedroom, she looked at the clock

on the bedside table. Half past three, the luminous hands told her.

She opened the window and breathed in the scent of dew-moistened grass and earth. Above her a bulging moon illuminated the garden, picking out in brilliant, magical whiteness the bark of the silver birches at the end of the lawn. It was all so peaceful out there, so undemanding, and it contrasted dramatically with the all-consuming terror she had just experienced.

Resting her elbows on the sill, Charlotte looked down at the tendrils of wisteria trying to reach inside the window. Peter would never have tolerated anything as untidy as wisteria. Peter.

She shuddered. It was the first time since the accident that she'd dreamt of him. She clasped her arms around her body, protecting herself against the thought of that blood. Why had she dreamt of that? It was odd. When she had been taken to identify Peter's body there had been very little blood. She had thought at the time that even in death Peter had been unwilling to give away any of himself. She wasn't proud of that thought now.

She wasn't proud either of the first part of the dream she had just experienced. Just what was happening to her?

She drew the curtains across the window and got back into bed, carefully so as not to disturb Mabel who was curled up, fast asleep, on what had once been Peter's side of the bed.

With a Hulme Welford jumble sale now under his belt, Alex decided it was time to give St John's a try.

He was met at the porch by Mrs Braithwaite and a woman whom he recognised from yesterday in the village hall. Mrs Braithwaite handed him a hymn book and an order of service. 'Glad to see you finally putting in an appearance, Mr Hamilton,' she said.

He gave her a nod of his head.

'Good morning,' said the other woman with contrasting friendliness. She sounded a little breathless. 'I'm Mrs Bradley. I do hope you'll enjoy your visit and come again. It's very old, you know, the church dates back to . . .'

'Really, Mrs Bradley,' interrupted Iris, 'we're working for the Lord, not the National Trust.'

'Thank you,' Alex said. 'I'm sure I'll find it most interesting.'

'Edifying, I should hope, Mr Hamilton. Reverend Jackson's theme today is following God's plan.'

'Ah yes,' said Alex. '"And he has showered down upon us the richness of his grace – for how well he understands us and knows what is best for us at all times."'

'Quite so,' said Mrs Braithwaite dismissively. 'Now come along, Mr Hamilton, there are other people behind you trying to get in.'

Alex chose to sit where he always did in any church, at the back and in the left-hand pew, and without even looking about him, he bowed his head.

A few moments later when he raised his head he found Charlotte was sitting next to him. She seemed startled when he looked at her. 'I didn't know it was you,' she said, and appeared to back away from him.

'What's wrong?' He noted the deep shadows around her eyes and her pale complexion. 'Am I *persona non grata* all of a sudden?'

She looked down, and he watched her turn her gold wedding band on her finger.

Charlotte felt Alex's gaze and knew she should answer his question. But what could she say? That he was the last person in Hulme Welford she wanted to be sitting next to that morning; that twice in twenty-four hours she had desired him, consciously and subconsciously. 'I'm surprised to see you here this morning, that's all,' she said at last.

'You're not the only one. Mrs Braithwaite has already given me a grilling. A little of that woman certainly goes a long way. Ah, I see we're off.' And picking up his hymn book, he got to his feet as the organ started up jauntily with 'Come Sing the Praise of Jesus'.

They were halfway through the second verse when a third person joined Alex and Charlotte in their pew. It was Barry Rogers. Charlotte recognised the now familiar jogging suit and flushed face, and once again noticed that he was positioned behind the stone pillar. Then as the service was drawing to a close he disappeared, as furtively as he had arrived, just as he had last week.

'I wonder why?' Charlotte said to Alex after she had explained this to him. 'Why does Barry sneak in and out of church each week? It's a bit odd, don't you think?'

Alex shrugged his shoulders. 'Maybe he's a late riser and has to get away early each time.'

'No, there's more to it than that. I bet you . . .'

'Gambling in the Lord's house, Mrs Lawrence, shame on you.' It was Iris Braithwaite looming large behind them both. 'And Mr Hamilton, I trust the sermon served you well?' Not expecting any kind of reply she was quickly off and moving towards her next prey. 'Now Mrs Haslip, I really must question the suitability of orchids in the altar flowers. Their costliness bothered me throughout the entire service. Reverend Jackson needs serviceable fauna, not exotic frippery.'

'Can't say I'd even noticed the flowers,' Alex said to Charlotte as they inched their way towards Malcolm Jackson.

'All I could think of,' Charlotte said, smiling for the first time. 'Kept thinking, what a lot of exotic frippery about the altar.'

'Hello Charlotte,' Malcolm Jackson's voice cut in. 'Good to see you again. How are things?'

'Fine,' she lied, and parrying with the kind of ease she despised, she said, 'Have you met my tenant, Mr Hamilton?'

'Always good to have new blood sitting in the pews.'

Charlotte flinched.

'Wouldn't be interested in ushering, would you?' Malcolm asked as he shook Alex's hand. 'It would give the congregation someone new to criticise,' he added, laughing.

'Why not?' Alex said.

Malcolm Jackson was amazed, for his sales pitch seldom worked. 'Right you are. I'll call round during the week with a copy of the rota for you.'

'You didn't have to, you know. You could have said no to Malcolm, most people do,' Charlotte told Alex as they waited to cross the road outside the church.

'Well, I'm not most people.'

Charlotte looked at him closely. 'You're not, are you, but then who or what are you?'

'That sounds like the corniest of lines from an old movie.'

'You're right,' she said, 'but the question still stands.'

'Tell you what, let me cut the grass for you this afternoon and then I'll tell you.'

'Okay. How about I do some lunch for us first?' She frowned and looked away from him, stared hard at the ground as they turned into Acacia Lane.

'That would be nice.' Alex was conscious of Charlotte's wariness. 'But only if you really want to.'

She stood still and looked up at him. 'Maybe we shouldn't. I wouldn't want people to . . . after all, Peter's only been dead a short while.'

He stared into her eyes which, in the leafy shade of the trees, were that same dusky violet he remembered so well from their first meeting. 'I presume it was only lunch you were offering.'

'For goodness' sake, you're beginning to sound like Derek now,' she snapped back at him.

'That's better, you don't look so . . .'

'Go on, what don't I look?'

He hesitated before speaking. It had struck him from the

moment he had met Charlotte that there was something wrong about her grief; he didn't know what it was, but knew only that something jarred. He felt at times that he forgot to treat her as a woman who had recently lost the man she loved, because she didn't behave like one. He said, 'I just feel that sometimes you're your real self and at other times it's as if you're trying to become the person you feel others expect you to be.'

'And what might that person be?' Charlotte said coolly.

'The grieving widow,' he said softly, still looking straight at her.

Charlotte said nothing, but walked on ahead, fast. Alex let her go, then after a moment's thought, he caught her up at the entrance to his part of Ivy Cottage. 'I'm sorry,' he said. 'Perhaps I shouldn't have said that.'

She turned on him and he braced himself for her anger. Instead she looked quite calmly at him. 'Can we carry on with this conversation over lunch?'

'How do you think Charlotte is coping?' Neville Archer asked his wife, as he pulled slowly away at the lights in Wilmslow. He was aware of the impatient Range Rover behind him, practically climbing into the boot of his tired old Volvo, but he would not be hurried. Moving into second gear, he added, 'I mean, really getting on.'

Louise looked up from the Royal Worcester teapot on her lap – the rest of that Sunday morning's car boot sale pickings were in the back of the car, but not this dear little teapot. Despite the small crack in the lid, it was a beauty, a real find. Stroking the spout, she said absentmindedly, 'How do you mean?'

Neville knew his wife wasn't listening. Louise's mind was on, around and inside that piece of china on her lap. Funny that something as small and insignificant as a piece of china should arouse such passion within his wife. Nothing else seemed to.

With him, of course, it was his gooseberries. Now that really was something to get excited about. The endless search to produce the ultimate berry, to nurse it through those first precious days of its infancy, watching it grow, until that exciting, poignant moment when it was time to pick it and give it up to be judged. Rather like children really – nurturing and sheltering them and then giving them up to life. Which reminded him: Charlotte.

'I was just wondering whether we should be doing more for her.' What he really wanted to say, but couldn't, was how inadequate he felt, how helpless he thought himself to be in matters of personal grief. He had been a GP all his working life, had coped admirably with gall bladders, chicken pox, herpes, chest infections and piles, but when it had come to Mrs Jenkins having a breakdown because Mr Jenkins had left her, or when he had had to tell Mr Forbes that his pretty young wife was dying of ovarian cancer, he had been useless, and he'd known it.

For no good reason that he could think of, he was convinced that Charlotte was hiding something. Whether it was from him specifically, or from everyone, he was not sure. Which was why he was now probing his wife. Had Charlotte discussed with her mother something she couldn't possibly tell him? He doubted this. He and Charlotte had always been so close.

'Look out!' Louise's voice crashed unexpectedly into his thoughts. He saw the brake lights of the car in front and pushed down hard on the brake pedal. The Volvo performed a splendid emergency stop, jerking Louise forward in her seat so that her nose almost tipped the glove compartment.

'I don't know what's the matter with you these days,' she said, straightening herself up, at the same time checking her precious teapot. 'You're so . . .'

Neville knew what she was going to say.

' . . . slow!' she said vehemently.

In response, he gripped the steering wheel tighter, his arms at a perfect ten-to-two position. 'You haven't answered my question,' he said holding back the desire to say, and you're so vague these days, you don't listen to a word I say.

'I don't know why you keep harping on about Charlotte. She's old enough to look after herself.'

He indicated to overtake a crawling refuse van, then pulled out. 'Don't you think that's being a little harsh? It was her husband who died, not a family pet. It was hardly an everyday occurrence for her.'

Louise glanced at the driver of the refuse van as they drew level. He gave her a crude wink. She looked away. 'For goodness' sake, Neville, can't you hurry up? And yes, I am well aware of the fact that it was Peter who died and not some nibbling hamster, but this is something Charlotte has got to sort out for herself.'

Neville pushed down hard on the accelerator, imagining for one delicious moment that Louise's cherished little teapot was under the pedal. A smile cracked his face and he pushed down harder. Speeding down the A34 towards Hulme Welford, he made up his mind to ignore his wife. He would go and see Charlotte and get her to talk to him. He would go tomorrow, when Louise was busy at the shop.

18

She was gulping the wine down, much too fast, she always did when she was nervous. But why was she nervous? Alex was the least intimidating man she had ever met.

They had started their meal sitting on Alex's patio, then when the May sun had proved too hot, they had retreated to Charlotte's favourite spot in the garden, to the welcome cool shade offered by the drooping branches of the fig tree. Each having eaten two helpings of spaghetti carbonara mopped up with chunks of garlic bread, they were now sitting back in their chairs, enjoying the feeling that only a pleasantly satisfied stomach can bring. Alex reached out for a grape from the Tuscan pottery bowl on the table between them.

Charlotte tried not to watch him, but she couldn't help it. His hands fascinated her, which was probably one of the reasons why she was drinking too much. Before the spoon incident at the jumble sale she hadn't given Alex's hands a second glance; now they seemed to be constantly on her mind. She shuddered involuntarily and looked down at Mabel at her feet. She lifted the little dog up on to her lap so that she had something to occupy her own hands.

'Are you cold? We could move back into the sun if you want?'

'Sorry? Oh I see, no, no I'm not cold, not at all.'

He smiled. 'Do you want to carry on that conversation now?'

Throughout the meal, they hadn't said a word about what Alex had said to her after church. It hadn't been a matter of skirting round the issue, it just hadn't cropped up. They had talked about all sorts of things: of Alex's love of small silver knick-knacks – hence the spoon; and the game that he and his brother played – who can find the most disgusting birthday present for the other – hence the tearful boy. And then he had told her about the book on trees he had bought.

'Did you know that the name rowan is believed to be derived from the Norse word *runa*?'

'Heavens, is it really?' she had said playfully, pretending to yawn.

'It means charm,' he carried on undeterred. 'Apparently rowan trees were planted outside churchyards and houses to ward off witches.'

Then she had seen the twinkle in his eye.

'I only mention it because I notice there's one at the end of your drive. With a bit of luck it should keep Mrs Braithwaite off your doorstep.'

She had laughed at that and at herself for momentarily accusing Alex of being dull.

But the issue had now been raised. What was she going to do, or say? What on earth had made her think that she could talk to Alex about her failing marriage? Why him? Why not Hilary? Why not her parents? Was it because Alex had never known Peter and she thought he would not sit in judgement of her?

'I . . . I'm not sure, to be honest,' she said. 'I don't think I can. I thought I could, but now I can't.'

He looked at her with a steady gaze, then turned away. 'You have a lovely garden. In London it was something I always wanted.'

'That's stupid,' she said, grateful for the reprieve. 'Why didn't you just buy a house with a garden?'

He leaned back in his chair and glanced up at the

drooping wisteria that covered the back of Ivy Cottage. 'Sometimes,' he said slowly, 'dreams are better than reality.' He picked at another grape. 'And anyway, the reality at the time was that I didn't have a free moment to indulge my fantasy. Work was the number one priority then.'

'Peter was like that. He would never admit it though.'

'Most men don't realise they're doing it. It's like falling in love, you don't mean to do it, it just happens. But it must be hard for a wife to accept.'

'It is, or rather, it was,' Charlotte said thoughtfully. 'But somehow you come to terms with the fact that you're no longer your husband's *numero uno*. It hurts though, and there's always a danger that . . .' But her voice trailed away. Should she tell him? Would he understand? Would he understand that eventually being second on the list makes you hate yourself and hate those around you, especially the one you once loved. 'But is work still your number one priority?' she asked, turning the conversation away from herself.

He laughed and rolled a grape between his thumb and forefinger. She wished he wouldn't do that. No she didn't. She wished he'd keep on doing it.

'I think that my very sitting here in my landlady's garden, drinking cheap supermarket Hungarian wine, proves that it isn't that important to me any longer. My eighty-hour weeks have long since gone, but then so has my company car, along with my smart address.'

'So you don't think Acacia Lane is grand enough for you?'

He laughed again and once more stretched forward to pluck a grape. Charlotte watched him carefully remove its small stalk and she shuddered again.

'Come on,' he said, getting to his feet. 'Let's get you back in the sun, you're obviously freezing.'

She tried hard not to laugh, and putting Mabel down on to the grass, she got up and started gathering up the lunch things. 'I've kept my side of the bargain,' she said, 'now it's your turn. The mower's that way.'

'Coo-ee, only me, all right if I come in?' Hilary appeared through the open conservatory door. Stepping into the kitchen, she joined Charlotte at the sink. 'I'm selling tickets for the fork supper next Saturday. I was supposed to be selling them after church this morning, only I couldn't because I wasn't there. I had to take Philip to an away match in Macclesfield – he scored the winning goal. He's really very good, you should come and see him play some time.' She put down her bundle of supper tickets and envelope of money, looked for a tea towel and automatically started drying the plates Charlotte had just washed. 'You've missed a bit,' she said, slipping one of the plates back into the soapy water. 'So, where was I?'

'Selling tickets for the fork supper I think,' Charlotte said, smiling to herself.

'Oh yes. Well, I've just been trying next door,' she nodded her head towards the kitchen wall that backed on to Alex's part of the house, 'but there was no answer, so I thought that maybe Alex was here with you.'

'Did you now?' Charlotte fixed her attention on the pan she was rinsing under the hot tap.

'This tea towel isn't very clean. Have you got another?'

'In the drawer over there.'

Hilary began rummaging through the chaotically filled drawer. 'Charlotte . . .' she said, but got no further as she was interrupted by the sound of a powerful lawnmower starting up. She joined her sister and looked out of the window. 'It's Alex,' Charlotte said unnecessarily, as a lawnmower appeared from behind the potting shed followed by Alex, stripped to the waist and now wearing shorts.

'I can see that,' Hilary said pressing herself hard up against the sink. 'Just look at him.'

'Hilary!'

Hilary slapped a hand over her mouth, as though to prevent any other impure thoughts from slipping out. 'I didn't mean, I only . . .'

Charlotte laughed. 'I know exactly what you mean and I happen to agree with you.'

'You do?' Hilary said, her hopes rising. Her sister was falling for Alex after all. Smiling to herself she stared out of the window as Alex pushed the mower towards the bottom of the garden. 'He's well tanned, isn't he?'

Charlotte tilted her head to one side as though looking at Alex's naked back from a better angle. 'Mm . . . I suppose he is.'

'Looks good in shorts.' Hilary decided to push the point home. 'Good looking altogether, wouldn't you say?'

Charlotte was about to respond when Alex reached the far end of the garden, turned the mower round and looked straight up at them. He waved nonchalantly.

They acknowledged him, then moved away from the window. 'Put the kettle on, shall I?' Hilary said, awkwardly.

They sat with their drinks at the table, Hilary just managing to keep one eye on the garden, but Charlotte with her back to it. 'It's a long time since we did any serious ogling, isn't it?' Hilary said.

Charlotte made no response. Hilary decided to be brave. 'You are allowed to, you know . . . just because you're a widow, it doesn't mean you're no longer a woman. You're going to have to try and remember what it was like in the old days, before Peter.'

Charlotte reflected on this, taking a sip of her tea. Pre-Peter. In those days Hilary had accused her of having a lascivious nature, but that was only because Hilary had been so taken up with David.

Hilary sensed Charlotte wasn't going to say anything more on the subject. She picked up her bundle of tickets. 'You'll come, won't you?'

Charlotte shook her head. 'I don't think so.'

'Why ever not?' Hilary's disappointment was obvious. She had been so sure that she could lure Charlotte and Alex together for the evening at the village hall.

Charlotte banged her mug down. Splashes of tea spilled over the table. 'I know exactly what you were thinking. One ticket to Alex and one to Charlotte. Do you really think I'm that naïve?'

Charlotte could feel her face colouring, her skin prickling with irrational hot rage. Suddenly she wanted to cry, to cry great sobs of . . . she didn't know what. Yes she did. Remorse. Guilt! It was there all the time, baiting her day and night. It had been there when she and Alex had had lunch together. A perfectly innocent lunch, but all the time she had felt it was wrong, wrong to have enjoyed Alex's company. And damn it, she had. She liked being with him. He was nice, amusing, attentive, and what's more she found him attractive. And now here was Hilary egging her on even further. Well, it wouldn't do. She would have to put a stop to it, here and now. It was time for her to take control. There would be no more 'Alex and Charlotte' because then there would be no more guilt . . . and no more dreams.

Common sense told her it was too soon. No woman in her right mind would let herself get caught up in another relationship only months after the death of her husband. It was madness. It was disrespectful. Yes. That was it. There had to be a decent period of mourning to be honoured. It was her duty. She may have failed Peter in marriage but she could at least do the right thing in death. She owed him that much. She almost sighed with relief, knowing she had hit upon infallible justification for not getting involved with Alex Hamilton. She had found the right weapon with which to fight off any temptation he offered.

Hilary peered over the top of her mug. She said quietly, 'You could always come on your own.'

'I know that,' Charlotte said calmly. 'Or I could bring a

friend with me.'

Hilary looked crestfallen. 'You could.' She decided to force her sister's hand. 'So that's two tickets, then.' She peeled off two orange cards from her bundle. 'That'll be five pounds.'

Charlotte went in search of her bag and wondered at what she had just done. Who on earth could she ask to go with her? She walked back into the kitchen and handed over a five pound note.

'So who are you going to bring?' Hilary said, putting her things together but not daring to look Charlotte in the eye.

For a split second Charlotte hated her sister. 'You'll just have to wait and see.'

Hilary had the grace not to push her sister any more. She headed for the door. 'Tell Alex I'll catch him later, will you? Bye for now.' She left.

Charlotte looked out of the window. Alex was halfway through the lawn now, deep in concentration. He had the look of a man completely at peace with himself.

Charlotte envied him.

Alex switched the engine off and pushed the mower into the potting shed. He noticed Charlotte standing at the kitchen window again. He noticed too the way she instantly turned away the moment she realised he had seen her.

He bent down to the mower and started to clean off some of the stuck-on bits of grass. But his thoughts remained on Charlotte. There were times when he felt sure that there was something she wanted to tell him – maybe not him specifically, just someone. There were other times though when she treated him as though he were Jack the Ripper.

He smiled to himself as he thought of Lucy's words, spoken to him so often: *Alex, I do believe you're a frustrated agony aunt, always trying to sort out other people's problems.*

'There's no need, you know.'

Charlotte was silhouetted in the doorway and Alex knew from the stilted tone of her voice that he had once again taken on the guise of Jack the Ripper.

'I can clean it myself,' she said.

He stood up. Sidestepping the mower, he moved towards her. 'It's no problem,' he said. What had suddenly happened between lunch and now? What had caused her to change? Was it something he had said? 'Perhaps I could become your fulltime gardener,' he quipped. 'I could move in here, into the potting shed.'

'And I could be your Lady Chatterley, I suppose.' Her words were heavy with sarcasm.

They stood in silence, each staring at the other, until Charlotte could bear it no more. She felt overwhelmed by the heady earthiness of the stifling shed, together with the sweet smell of fresh grass cuttings and petrol. She stepped back towards the sunshine and fresh air. As she moved Alex picked up his T-shirt which was hanging on the hook on the door. 'I'm sorry I upset you,' he said. 'It was only a joke.'

Charlotte wanted to apologise, but she knew she mustn't. She knew too that standing as she was, barely inches away from Alex and the warmth of his glistening body, that she wanted very much to pretend she was Constance Chatterley. She swallowed hard and tried to cling to her objective. 'I've a message for you from Hilary,' she said.

His face was unreadable.

'It's about the fork supper at the village hall next Saturday. Hilary wondered if you'd be wanting a ticket. Of course she realises that you've probably got better things to do on a Saturday night.' She forced herself to add a casual laugh.

Alex managed a laugh as well. 'What, and have Mrs Braithwaite commenting on my absence? No fear. You can tell Hilary I'll have a ticket. In fact, you can tell her I'll have two. I suppose it's okay for me to take a friend along?'

'The more the merrier,' Charlotte said, surprised. 'Actually, I'm taking someone as well.'

Throwing his T-shirt over his shoulder, Alex turned and walked away.

Damn! thought Charlotte, watching him stroll across the lawn. What on earth was she going to do now? Not only was Hilary expecting her to turn up with a man, but Alex was also bringing a partner. Hell!

19

What was happening to her? She never had sugar in her coffee. It was Peter who had sugar.

She had dreamt of him again last night. This time he was lying in a hospital bed, not in a normal ward but in a room that had been made into an office: a fax machine in one corner, an array of potted plants in another, a desk in the middle with Peter's attaché case, and Peter himself, lying on a bed beneath his faithful laptop computer. All this she was seeing through a glass window as she was trying to make an appointment to see her husband. But the attractive nurse was telling her that Mr Lawrence was too busy to see her right now, and could she come back later? 'But he'll be dead later,' she had screamed at the nurse. Then two policemen had led her away, saying they wanted to question her about the death of her husband.

Was she cracking up? Charlotte shook her head. Getting up from the table, she tipped her coffee – Peter's coffee – down the sink. She heard the sound of the letterbox being pushed open and went through to the hall.

She made herself another drink, and taking the letters upstairs to read she found Mabel curled up on the bed. The first letter was from her solicitor, something about investments Peter had made. She put this back in its envelope. The next was a handwritten letter with a Brussels postmark. She knew straight away who it was from. Christina Castelli.

Scanning through the first page Charlotte was not surprised by the lack of 'hope you're settling in' platitudes –

that was definitely not Christina's style. Instead it was a full account of a fat German industrialist and an Irish diplomat who had spent an entire evening singing in Gaelic to her. At the bottom of the second page was '. . . and so, Carlotta, I have booked a flight to Manchester and shall come to stay with you next month.' The letter went on to explain the exact date and time that Christina would be arriving, along with '. . . no need to meet me, I shall arrange for a taxi and arrive in time for cocktails.'

Charlotte laughed out loud. 'Cocktails!' she said. 'In Acacia Lane, just imagine.' She laughed again and tried to imagine Christina here in Hulme Welford: Christina and Iris Braithwaite . . . Christina and Derek Rogers! Lying back on the pillow, she reread the letter, squeezing it for more contact with her friend. Her thoughts were inter-rupted by the shrill ring of the telephone at the side of the bed. She picked up the receiver. 'Hello.'

'Charlotte?'

'Yes.' Her brain automatically ran through a list of possible male callers she might get at eight o'clock in the morning.

'It's me, Jonathan.'

'Jonathan!'

'I'm over in England on Friday, business, Birmingham, okay if I buzz up to see you, Saturday, about lunchtime, a bed for the night wouldn't go amiss?'

Yes, it was Jonathan all right, he always did speak like a telegram. 'Yes of course, I'll look forward to it,' she lied.

'Okay, see you.' The phone clicked and Charlotte was left with a droning sound in her ears and a stupefied expression on her face. She put the receiver down and nudged Mabel. 'So, we're to have the pleasure of Jonathan's company, how fortunate we are. Jonathan, King Kong of Hong Kong. Bet you'll dislike Peter's brother as much as I do.'

In eight years of marriage, Charlotte had only met her brother-in-law on a handful of occasions. The first time was by coincidence, at a party in London, not long after she and Peter had met. At the time she had no idea Peter had a brother, and coming out of their hostess's kitchen with two glasses of wine she had found Peter in the hall, admiring a large painting. Handing him his glass, she had kissed him lightly on the cheek, only to realise he was not Peter, and have it confirmed by the look of wonder on the man's face. Embarrassed, she had simply stood and stared, completely taken aback by the extraordinary likeness between this man and Peter. Peter had then appeared and he too, for a moment, had simply stood and stared.

'Surprise!' the man had said, taking a large mouthful of wine from the glass Charlotte had just given him.

'Another one of your passing-through visits, is it?' Peter said coldly.

'Needs must, when the devil drives. Aren't you going to introduce me?'

Peter turned to face Charlotte, his eyes narrow and dark. 'This is Jonathan, and as you've no doubt worked out for yourself, he's my brother.'

Driving home in the car afterwards, Peter had barely said a word, his tight-lipped expression telling Charlotte all she needed to know – that despite the striking resemblance there was no love between the two brothers.

Another occasion when they had met was in Singapore. It was then that Charlotte began to get a clearer picture of the intense rivalry between the two men. Jonathan was the elder brother by four years and neither of the two seemed able to forget this. 'As older brother, I insist on taking you two out for dinner,' Jonathan had said, when he arrived at their apartment, having just flown in from Hong Kong, where he lived and worked lucrative deals of gigantic proportions.

'I've already booked us a restaurant,' Peter had said, 'where the manager knows me personally.'

And so the evening had continued, with each brother trying to outdo the other, oblivious to Charlotte.

Now, after all these years, Jonathan wanted to come and see her. Why? Was it so that he could have one last shot at Peter – 'You see, little brother, I've got more staying power than you.'

The thought suddenly occurred to Charlotte that she could make good use of Jonathan while he was here.

*

It was just after twelve o'clock when the door bell rang and Mabel started to bark.

'Hello.' Neville Archer was standing on the doorstep. He bent down to stroke the little dog. 'Have you got time to see your old dad?'

'Come in,' Charlotte said, kissing his cheek.

He peered into rooms as he walked through to the kitchen. He could see that his daughter had got things more or less straight since Monday when he had helped her with the unpacking. A few pictures were hanging on the walls now, though there were still some propped up on the floor against the wall. Perhaps he should offer to help Charlotte put them up, or would she think he was interfering?

'How about some lunch? I haven't been out to the shops yet but I've got the remains of a bit of Cambozola and some crackers.'

He nodded and sat down at the table. 'Don't tell your mother. I haven't been allowed Cambozola for six months – too many calories.'

They laughed conspiratorially. Neville felt reassured. She was still his ally after all. He waited until Charlotte had sat down with him at the table before embarking on what he had to say. 'Charlotte,' he helped himself to some cheese, 'I know you could tell me to mind my own business, or you could of course throw me out, or simply lie, but just how are you really feeling? I know I'm not much good at this kind of thing, as I'm sure your mother would be the first to agree . . .'

'Has Mother sent you here?' Charlotte wondered at her

father's words which had come out like a well-prepared speech.

'No. As a matter of fact, she thinks I've gone to see Ron Wicklow about the gooseberry show.'

'You lied to Mother. Why?'

Neville shrugged. He felt like a small boy caught with apples in his pockets. 'I . . . I was worried about you and wanted to know . . .'

'Oh Dad.' She reached out and touched his arm, finding comfort in the feel of his old tweed jacket – he had always dressed like a country doctor and still did. With a sudden surge of emotion she remembered vividly, waiting outside his surgery, as a child, listening to two elderly women discussing her father: 'He's such a dear man, I'd love to take him home and put him on the mantelpiece.'

'I've been worried about you,' Neville pressed on. 'Losing Peter like that, so suddenly, must have been awful. I just want you to know that I'm here if you need me.'

She felt tears welling up, but she battled against them and passed him the plate of crackers. 'We've always been close, haven't we?'

He nodded his head. They were on uncharted territory now and he didn't trust himself to speak.

'We've always sort of known what the other was thinking.'

Again he nodded.

'At the moment though, you couldn't possibly guess what's going on inside my head . . . I wouldn't want you to.'

Still he said nothing, convinced now that there was something his daughter was holding back. If he waited long enough she'd talk to him, it would all come out.

'Do you want some more cheese?' she said, pushing the plate towards him.

He shook his head.

'You see, it's not as everyone thinks. Everyone thinks that

I . . .' She got up from the table and started fiddling with the kettle.

It was no good. He couldn't take it any longer. He had to say something. 'Charlotte . . .' But he got no further because the telephone rang. Was that relief he saw on his daughter's face as she went out to the hall to answer it?

He watched Charlotte through the open door as she picked up the receiver. 'Hello Mum,' she said. He shook his head and then pretended to hold a gun to his temple. Charlotte tried hard not to smile. 'What, here, you think Dad's here?' She put her hand over the mouthpiece of the receiver and whispered, 'Ron Wicklow's just been on the phone asking for you.'

'Oh heavens,' groaned Neville.

Charlotte packed her father off to meet his fate, cleared up the lunch things and went outside. She collected a few tools and the wheelbarrow from the potting shed, and headed off towards the bottom of the garden.

The flower beds had not been tended in a long while; the death of Mrs Clifford senior must have put the garden very low on the list of priorities for the Clifford family. Death was like that. Or was it? Another person might have absorbed themselves into a regime of digging, weeding and pruning, worked all hours so as not to think of their loss. Perhaps that was what she should do. Throw herself into something, so that she didn't have time to keep blaming herself, would not keep feeling the need to confess. She had almost told her father, had been so close to telling him everything. She dug deep and vigorously into the heavy clay soil. 'Ashes to ashes, dust to dust,' she suddenly said out loud.

Alex put the phone down and made some hurried notes on the pad on his desk – a company over in Knutsford wanted to update their current stock control system.

He looked out of the window. At the bottom of the garden he could see Charlotte with a fully loaded wheelbarrow. Immediately he was working out what excuse he could use to go and talk to her. He smiled to himself. He was off again.

He went through to his small kitchen and put the kettle on. He would take her a cup of tea.

He made his way down the garden and stood some twelve feet away from where Charlotte was digging. She was talking to herself. No, not talking, it was more like a chant: 'Ashes to ashes, dust to dust,' she was repeating over and over again. He stood still, not knowing what to do. It was obvious she had no idea he was there. He felt like an intruder, and was about to step slowly backwards when from behind him came the sound of yapping. Mabel was scuttling across the lawn.

Charlotte turned round sharply. 'How long have you been there?' Her faced flushed and he noticed a long smudge of earth across her right cheek. He wanted very much to wipe it away for her.

'Thought you'd like a tea break,' he said, ignoring her question.

'Oh, thank you.' She dropped the spade and pulled off her gardening gloves. 'I was miles away, I didn't hear you coming. Have you been working?' Her words were rushed in a conspicuous attempt to overcome her embarrassment. He handed her the mug.

'Yes,' he said, thankful that for the time being he didn't seem to be Jack the Ripper. 'I think I've just gained a new client, over at Knutsford. How long do you think it will take me to get there?'

'Not long,' she said, flicking her hair out of her eyes. 'About thirty minutes. Parking can be a devil though. I should give yourself an extra ten minutes to be on the safe side.'

Glad to be able to talk to her, Alex carried on. 'So what's Knutsford like?'

'Nice, but very twee. Black and white like Hulme Welford, except more upmarket. They've got Mrs Gaskell while all we've got is Iris Braithwaite.'

He laughed.

Charlotte drained her mug and handed it back to him. 'Thank you, I enjoyed that.' He noticed her looking over his shoulder. 'It looks like one of us has a visitor,' she said.

Alex turned and saw Barry Rogers coming towards them.

'Congratulations!' he said. 'I hear you passed your driving test on Wednesday. Well done.'

Barry pushed at his glasses. 'I think I was just lucky.'

'Nonsense,' said Charlotte. 'No such thing as luck.'

'I hope there is. I had my first physics exam this morning.' He pushed his hair back, which like his glasses slipped straight back to its familiar place.

Charlotte groaned. 'How did it go?'

Barry smiled, which had the effect of altering his earnest face completely. 'It was okay actually, easier than I thought it might be.'

'Good for you,' Alex said. 'What else are you doing?'

'Chemistry starts tomorrow, next comes biology and then economics. They're spread out over three and a half weeks.'

Charlotte groaned again. 'You poor boy. But what brings you here? You've not come to me for private tuition I hope?'

As suddenly as the smile had appeared so it vanished. Barry looked awkwardly at them both.

Alex could see how tense he was, and thinking it might be to do with the Charlotte and Derek incident, he said, 'I'll be off then.'

'No, no, don't do that.'

Again a nudge of the glasses and a hand pushing fruitlessly at his hair. 'I'd like to speak to both of you, if that's all right.'

'Sounds ominous,' Charlotte said, leading them towards the chairs which she now kept permanently by the fig tree.

'It hasn't got anything to do with your parents, has it?' she added cautiously.

'No, certainly not, well, not directly anyway. I suppose I should apologise for what I said to you in church that morning. I don't normally go around . . .'

'I'm sure I'd have done the same if I'd been in your shoes.'

'Well,' said Alex, setting the empty mugs down on the table, 'how can we help you?'

'It's a bit difficult.' Barry squeezed his large frame into one of the flimsy chairs. 'I'm not sure where to start, and please don't say at the beginning.'

'I'm tired of clichés myself,' Charlotte smiled. 'Carry on, just as you want.' Her words were warm and sincere and Alex realised that here was the real Charlotte, relaxed and eager to help. Barry posed no threat to her. It was he himself who somehow caused her to smell danger. Why?

'You see, it's true, isn't it?' Barry was saying. 'Most people at some stage in their lives feel something, experience something, that they know will change their lives for ever.' He turned his earnest face up at them both, seeking confirmation of this statement.

Alex nodded and Charlotte leaned forward in her chair, as though willing Barry on.

'Well, I guess I've just reached that point in my life and I'm not sure what do to about it.'

Alex rubbed his chin thoughtfully and for a split second Charlotte's attention was drawn away from Barry and was absorbed in Alex's hands.

'So what you're saying,' Alex said, causing Charlotte to concentrate again, 'is that something has happened to you recently, something that has changed your understanding of your life?'

'Yes, that's exactly it.' Barry looked visibly relieved. 'I felt sure you'd understand. That's why I came to you.'

Charlotte thought about this for a moment. What was it about Alex that had this effect on people? What made people want to confide in him? First her, now Barry. She couldn't understand it, nor this conversation. What were they talking about? Was it a girl? Had Barry fallen in love? She took her courage in both hands. 'So what's her name?'

At first Barry looked confused, then he smiled, again a smile which transformed his serious teenage face into that of a dazzling young man. 'I think, Mrs Lawrence,' he said politely, at the same time making Charlotte feel like Old Mother Hubbard, 'that perhaps I've misled you.'

'Oh,' said Charlotte, 'but I thought . . .' And then another idea came into her head. 'Oh,' she said again, 'you mean it's a . . .'

Alex cut in swiftly. 'I think Barry should spell it out for us.' He looked at Barry and smiled encouragingly.

20

Barry felt better for having talked it through with someone else. Now all he had to do was tell his parents.

It certainly wasn't going to be easy. Bewilderment would come first with his father, then it would be ridicule. Tiffany would be okay. She'd tease him for a while and then get bored with it all. His mother he wasn't so sure about. It was difficult at times to know what she thought.

He could hear his parents down in the kitchen, not talking to one another, just moving about. He decided the time was right, breathed in deeply, got up from his desk and went downstairs.

They started supper in silence. Tiffany's chair was typically empty. Without her, Barry didn't want to say anything. But the longer he waited the more he could feel his nerve going. Perhaps he could tell them tomorrow, after his chemistry exam? He ran his hand nervously through his hair. 'I had my first physics exam this morning,' he said.

His mother looked up from her plate of salad. 'Oh, I'm sorry, I forgot all about that.' She looked genuinely pained at this parental oversight. 'How did it go?'

'Cost of the fees at that school, he'd better have done all right,' his father said, reaching for the jar of mayonnaise. 'Only joking, Bas. How was it?'

'Okay, I think. I was lucky, I'd revised the right bits.'

'You're late,' Cindy said, looking over Barry's shoulder as Tiffany sauntered into the kitchen.

Still cyclamen pink, Tiffany ignored her mother and

pulled a face at the sight of the salad on her plate. She sat down and smiled at Barry. 'So, how was it?'

'If you'd been here when you were supposed to be,' Cindy snapped, 'you would have heard.'

Still ignoring her mother, Tiffany said, 'Tell me later, Barry.'

'Actually,' Barry said carefully, putting his knife and fork down on his plate, 'I've got something I want to tell you all.'

His father viewed him speculatively and then a broad smile covered his face, and, brandishing a large radish on the end of his fork, he said, 'You sly old devil, you've gone and got yourself a girl, haven't you? I told you that car would do the trick.'

'Give it a rest, Dad,' Tiffany said. 'Let Barry speak.'

'Watch your step, young lady. You're not so—'

'Look,' Barry interrupted, raising his voice slightly, 'this is hard enough for me to say without you lot arguing as well.'

Cindy looked up sharply. 'Hard enough?' she repeated. 'Why, what have you done?'

'Oh my God,' Derek said slowly looking at his son across the table. 'You've gone and got a girl pregnant, haven't you? All that crap about not being interested in girls and studying like mad was just to fool us. Bloody hell! I'd have expected even you to know about safe sex.'

'What, like you?' Cindy's voice was as brittle as the look she gave her husband.

Barry got up from the table, scraping his chair noisily on the tiled floor. A silence followed as everyone looked up at him. 'Look, Dad,' he said, 'this has absolutely nothing whatsoever to do with a girl.' He had their attention now and so pushed on, trying to gain confidence through momentum. 'I've recently discovered something about myself that I feel I need to share with you, something that may surprise you.' He paused as he sought the right words.

His father threw down his knife and fork on the table. He

too stood up and looked Barry straight in the eye. 'Well, you can pack your bags now. You can bugger off somewhere else, anywhere, so long as I don't have to set eyes on you.'

Three pairs of eyes stared at Derek in astonishment. 'Not only,' he said, looking at his wife and then back at Barry, 'not only is he a stuffed Henry, but he's a bloody great screaming poofter.' He turned away from them all. 'I need a beer,' he said, reaching for the fridge.

Cindy's eyes filled with tears as she pushed her plate away and bent her head down over the table. Tiffany got to her feet and stepped towards Barry. She put her arm around him. 'If he goes,' she said dramatically, 'so do I.'

'Good!' shouted Derek, slamming the fridge door shut and yanking at the ring pull on his can of beer. 'Good bloody riddance to the pair of you.'

'But Dad . . .' It was Barry, his voice strangely calm and assured.

'Don't "but Dad" me anything,' Derek rounded on him. 'You've betrayed us all. You filthy . . . homosexual!' He almost spat out the last word.

'But Dad, I'm not a homosexual.'

'Not a homosexual? Then what do you call yourself, got some other bloody fancy name for it, have you?'

'My sexuality doesn't come into this at all,' Barry said.

'Then what the hell does?'

'God does.'

'God!' shouted Derek. 'And just what is that supposed to mean?'

'It means I've become a Christian.'

Frothy bubbles spurted across the kitchen floor as Derek choked on his beer. 'A what?' he gasped.

Barry was fully in control of himself now. 'A Christian, Dad. You know, someone who believes in Jesus Christ as his personal saviour.'

Derek suddenly looked very pale and dazed as he slumped back heavily against the worktop, speechless.

'Muffin 'ell, Barry,' said Tiffany, 'that really has shut Dad up.'

'Perhaps we could all sit down again,' Barry said quietly, aware how drawn his mother looked as she sat completely motionless at the table. Dutifully his father and sister sat down. Feeling better than he had for weeks, Barry picked up his knife and fork and said, 'Anybody want to say anything?'

'So, um . . .' Derek said at last, 'so what exactly does this mean – orange dresses and tambourines?'

Barry laughed and nudged his glasses on his nose. 'Dad, I'm not about to create a Fort Waco here in Acacia Lane.' His words were light, almost flippant, in an attempt to lighten the mood around the table.

'But you haven't been confirmed or anything,' Tiffany said.

'I know. More importantly, I haven't even been baptised.'

'I wanted you both baptised,' Cindy said, her first words in more than ten minutes. 'I wanted you both baptised when you were babies.'

'Only because you wanted a new dress and a party out of it,' Derek fired at her, tossing back the last of his beer.

'I did not!'

'Well, I think it's brilliant,' Tiffany said, sensing a row about to start up again. 'At least now we might get some much needed morality in this house.' She fixed her eyes on her father.

For the first time in his life, Barry saw his father flinch.

By eight o'clock they had finished their meal, which, on reflection, Barry thought must have seemed like an eternity for his parents, sitting there as though the Archbishop of Canterbury had just dropped in. They both seemed relieved when he said he was going out for a short while.

Barry knocked on Alex's door.

'How bad was it?' Alex led him through to the small

uncluttered sitting-room.

'I'm amazed you didn't hear all the shouting. Poor Dad, he thought I was trying to tell him that I was gay.'

'Oh Lord,' Alex said. 'But then, parents have such a tough time of it. I suppose it's only natural they jump to the wrong conclusions, which are usually their worst fears.'

'I hadn't thought of it like that, but you're right. To Dad, sexuality is all.'

'So, what happens next?'

'I go home and get myself ready for my chemistry exam tomorrow morning.'

21

'Left you nicely, didn't he?'

Charlotte swallowed hard, not for the first time in the two hours since her brother-in-law had turned up, driving an oversized hired Mercedes and carrying his Ralph Lauren garment bag and matching leather briefcase.

She looked across the sitting-room at Jonathan in his expensive, crisp suit, his long legs sticking out from the sofa, and felt repelled by his air of being entirely at ease, wherever he was. But what had really taken her by surprise was the shock of being with such a tangible reminder of Peter. She hadn't prepared herself for that, hadn't thought how disturbing it could feel to be face to face with a man who looked so similar to her dead husband. Even the way Jonathan picked minuscule specks of fluff off his jacket sleeve put her in mind of Peter.

'Lucky old you.'

Charlotte looked up at Jonathan. 'Lucky old me,' she repeated. 'How's that exactly?'

Jonathan crossed his legs. 'All that money Peter must have left you.'

Charlotte got up from her chair, trying to keep a rein on her anger. How typical, how bloody typical that Jonathan should show no sign of missing his own brother, but only show a keen interest in how well off Peter had left his widow. And why? Why the hell should Jonathan care about how much money she had, when he himself had bank accounts scattered far and wide? Did he feel cheated? She breathed in deeply, determined to stay calm. She had to keep Jonathan sweet until tomorrow morning, then she could tell him what she really thought of him. If she blew it now, she would lose her 'date' for the evening down at the village hall.

'Nice place you've got yourself, Charlotte. An expensive but worthwhile investment, I shouldn't wonder.'

She nodded. How dare he! How dare he talk to her like this. What right did he have to make these assumptions? Or was she angry because it was almost as though Jonathan knew the truth: that Peter's death had left her better off – in all ways. She looked out of the window trying to take her mind off this dreadful man sitting a few feet away from her. 'I can't dispute that Peter has left me comfortably off, so I suppose, as you say, I am indeed lucky.' She turned to face Jonathan once more. 'But you know, there's more to life than how much money is involved. Wasn't it John Ruskin who said "The only wealth is life itself"?'

He smiled, like a weasel. 'Helps though.'

Charlotte pushed her nails hard into the palm of her hand. 'Coffee?'

'Black, no sugar.'

She escaped to the kitchen and vented her anger by rattling mugs and spoons until she realised that she was no longer alone. Jonathan was standing in the doorway. He came towards her. She suddenly felt uncomfortable.

'You'll soon marry again of course, won't you?' he said.

She could feel his hot breath on her neck and moving away from him she wondered at this statement. The very idea was preposterous. Why would she want to replace one man with another, who in the end would probably do exactly as Peter had done – turn her into second best. No. The answer was no. She would not marry again.

She looked out of the window and saw Alex walk across the lawn in front of his part of the house. He was carrying a glass of beer in one hand and a book in the other. She watched him settle himself down on the grass. Why wasn't that man ever at work? she thought angrily to herself. She turned round sharply to face Jonathan.

'No, I have no intention of remarrying,' she said, smiling sweetly up at him. 'Just in case that was a proposal from you, Jonathan.'

Derek switched off the lights in the salon. It had been a busy Saturday and they had finished late, leaving him no time for a session in the gym and a sauna before going out for the evening. A village hall jamboree was far from his idea of a good night out, but it would do no harm for the business for him and Cindy to be seen socially in the village. And of course, there was always the prospect that Charlotte would be there.

He hadn't seen Charlotte since that farce of a jumble sale last Saturday and what with the ridiculous number of problems at the Wilmslow and Altrincham salons, he hadn't had any free time during the week to slip next door. What really bothered him, though, was that her tenant might be doing more than his fair share of '*slipping next door*'.

Going up the stairs in the main part of the house, Derek could hear Tiffany's hi-fi playing loudly in her bedroom – The Doors, yet more revival music. A spark of annoyance flickered within him as he stood and listened to 'Come on Baby Light my Fire'. He hated nostalgia. It served no purpose other than to remind him he was getting older.

He moved further along the landing and paused outside Bas's room. Silence. Probably down on his knees, Derek thought caustically. Immediately he regretted this thought. He didn't know why, but he did, and that disturbed him. He never regretted anything. He remained standing outside his son's room, half tempted to go in. But what would he say? What could he say? He shook his head. Just what was happening to his family? He didn't understand any of it.

Tiffany running around like a liquorice allsort and now Bas turning into some bloody kind of monk! Brother Bas! He shook his head again, it was all beyond him. Religion was for weirdos, for those cranks and loonies too weak to get through life without some kind of mental crutch. So where did Bas fit in?

'Hello Dad.'

Derek started and turned round to see Barry standing behind him. 'Bas,' he said, feeling unaccountably pleased to see his son, all six foot two of him and looking anything but a crank or a loony. 'I thought you were in your room.'

'No, I've been down at the village hall helping to get things ready for tonight. I went to see Malcolm Jackson earlier and he kind of roped me in.'

Derek looked uneasy.

'I went to see him about being baptised. He said he could do a service later in the summer.'

'I see,' was all Derek could think to say. He could sense that his son had something else to tell him. He watched him push his glasses up on to the bridge of his nose.

'Dad, I'd like you and Mum to be there, Tiffany too.'

Derek gaped. 'Oh no, I don't think . . . I mean, we can't . . . not Tiffany, not the way she looks.'

'Dad, it really doesn't matter what she looks like. But you don't have to come if you don't want to. I . . . I don't want to embarrass you. I understand.'

Derek looked at his son. All at once he felt like the biggest shit that had ever walked the earth. Unable to meet his son's gaze, he pushed his hands deep into his pockets and looked down at his shoes. At last he raised his head. 'Okay, if you want us there, we'll be there. But you'll look a right prat in a christening gown. I'll buy you a decent suit.'

'Thanks, Dad, that's great.'

They stood facing each other, suddenly not knowing what else to say, with the noise of thumping music invading the silence between them.

The moment was broken by the sound of a door opening followed by Tiffany. 'You look dead serious,' she shouted above the music. 'Been arguing again?'

Derek and Barry exchanged looks and both laughed.

'What's got into you two?' Tiffany said.

Inexplicably, Derek felt an unfamiliar rush of warmth run through him for his children. Wondering where Cindy had got to, he said, 'Where's your mother?'

'She was having a lie down earlier, said she had a headache,' Tiffany answered.

'Well, you can turn that bloody din off then,' Derek said. 'How do you expect her to rest with all that noise going on?'

Baffled, Barry and Tiffany looked at each other. Consideration – from their father?

'Oh Lord, where have I put it?'

'Put what?' David asked Hilary, as she pushed past him like an express train.

'The key,' Hilary shouted. 'The key for the hall, for tonight.'

David always knew when his wife was panicking. She seemed to grow six inches taller and her nostrils flared imperceptibly. Experience had taught him that in these situations there was usually very little he could do. Years ago he had been stupid enough to think that it was his job to take control of the situation, but now he knew better. He stood back patiently watching, while Hilary gave the oak chest of drawers on her side of the bed a ruthless body search.

'I had it earlier when I came back after setting up all the tables,' she said.

David cleared his throat and decided to risk it. 'What did you have on this afternoon?'

'Oh don't be so stupid, David. Of course I've already thought of that. I'm not that daft.' She let out a cry of frustration as she slumped down on to the bed, sitting heavily on the dress she had just spent ten minutes ironing. 'I was so looking forward to tonight,' she moaned. 'I thought for once I had it all carefully organised: the tickets, the food, the drinks. Everything. And now I've gone and lost the wretched key and no one will be able to get into the hall. What *will* everyone think of me?'

David took a cautious step towards the bed. 'Can't we borrow Brown Owl's key?'

Hilary sniffed dismissively. 'No. She's gone rambling in the Peak District this weekend.' She reached for a tissue and blew her nose. 'I've got exactly one hour to find this key,' she said, determination rising in her voice, 'and find it I will.'

Knowing there was nothing he could say or do, David sat down on the small boudoir chair in the corner of the bedroom, at the same time being careful to move to one side Hilary's jeans. He remembered having seen her wearing them earlier. Wouldn't do any harm to check, he thought. Fumbling furtively so as not to alert Hilary that he had doubted her, he searched all the pockets. To his relief he touched cold metal, but there was something with it, something lacy. 'Hilary,' he said, 'what's this?'

'For goodness' sake, David, don't bother me now,' she replied tersely, rushing past him and heading full tilt for the *en suite* bathroom.

He followed her in and closed the door behind him. 'I've got something for you.' He held up a large key and waved it in front of her.

'David, you wonderful man! Where was it?'

'Your jeans.'

She looked puzzled, at the same time seeming to shrink back to her normal size. 'But I checked the pockets,' she said, 'truly I did.'

'The back pockets?'

She shook her head and reached out for the key. But David snapped his hand away. 'Not so fast.' With his other hand he dangled something red and lacy in front of her.

'What's this, darling?' he said. 'Something you've been hiding from me?'

Flushing as red as the G-string in David's hands, Hilary blurted out, 'It's not mine. I found it at the jumble sale. Derek Rogers wanted it and I wouldn't let him.'

David laughed. 'Well that wasn't very sporting of you, was it?'

'You don't understand.' She was flustered. 'Iris told me to get rid of it and I forgot and somehow it ended up on the table with all the other clothes and I . . .'

David looked at his wife. 'Ah, and there was I thinking you'd got me something special.' He pulled Hilary to him and kissed her, leaving her in no doubt what was in his mind.

'The children,' she said.

'They're watching the telly.'

'We haven't got long . . . Tiffany will be . . .'

He kissed her again. 'I'm claiming my reward for finding the key.'

22

For the third time in five minutes, Charlotte looked at the broken lock on the bathroom door. Jonathan was taking a shower in the guest bathroom, but there was something about the way her brother-in-law had been acting during the day that had seriously unnerved her. In the eight years she had been married to Peter, Jonathan had never once paid her the slightest bit of attention, now suddenly he seemed overly attentive.

Sitting in the bath, she wished fervently that she was one of those glamorous women you see on television who always have froth-filled baths, so that if a surprise guest just happens to drop in only a pair of perfectly tanned shoulders peep seductively above the bubbles. As it was, her own stark, white nakedness was all too apparent in the clear bathwater.

She lay back and tried to relax, wondering how to control the events of an evening that seemed to stretch dauntingly ahead of her. She had finally dared to ask Jonathan – while sitting out in the garden – if he would mind taking her to the fork supper. From the look on his face, at first she thought he was going to turn her down. Then he had smiled and said, 'How quaint. What time?'

Resting one foot on the hot tap, Charlotte considered her objective for the evening: to throw her sister off the scent and to convince Alex she was in no need of his attentions. To this end, she would have to achieve the impossible – to appear thoroughly at ease with Jonathan at the supper and to remain at his side throughout the entire evening. Tonight, she had to be seen as a woman who needed no outside help in re-establishing her life.

She closed her eyes and doused her face with the strawberry-shaped sponge. She shook the water off her face and tried harder to relax. Smiling was supposed to be helpful here. It struck her that it might be a good idea to practise thinking of Jonathan and smiling at the same time – after all, she would have to do plenty of that at the village hall this evening. She parted her lips and grinned inanely. She caught sight of herself at the end of the bath in the reflection of one of the shiny chrome taps. The distorted convex image made her smile more naturally. She covered the tap with her foot and thought how tonight she was going to prove to herself that she could handle not only Jonathan, but all the rest of them who seemed so intent on organising her life. She breathed out deeply, having convinced herself that all would be well.

Then all hell broke loose.

'God dammit, what the bloody hell's been going on here? I leave my room for ten minutes . . .'

Charlotte sat up at the sound of Jonathan's angry voice on the landing. She heard barking followed by a sound that had her springing out of the bath and reaching for a towel. It was Mabel, yelping.

She threw open the bathroom door. There was Jonathan, a towel around his waist, holding up in one hand a mangy-looking tie, and in the other hand Mabel, grasped firmly by the scruff of her neck, eyes bulging, teeth bared.

Charlotte acted without thinking. She kicked Jonathan in the shin, twice, and then she reached out for the little dog. Hugging the whimpering animal to her, she pushed past Jonathan and slammed her bedroom door shut. Only then, as she sat down on the bed to look at Mabel, did she realise that her towel had gone.

*

165

'Now remember, Neville, avoid all the dishes with mayonnaise.'

'Yes dear.'

'Did you remember to lock the back door?'

'Yes.'

'I hope Malcolm doesn't make a long speech like he did last year. I seem to remember hearing your stomach rumbling throughout most of it. Just look at that.' Her hands full of quiches, Louise nodded towards David's Volvo. 'You'd think they'd have walked, wouldn't you? Did I tell you that Hilary said Charlotte would be coming tonight? Apparently she's bringing a friend. I wonder who. I mean, she doesn't really know anyone here, does she? Neville, are you listening to me?'

'What?'

'Oh never mind. But remember what I said about the mayonnaise.'

'Mrs Parker, the music is far too loud, turn it down. If I've told you once, I've told you a hundred times, my shattered nerves just won't take that kind of volume.'

'But I don't know how to, Mrs Braithwaite. There are so many switches and dials.'

'Well, don't just stand there in the way. Let me through.'

Easing herself out of the small boxed-in area that contained Malcolm Jackson's state-of-the-art CD player and amplifier, Hilary escaped to the safety of the kitchen at the back of the hall. Within seconds the sound of Mantovani – Iris's own personal choice – was blaring through the hall. Then there was nothing, just an awkward silence, leaving people stuck mid-air in unfinished sentences.

'Mrs Braithwaite, allow me,' said a worried Malcolm Jackson moving swiftly across the wooden floor to ensure that no further harm came to his most prized possession. 'This knob here, the one marked volume, you have to make sure that the needles are both synchronised, that way you avoid overloading the . . .'

'Quite so, I'm sure, Vicar. But I can't stand around here all evening discussing synchronised needles. I have work to do in the kitchen.'

Malcolm sighed with relief and moved off to greet more of his parishioners at the door. 'Ah, Louise and Neville, good to see you.'

'Hello Malcolm,' Louise said. 'Excuse me if I don't hang around. I must get these quiches on the tables.'

'Evening Malcolm,' Neville said as the two men shook hands. 'Anything I can do?'

'That's kind, but I think everything's under control now. Between your daughter and Mrs Braithwaite, we all seem to be more or less whipped into shape.'

'That's our Hilary for you.' Neville moved off to get himself a drink. He could see his son-in-law behind the drinks table, acting as barman. He joined the queue. 'Need any help?' he called out above the rumblings of conversation ahead of him.

'No thanks,' David called back. 'I think I can manage.'

Eventually it was Neville's turn.

'What can I get you? I've got red wine, white wine, some dreadful non-alcohol stuff, lager, beer, orange juice, Seven-up, or mineral water?'

'I'll have some red wine, please. Are you sure I can't help you?'

David smiled. 'No, that's all right. You go off and enjoy yourself.'

Seeing the queue of people waiting behind him to be served, Neville paid for his drink and wandered away. He stood beneath a curling photograph of the Queen and tried hard not to allow his sense of isolation to overwhelm him. He was no good in a large gathering such as this, unable to march in step with the rest of the parade. He looked at his watch and wondered where Charlotte was.

*

Alex and his guest entered the hall and were greeted by Malcolm Jackson. 'Ah, I see you've brought some liquid refreshment. Put it on the table at the back there where David Parker looks like he's being mobbed.'

Pushing through the crowd of villagers, most of whom he had never seen before, Alex guided his guest through to the bar. 'David,' he said, 'these bottles any use to you?'

'Hello Alex. Yes, they'll do nicely, thanks.' David took the two bottles of white wine from Alex and added them to his stockpile. 'Hilary mentioned you might be coming,' he said. 'And with a friend.'

David's eager eyes rested predictably on his guest's face, so Alex made the necessary introductions. 'David, this is Heather; Heather, this is David, one of my neighbours and my landlady's brother-in-law.'

'You're not from around here, are you?' David said. 'I'm sure I would have remembered you if I'd seen you before.'

Alex smiled to himself at this hackneyed line which David had delivered with true conviction. For indisputably it was true. With her young, willowy figure, powder-blue eyes and curly blonde hair, Heather fitted neatly into that category of female that was all things to most men. He had met her only a few days ago in Knutsford, where she worked as a receptionist at the company which had approached him earlier in the week about some consultancy work. While handing in his visitor's badge on his way out of the building he'd asked her out for lunch. They had eaten in a crowded wine bar in King Street and he had let her do most of the talking, while he sat and questioned his motives for being there at all. He had never once used a girl before and yet here he was doing exactly that. And all because of Charlotte.

When he had told Charlotte he would be taking a friend to the fork supper he had said it as a knee-jerk reaction to her sudden change in mood towards him. That evening, though, he had regretted his words. But following their conversation in the garden with Barry later that week when he had seen how relaxed she was in somebody else's company, the thought had occurred to him that if he backed off she might feel more comfortable in his presence. He had reasoned that if he was to take someone else to the supper, there was a chance he would still be able to enjoy Charlotte's company without causing her to feel threatened in anyway. The one question in all of this he hadn't asked himself was why he was prepared to go to such lengths to be with Charlotte.

By the end of the meal his plan was fixed. 'A fork supper,' Heather had repeated. 'I've never been to one of those. What should I wear?'

'Casual,' he had answered, feeling almost sorry for her. A nightclub in Manchester was probably more what she was used to.

'What can I get you?' David asked Heather.

'I'd love a 20-20.'

'Ah,' David said, looking at his supply of bottles. He didn't have a clue what he'd just been asked for. 'Try again.'

'Malibu and Coke?'

'How about a glass of white wine?'

'And a beer for me please.' Alex looked around him. So this was a village hall fork supper. He'd never been to such an event before. It was busier than he had imagined it would be, with people appearing to enjoy themselves – more than he thought might be the case. He tried to pick out a few familiar faces. There was Hilary over by the kitchen hatch looking flushed and agitated; Louise Archer chatting to a middle-aged woman whom he didn't know; Ted the Toup being told in no uncertain terms by Iris Braithwaite not to smoke and Neville Archer standing on his own looking up at a gaudy photograph of the Queen. 'Come on,' Alex said, taking their drinks from David and leading Heather by the arm. 'Let me introduce you to my landlady's father.'

They inched their way through the crowd. 'Hello Neville.'

He swung round. 'Good to see you again, Alex.'

'This is Heather.' Alex hesitated before adding, 'A friend.' They shook hands. 'No sign of Charlotte, then?' Alex said lightly, looking up at the Queen.

'No. And to be honest, I could do with her here. I'm not much good in these situations. Never know what to say to people. I find it difficult to make small talk with those I've seen without their clothes on.'

Alex laughed. Seeing the look of surprise on Heather's face, he said, 'Neville's a doctor.'

'*Was* a doctor,' Neville corrected him. 'Now I'm just a . . .'

'Just a what?' It was Louise, with a handful of peanuts.

'Nothing, dear,' Neville said, looking longingly at the nuts.

Louise turned to Alex. 'How are you, Alex? I hear you've taken up gardening.'

'Are you ready, Jonathan? It's time we were going.'

The question, called through the guest room door, sounded ludicrous. But Charlotte could think of nothing else to say to this man for whom she cared so little and whom she had just physically assaulted, not to mention cavorted naked in front of.

The door opened and she offered a smile. 'Look, Jonathan . . .' she started to say.

'Thirty-six pounds, that tie,' he said.

She breathed in deeply. 'I can write you out a cheque if you like, or perhaps you would prefer cash?'

He ignored her and turned back into the bedroom.

He reached for the jacket which completed his dark navy Yves St Laurent suit. He looked at himself in the full-length wardrobe mirror before stooping to pick up a towel from the floor. He handed it to her. 'Yours, I believe?'

She coloured and took it from him. 'Thank you.'

His garment bag lay packed on top of the bed. He picked

it up. 'A hotel for the night is the best thing.'

'No,' she said, 'don't do that.'

He looked at her closely.

'There's no need, Jonathan,' she said, and biting back every instinct within her, she added, 'I'm sorry, I shouldn't have kicked you like that. I don't know what came over me.'

He continued to stare at her in silence, as though assessing her, and then suddenly his face broke into that familiar weasel-like smile. With a patronising shake of his head he said, 'God, Charlotte, you're going to need a man in your life again, and soon.'

She didn't trust herself to say anything to this preposterous remark, so she turned away and moved towards the stairs. 'We'd better go,' she said. And with each step she took, she prayed, Please God, just get me through this evening.

It was still light as they walked the short distance to the village hall, Jonathan being careful just where he placed his expensive shoes. They were silent until they had almost reached the hall, when Charlotte, conscious that Jonathan looked dressed more for dinner at the Ritz than a village beanfeast, said, 'You'll find it all terribly simple, Jonathan, not at all what you're used to.'

He said nothing.

She laughed brightly and slipped her arm through his. He looked taken aback. Her public performance had begun.

Inside the hall, Charlotte saw Alex straight away, and knew too that he had seen her. Automatically she smiled up at Jonathan. 'Come on,' she said, 'I need to . . . I mean . . . I want to introduce you to someone.'

For a moment, the two couples stood facing each other, like four advancing pawns on a chess board. 'Hello Charlotte,' Alex said. She nodded back at him and placed her hand on Jonathan's arm. 'I'd like you to meet Jonathan. He's stopping the weekend with me.' Was it her imagination, or did she detect a slight lift of the eyebrow?

'Hello,' Alex said, taking in the contrast between his own jeans and plaid shirt and the immaculate suit in front of him.

'And you are?' Jonathan enquired.

Alex couldn't help himself. 'Alex Hamilton. I live with Charlotte.' He felt Heather stiffen at his side, saw the horrified expression on Charlotte's face, but most of all, the look of surprise on her companion's.

Charlotte laughed, a little too loudly. 'What Mr Hamilton is trying to say is that he's my temporary tenant in the granny annexe.' She emphasised the word 'temporary' and threw Alex a wait-till-I-get-you-home look.

'But you can't be his landlady?'

Charlotte looked at Heather, twenty-two at the most, she reckoned and with a waist to match. 'Why ever not?' she asked.

Heather looked at Alex accusingly. 'You told me your landlady was bad tempered and rude. I was expecting someone much older.'

Alex felt Charlotte's eyes blazing at him. He laughed awkwardly. 'No, no, that was Iris Braithwaite I was describing.'

'So,' said Jonathan, obviously bored with the conversation, 'what are you in?'

That did it. Now Alex knew for certain that he didn't like this so-called friend of Charlotte's. 'The village hall actually,' he replied. 'Can I get you and Charlotte a drink?' Alex noticed Charlotte biting her lower lip. Was that a slight smile she was trying to hold back?

'I'll get them,' Charlotte said. 'White wine do you?'

'A well-chilled Chardonnay would be out of the question, I suppose?'

Alex tried not to laugh and followed quickly behind Charlotte as she moved off to the bar. 'I'll give you a hand,' he said.

'There's no need,' she hissed back at him. 'I can manage.'

'Of course you can,' Alex said, as they joined the queue. 'I know that. Who's your friend?'

She smiled. 'Oh, we go way back.'

Alex pushed his hands into his pockets. 'Nice suit he's got on.'

'And what's that supposed to mean?'

'Nothing, nothing at all,' he said innocently. 'Nice suit in the right place, that is.'

'As a matter of fact he's just flown in from Hong Kong and that's all he had with him.'

'Oh,' Alex said, nodding his head in an exaggerated fashion, 'that explains it.'

'So what time do you have to get your little friend home?'

'*Touché.*'

They took the glasses of wine back to where they had been standing, only to find that both Jonathan and Heather had disappeared. 'Ah well,' Alex said, 'that just leaves you and me.'

'So it does.' Charlotte looked anxiously round the hall for Jonathan.

'And what was all that about me being a temporary tenant?' Alex said.

'Well, you are. You'll be wanting to buy your own house soon, won't you?'

Alex frowned. That of course had been the original plan, but now he wasn't so sure.

'And how dare you describe me as being bad tempered.'

'And rude,' he added helpfully.

'I've a good mind to evict you.'

'Hello you two.' It was Hilary. 'Having a good time? Don't tell me your dates have stood you up, then?'

Charlotte glared at her sister.

'We seem to have lost them,' Alex said. 'They're here somewhere.'

'What do they look like? I might have seen them?'

'His,' Charlotte said, 'looks as though she ought to be home in bed by now.'

'And hers looks like he's lost his briefcase.'

'Oh well,' Hilary said brightly, not really listening, 'I'm sure they'll pop up. We're just about to serve the food, but whatever you do, don't touch Iris's lentil dip. I was on the loo for days after it last year. Oh look, Derek and Cindy at last.'

Following behind Cindy was Derek, pushing an ostentatious hostess trolley. 'Coming through,' Derek yelled, scattering people in his wake as he steered the trolley at full speed through the crowded hall.

'I'd better go and see what they've brought,' Hilary said. 'It looks a lot, whatever it is.'

Left alone again, Alex said, 'Your father was looking for you earlier. He's a nice man. I like him.'

Charlotte smiled. 'I'm still going to evict you though.'

'Come on, let's get some food. I'm starving. You can serve me notice while I'm eating.'

'I think, everybody,' Malcolm Jackson shouted, turning the music down, at the same time halting the raised cutlery over the bowls of rice salads and quiches, 'that we should now take this opportunity to bow our heads and give thanks . . .'

From nowhere, a loud scream filled the obediently drawn silence. Alex saw Hilary slump against Louise, who in turn gasped loudly. Wide eyed and staring, both women looked as though they had been turned to stone. He followed their gaze and found himself looking at Charlotte's friend Jonathan, standing next to Heather.

'Damn!'

He turned to Charlotte at his side.

'Damn,' she said again.

'For goodness' sake Charlotte, why on earth didn't you tell us?'

'Yes, Mother's right, why didn't you?' Hilary said, as they stood in the hall kitchen. 'He's family, after all.'

Charlotte bristled. 'No, he's not. None of you know him,

and anyway, you wouldn't want to know him, he's a pig.'

'Charlotte!' Hilary remonstrated with predictable horror. 'He's Peter's brother.'

Charlotte pursed her lips.

'Well,' said Neville, feeling he ought to contribute to the conversation in some way. 'He's certainly the spitting image of Peter, isn't he?'

Hilary shook her head. 'I couldn't believe it when I saw him. I was so convinced it was Peter . . . a ghost . . .' Her voice trailed away. 'I feel a bit of a fool now.'

'Seeing as we've all recovered from the shock,' said Louise, 'I suggest we all go out there and at least introduce ourselves to Peter's brother.' She threw Charlotte one more reproving look and led the way, followed by Hilary, then Neville and finally Charlotte, who dragged disconsolately behind. Her plan had misfired because she had failed to take into account the simple fact that anyone who had known Peter would be struck by Jonathan's likeness. But she hadn't thought that anyone would go so far as to think he was Peter's ghost. Silly Hilary. And how typical of her to jump to such a ridiculous conclusion.

She chewed unhappily on her lower lip, knowing she had made rather an idiot of herself. How on earth had she thought she could get away with such a half-baked scheme? Convincing Alex that Jonathan was an old flame from way back was one thing, but thinking she could fool her family was another.

In the main part of the hall the other party-goers seemed to have forgotten about the commotion. Frank Sinatra had replaced Mantovani and the general ambience indicated that everyone was having a jolly good time.

'Suddenly I don't feel hungry,' Charlotte said despondently to her father.

'Come on, you'd better try something. Tell me which dishes have got mayonnaise in them. I want to try them all.'

*

175

Over at the bar, David was pouring out a glass of wine for Derek.

'You mean Charlotte's husband looked just like that jerk in the suit?'

David tried not to smile as he handed Derek his drink. 'Pretty much like him. But how about the blonde piece? She came with Alex, but seems to have abandoned him now.'

Derek laughed. He looked about the hall, trying to track down Alex. He found him eventually, balancing a plate of rice and an empty glass in one hand and a fork in the other, listening attentively to Iris Braithwaite. 'Looks like our Alex prefers older birds,' Derek said. He took a gulp of his wine. 'That's disgusting,' he shuddered, 'like gnat's pee. What the hell is it?'

David looked at the bottle. 'I'm sorry. I've given you the non-alcoholic wine by mistake. Iris Braithwaite insisted we have some, says alcohol is the way to hell.'

'Well, don't just stand there, give me a one-way ticket,' he said. 'No, on second thoughts, make that two tickets to hell.' And taking the glasses from David, he sauntered in the direction of Alex and Iris Braithwaite.

'Evening, Mrs Braithwaite,' he said sidling up to her. He nodded to Alex. 'Thought you'd like a drink.' He handed her a glass. 'I must say, this non-alcoholic wine is very good. I could become quite an addict.'

Alex looked at Derek, wondering if he'd heard right.

'I'm pleased to hear that,' Iris said. 'Alcohol is the way to—'

'Hell,' Derek finished for her. 'That's so true, Mrs Braithwaite.'

Again, Alex wondered if he'd heard correctly. 'Well, if you'll excuse me, I'll just go and help myself to some more food.'

'Try some of my lentil dip. There's lots left,' Iris said after him. She raised her glass and drank from it. She winced, drawing in her lips like a cat's bottom.

'Quite dry, isn't it?' Derek said smiling. 'It's an acquired taste.'

Helping himself to a slice of spinach quiche, Alex found himself standing next to Cindy. 'Hello,' he said. 'I've just left Derek extolling the merits of alcohol-free wine to Iris Braithwaite.'

She looked at him as though he were mad. 'I doubt that somehow.'

'I should go easy on that lentil dip,' he said. 'Hilary told me earlier it has rather a lethal effect the next day. How's Barry?'

'Barry? He's fine, why?'

'I was thinking about his exams. He seems a bright lad, he should do well. I expect you'll miss him when he goes off to university?'

Cindy picked up a stuffed tomato which she added to her sparsely filled plate. 'I suppose I will. Though to be honest with you, even when he's at home, we hardly ever see him. Just shuts himself away in his room mostly.'

Moving away from the tables of food, they located a couple of chairs and sat down. Over on the other side of the hall, Alex could see Derek at the bar again. He watched with interest as Derek carried two full glasses of wine in Mrs Braithwaite's direction. He turned back to face Cindy and was surprised to see her with her hand over her mouth. Her eyes were watering. 'Lentil dip?' he asked.

At about half past ten, when Charlotte was helping her sister to make sixty-two cups of coffee, she realised that something was wrong. Iris Braithwaite had a distinct pink edge to her. An election-winning Margaret Thatcher sprang to mind as Charlotte watched Iris bobbing about the hall, talking animatedly to everyone as though they had just returned her to high office. Even her handbag was swinging from her arm *à la* Maggie. Charlotte decided to go and investigate.

Armed with a cup of coffee, she caught up with Iris as she

laid a hand on Alex's shoulder. 'Mrs Braithwaite, cup of coffee?'

Iris spun round at the sound of Charlotte's voice. 'Certainly not,' she announced. 'I want some more of that delicious alcohol-free wine that nice Mr Rogers has been giving me. Kindly fetch me some while I talk to your lovely young man.'

Charlotte took a discreet sniff at Iris's powdered face. She looked at Alex and mouthed the incongruous words, 'I think she's drunk.'

Alex thought fast. 'There's none left, Mrs Braithwaite,' he said.

'What!' shrieked Iris, causing those around to look at them. Alex and Charlotte moved closer to Iris, trying to shield her from view.

But Iris was having none of it. 'I want a drink,' she said like a determined four-year-old. 'Where's Mr Rogers?' And turning away from them, she hurried off to look for Derek. Charlotte and Alex saw her track him down by Malcolm Jackson's hi-fi, sorting through the selection of CDs and cassettes. He seemed alarmed at her approaching figure and quickly moved away.

'Oh, oh, you naughty man,' giggled Iris, increasing her step. 'Running away from me, are you?'

Derek looked genuinely horrified and sped off. Then disaster struck. Iris, in her haste to catch up with Derek, tripped over an electricity cable running from the hi-fi to the main power socket. She reached out to hold on to something secure, only to plunge the hall into complete darkness by pulling the fuse box off the wall.

Amongst the general crashing about that followed – the screams of mock horror, the giggling, the sonorous tones of the vicar requesting everyone to remain calm and one ridiculous voice calling out 'Let there be light' – there was one, very loud crash, accompanied by an even louder cry and an expression that was quite out of place at a church fund-raising event.

Neville, who had been hiding out in the kitchen at the time of the black-out, managed to find a box of candles and some matches on a shelf above the coffee urn. It wasn't long before a procession of candle bearers, somewhat akin to acolytes, miraculously emerged from the kitchen and streamed out into the main body of the hall. And a voice, presumably the same one that had said 'Let there be light', called out, 'And then there was light.'

The air of wreckage everywhere was surprising. Chairs had been knocked over, along with one of the tables that had been heavily laden with rice salads. In the flickering candlelight, the floor looked as though it was covered with a thousand stunned maggots. A ripped curtain, complete with track, lay in a bedraggled heap on the floor.

'I think I've broken something!' came a cry from the semi darkness. Recognising her husband's voice, Cindy carefully made her way over to Derek, lying sprawled out on his side. She bent towards him, then stood up again. 'What's that all over your back, Derek?'

'I think it's dog crap!' he shouted, wincing with pain. 'I bloody well slipped on it.'

Somebody laughed. 'I think you'll find that's Mrs Braithwaite's lentil dip.'

23

'Start spreading the news, I'm leaving today . . .'

'Please, Mrs Braithwaite, be quiet, someone will hear you,' Charlotte pleaded with the older woman who was held firmly between Alex and herself as they slowly made their way, in the dark, from the village hall towards Acacia Lane.

But Iris was not to be put off. ' . . . I want to be a part of it, New York, New York . . .'

'Come on, Mrs Braithwaite,' coaxed Alex, 'we're taking you home.'

Iris beamed back at him, and then kissing him on the cheek continued with ' . . . These vagabond shoes are longing to stray right through the very heart of it, New York, New York . . .'

Charlotte started to laugh. Iris at that moment slipped away from Charlotte's grip and swung round to face Alex, and staring him in the eye she sang at him, her deep contralto voice wobbling just slightly off key, her pronunciation, though, surprisingly clear for one so drunk, ' . . . I want to wake up in a city that doesn't sleep and find I'm king of the hills, top of the heap . . .' And in a moment of inspiration, Alex threw his arms round Iris and started to tango with her, skilfully edging her towards The White Cottage.

Charlotte followed behind as best she could. Tears were rolling down her cheeks, she was helpless with laughter. 'I don't think I can take much more of this,' she groaned, bent double and with her legs crossed. 'I think I'm going to wet myself.'

'Well, before you do, see if you can find her key,' Alex called over his shoulder as they approached Iris's gate. 'It's probably in her handbag.'

Charlotte reached forward but Iris pushed open the gate and, dragging Alex behind her as though *she* were leading the way home, she marched him up the path. She rummaged in her handbag and pulled out her door key. She snapped the bag shut and promptly pushed the key through the letter box. She turned and looked at them both, her eyes wide with surprise. 'The keyhole's grown,' she said, and rocking from side to side as if on a tilting ship, she sang out, ' . . . I'll make a brand new start of it in old New York and if I can make it there I can make it anywhere . . .'

'Now what do we do?' Charlotte said. 'Break a window?'

'Certainly not, Mrs Lawrence,' said Iris sharply, breaking off from her singing, 'not when there's a perfectly good key hidden in the back garden.'

'Come on,' Alex said 'let's go a-hunting.'

Iris was off again. 'A-hunting we shall go, a-hunting we shall go . . .' she sang as she led the way, almost breaking into a jaunty little skip as she cornered the house.

'Mind my pelargoniums, Mr Hamilton, I believe you're perry close to them, I mean, peril, peril, perilously close to them. Who's that hiding in the dark?'

'It's me, Mrs Braithwaite, Charlotte Lawrence.'

'Well, what on earth are you doing in my herb garden at this time of night?

'Mrs Braithwaite,' Alex interceded patiently, 'can you find the key?'

'Well of course I can, young man, but you'll have to close your eyes while I get it, and you, Mrs Lawrence, you too.'

Amazingly Iris not only found the key, but managed to insert it into the lock and open the back door. They stepped into the kitchen, Alex fumbling blindly for a light switch.

He found it at last and steered Iris towards the hall. Charlotte said, 'I'll get her up to bed, you make her some coffee.'

'I'd better find her a bucket, or something,' Alex said. 'She's likely to be as sick as a dog at some stage in the night.'

'Did somebody mention my dog? Where is Henry?'

Alex and Charlotte looked at each other. It was a good question. Where was Iris's spaniel? Surely he should have barked the house down by now with all the din they had just been making outside in the garden.

'Come on, Henry,' Iris cooed, 'come to Mummy.'

'Get her upstairs,' Alex said. 'I'll look for him.'

'Let's look upstairs for Henry, shall we, Mrs Braithwaite?' Charlotte said, taking her by the hand. 'I expect he's waiting for you up there.'

Iris looked pleased. 'Henry,' she called out with each stumbling step, 'Henry, Mummy's coming.'

Alex found Henry in the sitting room, curled up in his basket. He knew straight away that the dog wasn't asleep. He was dead.

'Oh my darling Henry,' wailed Iris. 'He was my only real friend, the only one who truly loved me . . . even Sidney didn't really love me. Poor little Henry, he was only eleven years old, he should have lived until he was at least fourteen. Why has he died?' Her grief was enormous, she was inconsolable.

'I wish Henry hadn't chosen tonight to snuff it,' Charlotte whispered downstairs in the kitchen, when they had at last got Iris off to bed. 'For just a few moments Iris seemed . . . well, sort of happier than I've ever seen her. It seems like a particularly cheap and nasty trick on God's part, don't you think?'

Alex shook his head. 'I'll dig a hole in the garden tomorrow for him. I suppose that's what she'll want.'

'Alex?' Charlotte suddenly said. 'Why are we here?'

'What, you mean planet earth and all that?'

'No. I mean, why did *we* get Iris out of the village hall and bring her home?'

'You mean why didn't we just abandon her to the public humiliation that everyone thinks she probably deserves?'

'Yes, that exactly.'

'Because we're nice people, I suppose.'

'Are we?'

Alex laughed. 'Charlotte, I'm too tired for this, go home. I'll stay on here in case Mrs Braithwaite is ill in the night.'

Charlotte looked hard at Alex. 'What is it with you and vomiting women?' she said. 'Anyway, shouldn't you go and see what's happened to your little bit of moorland Heather?'

He laughed again. 'I don't think I'll bother. I expect she's being well looked after by your . . . by Jonathan . . . do you mind?'

Charlotte shook her head. 'No.' She decided to come clean. 'I guess you got the gist of all that fuss earlier in the evening, didn't you?'

'That Jonathan is Peter's brother? Yes, I did. Does he look very much like Peter?'

'The first time I met him, I thought he was Peter.'

'But that must be so . . .' he paused, making sure he used the right word, 'difficult for you.' He knew from experience how painful it was to be physically reminded of someone you'd loved and lost.

Charlotte picked up the mugs on the green Formica-topped table and carried them to the sink. 'I didn't think it would be, but you're right. It was quite a shock seeing him coming up the drive this morning.' She rinsed the mugs out, and then turning round, she found Alex standing behind her. Only that afternoon, Jonathan had been standing behind her in much the same way, and only a couple of weeks ago, so had Derek.

She looked up into Alex's face. Blue eyes. She hadn't

noticed their colour before, nor that there was a small white scar just below his left eyebrow. His lips were parted and she felt he was about to say something. Her heart began to beat faster.

'Charlotte —'

'No, please don't say anything.' And with the slightest of movements she leaned towards him, knowing what it would mean, knowing also it was what she wanted. He reached out to her and the touch of his fingers against her cheek made her turn and kiss his hand. He kissed her and she held him tightly, frightened he might stop, thinking only how much she wanted him.

But from upstairs came an unmistakable sound.

'Another time perhaps,' Alex said calmly, looking into her eyes and tracing the outline of her cheek with his hand.

Charlotte swayed slightly. She felt anything but calm. She swallowed back her disappointment and followed Alex out of the kitchen.

It was three o'clock in the morning when they finally settled Iris Braithwaite. They collapsed on the sofa in the sitting-room — Henry and his basket having been moved to the dining room as his makeshift chapel of rest.

Charlotte said, 'You know, I don't understand how all this happened. How on earth did Iris end up drunk? She never drinks alcohol.'

'I think you'll find that Derek had a lot to do with it,' Alex said, yawning and putting his arm around Charlotte.

She kicked off her shoes, tucked her feet under her and snuggled up to him. 'How stupid I've been. Of course, that's what Iris said, didn't she? She wanted some more of that lovely non-alcoholic wine Mr Rogers had been giving her. Poor Iris. She's lost her dignity, her reputation and her little Henry all in one night.'

She looked up at Alex. His eyes were closed. She didn't know whether she was feeling lightheaded from being so tired or was still reeling from the shock of what she had instigated in the kitchen, but she was aware of an added frisson of pleasure and expectancy running through her.

'Alex?'

'Yes.'

'What would have happened in the kitchen, if Iris hadn't . . .?

He opened his eyes. 'You mean, would I have made love to you there and then on the kitchen table?'

'I didn't mean . . . well yes, okay then, is that what you would have done?'

'No, Charlotte. I wouldn't have made love to you.'

She sat up straight. 'Why?' She felt affronted. 'Why not? she repeated.

'Come on, Charlotte, it's late. Can't we talk about this tomorrow?'

'No. I want an answer. Would you now, for instance?'

He looked at her, confused. 'Am I dreaming this conversation, or have I missed a huge chunk of it?'

She moved away from him and went and sat in one of the armchairs. 'It seems Iris is not the only one to have made a fool of herself tonight.'

24

Derek lay awake in the strange bed. The injection he'd been given had wiped out the excruciating pain, but not his anger and the humiliation he had felt lying on the village hall floor. He shuddered at the memory of all that revolting muck he had lain in – nobody was ever going to convince him that it was something edible he had slipped on. Thank God there had been a 'doctor in the house'. Neville Archer had never struck him as a particularly competent man before, but he had certainly shown his mettle, clearing away all those gawping onlookers and sending someone off to call for an ambulance.

A broken leg was his reward for showing up at the village hall jamboree, but that wasn't all – that fool of an ambulance man had ripped his trousers! Eighty quid those trousers had cost him last month. Fine bloody evening it had turned out to be and not even a moment of it spent with Charlotte. And where was she when he was lying on the floor in agony? Bloody scarpered with that Alex, that's where. He'd seen them leaving together.

And now here he was alone, three-thirty in the morning and surrounded by stale bodies in striped flannelette. Thank heavens he'd had the presence of mind to make Cindy pick up a pair of decent boxer shorts on the way to the hospital. He eased himself upright and craned his neck forward to see if any of the nurses were about. Ah yes. There she was, sitting at her illuminated desk, the pretty young blonde one, Nurse Wilkins, who earlier had helped him into bed. She was bent over a book with her hands around a mug in front of her.

Derek pressed the green button just above his plastic jug of water. 'Nurse,' he called out. Hurried squeaking steps sounded out across the thick linoleum floor.

'Yes, Mr Rogers, what is it?'

'Hello,' he said brightly, as though she were a wine bar waitress coming to take his order.

'Ssh . . . you'll wake the others. Now what's the matter?' Though young and recently qualified, Nurse Wilkins was already astute enough to know what her newest patient was up to.

'Come and sit here,' Derek said, patting the side of his bed, 'and I'll tell you.'

Nurse Wilkins smiled and turned to go, but Derek let out a loud groan, which had her instantly bending over him, giving him a closer inspection.

'That's better,' he said. 'Come and talk to me, I'm lonely.'

'It's very late, Mr Rogers, you should get some sleep.'

A smile spread across Derek's face. 'I can't. I'm not used to sleeping on my own.'

'Somehow that doesn't surprise me,' Nurse Wilkins said, contemplating her healthy-looking patient, with his bare tanned chest and roving eyes.

'So, now that I've thoroughly captivated you, tell me your name. Mine's Derek.'

'It's Rosemary and I really should be getting back to my desk now.'

Satisfied that he had made a sufficient enough impression, Derek said, 'I'll see you in the morning, then, before I'm wheeled away to meet my fate on the operating table.'

'Sorry. Tomorrow you'll be in the capable hands of Nurse Baker. You'll like Nurse Baker.'

'I will?'

'Nurse Baker's very nice, very accommodating. Good-night.'

187

'Goodnight Rosemary.' At last Derek was beginning to feel the onset of sleep as the lingering humiliation he had experienced earlier began to fade.

'I tell you I'm right,' Hilary said. It was ten minutes past eight the next morning and she was looking out of the bedroom window across the road towards Ivy Cottage. 'Charlotte didn't go home last night, none of the curtains have been drawn and that Mercedes has gone as well.'

'What?' David said, peering out from beneath the corner of the frilled duvet cover, which had wrapped itself around his head making him look as though he was wearing a baby's bonnet.

Hilary appeared from behind the curtain. 'Come on, David, it's perfectly obvious what happened.'

David tried hard to think. It was Sunday morning, the one day of the week when he was sure of a lie-in; most Saturdays he was in the office persuading people to buy their dream house – nightmares, more like it, as some of them discovered. Nightmares, that rang a bell. Yes, last night, chaos down at the village hall. He turned over, pushed his head under the pillow and thought about Derek Rogers lying there on the floor. While Neville had been sorting Derek out, he had made himself scarce and hidden in the kitchen so that no one would see him laughing.

It had been a funny old night, one way and another. That business with Charlotte and Peter's brother had triggered events. Fancy Charlotte not telling any of them Jonathan was coming. On the other hand he was a complete jerk – bit like Peter really – maybe that was why she had kept him quiet.

He certainly had a condescending way with him, David thought. 'Real estate,' Jonathan had said, shaking his head dismissively, when David had introduced himself after the furore of Peter's 'resurrection' had calmed down. 'What's your turnover?' he had gone on to ask. Mind your own business, David had wanted to tell him, but instead he had plucked an astronomical figure out of the air and then quadrupled it. Even that had been pushed aside as Jonathan went on to explain in detail why, in general, the British made such lousy businessmen. 'No balls,' seemed to be the long and short of it.

Finally he had been rescued by Neville appearing at his side, and he had escaped to man the bar once more. Then later on he had hardly been able to believe his eyes as he watched Old Ma Braithwaite chase Derek round the hall, until they were all plunged into complete darkness, only to discover, when some candles had been found, Derek lying on the floor clutching his leg.

As though picking up on his thoughts, Hilary said, 'Funny that when the ambulance came there was no sign of Charlotte or Alex. That's why I'm so sure –'

'You can't be sure of anything, Hilary,' David said grumpily from beneath the pillow, 'but wherever Charlotte is, I hope she's getting more sleep than I am.'

Giving up on David, Hilary got dressed and went downstairs, to find Philip and Becky in their pyjamas at opposite ends of the sofa, imbibing their weekend diet of brain-wasting pre-breakfast television. 'How long have you been down here?' she asked.

'Only ten minutes,' Philip said, never taking his eyes off the screen.

Becky unplugged her thumb from her mouth. 'We've seen *Sonic the Hedgehog*, *Disney Club* and *Scooby-Doo*.'

'That's an awful lot just in ten minutes.'

Philip scowled at his sister. 'Bigmouth,' he said. 'When's breakfast, Mum?'

'When you're both dressed you can get your own. I'm popping over the road to see Auntie Charlotte. I'll be back in a moment and then it won't be long before we're due at church.'

'Ooh, can I come?' Becky asked, bouncing off the sofa. 'I

want to see her little dog. She didn't bring it when she came to babysit.'

'No,' Hilary said. She wanted to go and snoop about in private, to prove to herself that she was right and that Charlotte had spent the night with Alex. But then a thought struck her. Supposing her sister was there after all? If she took Becky with her at least she had a perfect excuse for calling so early – to see if Charlotte would let Becky play with Mabel. She smiled at her daughter. 'All right then, but hurry up and get yourself dressed. I'll wait for you in the kitchen.'

As they crossed the road, Becky ran on ahead to ring the door bell. To her dismay she found she was too small to reach the button. While she waited for her mother to come up the drive she pushed open the brass letter box and peered inside. Mabel came yapping towards her. Becky poked a small finger in, then seeing that Mabel could jump quite high, she withdrew it quickly with a high-pitched squeal.

Hilary pressed the door bell, which in turn brought on a further burst of yapping. Hilary looked pleased. Here of course was her excuse – she had been worried about Charlotte's dog, she had heard it barking.

'Do you think Auntie Charlotte's still in bed, Mummy?'

'Quite likely,' she said and brought out a bunch of keys from her pocket.

'Will one of our keys work in Auntie Charlotte's key-hole?'

'Ssh,' Hilary said, turning the key in the lock, suddenly realising that if her sister was with Alex, they were, after all, only next door. 'No,' she whispered in answer to Becky's question. 'This is an Ivy Cottage key.'

'Did she give it to you?'

'Yes,' lied Hilary. She knew her sister would never get around to giving her a spare key, so she had taken the precaution of having an extra key cut, just in case . . . just in case of an emergency such as rescuing a small dog, she thought, absolving herself of any accusation Charlotte might throw at her.

'Shouldn't we come back later if she's still in bed, Mummy?'

'Just be quiet, Becky.'

Hilary pushed against the door and was immediately confronted with Mabel dancing excitedly around her feet. 'You play with Mabel while I nip up and see Auntie Charlotte.'

She went slowly up the stairs, calling Charlotte's name quietly as she went, then crept along the landing, checking the bedrooms. All were empty. With a smile on her face she went back down the stairs. As she reached the bottom step she heard Becky say, 'Oh, you naughty little dog. Look at all the puddles and splatter-pies you've made.'

Hilary grimaced at the scene in the kitchen. She stepped cautiously across the floor as though tiptoeing through a minefield. She made it to the back door and let in some much needed fresh air, then opened the cupboard under the sink where only a couple of weeks ago she had put a selection of cleaning fluids.

'Let me help you, Mummy,' said Becky, bored with Mabel and liking the look of one of the aerosol cleaners. She made a grab for it.

'Watch where you put your feet!' shouted Hilary. But it was too late. Becky skidded on a wet patch, sending her legs in different directions, until she lost her balance altogether and ended up sitting down with a bump in one of Mabel's puddles. She started to wail.

Sensing some excitement after a night on her own, Mabel pattered across the floor and climbed on top of Becky.

'Get away,' Becky squealed, 'get away from me, it's all your fault.'

Mistaking Becky's pushing for playfulness, Mabel sank her teeth into the sleeve of Becky's sweatshirt and with her tail waving in the air like a high speed windscreen wiper, she started to pull, shaking her head from side to side and giving off an occasional growl. Becky pulled sharply in the opposite direction and tipped backwards with Mabel still attached. Hilary made a desperate attempt to prevent her daughter's fall but she wasn't fast enough. She watched helplessly as Becky's head landed in the inevitable with a soft splat.

Hilary and Becky retreated from the mayhem of Ivy Cottage to the relative quiet and hygiene of The Gables. Becky was hysterical by now and Hilary was only seconds away from slapping her daughter as she stripped off Becky's sodden leggings and sweatshirt. She was throwing the clothes in the washing machine, when David appeared in the kitchen.

'What the hell's going on?' he shouted above the noise of Becky's screaming.

'Daddy!' she shouted. 'I fell in Mabel's—'

'We had a little accident,' Hilary said, trying to sound quite calm, knowing that David would never understand what she had been doing over the road at Ivy Cottage.

'I'm never, never, ever going over to Auntie Charlotte's again,' whimpered Becky.

David looked at Hilary and noticed that she was looking anywhere but at him. 'What were you doing over at Charlotte's? I seem to remember you saying something earlier about knowing that she wasn't there.'

'I was worried about her dog, if you must know.'

David laughed, not with humour. 'You were snooping, weren't you?' Not expecting an answer, he turned to go, but then looked back at his wife. 'Well, was she there or not?'

25

When Charlotte woke up in Iris's sitting-room, she was stiff and cold. Alex was still asleep on the sofa. Seeing him she remembered how angry she had felt last night, not so much with Alex, but with herself.

After all her resolute determination not to get involved with Alex, she had allowed herself to do a complete U-turn. Kissing him and being in his arms had made her want him more than she would have imagined possible. Had the circumstances been right last night she knew she would have made love with Alex. But then later he had made it only too clear that he wasn't interested. She had fallen asleep stinging with hurt pride and the decision firmly resolved in her mind that it was not going to happen again. His rejection had, once and for all, established their relationship. From now on he was merely her tenant.

She drew the heavy velvet curtains and looked out over Iris's front garden, trying to decide what she was going to say to Alex. When she turned round he was sitting upright and rubbing his face. 'Good morning,' he said.

She walked over to the fireplace and rested one hand on the mantelpiece. 'Alex . . .'

'You're not going to give me a lecture on snoring, are you?'

'Alex,' she started again, conscious that the tone of her voice was at odds with his. 'What happened last night was . . .'

He looked at her for a moment, then stood up. 'Charlotte.

Do I take it you're referring, and stop me if I'm wrong, to us kissing each other last night? Because if you are, I have to tell you, from where I was standing it was pretty enjoyable. I don't know what went through your head afterwards, but I was left with the distinct impression that yet again I had done something wrong. For the life of me I can't think what.'

'That's rich. It was you who said . . .'

'Said what?'

'Oh nothing. Forget it.'

'No, go on. Tell me.'

'You said you didn't want to make . . .' she moved away from the mantelpiece, over to the window, 'so on the basis of that it would be better all round if . . .'

'My God, I don't believe it, you think . . .'

'Alex, will you let me finish? I acted without thinking last night.' She took a deep breath. 'I can't handle being on this emotional roller coaster any more, so I would prefer it if we got things sorted out between us. You're my tenant. Let's just keep our relationship on that level from now on.'

'This is ridiculous. I only meant . . .'

'Please, Alex.'

He shrugged his shoulders. 'You don't give me much choice, do you?'

Alex pushed hard on the spade, forcing it down into the soil as he began digging Henry's grave. Charlotte bloody Lawrence! What was she doing to him? *She* was tired of being on an emotional roller coaster? Well, so was he for that matter. Enough was enough. But how could she be so dense? He hadn't meant that he didn't want to make love to her. He'd said those words, yes, but only because he didn't want her to think he would take advantage of her when she was still so vulnerable. Why couldn't she see that? He pushed on the spade again. And who in their right mind would want to make love in Iris Braithwaite's kitchen?

Instantly some of his anger vanished at the thought of Iris catching him with his trousers down.

Charlotte watched Alex in the garden, to convince herself that she could now regard him quite dispassionately. She found she could, and picking up the kettle from the cooker, she filled it at the enamel sink. She placed it on the gas ring and struck a match. Last night she had done exactly the same, but then she hadn't noticed her surroundings. This morning though, with the early morning sunlight pouring in through the spotlessly clean window, the kitchen was picked out in detail like a 1950s film set. Everything about it was cluttered and unfitted, with bulky appliances which Charlotte could remember from her own childhood along with the same green and cream colour scheme – where others had moved on, Iris had not.

As she waited for the kettle to boil, Charlotte picked up the mugs she had rinsed out last night and looked around for some tea. There was no sign of a tea caddy on the green Formica worktop between the cooker and sink, so she slid back one of the plastic doors on the freestanding unit. Coffee, but still no tea. She noticed a door off the kitchen and pulled it open. As she'd thought, it was a larder. She was instantly reminded of her grandmother. Granny Archer had been a notorious hoarder. From the looks of things, so was Iris Braithwaite.

On the highest shelf Charlotte could see a tin of Bird's Custard Powder, and she knew that if she were to look inside, the ancient-looking tin would be half empty just like Granny Archer's, and its contents rock hard. Her eyes roaming the shelves, Charlotte counted ten rusting tins of evaporated milk, eight polythene-wrapped bags of sugar, four packs of Bisto, numerous jars of fish paste, rows of tinned pears and peach slices, and half a dozen bottles of gravy browning. The kettle began to whistle. Charlotte went to turn off the gas and then returned to the larder to continue her hunt. Surely amongst this hoard of goodies there had to be at least one packet of tea?

On the lowest shelf, crammed with tins of Campbell's soup and pilchards in tomato sauce, Charlotte saw an old Cadbury's tin commemorating the Queen's Coronation. She remembered Granny Archer's identical tin – Hilary had it now and kept old buttons in it. Out of curiosity, she took it down from the shelf and carefully prised the lid off. She wasn't expecting tea bags, but she was surprised to find a selection of used birthday-cake candles, along with some small plastic cake decorations. Iris had never had any children. She noticed that all the cake decorations were a variation on the same theme – a dog holding up a paw, a dog curled up in a basket and a dog with a bone in its mouth. Moving these objects to one side of the tin, Charlotte caught sight of a faded, stained envelope at the bottom. Ashamed of her nosiness but unable to stop herself, she opened the envelope and pulled out a set of photographs. Each photograph showed Iris's dog sitting in front of a decorated cake with writing in shaky blue icing that read 'Happy Birthday Henry'. Charlotte counted the photographs. There were exactly eleven.

'Damn!' she said out loud, and screwing up her eyes in a futile attempt not to cry, she pushed the tin back on the shelf and closed the larder door behind her. As she wiped away her tears with the palms of her hands, Alex came into the kitchen.

'You all right?' he asked.

She told him about the tin and the photographs of Henry. 'It's silly, isn't it?' she said. 'But it's always the trivia in life that gets to you. I saw poor Henry quite dead last night and that didn't upset me, but put a collection of sentimental plastic bits and pieces in front of me and I'm a hopeless wreck. Why do you suppose that is?' She paused, but not long enough for Alex to answer her. She went on, her words hurried and full of restrained emotion, 'Do you know, when

I was told Peter was dead . . . I didn't cry . . . Can you believe it? I didn't cry, not one tear.' She bit her lower lip, clenched her fists, held her breath, all to keep her body in check, to stop it trembling and betraying her completely, but no matter how hard she tried she could not hold back the tears.

'Charlotte,' Alex said, 'you must—'

'No,' she said without looking at him. 'Don't. Just leave me . . .'

'I have only vague memories of last night . . .'

They both spun round to see Iris Braithwaite, looking pale and gaunt, framed in the doorway. She was wearing a dressing-gown and somehow managed to appear strangely majestic.

' . . . but I remember enough,' she carried on, 'to have woken up with the distinct impression that for some unaccountable reason I behaved very badly. I would prefer it if you never mentioned or referred to the event again. And now . . .' she hesitated slightly, as her voice began to waver, 'I would appreciate, Mr Hamilton, you taking Mrs Lawrence home, who, for her own reasons, seems to be quite overwrought. I would very much like to be alone with my poor Henry now. Thank you for being so kind as to dig a hole for me. I watched you from my window. You made a good choice, beneath the magnolia tree . . . it was planted the same year Henry came to live . . .'

Unable to continue, she went back upstairs.

They left The White cottage in silence. Aware now that his role had been so clearly defined, Alex knew he had no right to intrude upon Charlotte's unhappiness. But he couldn't help wondering how much longer she would be able to fight back the need to free herself from the prison of her own making. For that was what it was, and he knew all about self imprisonment. Standing in Iris's kitchen he had seen the pain in Charlotte's tormented face, and had recognised it as the same pain he himself had once experienced. Guilt. As surely as Charlotte was a willing prisoner of her guilt over Peter's death, so he too had been held captive after Lucy's death.

'I feel so angry,' Charlotte said, suddenly coming to a stop.

He looked at her, but she was turned away from him, staring up the drive of In The Pink. 'It's all *his* fault. How *dare* he come here with all his flash charm and ruin Iris's life. He's got no right hurting people like that.' She turned on Alex, her face flushed with angry indignation. 'I've got a good mind to go and have it out with him. Coming?'

Halfway up the drive, they were met by Barry jogging towards them.

'Is your father up?' Charlotte demanded.

Barry looked startled. 'I'm sorry?' he said, pushing a nervous hand through his hair.

'I asked if that rotten stinking father of yours was up yet? Probably enjoying a good laugh, is he?'

'Dad isn't at home, he's . . .'

'Out ruining somebody else's life, no doubt,' Charlotte said hotly.

'Look, Charlotte,' Alex intervened, knowing that Charlotte was taking out her frustration on the nearest person to hand, 'this has got nothing to do with Barry. Leave it till later, when Derek's back from wherever he is.' He tried to lead Charlotte away, but she was firmly rooted to the ground.

'Actually Dad won't be home until he's been discharged from hospital.'

'Ah, somebody got to him before me, did they?'

'Hold on a moment, Charlotte,' Alex said, placing a hand on her arm. 'Why, what's happened?' he asked Barry.

Slowly, Barry's earnest face cracked into a cautious smile. 'Dad broke his leg down at the village hall last night. I thought you were there. Surely you saw what happened?'

Two blank faces stared back at Barry. 'We left early,' Alex volunteered.

'Apparently the power went off and Dad slipped and . . .'

'And broke his leg,' finished Charlotte. 'Well thank goodness there's still a spark of justice in the world.'

'I'm going to see him later, do you want me to pass on a message?'

'No need. I think I'll go and see him in person.'

When Charlotte got back to Ivy Cottage she was horrified and shocked – horrified at the state of the kitchen and shocked that she could have forgotten poor Mabel so completely.

After cleaning up, feeding Mabel and generally making a fuss of her, Charlotte decided to take the dog for a walk down by the mere. She set off down Acacia Lane and turned left on to the footpath between In The Pink and The White Cottage. She peered through the neatly trimmed privet hedge to see if Mrs Braithwaite was about. There was no sign of her so Charlotte pressed on, down the hill, towards the mere.

It was a beautiful morning with clear blue skies. While Mabel scampered on ahead, snuffling around in amongst the fir trees, Charlotte followed slowly behind, enjoying the moment of freedom. Freedom. It seemed she had been searching for this commodity all her life. Was this the only way to experience it? To be utterly alone? For it seemed to Charlotte, standing there in the clearing, over-looking the still water and breathing in the sweet smell of pine, that whenever people were involved, restrictions were applied and demands made. In her experience even the nicest of people pushed others about for their own purposes.

Calling Mabel to heel and turning for home, Charlotte thought of poor Iris again. She wondered how she must be feeling right now. All at once the anger she had felt standing there on the driveway of In The Pink came flooding back. Derek!

Charlotte lied to the nurse, saying she was 'family', then walked through the ward towards Derek's bed at the far end. It was seven-thirty and the ward was packed with evening visitors.

'Charlotte!' he called out, seeing her. Huddled visitors and patients all looked up as she made her way past them. 'My mistress,' Derek said loudly, with a big grin on his face.

'Shut up, Derek,' she said, when at last she stood over him.

'What, no kiss, not even a peck on the cheek?'

She glared at him. 'Not after what you've done.' Her voice was raised and unmistakably angry and everyone else in the ward was making a poor job of pretending not to be listening.

'After what I've done? What on earth are you talking about? Here I am, recovering from major surgery, and you accuse me . . .'

'I said shut up, Derek. I don't know how that family of yours puts up with you.'

'Must be my magnetic . . .'

'I said shut . . .'

'All right, all right, you've used that line,' Derek said frowning. 'And anyway, you sure you're not muddling me up with somebody else? I'm Derek Rogers, he of the compound fracture fame.' He pointed to the end of the bed. 'They've put a pin in my tibia-whatsit or something or other. I've been very brave. Surely I deserve just a little sympathy from you? One kiss would do it.'

'You're despicable. What you did last night was pathetic.'

'Charlotte, a guy can't help breaking his leg . . .'

'Not that. What you did to poor Mrs Braithwaite, that was such . . .'

'A laugh, I thought,' Derek said smiling. 'Got her a touch frisky, didn't it, relaxed the old bird a bit?'

'You've ruined her!' Charlotte shouted. 'And you don't give a damn, do you?'

'Oh come on, Charlotte,' Derek retorted with equal volume, 'don't exaggerate. You talk as though I'd raped her.'

An audible gasp rippled round the rest of the ward.

'Well, you might just as well have done. She's lost all her dignity and reputation in one go. She'll be the laughing stock of the village.'

'Rubbish! She was that already and why the hell are you so defensive on her behalf? I would have thought after what she'd done to you, you would have been pleased with what I did, grateful even.'

'You . . . you don't understand, do you?' It was hopeless. Charlotte turned her back on Derek and rushed out of the ward, goggled-eyed faces following her as she went.

'Too bloody right I don't!' Derek threw after her, and then, as all faces turned back to look at him, he shouted angrily, 'Oh, sod off, the lot of you!'

What a day! Derek thought to himself, reaching for his jug of water – a day that had begun with Nurse Baker, of whom he had had high hopes, who had turned out to be a mustachioed, red-haired Cliff Baker and was probably as bent as a Uri Geller fork. He took a gulp of his water and looked up to see Cindy and Barry coming towards him.

'What did Charlotte want?' Cindy asked sharply, as she stood at the end of his bed. 'We passed her on the stairs. She looked upset.'

'If you must know, she's just been giving me a right mouthful and I don't mean we were snogging. Ask this nosy lot here,' he said, gesturing with his hand towards the rest of the ward, who were all, once again, not so discreetly tuning in.

Barry looked down at his father. 'Alex said you got Mrs Braithwaite drunk last night. Is that true?'

'Isn't anyone at all interested in how my operation went?

I reckon I'm bloody lucky to be alive.'

'Well, is it true?'

'Of course I didn't,' Derek said, turning away from his son and looking out of the window. In the car park below, he could see Charlotte getting into her car. He watched her slam the door shut and then slump over the steering wheel, her hands covering her face.

'Dad?'

Derek turned and faced Barry. 'Okay,' he said irritably, 'so what if I did?'

'You stupid bloody fool,' Cindy said with undisguised contempt.

'I thought it would be a laugh.'

'Alex says Mrs Braithwaite's dog died last night,' Barry said.

'Oh Alex says this and Alex says that,' shouted Derek. 'I'm sick of that man.' Heads again turned their way.

Cindy suddenly smiled. Jealousy! How wonderful that at last her husband should have come to know that most self-destructive of emotions. 'Well, we're all sick of you,' she said, and walked away, her head held high as all eyes followed her down the ward.

Derek looked at his son. 'Are you leaving as well?'

Barry nudged his glasses. 'Not if you don't want me to.'

They stared at each other. Then Barry walked slowly round the bed and sat in the chair between the window and his father.

'Been a bit of a plonker, haven't I, Bas?'

'You could say that, Dad.'

26

My dear Carlotta, I am so very sorry, but I shall not be able to come and visit you this month. I have to be in Rome for a funeral. I think it will be quite a party! Forgive me for disappointing you. Love, Christina.

'No!' said Charlotte out loud, looking down at the letter in her hand which had just arrived by that morning's second post. 'No, I won't forgive you. I want you here with me.'

Charlotte had found Hulme Welford strangely quiet for the past five weeks. Flaming June had been and gone and for once had lived up to its name, being hot and dry, but July so far had been a wash-out, forcing people to stay indoors, abandoning their gardens to the daily downpour of torrential rain, which left delphiniums battered and cheap barbecues to fill up with water and rust.

Charlotte had put her time to good use, though, spending most days up a ladder with a paintbrush in her hand. She had even taught herself to stencil and had festooned the kitchen walls with wisteria and the bathroom with ivy, echoing exactly the exterior of the house. She was really quite pleased with her efforts at decorating. But she didn't feel pleased now. She had been looking forward to Christina coming to stay, had even decorated a bedroom specially for her. There was so much she wanted to talk to Christina about. What with all the rain and being cooped up inside the house, she felt as though she hadn't talked properly with anyone for weeks.

Everyone, it seemed, was busy. There was Dad with his gooseberries – trying to protect them from all the rain – and Mum with her shop and the passing holiday trade; even Alex, who previously had seemed always to be around, had been absent recently. Charlotte had missed their chats in the garden. Occasionally she would hear music coming through the wall, but Alex was a good tenant and the music was always to her liking, and never intrusive. She sometimes heard him going out early in the morning and not returning until late. Some nights, he didn't come home at all. She wondered what he did then. Was he with Heather? Perhaps not, not after Jonathan.

The last she had seen of Jonathan had been when she had got back from the hospital after giving Derek a piece of her mind and found him waiting for her on the doorstep. 'I need my things,' he had said, with not a hint as to where or what he had been doing since the previous evening. And then he had gone, accelerating smoothly down Acacia Lane in his hired Mercedes.

She had seen hardly anything of Hilary either. Her sister had been busy organising just about every end-of-term social activity for children and parents alike, at the same time getting ready for their annual camping holiday. Only two days ago Hilary had sat in the conservatory with Charlotte, the rain coming down like stair rods on the glass roof above their heads, and had said, very smugly Charlotte thought, 'Well, at least we'll be able to rely on the weather in Haute Provence.' They had set off yesterday morning, the Volvo weighed down with patched canvas, Marmite, Ribena, mosquito repellant, water-purifying tablets, factor twenty sun cream, as well as several bagfuls of pre-holiday tension. They were supposed to leave at the crack of dawn according to David's itinerary, but at nine o'clock he was still sitting in the car, revving the engine and waiting for Becky, who that morning had started complaining of an upset tummy, to get off the toilet.

She heard Mabel scratching at the conservatory door and went to let her in. The little dog was drenched. Charlotte picked up a towel and rubbed her down. The door bell rang.

'Hello Tiffany,' Charlotte said, opening the door.

'You okay for a visitor?'

'Yes, of course, come in. I was just about to indulge in some comfort eating. Fancy joining me?'

They sat in the kitchen, Charlotte loading crumpets under the grill and Tiffany absentmindedly carving patterns in the butter. With her head bent over the table, Charlotte could see that Tiffany's own natural colour was showing through the defiant puce of the rest of her hair. She was no longer wearing the elaborate beehive, but a plait, which hung down her back like a stick of rock. Not for the first time Charlotte wondered how on earth Tiffany had got away with it at school. Didn't teenagers get expelled for such things?

'The house seems so empty without Barry,' Tiffany said, looking up at Charlotte. 'It's dead boring not having him around. I know he's quiet and all that, but at least, when he's there, I can . . .'

'Annoy him?'

Tiffany laughed. 'Isn't that what brothers are for?'

'Sisters too,' Charlotte said with a smile.

'You know, I don't think Dad can work Barry out. He's paid for us both to have a dead expensive education, expecting at least one of us to end up as a smart something or other, you know, an accountant or a barrister, something boring like that. Dad thinks you've got to spend money to make money.' She laughed scornfully and plunged the knife deep into the butter. 'And Barry's gone off to do charity work in an orphanage in Rumania for the summer. Ironic or what?'

'Have you heard from him yet?' Charlotte asked, setting a plate of hot crumpets down on the table.

'Yes, we got a letter yesterday. He's been sprayed for fleas and lice and is helping to install twelve new toilets.'

'Well, at least he's doing something positive,' Charlotte said, sitting down and passing Tiffany a knife and a plate.

'Meaning I'm not, I suppose.'

Charlotte shook her head. 'No,' she said emphatically. 'Meaning *I'm* not.'

'Do something, then.'

'Like what?'

'Hang on,' Tiffany said, balancing a thick slab of butter on a crumpet, 'isn't that supposed to be my line? I'm the awkward teenager, you're supposed to be the one with all the answers.' She took a huge bite of the buttery crumpet, and with her mouth full, said, 'Why don't you just get a job?'

Charlotte looked up from her plate. 'I know that's the answer. The trouble is I haven't got a clue what I really want to do.'

'There must be hundreds of things you could have a go at. I'll prove it to you. Got a newspaper?'

Charlotte went through to the sitting-room and came back with a copy of the *Chronicle*.

'Right,' said Tiffany, taking it from her and lying the relevant pages out on the table. '"Receptionist required, must be smart in appearance."' She looked at Charlotte in her jeans, paint-splattered sweatshirt and hair scraped back in a rubber band. 'Well, we'd have to get Mum and Dad to tidy you up a bit.' She continued with the advertisement. '"Must have excellent communication skills and knowledge of Monarch system."' She lifted her head. 'What's a Monarch system?'

Charlotte shrugged. 'A computer for Royals? Helps them to foul up perhaps.'

'Okay then,' Tiffany grinned, returning to the paper. 'How about "Efficient organiser and administrator, must be confident and discreet and able to act under pressure."'

Charlotte gave a short derisive laugh. 'I think I've got enough pressure in my life just at the moment.'

Undaunted, Tiffany carried on. 'Well, that rules out secretarial and administrative. How about domestic? Some poshy over in Prestbury wants a housekeeper. You've only got to be conscientious and like children.'

'Grilled or fried?' laughed Charlotte.

'You're not taking this seriously at all, are you?' Tiffany said, throwing the paper on the floor.

'Let's forget about me. How's your dad's leg?'

'Covered in kisses,' Tiffany said in disgust. 'Every woman who comes into the place wants to sign her name on his plaster. By the way, did you know he tried to apologise to Mrs Braithwaite?'

'No, I didn't,' answered Charlotte, wondering what crass things Derek might have said.

'She wouldn't even speak to him, just slammed the door in his face. He said she looked awful, well, worse than she normally does.'

Charlotte frowned. She had been worried about Mrs Braithwaite for some time now. Ever since that dreadful night at the village hall and Henry's death it was as though Mrs Braithwaite had disappeared from the village. Nobody seemed to have spoken with her; nobody knew whether she was hiding her grief or her embarrassment, or even both. 'When was that exactly, when did your father see her?'

Tiffany thought for a moment. 'Ages ago, I think, before all this rain started anyway. Why?'

'I don't know, I just feel uneasy about Mrs Braithwaite. Even Hilary, before she left for France yesterday, said she hadn't seen her about, and Hilary usually sees most things going on in Hulme Welford.'

'Surely someone must have seen her down at the shops.'

'Apparently not.'

'What's she eating, then?'

Charlotte thought of all the jars of paste and tins of pilchards in Iris Braithwaite's larder and feared the worst.

*

In his study at the Vicarage, Malcolm Jackson pulled the telephone towards him and dialled a number from his parish address book. He waited and waited. At last he heard Neville Archer's voice.

'Hello Neville, it's Malcolm. You all right? You sound out of breath.'

'I'm fine. I was in the garden.'

'What, in this weather?'

'Especially in this weather. I was making sure I'd got enough rhubarb leaves covering the gooseberries. It's only a couple of weeks to go until the big day.'

A smile flickered over Malcolm's face. 'Oh yes, of course, the gooseberry show. I'd forgotten about that. How are they doing?'

'Best not say, not over the telephone, careless words, etc.'

They both laughed. Gooseberry growers were notorious for their rivalry and secrecy, and sabotage was not unheard of.

'So what can I do for you, Malcolm?'

'Actually, Neville, do you think you could leave the gooseberries for a short while and bob round? There's something I'd like you to do for me.'

Neville approached The White Cottage in the drizzling rain, taking each step with increasing trepidation. 'She might listen to you, Neville,' Malcolm had said. 'For so long in her life you've been a figure of standing in the village. You were her doctor for goodness knows how long, she's more likely to listen to you than anyone else. She's got to realise that we all care about her, that she can't hide in her house for ever, for whatever reason. She's got to come out.'

On the doorstep, Neville didn't feel a figure of any standing whatsoever. He lifted the brass knocker and brought it down sharply. He counted to twenty and knocked again, and then again. He bent down, pushed open the letter box and peered inside. 'Mrs Braithwaite,' he called out nervously. 'Are you there, Mrs Braithwaite?'

Why nervously? What was he afraid of? Afraid that they, that he, had left it too late, that Iris was lying on the floor . . . dead?

Why did he imagine Iris lying dead *on the floor*. Why be so dramatic? Why not just imagine her in her favourite comfy armchair? Not every old person living alone had to die on the floor. Stop being so useless, Neville Archer! he told himself. Get on and do something! Smash a window, do something heroic for once in your life. But be careful, let the gas out before you go in. Gas? Who mentioned gas? He breathed in deeply, then exhaled slowly. One more time and then I'll call the police, he told himself. 'Mrs Braithwaite,' he shouted through the letter box again, 'it's me, Dr Archer.'

'I can see that perfectly well, Dr Archer.'

Neville spun round at the sound of Iris Braithwaite's voice.

'Though why you should be shouting through my letter box for all the neighbours to hear, I really cannot think.'

'Mrs Braithwaite!' he said, revelling in the fact that Iris was looking wonderfully alive and not gasping her last in front of the gas cooker.

'Perhaps you would be so good as to help me with my case. It's heavy and I've just walked with it from the bus stop.'

'You've been away, then?' Neville said, watching Iris unlock the front door.

'My word, Dr Archer, retirement has done nothing to weaken your diagnostic powers, has it? Well of course I have, you don't think I've been shopping with a suitcase, do you?'

'It's just that we were all so . . . Neville hesitated.

'Come on, Dr Archer, in with that case, if you please, and what were you all?'

'Pleased to see you back,' Neville said smiling.

In the hall Iris freed herself from her raincoat and stared at Neville. 'Well, that's very civil of you.' Then removing her plastic rain-hood and patting her hair into place, she said, 'Now don't let me keep you. I'm sure you must have plenty to do.'

'Yes,' he answered, edging towards the door. 'Been anywhere nice?' he ventured, realising that Iris was exhibiting a tan that could not possibly have been acquired anywhere in the North of England during the past few weeks.

'Yes, as a matter of fact, somewhere very nice. Goodbye.'

27

When, three weeks later, the removal of his plaster cast coincided with two days of continuous sunshine, Derek decided to hold an impromptu barbecue. It was early Sunday morning and he sent Tiffany off to invite the neighbours. He told her to ask Louise and Neville. 'And you'd better ask Old Ma Braithwaite,' he added, 'and that vicar bloke.'

'The vicar?' Tiffany said, astonished. 'Why him?'

'I want to see what kind of man is going to baptise my son. I want to know whether he's into choirboys or not.'

Both the vicar and Iris Braithwaite sent their apologies, or rather Malcolm Jackson did. Iris informed Tiffany she would rather sup with the Devil. Undaunted, at one o'clock, resplendent in knee-length shorts, espadrilles, sunglasses, and with his hands stuffed inside the mouths of a pair of crocodile oven gloves, Derek greeted the rest of his guests, as well as their plates of microwave-defrosted meat and freezer-chilled bottles of wine. He was an incongruous sight with one evenly tanned leg and an elastic support stocking covering the lower part of his other leg which was white and scrawny. He was leaning on a walking stick, but mostly he used this to direct operations.

'Meat over there,' he said, pointing with the stick to the hostess trolley they had all seen at the fork supper, 'and booze over here, where I can reach it easily. A guy can only hobble so far. Tiffany, go and tell your mother to bring out that sangria I made earlier.'

Alex felt Charlotte wince at his side. They had arrived at the same time, though not together. He hadn't seen her to talk to in ages. Their landlady–tenant relationship had consisted of fleeting glances of each other, and that was all. Earlier in the summer their lives had been unexpectedly thrust together, but after that morning in Iris's kitchen they had gone their separate ways; and if he was truthful with himself, despite missing her company, life had been a lot more straightforward since then.

Standing slightly apart from the rest of the group, which numbered Louise and Neville and Hilary and David, along with their children, Alex turned to Charlotte. 'Good thing Mrs Braithwaite isn't here,' he said.

She responded with a slight smile, though enough, he noticed, to set off those two dimples either side of her mouth. He couldn't read her eyes, for they were hidden behind dark glasses.

'Anyone found out where she went on holiday?' he asked.

'No,' she answered. 'Apparently she's been quite secretive about it, hasn't told a soul where she went. Dad reckons it's the first holiday she's had since she brought Henry home as a puppy.'

Alex looked directly at Charlotte, and – conscious that he was shifting a gear or two – said, 'To be honest, I'm surprised to see you here. Aren't you still angry with Derek?'

Charlotte returned Alex's unwavering gaze for a moment, then looked away towards Derek, who was prodding indiscriminately at the fake hot coals of his gas-fired barbecue. At the same time he was chatting to her mother and leaning on his stick. 'It's hard to stay mad with such a fool,' she said.

'And are you still mad with me?' he ventured.

'No,' she said.

He noticed there was no hesitation in her reply. 'Friends, then?'

She nodded. 'Friends.'

'Fancy a stroll?'

'Yes, if it means getting out of having to drink Derek's lethal sangria.'

They wandered down to the bottom of the garden, away from the smoke and the sound of Becky and Philip starting to argue, and Hilary and David telling Neville, yet again, about their eighteen hours of hell on the French roads coming back from Haute Provence.

'How have you been?' Alex asked, as they sat on a white-painted wrought-iron garden seat, overlooking a small pond with a spouting cherub and an ugly-looking ornamental toad.

'Quiet, but busy,' she answered. 'In fact I've struck up quite a relationship with Mr Dulux. How about you, you don't seem to have been around as much?'

'I've been busy with several . . .'

'You're not going back to your eighty-hour weeks, are you?'

'Would you be disappointed in me if I was?'

'Yes,' she said, 'I would. I had high hopes for you, Alex. I thought you were a real 'nineties man.'

Was it his imagination or was she more at ease, not just with him, but with herself? 'Oh don't worry about me, I'm way ahead in the emancipation of men stakes. I already organise my work schedule around *Neighbours* and *Home and Away*.'

'Now you have disappointed me. I had you down as an Anne and Nick fan.' She pushed her sunglasses up over her head and closed her eyes. 'After all that rain this is wonderful. I feel as if I'm on holiday.'

'Do you think you'll go away this summer?'

'I shouldn't think so,' she said. 'I know it sounds like I'm being a bit of a wimp but I don't much fancy a holiday alone. And before you say anything, I'm too old for Club Eighteen and too young for a bowling holiday in

213

Bournemouth with a bevy of grey-haired grannies. I'd rather stay at home.'

An idea occurred to Alex. 'Charlotte?' he said. 'Do you trust me?'

'What an extraordinary question,' she said, reminded of the morning she had discovered Alex cleaning her kitchen floor when he had given her that hangover cure – 'Trust me,' he had said then. 'Why, what have you done?'

'It's not so much what I've done, as what I'm about to suggest.'

Charlotte opened her eyes. She fixed her attention on a blackbird some six feet away, basking in the sunshine, its feathers so plumped up it looked like a sooty powder puff. 'Go on,' she said.

'I'm going to stay with some friends next week, over in Yorkshire. I've known them since we were at university together.'

'That's nice. I hope you have a lovely time.'

'Why don't you come with me? It might be fun for you to get away for a few days.' Was he pushing it? Was he already putting their re-established friendship in jeopardy?

She kept her eyes on the blackbird. Recently her life had begun to show signs of becoming trouble-free, with each day gently easing itself into the next. She had even started to feel better, the dreams had stopped and she couldn't remember the last time she had cried. Would going away with Alex complicate things again? But surely they were both over all that nonsense now. 'I don't know what to say,' she said at last.

'I am only offering you a few days in Yorkshire.'

'I know that. If I thought it was anything else I wouldn't be considering the idea.'

'Say yes, then, and before Long John Silver gets bored with his alfresco Keith Floyd impersonation and comes yo-ho-ho-ing down here to rout us out.'

She laughed.

'Hey you two,' shouted Derek, right on cue, 'quit your canoodling in my bushes. I've got a lovely steak for you, Charlotte. Alex, I'm sorry but your burger's burnt.'

'Subtle, isn't he?' Alex said, as they began walking back to the house. They hadn't got as far as the patio when Tiffany called from the kitchen french door.

'Dad, there's a man on the phone for you.'

'Well bring it out here. What's the point in having a mobile phone if it's stuck in the kitchen the whole time? You don't expect me to be Linford Christie with this leg, do you?'

Coming out into the garden and rolling her black-lined eyes, Tiffany slapped the phone down into her father's hand. He poked her with his stick.

'Hello,' he said, 'Derek Rogers here . . . yes, that's right . . . what, what kind of . . . what do you mean you don't know . . . what kind of agency are you . . . you send my son . . . too right I'm worried, pal!'

Derek pushed the aerial in and tossed the phone on to the pink-frilled hammock behind him.

'What is it, Dad?' asked Tiffany, seeing the look on her father's face.

'You'd better go and tell your mother. Bas is being flown home from Rumania . . . he's ill, caught some . . . they don't know what. He'll be at Manchester, about six.'

'He'll be fine,' Hilary said brightly, looking inanely about her. 'It'll just be some kind of tummy bug, you know what these foreign places are like. Last year in the Dordogne we . . .'

'They've arranged for an ambulance to be there at the airport,' Derek said flatly.

Nobody said anything else.

They were met at the airport by a small nervous man in baggy trousers and a creased shirt. 'Mr and Mrs Rogers? I'm from Aid Now and I'd . . .'

'I don't give a shit about you,' Derek shouted, pointing an accusing finger at the man, 'so shut up until you're spoken to.'

An airport official escorted the tense group to a private lounge. 'We'll let you know the minute the plane lands,' he said. 'I'm afraid you won't be able to see your son straight away. We have a medical team on standby . . . we need to know whether he's infectious.'

When the man left them, Cindy began to cry and Tiffany put her arm round her mother's shoulders. She was shocked to feel how thin and insubstantial her mother really was – her mother, who had always seemed to be rock solid, fighting Tiffany every step of each day.

Derek breathed in deeply, and stood and glowered over the man in baggy trousers.

They saw the plane land and then watched in helpless disbelief through the triple-glazed window as a stretcher was carried down the steps of the aircraft and was pushed into the awaiting ambulance.

At the hospital Cindy looked through yet another glass window at her son. 'I can't believe this,' she said, 'I can't believe he's going to die.'

'He's not,' Tiffany almost growled. 'He's bloody well not going to die.'

Derek turned away from the sight of his son, twitching spasmodically, suffering God knows what. It was too much for him. 'I'm going to look for that doctor. It's been long enough for them to know something by now.'

Before he even got to the door it was opened by the young doctor they had spoken to earlier, a man who looked as though he would be more at home on a rugby pitch than in an intensive care ward. He came into the room, filling the small space. 'We've performed the lumbar puncture,' he said briskly, 'and it's as we thought; your son has mening-itis. I think you should prepare yourselves for a long haul.'

He turned away from them and looked through the glass at Barry and two nurses who were hovering over him. 'I have to tell you, the delirium may well wear off quite soon, but there's a strong possibility that he could lose consciousness.'

'Will he . . .?'

The young doctor looked kindly at Cindy. 'We know exactly how to treat your son, Mrs Rogers, it's more a question of timing. If we can treat the illness in the early stages, there's a good chance of a full recovery, but . . .'

'What you mean,' Derek said, cutting in, 'is that we might be too late in Bas's case.'

'Dad,' shouted Tiffany, 'stop it!'

'I'm sure you'd like to see your son now,' the doctor said simply. 'First though, I'll show you where you can wash and put on some gowns.'

They stood at the foot of the bed, staring down at Barry's restless body. Tiffany was the first to move forward. 'Oh Barry,' she cried, bending over his flushed, sweating face. 'Barry, what have you done?'

Slowly, as though using all his strength, Barry opened his eyes. Tiffany could see he was trying to focus on her. 'Tiffany?' he said faintly.

'Yes,' she said, 'it's . . .' Then moving away from the bed, she began to cry quietly.

Cindy came forward, her hand covering her trembling lips. Behind her, Derek leaned over towards his son, and swallowing hard, he said, 'So Bas, it's your turn to be a bit of a plonker, is it?'

Barry's eyes closed.

They took it in turns to stay awake by Barry's side throughout the night, even though a nurse was constantly monitoring his progress. Each watched helplessly as Barry's restless, fevered body thrashed from side to side. A drip was in place, its plastic bag of liquid vanishing steadfastly into Barry's arm.

At about four in the morning, as Derek felt himself falling into a much needed sleep, he was brought up with the strongest of feelings that something was wrong. His son wasn't moving. 'Bas!' he cried, convinced that Barry was no longer breathing. There was no sign of the nurse, so he stumbled out of the room, forgetting his stick and trying to ignore the pain shooting through his leg. 'Help! Somebody come quickly,' he shouted down the empty corridor. At once Tiffany and Cindy were at his side, along with the nurse. 'He's not moving . . . I think he's . . .'

The nurse pushed past him and went to Barry. 'He's unconscious,' she said, hurrying out of the room. 'I'll fetch Dr Bawton.'

Alone again, Cindy sat by her son. She reached out her hand and eased back his damp hair. It was such a simple gesture, but that lock of hair was such an integral part of her son's make-up. She felt Tiffany and Derek moving behind her. 'I want him baptised,' she said quietly. 'He's to be baptised, just as he wanted.'

Exhaustion, fear and bewilderment made Derek unusually quiet. He greeted Malcolm Jackson in the waiting-room with nothing more than a nod, taking him through to Cindy and Tiffany and Bas. What was there to say anyway? He listened to the vicar talking about Barry's courage and about pulling through and then about them joining him in a moment of prayer.

'I usually like to kneel,' Malcolm Jackson said, 'but if you'd feel more comfortable standing, that's fine.'

Derek watched the others to see what they would do. They knelt, and so he got awkwardly down on one knee. He couldn't concentrate on anything that was being said. He could only think how scared and isolated he felt, kneeling alone on his side of Bas's bed. More than anything he wanted to run away from this room, to be outside in the sunshine, in their garden, where only yesterday they had been drinking sangria and burning cheap steak. Oh God, he wasn't strong enough to cope with this.

At last it was over and they were getting to their feet. Derek limped over to the window and looked out over the car park. In the background he could hear more kind words being said. Then he lost it. Something deep inside him exploded and, bringing his fist down on the windowsill, he shouted, 'What's the bloody sense in all this?'

28

'This doesn't feel at all right,' Charlotte said, as the Elton John cassette came to an end. Alex looked across at her briefly, wanting to keep his eyes on the motorway ahead. They were on the M62, just passing Hollingworth Lake, and for most of the journey neither of them had spoken much. He wondered whether Charlotte was beginning to regret coming.

He didn't know which had most surprised him; his impulsiveness while sat in Derek and Cindy's garden, or Charlotte's agreement to come away with him, and without any real persuasion on his part. All he could be sure of was that the anticipation he had experienced over the past few days at the prospect of spending some time with Charlotte had made him face up to how he really felt towards her. When they had first met at Hilary's, he had been intrigued by her. Intrigued because she had seemed determined from the word go not to like him. She had been on the attack as soon as Hilary had introduced them, and had been in that position ever since . . . until now possibly. When she had told him Derek had kissed her he had realised then that what he felt for her was more than just passing curiosity. Imagining Derek kissing Charlotte had not set him off down the path of jealousy as he might have supposed, but had made him want to protect her from any further advances from Derek . . . or any other kind of roué for that matter. From that moment on he had wanted Charlotte for himself, and the whole of her, not just the fragments she was prepared to share. During their brief time apart he had almost convinced himself that his feelings for her had changed. But they hadn't. He still wanted Charlotte, and now that he had somehow gained her trust, he didn't want to risk losing it.

'I said this doesn't feel right,' Charlotte repeated, looking pointedly at Alex.

'I'm sorry,' he said. 'I was miles away.' He pulled out into the fast lane and overtook a shirt-sleeved man in a Cavalier, his jacket hanging limply behind him on the specially designed hook. 'So what exactly doesn't feel right?'

'Oh, I don't know . . .'

'Come on, you can do better than that.'

'It feels . . .' She looked out of the window, realising that at some stage during the journey, the landscape had changed – ribbons of dry-stone wall had replaced the familiar hawthorn hedges of her native Cheshire. 'I feel bad about Barry. It's as though we don't care by coming away.'

'I know what you mean, but Barry could be in a coma for ages. Somehow life has . . .'

'Oh please no, not that old number,' Charlotte said. 'You're beginning to sound like Hilary.'

Her defiance made him want to smile; it was one of her traits he had missed these past few weeks. 'I called in at the hospital last night,' he said. 'Cindy was on her own. She looked worn out.'

'I know. Tiffany burst into tears when I went and poor Derek couldn't even talk to me.'

They drove on in silence, until Alex indicated to come off the motorway. 'Nearly there,' he said.

Charlotte tried to block out her anxiety for Barry. Instead she began to wonder what Alex's friends would be like. He had barely said a word about Sally and Stephen, other than to say that he was sure she would like them and that they had a five-year-old son called Mark. She stole a quick glance at Alex, thinking how little she really knew about him. It wasn't so much that he was a secretive man, it was more that he seemed to prefer encouraging others to talk about themselves. Initially this had disturbed her – he had probed a little too deeply for her liking. Then he had frightened her, or rather her own response to Alex had made her scared of him. She hadn't expected to feel such a physical attraction to another man so soon after Peter's death. It had taken her completely unawares and she had found herself out of her depth, floundering through her inability to cope with her confused emotions. It had been her misreading of the situation that had led to all the problems, she could see that; she had simply read too much into Alex's relationship with her and had over-reacted. Thank goodness she had come to her senses and she could now enjoy Alex's friendship on a more down-to-earth level. He was good company and made her laugh, and since their truce he had stopped probing. Which was why she had decided to accept his invitation. A few days away from Hulme Welford might even help her to start thinking more clearly about what she was going to do with her life. She had spent long enough licking her wounds; it was time to think of the future.

'You're quiet. You okay?'

'These friends of yours,' she said, 'what are they like? Green wellies and Labradors?'

Alex laughed. He slowed the car down, eased it round a sharp corner and then turned through a gate that led into a small cobbled courtyard. Turning the engine off, he said, 'Do I look like the sort of man who has friends out of a Jilly Cooper novel?'

Charlotte gazed up at the house in front of them. It was lovely, possibly more than a century old. Its original light stone was now, in parts, blackened with age and dotted with small, staring, mullioned windows. Around the front door was an assortment of stone-coloured tubs, but not one was filled with the usual summer array of geraniums and lobelia. Instead, the pots were home to burgeoning tomato plants.

She got out of the car and instantly the front door opened and out came a petite blonde girl in jeans and an oversized T-shirt. Her hair was tied up on top of her head in a loose knot, and wisps of it framed a pretty face that was almost angelic in appearance. Charlotte thought she looked about nineteen and that she couldn't possibly have been at university the same time as Alex.

The girl rushed to Alex's side of the car and kissed him delightedly. Their pleasure at seeing one another was obvious, especially when Alex picked her up and swung her round.

'Stop it, Alex,' she called out, 'and let me say hello to Charlotte.'

Alex did as he was told and introduced them.

'Come on in. Don't bother about your luggage, Alex can see to that later. Can't you?' Sally said, looking over her shoulder as she steered Charlotte inside. 'I've just pulled some scones out of the oven, would you like one? I've even got some cream.'

She took them through to a large welcoming kitchen – welcoming because of the smell of baking and the fact that it was so colourful and looked as though it had evolved through use rather than careful planning. There was a large dresser painted royal blue, which dominated the room. It was packed with books rather than artfully placed pieces of china. In the centre of the stone-flagged floor was a table which held a further assortment of books and the floury remains of a baking session. The walls were covered in wrinkled pieces of artwork. Charlotte presumed the artist himself was the small blond-haired boy at the far end of the kitchen sitting with his back to her. Like Becky and Philip, he was engrossed in watching the television in front of him, but unlike Becky and Philip, the sound of the television was not at blaring pitch.

'I'll just go up and tell Stephen you've arrived,' Sally said, darting out of the room.

Charlotte watched Alex walk over to Mark. He said nothing until he was directly in front of the child. When the boy saw Alex he leapt excitedly to his feet. Alex gathered him up in his arms and brought him over to Charlotte. 'Mark, this is my friend Charlotte.' His voice was strangely slow.

'Hello,' she said, a little shyly and somewhat surprised at how gorgeous this particular child was. But there again, the only children she even vaguely knew were Philip, with his belligerent face, and Becky with her many pouting madam expressions.

An open smiling face looked at her with undisguised curiosity, but soon turned back to Alex. 'Uncle Lex,' Mark said, slowly and in a distorted voice, 'play monsters?'

Alex smiled and then put him down on the floor. 'Later, Mark,' he said slowly. 'Let me say hello to your father first.' Satisfied, Mark went back to the television and Alex joined Charlotte.

'Is he deaf?' she asked in a low voice.

'Yes. So there's no need to whisper. But isn't he great?'

'God, life's a bitch, isn't it?'

'I wouldn't say that.'

'Stephen!' The two men hugged each other with unrestrained affection, Charlotte noticed, and in a way so few men feel able to do. Alex introduced Charlotte.

Stephen smiled at her as he shook her hand. He was slightly taller than Alex and almost as blond as his pretty wife. It wasn't hard to see how between them they had created such a beautiful child.

'I hope my coming hasn't put you to any extra trouble,' Charlotte said, wanting to sound genuine but suspecting she sounded terribly trite.

'Not a bit of it,' Sally said, coming into the kitchen. 'Stephen, why don't you take Charlotte into the sitting-room and Alex can help me get some tea together.'

Leading the way but still within earshot of his wife, Stephen said, 'Round here we call Sally the Ayatollah. We pray to her at least six times a day.' A pair of rolled-up children's socks came flying through the door and hit him on the back of his neck.

He took Charlotte into a large square room with deep mullioned windows which overlooked the garden and a vast landscape of open moorland beyond. Late afternoon sunlight filtered through the windows giving a brilliant, almost theatrical light to the room. Like the kitchen, this room was no slave to fashion either, but held an eclectic assortment of homely-looking armchairs and tables, with a patchwork of paintings on the walls ranging from bucolic landscapes to a stunning watercolour portrait of Mark. There was a silver-framed photograph on a windowsill that caught Charlotte's eye. It was of Stephen and Sally on their wedding day and Alex was there too, with his arm round . . . a girl who looked just like Sally.

Stephen gestured to a squashy armchair for Charlotte. He sat down opposite her. 'You've caught us on a good day,' he said. 'The sun has barely shown itself all week. With a bit of luck, you and Alex might even be able to go on some decent walks. He has warned you about his passion for walking, hasn't he?'

'No, he's kept quiet about that.'

'Hold on, Stephen,' Alex said, coming in to the room with a large tea tray, 'you're not giving away all my secrets, are you?'

'I wouldn't dream of it,' Stephen said.

Later that evening, while Stephen and Alex were both upstairs putting Mark to bed and Charlotte was helping to prepare supper, Sally caught her off guard. 'Alex told us your husband died earlier this year . . . in a car crash, he said.'

Charlotte concentrated hard on scraping the potato in her hand. 'Yes,' she said, simply. She felt annoyed at this untimely reminder of Peter. The day had been going so well. 'So what else did he tell you about me?' The thought occurred to her that perhaps Alex had asked Sally to do his probing for him.

Sally stopped what she was doing. She put the vegetable knife down on the chopping board. 'I'm sorry,' she said, 'I shouldn't have said anything. Here, have some wine and you can tell me to mind my own business.'

Grateful for Sally's change of tack, Charlotte took the glass from her. She remembered the silver-framed photograph she had seen earlier and asked, 'Is that your sister in the wedding photo of you and Stephen, in the sitting-room?'

'Yes, my twin sister Lucy,' Sally replied, bending down to the oven and sliding a large casserole in. 'She died seven years ago.'

Her voice was matter of fact, in a way Charlotte felt sure hers would never be when talking about Peter's death. 'It's my turn to be sorry now,' she said.

'Don't be. It doesn't hurt any more to talk about her. You're not intruding on my grief . . . like I just did with you. It was crass of me. I should have realised it would be too soon for you to talk about your husband with somebody you hardly know.'

Was that another attempt to get her to open up, Charlotte wondered? She chose to ignore it. 'Was it a sudden death?'

'No. Leukaemia. It took her sixteen months to die . . . it was a long and painful time for us all . . . especially for Alex.' She saw the look on Charlotte's face. 'You did know that he and Lucy were . . .'

'No,' Charlotte said, her heart suddenly heavy with sadness for Alex. Why had he never said anything? Was it possible he was still in love with the memory of Lucy?

'You know, Lucy and I could never fool Alex,' Sally said, adopting a more cheerful voice. 'We led all our boyfriends a merry old dance. We'd swap dates and they'd never know. We even fooled poor Stephen. But Alex was the only one who could separate us. I used to joke that it was his sixth sense. Once he threatened to put us both over his knee if he ever suspected we were trying it on with him.'

'And did you?'

Sally laughed. 'Lucy was all set to give it a go but I chickened out. Believe it or not, I was the more timid of the two of us.'

'You must miss her. How did you come to terms with losing someone you were so close to?'

'This might seem strange but I don't think in terms of having lost her completely. Maybe because we were twins I feel a bit of Lucy is still with me.'

'And Alex, how did he . . .?'

'It was so much harder for Alex. When Lucy died it was as though she took away his future. He had spent so long determined he was going to live the rest of his life with her. I had Stephen. But Alex had no one. He was alone and has been ever since.'

29

As they were finishing breakfast the next morning, the telephone rang. Stephen went to answer it in his study. He came back after a couple of minutes. 'Sorry,' he said, picking up the remains of his toast, 'but I'm going to have to leave you. One of the surgeons has gone down with tonsillitis, so bang goes a rare day off.' He turned to Sally. 'I'll give you a ring when I think I'll be able to get away.'

'You didn't tell me Stephen was a surgeon,' Charlotte said, when Sally and Mark had gone to the front door to wave goodbye to him.

'I didn't think we needed to pin identity labels on everyone,' Alex said, getting up from the table and starting to clear away the dishes.

Charlotte laughed. 'What a horrid, nasty man you are.'

At Sally's insistence, Alex and Charlotte were sent out on a walk. Mark's disappointed face peered from the doorway as they set off.

They turned left at the gate and set off along the open moorland road. At a fork in the road Alex chose the right one and led Charlotte uphill until they came to a footpath, which took them to a small craggy outcrop. A dozen or so frightened rabbits scampered away at the sound of encroaching footsteps, their lean bodies slithering into crevices hidden deep in the rocks. A bird flew overhead and Charlotte watched Alex raise his head, shading his eyes against the sun. 'A curlew,' he said, coming to a stop.

'I'll take your word for it,' she answered, her eyes

remaining on Alex. Since her conversation with Sally last night she had been unable to stop herself thinking of Lucy and the devastating effect her death must have had on Alex. But the most persistent thought running through her mind was what it must have been like for Lucy to be loved in such a way. Plainly Alex had adored her.

From where they stood, they had a clear uninterrupted view of a landscape of endless moorland. The purple heather was at its best, with a summer fragrance that carried lightly on the wind. Charlotte sat down on one of the rocks, letting the moment last. The sprawling landscape held a quietness that right now she needed. There was a timeless quality about it that meant just here, just now, she was held in its reassuring vacuum. 'Thank you,' she said, looking up at Alex.

'What for?' He joined her on an adjacent rock.

'For this, for bringing me here.'

'It was a risk though, wasn't it?'

She smiled. 'I hadn't got you down as a gambling man.'

'Full of surprises, me.'

'Mm . . . you're right, you are.' Charlotte decided it was now or never. She wanted Alex to tell her about Lucy. She knew if she didn't hear the words from him she would never be able to rid herself of the memory of what Sally had told her last night – *He was alone and has been ever since.* 'Sally told me about her sister dying.'

There was no shocked response from him, as she might have thought. 'Did she tell you about Lucy and me?'

'A little. She mentioned . . .'

'Come on.' He stood up and took her hand, pulling her towards him. 'Let's walk and I'll tell you about my dark and murky past.'

They left the crags behind them and followed the foot-path out across the purple heather. 'The four of us were all at university together,' Alex told her. 'We were a mixed bag to say the least. There was me, a complete freak as far as computers were concerned, and Stephen studying medicine. We were in our third year and both lodging with Mrs Holroyd. Remember, I told you about her? Then along came Sally and Lucy, into the house next door. They were both studying psychology – they really were identical, in everything. There were times when Stephen couldn't even . . .'

'Yes, Sally told me how he had trouble telling them apart, but that you always could.'

'Don't ask me how, I just knew.'

'I'm sorry, I interrupted. Carry on.'

'It wasn't long before I knew that I wanted to marry Lucy. I asked her several times and each time she turned me down, but refused to give a reason. Then we graduated and both ended up in London, independently of each other, but friends, close friends. I was working with Henderson and Wyatt and in a better position to ask Lucy to marry me, so I asked her one more time. Over dinner in her flat she told me she would never marry anybody and she explained why. She had this recurring dream – she'd had it since she was a child – that she was going to die before the age of thirty. She didn't want anyone to be saddled with that kind of heartbreak . . . she was so certain she was going to die.'

'But that's awful. Surely you must have convinced her otherwise.'

He shook his head. 'I managed to persuade her to live with me, and then, two years later, she was diagnosed as having leukaemia. She carried on working for as long as she could but she spent more and more time in hospital, until the doctors said there was nothing else they could do. She pleaded with me to bring her up here to Yorkshire to be with Sally and Stephen. They'd settled here by then. They nursed her to the end. Sally gave up her lecturing job at Leeds and I tried to spend as much time as I could helping . . . and just being there with Lucy. We all became very close during that time. I suppose the text books would call it a bonding experience.'

When he didn't carry on, Charlotte reached out to him. She touched his arm with her hand. 'Oh Alex. How *did* you cope, when you loved her so much?'

'I . . .' He looked down at his arm and without thinking he picked up Charlotte's hand, turned it over and pressed her palm to his lips, closing his eyes momentarily. 'It was Sally who held me . . . held us all together.' He lowered Charlotte's hand, but kept it at his side. 'She's incredibly strong. Nothing ever fazes her, not even after Mark was born and she and Stephen realised he was deaf.'

'Yes, I could see when she talked to me last night that there was a lot more to her than her youthful good looks.' But Charlotte wasn't only thinking of Sally's strength of character and courage, but of the determined love Alex once had for another woman. To be loved like that . . .

'Shall we go back to the crags now? There's something I'd like to show you.'

They stood where they had been an hour earlier. Small puffy white clouds had bubbled up and were hanging listlessly in the blue sky; the persistent cry of curlews overhead provided the only sound to penetrate the emptiness of the landscape.

'What did you want to show me?'

Alex guided her round to the back of a massive rock, weathered smooth by wind and time. 'Stand just there,' he said, 'about four feet away from the rock, and tell me what you can see.'

She laughed, feeling slightly silly, but did as he asked. 'Nothing in particular, just a large dark stone.' She turned to face him. 'Is that it?'

'Charlotte – I asked you this before – do you trust me?'

'For goodness' sake, Alex, what is all this?'

He took a step closer to her. 'That large dark stone, as you call it, represents Peter.'

She stepped away from him and pushed her hands down

deep into the pockets of her jeans. She felt cross with Alex for reminding her of her failed marriage. And anyway, she had all that under control now. She had already begun to close that particular box in her life. 'I thought I was supposed to come here to get away from my problems.'

Why had he started this? What was he doing risking everything with her all over again? But Alex's instinct told him that something was stopping Charlotte from putting Peter to rest, and he suspected he knew what it was. 'I think it's time you started facing up to the main problem in your life,' he said.

'Oh yes,' she said, scathing sarcasm ringing in her voice. 'And what would that be, Mr Know-it-all?'

'I'm only guessing, but for some reason I think you're blaming yourself for what happened to Peter. Am I right?'

'That's rubbish,' she shouted defiantly. 'And what gives *you* the right to make assumptions like that?' She started to walk away from him. She was furious. Why couldn't he leave her be? They had been happy a few moments ago. Why did he have to keep spoiling things?

'Because,' Alex called out, catching up with her, 'when Lucy finally died . . . I felt such relief that it was all over. Suddenly I was free of the daily burden of grief that I'd experienced for two years. But that feeling of freedom soon passed and guilt took a hold of me and I nearly screwed up completely. I think guilt is your problem and, believe me, I know about it.' He was almost shouting at her now. He hadn't meant to, but he wanted to convince Charlotte that she was not alone.

She faced him. 'So what happened to you?'

'I pushed myself harder and harder at work, got more and more run down. Then Stephen came to stay. He saw the mess I was in and insisted I came back here to rest. One day Sally brought me to this very place and stood me behind that rock. She asked me what I could see and my answer was more or less what you just said, except I emphasised the darkness . . . for me the whole world had been eclipsed by what I was doing to myself.'

Charlotte swallowed hard. 'What did Sally say next?'

Alex led Charlotte back to the rock. When she was standing where she had stood a few moments ago, he said, 'Step back six paces and tell me what you can see now.'

She wanted to shout, oh stop all this nonsense, it's so facile, but instead she said, 'I can see . . . how much do you want me to tell you?'

'Everything you see.'

'Blue sky, white clouds, a bird flying, dry-stone walls, grass, some sheep, small houses over there, a church.' Without looking at Alex, she said, 'Is that where Lucy is buried?'

'Yes, but don't change the subject. Do you want to know what Sally said next?'

'Okay.'

'She told me it was time to step back from my boulder of guilt and take a look at the world behind it.'

'That's very interesting,' she said, 'but I'm over Peter's death, and I certainly don't have a problem with guilt.' She gave the rock a vicious kick and once again started to walk away.

But Alex was ready for her. He placed a firm hand on her shoulder and pulled her round to face him. 'Charlotte,' he said gently, 'stop pretending. Try talking to someone about it. Surely you must have a friend you could talk to.'

'No,' she answered. 'We were on the move so much I didn't make many close friends. Anyway, they're too busy, too wrapped up in their own lives and marriages to listen to me . . . apart from that, they all think that Peter and I . . .'

'Peter and you what?'

She remained silent, turned her face away from him.

And then he knew, understood at last what Charlotte's real pain was about. How stupid he had been! He had wondered at the time about those words she had uttered in the garden at Ivy Cottage, about her life in Belgium – *It was empty and cold and I hated it*. But that wasn't about her life in Belgium at all, that was her life with Peter. He said, 'So they all think that you and Peter had the perfect marriage? That you of all people couldn't possibly have stopped loving your husband. Is that it, Charlotte? Charlotte, talk to me.'

'Yes!' She yelled back at him. 'Yes, yes! Only hours before Peter died I'd asked him for a divorce . . . there, you're the first person I've told. Are you satisfied now?' Her words were angry and filled with pain as though they had been extracted from her under torture. And then suddenly her anger subsided and she fell against Alex and allowed him to lead her back to the rocks. There they sat, her shaking body held tightly against his own, while she sobbed and sobbed.

'I killed him, didn't I?' Charlotte said, when at last she had calmed down and had managed to tell Alex what had happened that snowy February morning and what had led to it. 'I upset him and he was in no state to drive. I shouldn't have let him go . . . I should have . . .'

Still with his arms round her, Alex said, 'But it was Peter who chose to walk out of the apartment that morning, it was Peter who was behind the wheel of his car, not you –'

She pulled away from him and shook her head. 'But Alex, if I hadn't said anything, Peter would still be alive today. I'm sure of it.'

'Would he, though? He would still have driven on that same road, he would have been just as determined to get to his meeting in Luxembourg . . . would have encountered that same patch of ice.'

'Yes, but that conversation did take place and it must have affected the way he drove.'

'Look, Charlotte, you have to come to terms with the fact that we can't control other people's reactions, it's just not possible. What happened to Peter happened because he chose to make that journey.'

He took her hand in his and squeezed it gently. She sighed and leaned against him again. They sat in silence for a while, until Alex placed a hand under her chin. 'Okay now?' he said in a low voice.

'Yes.' She lifted her head. Her eyes fixed on him were heavy with sadness and wonder. His heart twisted with compassion and he stroked the stray wisps of hair away from her face. Her eyes closed at his touch. He kissed first one eye, then the other, and then he kissed her on the lips, tentatively at first, but when she responded with an eagerness that matched his own, he cradled her head and tilted her back on to the flat surface of the rock. The touch and feel of her body clinging to him filled him with desire. Then in the distance he heard voices, children's voices. He tried to ignore the noise, hoping he was imagining it, but Charlotte's body was shaking. He looked down into her face, concerned. But she was laughing, her eyes wide open and reflecting the blue sky above. 'God, you're beautiful,' he said. 'Do you suppose we're always going to be interrupted?' He sat up and pulled her towards him as the voices came nearer.

She sprang to her feet, still laughing as a Scout troop weighed down with enormous backpacks passed by. 'We'll have to see, won't we?' she said.

They headed for home, hand in hand.

That evening, Charlotte and Sally were left alone while Stephen and Alex disappeared off to the pub for a pint of beer. It was a warm evening and they sat out in the garden with a bottle of Chianti and a large bag of peas to shell for supper. Charlotte began to tell Sally some of what happened on her walk with Alex that morning.

Looking up from the bowl of peas on her lap, Sally said, 'Why do you think you and Peter got married in the first place?'

'I think he only asked me to marry him because his

235

parents didn't approve of me. They thought I was just a shop girl. The fact that it was my own shop was immaterial to them. I wasn't good enough for their son and Peter wanted to get his own back. In fact I don't think he would have married anyone who his parents actually did approve of.'

'So why did you accept?'

'Because . . . oh dear, this is going to sound pathetic, but I truly believed I could undo all the harm of Peter's upbringing.'

'Saint Charlotte the Saviour, eh?'

'That's not nice,' Charlotte said, but she smiled all the same.

'So, you married and then found you didn't have the necessary saintly qualities. But what made you want to take that final step to end your marriage?'

Charlotte snapped open a pea pod and popped out the peas. She put one in her mouth. 'It was when I knew that Peter was always going to put work first, that he didn't need a wife, simply someone permanently on hand to massage his ego. Then I knew I couldn't carry on as we were. Selfishly, I suppose, I wanted more . . . I wanted to be loved.'

'Nothing particularly selfish in that.'

'Okay then, you might be able to convince me that I shouldn't feel guilty about wanting to be loved, but how about the fact that I'm responsible for Peter's death?'

Sally put her bowl of peas down on the grass and picked up her wine glass. 'You're *not* responsible for Peter's death. It's possible that you want to believe you're to blame, and then not forgive yourself for it, because you want to keep punishing yourself. It can be an insidious self-defence mechanism against grief. Focusing on the injustice means that you can't forgive yourself, can't grieve properly. Does that make any sense, ring any bells?'

Charlotte leaned back in her chair. 'Oh yes,' she said. 'Yes, it certainly does.'

'More Chianti?'

'Mm . . . please.'

As Charlotte reached forward with her glass Sally said, 'Now, what are you going to do about Alex? You do realise, don't you, that you're the first woman he's allowed himself to fall in love with since Lucy?'

30

They drove back to Hulme Welford after breakfast the following day. Mark was disappointed that Alex wasn't staying longer. 'Come again,' he shouted as Alex started up the engine. And while Stephen said goodbye to Alex, Sally came round to Charlotte's side of the car.

'Now remember,' she said, 'stop being so hard on yourself.'

Charlotte leaned out of the car and gave Sally a kiss on the cheek. 'Thanks for everything.'

Once they had left the Pennines behind them and they were skirting round north Manchester, Charlotte realised that she was going home reluctantly. She had hoped her time away from Hulme Welford would give her the opportunity to think more clearly about her future. It hadn't. Her disclosure to Alex had left her battered and bruised, but it had made her see that she had been kidding herself that she was getting over Peter. Sally was right: she hadn't allowed herself to grieve for Peter, she had been too frightened of the consequences.

And Alex. What was she to do about him? Again she could no longer ignore what had been staring her in the face all these weeks. But love? Perhaps Sally was wrong. Maybe Alex might never be able to love another woman. Could anyone ever replace Lucy? Could she . . . did she want to?

With so much of the past hanging over her, Charlotte knew there was a lot she had to consider before she could even contemplate the future. She had to speak to Alex, and soon, but she didn't know where to start.

'You've got something to say, haven't you?'

She looked across at Alex. 'Sally mentioned you had a sixth sense.'

'That's great coming from her. I've never known anyone more perceptive.'

You're the first woman he's allowed himself to fall in love with . . . 'And is she always right?'

'Usually. But I'm an amateur compared to her. I only know when you've got something important to say because you frown slightly and you get three lines, just here.' He took his eyes of the motorway briefly and placed a finger on her forehead.

Her stomach lurched as he touched her. 'You're right though,' she said watching his hand move back to the steering wheel, 'I do have something I want to say.'

'Go on, then.'

'No, not now. Later. I need to think first.'

'How about tonight, then? I'll cook us a meal, and you can talk.'

'I don't . . .'

'Look,' he said patiently, 'I want to call on Cindy and Derek and then perhaps go and see Barry in hospital. Do you want to come with me? We could talk afterwards.'

'You're very sure Barry's still alive, aren't you?'

He moved his hand from the wheel and rested it on her knee. 'If there's one thing my time with Lucy taught me, it was never to give up hope.'

'But she *died*, Alex,' Charlotte said, mystified.

'Yes, but *I* didn't . . . I thought my life would end when hers did, but it didn't.'

They tried calling at In The Pink later that afternoon and found the whole place shut. They drove on to the hospital where, at Barry's door, they were greeted by Tiffany. 'Come in. We were just talking about you two.'

'You were?' Alex smiled and walked over to the bed. 'Hello Barry, how's it going?'

'Surprisingly good, considering. Just tired, mainly.'

Charlotte couldn't believe what she was seeing. There was Barry, sitting up in bed wearing his familiar glasses, with a book lying open at his side. He looked pale and tired, and was still attached to a drip, but there was no sign of death about him, nor that there ever had been. She was so pleased! She went straight up to Barry and gave him a kiss, and then, sensing his embarrassment at her unexpected display of euphoria, she said, 'We've all been so worried about you.'

'Sorry to have been a nuisance,' he said, pushing his glasses up on his nose.

'Muffin 'ell, will you listen to him!' Tiffany shouted. Get him to tell you his exam results, they came this morning.'

'No, Tiffany, they don't want to know about that.'

''Course they do.' She turned to Alex and Charlotte. 'They're brill. Pure genius, this lad.'

Barry picked up the piece of paper by the side of his bed and passed it to Alex.

'A for physics,' Alex read out, 'A for chemistry, A for biology and, wait for it, A for economics. I'll say one thing for you, Barry, you're consistent. Well done!'

'Yes,' agreed Charlotte. 'Congratulations! I used to hate people like you at school. Your parents must be delighted, and I don't just mean with your exam results.'

'Dad's been a real head-case,' Tiffany said. 'He was here on his own when Barry came round on Tuesday.' She laughed. 'I'm not sure Dad's the first person I'd want to see after being in a coma!'

'Don't be so hard on him,' Barry said.

'What?' she cried. 'After the things he's said to you?'

'It's just his way.'

'So where are your parents?' Alex asked. 'We called in at your place, but there was no sign of anyone there.'

'The salon and everything's been shut since Barry's been here, but Mum and Dad are somewhere in the hospital. They went off to find the doctor to see about Barry coming home. We're hoping it'll be in a few days, or rather Dad is – he won't want to be paying for this private room for too long, will he? So anyway, you two been away or what?'

'Stop being so nosy, Tiffany,' Barry said.

Alex laughed. 'So that's what you were talking about when we arrived.' Worried that Barry was more tired than he was letting on, he added, 'We'd better be going, don't want to wear out the patient.'

'We reckon you've been away, *together*,' Tiffany persisted.

'Correction,' said Barry. 'That's what my sister thinks. Honestly, Tiffany, you get more like Dad every day.'

'Bloody well don't!'

Charlotte looked at Alex and realised that he was leaving it up to her to decide what to say. 'You're absolutely right, Tiffany. Alex took me to see some friends of his.'

Tiffany was triumphant. 'Told you,' she said, looking at her brother.

'You know,' Alex said, in the car on the way home, 'I don't think I can take the suspense any longer. Do you want to tell me now what it is that's on your mind?' Since their drive back from Yorkshire, he had been conscious of Charlotte's preoccupation with her own thoughts and he suspected that it had something to do with what she wanted to talk to him about. He sensed it wasn't good.

'Yes, perhaps you're right,' Charlotte answered distantly, 'now is probably as good as later. I just want to say how grateful I am for these past few days. You were right about many things, especially my liking Stephen and Sally.'

'So, why is it I detect an unspoken "but" in what you've just said?'

'Alex, both you and Sally made me see that I haven't

really begun to get over Peter . . . Sally also said . . .' Charlotte paused, unsure just how to carry on. In her mind, she had worked out exactly what to say to him, it had sounded perfectly reasonable when she had gone over it earlier, but now she didn't seem so convinced. Sitting close to Alex in the car, watching his hands on the steering wheel, she was reminded of their time at the crags, when his hands had caressed her with such tenderness. The memory was so provocative she could almost feel the weight of his body against her own, could remember exactly the sensation of his mouth on hers. She shifted awkwardly in her seat.

'She told you I loved you, didn't she?' Alex said, bringing the car to a stop at a red traffic light. He turned and looked at her.

'Yes, she did.'

'So where does that leave us?'

'Oh Alex, I don't know. I feel so confused. I don't want to lie to you, it wouldn't be fair. I just don't think I'm capable of loving anyone, not after . . .'

'But you might feel differently in time.'

'Please, please don't push me.'

The traffic lights turned to amber, then green, and they completed the rest of the journey in silence.

Sat in his office, Alex was strangely calm. Surely he hadn't really hoped for more. He had been a fool to think that anyone who had gone through what Charlotte had would be inclined to take up with another man so soon. He had to give her space, so that she could get over Peter's death properly. She may not have loved him when he died, but she still had to go through some sort of grieving process for the man she had been married to for eight years; a process which up, until now, she had avoided.

Patience. That's what was called for. Let's face it, he had been patient with Lucy for all those years. He stared into the VDU screen in front of him, its blank whiteness waiting expectantly for him to fill it. He switched it off. Why, he wondered, did he fall for women who were determined to keep him at arm's length? Why couldn't he be satisfied with the Heathers of this world?

31

When Barry was discharged from hospital, he was welcomed home by the residents of Acacia Lane. Even Iris Braithwaite surprised everyone by calling round. 'A pot of honey for your son, Mrs Rogers. I recommend two spoonfuls a days, soon have him back on his feet.' Then Charlotte herself received a surprise.

She had just got back from the supermarket and emptied the car, when she looked out of the kitchen window and saw Alex sitting in the garden talking to an extraordinarily glamorous woman. It was a while before Charlotte realised who it was, because initially the combination of this particular woman sitting in this particular rickety old garden chair beneath her fig tree threw her completely.

'Christina!' she shouted, rushing outside. 'What on earth are you doing here?'

'Carlotta, my darling,' Christina said, rising elegantly from the old chair, 'I have been waiting here for you, so long.' She wrapped her graceful arms around Charlotte and kissed her several times. Then standing back, she gave Charlotte a long hard stare. 'You still look dreadful, but slightly better than when you lived in Brussels. Carlotta, why are you looking like that, as though you weren't expecting me?'

'That's because I wasn't expecting you.'

'Did you not receive my letter, telling you I was coming?'

Charlotte shook her head. 'Sorry, no letter.'

'Oh, that is too bad. Then there is nothing else for it. I

shall leave you to recover from your shock and return tomorrow. Perhaps that would suit you better?' She offered Alex one of her most seductive of smiles. 'I am sure Mr Hamilton here would provide me with a bed for the night.'

Alex smiled, until Charlotte threw him a keep-out-of-this look. 'Don't be so silly, Christina,' she said. 'I'm delighted you're here. It's just that there's nothing ready for you and the house is such a mess.'

Christina shrugged her shoulders dismissively. 'What else do I need? I have your company and your nice Mr Hamilton to amuse me.' She laid a perfectly manicured hand on his arm. 'Oh yes, I have everything I could possibly desire.' She seemed to add an extra emphasis to the word desire. Charlotte began to feel uneasy.

'And why, Carlotta, have you never written to me of your charming neighbour? If I had been you I would have written of little else.'

Trying hard not to laugh, Alex got to his feet. 'I think I'd better leave you to it. I have some work I need to get on with.'

Christina looked up at him. 'I am so sorry to have kept you. But Carlotta darling, could we not invite Mr Hamilton for dinner?'

'I'm sure,' Charlotte said firmly and giving Alex a warning glance, 'that Mr Hamilton has far too much work to do to spare us any of his valuable time.'

'I have?' asked Alex.

'You have,' Charlotte repeated. 'You've probably got enough to keep you busy for days.'

'Oh, stacks to do,' Alex said, making a move towards his part of the house. 'I shan't surface for weeks probably. Goodbye.'

'Well,' Christina said, in a voice designed to carry, 'what a most desirable man and those gorgeous blue eyes. Have you slept with him?'

'Christina!' cried Charlotte in a shocked voice, watching

245

Alex as he disappeared inside. Had he heard?

'What, what have I said? He's young, he's handsome, he's amusing and he's living in your house with you. Why in heaven's name do you not sleep with him?'

That, thought Charlotte, is the million-dollar question.

Charlotte unpacked the shopping and stuffed the empty carrier bags into the bin, ignoring Hilary's imaginary voice in her head reminding her of the recycling banks in the village. What on earth was she going to give Christina for supper that night? She pulled open the fridge, knelt down and stared at all the food she had just bought. She waited for inspiration to come, but it was no good – she had only chosen convenience foods in the supermarket. They would have to go out to eat. She'd drive them over to Knutsford, plenty of upmarket restaurants there to impress Christina with.

Charlotte opened a can of dog food for Mabel and was putting the dish down on the floor by the back door when a cloud of expensive perfume came into the kitchen, followed by Christina. She was dressed in a close-fitting, red and white striped dress, which would have made anyone else look like a stick of candy, but on Christina looked stunning.

Mabel obviously thought so too. Giving her dish of food not a second glance, she pattered across the kitchen floor, looked up at Christina and rolled over on to her back, her paws hanging limply in the air.

'Oh, what a perfectly splendid little *bambino*,' Christina cried. She bent down to Mabel and rubbed her tummy. 'Carlotta, you have much to tell me, I think. Why don't you take me out to one of your famous pubs for supper?'

Charlotte laughed. 'I don't think the Spinner is quite ready for you, Christina.'

'But I am ready for the Spinner. Come on, Carlotta, where is your sense of fun? Let me get you out of those drab clothes and into something to set the Spinner on fire.'

It was impossible not to catch Christina's infectious humour and it made Charlotte realise that up until that point she had acted quite churlishly towards her friend. She wondered why. Was it because Christina had flirted so outrageously with Alex in the garden?

They opened the wardrobe doors in Charlotte's bedroom and got to work. 'Too dull,' Christina said, as Charlotte took out a smart pair of fawn-coloured trousers. 'Too morbid,' she sighed in response to a black pair. 'Come on, Carlotta, go for lightness, lightness of heart and spirit. Oh, I can see I came just in time to save you from dying of dullness. Ah here, wear this.'

Charlotte looked doubtfully at the strapless cream dress in Christina's hands. She hadn't worn it since last summer, when she had gone with Peter to Nice, he to give a presentation at the company conference and she to sit next to him at the dinner afterwards and bask gratefully in his reflected glory. After the meal the chairman had stood up and thanked all his hard-working colleagues for their unstinting loyalty to the company, telling them to keep up the good work. Not a word did he say to those wives present who had given up so much of themselves to travel with their husbands so that they could feel fulfilled; not a word of thanks to those wives who had given up their own careers and possibly their children to boarding school for the sake of continuity in their education. When the last of the liqueurs had been tossed back and the cigars stubbed out, Charlotte had tried to tempt Peter into a walk along the beach, but he had refused, preferring instead the company of his overhead slides for another presentation he had to give the following morning. And so, beneath the midnight sky, her shoes in her hands, Charlotte had walked along the water's edge alone.

'Okay,' she said. 'I'll wear it.'

She slipped into the dress and sat on a stool in the bathroom to let Christina see to the rest of her. First her friend wove her hair into a French plait. Then came her face. Looking with disgust at Charlotte's haphazard collection of make-up, Christina fetched her own. When she declared that she was finished, Charlotte looked apprehensively into the mirror. She was delighted. The shadows under her eyes had magically disappeared and somehow Christina had managed, with a few simple strokes of powder, mascara and lipstick, to give her a facelift. She looked good and she felt wonderful.

'And now,' Christina said, 'you must wear my perfume. We must not clash, we must not compete with each other.' She sprayed Charlotte liberally. 'There now, you are ready, and I think it would be nice for us to have a chaperon for the evening.'

'No,' Charlotte said vehemently. 'Alex is busy.'

Christina laughed. 'What a charming idea. But no, I was thinking of your little *bambino*. This is strictly a girls' night out.'

When they strolled arm in arm down Acacia Lane Charlotte was aware of a strange feeling bubbling up inside her. It wasn't until they got as far as the village hall that she recognised what the strange feeling was. She felt incredibly sexy. Tottering along on her high heels, wearing her girlfriend's lipstick and feeling as radiant as a star, she was nineteen again. With sadness, she knew she had never felt like that with Peter. How out of touch with her emotions she had become . . . until now. She caught her breath. Oh Alex. There it was. The truth, at last. Alex had unwittingly frightened her because he had made her come to know what she had been missing all these years and as hard as she had tried to resist him it had only made things worse, had made her want him all the more.

They made a predictably striking entrance at the Spinner, causing heads to turn and Ted the Toup to lose contact with the cigarette drooping out of his mouth; it plopped and fizzed into his beer. While Charlotte herself wasn't entirely comfortable with the position of centre stage, she knew Christina was perfectly at ease. For Christina there was no other position.

Hoping there would be fewer people outside, Charlotte led the way through the noisy public bar and out to the garden. They sat in the evening sun at a large wooden table with two benches either side, and the landlord came out personally to serve them. He took their order with a flourish of efficiency that would have even impressed Iris Braithwaite.

'Now Carlotta,' Christina said, when they were alone, 'how have you been? Your letters tell me nothing about you, only about your sister and your parents, oh, and a Mrs Britwit.'

'Mrs Braithwaite,' Charlotte corrected, with a smile.

'Now, tell me about yourself. Are you happy?'

'I'm happier.'

Christina shook her head. 'That is not good enough. Let me ask you this: would you rather be back in Brussels in that miserable apartment with that miserable husband of yours?'

'Christina, you can't ask things like that.'

'But I just have.'

'Well, no. No, I wouldn't want to be back there.'

'Good, so we have progress, now all you have to do is forgive yourself.'

Charlotte looked up sharply. This was exactly what Sally had told her. Was there a conspiracy? 'Why do you say that?'

'Because it's true. I was there with you in Brussels, I saw how unhappy you were. I knew why too. I knew that you felt guilty because you could not make yourself fit your husband's requirements. Few wives truly can. I knew too that you did not love Mr Carlotta . . . and that Mr Carlotta did not love you. So simple really. Nobody's fault, so nobody to blame, just forgive and—'

'But you can't forget,' Charlotte interrupted.

'No, I was not going to say forget, I was going to say *move on*. You should be a Catholic like me: you get forgiven every week and you move on.'

Charlotte laughed and then she frowned. 'Would you like to hear a confession?'

'Why not?'

'Remember the morning Peter died?'

'Yes, I remember it well, all that snow.'

'While we were having breakfast I asked Peter for a divorce.'

Christina looked across the table at her friend. She took Charlotte's hand. 'Oh my poor little Carlotta, so that is why you are still sad, I see now. But why did you not tell me?'

'Because . . .'

'Because you are so very English.'

'And you are not, if you don't mind me saying,' said the landlord of the Spinner as he put their tray of food down on the table.

'My dear man,' smiled Christina, 'how clever of you. What gave me away?'

The man beamed. 'Oh you know, little things.' He passed them their chicken and chips. 'The drinks are on the house,' he added, almost bowing as he made his exit.

'Tell me, Carlotta, here is a phrase I do not know – the drinks are on the house. What does it mean?'

Charlotte laughed. 'It means, they're free, because the landlord of the Spinner has fallen in love with you, Christina.'

'That is good, we shall come here tomorrow, I think,' she said, spearing a huge chip with her fork. 'And why have you not fallen in love with Mr Hamilton?'

Sprinkling salt on to her meal and then some vinegar, Charlotte said. 'To be honest, Christina, I think I probably could fall in love with him.'

'That is very good.'

'No, it's not good. I don't want to fall in love with him, or anyone else for that matter. Not at the moment.'

'Oh Carlotta, you make your life so very difficult.' She speared another chip. 'Delicious,' she said, putting it to her lips and managing to make it look like an erotic act. 'Now I will tell you all about my friend Henri the Diplomat. He's so beautiful and with legs to die for.'

Glad the pressure was off her, Charlotte said, 'You must be missing him.'

'I had thought I might, but that was before I met your delightful Mr Hamilton.'

Charlotte laughed. But Christina looked serious. 'Why are you laughing? What is so funny?'

'Come on, Christina, Alex is too nice to be added to your list of . . .' She paused, list of what? What did one call Christina's men friends? Were they clients or lovers? She settled for the latter. '. . . Lovers.'

'I think a little souvenir of England to take home might be nice though.'

Charlotte looked shocked. 'But you can't . . .'

Christina smiled. 'Oh, but I think I will. After all, you do not seem to want him, do you?'

32

'Just thought I'd pop round,' said Hilary coming through the open conservatory door. 'Heard you'd got a friend staying.'

I bet you did, thought Charlotte, knowing that last night's visit to the Spinner would have the village spinning on its axis in a tizzy of excitement and curiosity for days to come. And all because Christina had insisted, in a loud voice, that the Spinner wasn't the real thing. 'How can it be so, there is no piano, there is no one singing?' Hearing this, the landlord had fetched his son's keyboard down from upstairs and called upon Mr Phelps, the church organist, to come out of the snug and put his hands to good use. With everyone gathered round him ready to sing, including Christina and Charlotte, Mr Phelps rose to the occasion and surprised them all by revealing his true musical bent, which was honky-tonk. He opened up with 'Down at the Old Bull and Bush' and then moved through a repertoire that included 'We'll Meet Again', 'I'm Getting Married in the Morning', and because he knew Christina came from somewhere across the Channel he played 'Viva España' again and again, until Ted the Toup demanded 'The Birdy Song'.

'I heard there was a bit of a party down at the Spinner last night.' Hilary already knew all the details of last night's goings-on. Ted had been only too willing to impart his news when she had gone to pick up her copy of Hello!

'I danced with a fancy foreign piece last night,' he had

told her with relish. 'She's a friend of your sister's from abroad, you know, got a real body on her, too.'

'So where is she, this friend of yours?' Hilary pursued.

'She's not here,' Charlotte said, scrubbing hard at a particularly stubborn stain on the cooker hob she was cleaning.

'Oh, you mean she's gone home, already?' Hilary was unable to keep the disappointment out of her voice. She had rushed straight from Ted the Toup's to Charlotte's in the hope of meeting this incredible creature, who had apparently enslaved both Ted and the landlord of the Spinner in one fell swoop.

'She's out with Alex,' Charlotte answered through clenched teeth. 'He's taken her to see the Italian Gardens at Tatton.'

Hilary was shocked. She had thought that things were more or less in the bag, ever since Tiffany had told her Charlotte and Alex had been away together. But if Ted's description of this woman was anything to go by, then Alex was in serious danger. 'Why on earth didn't you go with them?'

'Because I had a headache,' Charlotte snapped back, 'and I didn't feel like it.' Reluctant as she was to admit it, this was not the truth. Over breakfast Christina had suggested they go out for the day, suggesting also, 'We could take your lovely Mr Hamilton with us?'

'Look, Christina,' Charlotte had said on the edge of losing her temper, 'let's just get this clear. Alex Hamilton is not my lovely anything, okay?'

'Okay, okay, but let's invite him anyway . . . I think I would very much like him to be my lovely something for the day.'

Before Charlotte could stop her, Christina was next door inviting Alex to accompany them on an outing. Even worse, Alex proposed a trip to Tatton to show Christina the Italian Gardens. At the last moment, in a desperate attempt to sabotage things, Charlotte feigned a headache – a headache that had all the potential of a full-blown migraine.

'My poor Carlotta,' Christina sympathised, 'you must rest, you must stay out of the sun. I will put you to bed and there you will stay. But we cannot possibly disappoint Mr Hamilton. I shall try my best to amuse him in your absence.' She settled Charlotte in bed, pulled the curtains across and ignored her protestations of suddenly feeling so much better. 'No, no, you are only trying to be brave,' Christina insisted, shutting the bedroom door softly behind her and then the front door with a resounding bang.

'What time did they go out?' Hilary asked. 'And when are they due back?'

'What is this, Hilary, the Hulme Welford Inquisition?'

'I only asked.' Hilary decided she had better change the subject. 'What are you wearing to Barry's confirmation tomorrow?'

Charlotte moved over to the sink and rinsed out the cloth she had been using to clean the cooker. 'I really don't know. I haven't thought that far ahead.'

No, thought Hilary, I'm not surprised, not with Alex being seduced in amongst the topiary, right now this minute. 'Shall I help you choose something?'

'No!' shouted Charlotte. 'No, and I just wish everyone would leave me alone.'

Hilary tactfully withdrew to The Gables. Her only hope was that if her sister was ruffled by the fact that Alex was out with Christina, then all was not completely lost.

It was nearly ten o'clock that evening when Charlotte heard Alex's car pulling up on the drive, followed by the sound of Christina's light tinkling laughter. But it was well past midnight before Christina came and rang the door bell.

Charlotte let her friend in and tried to show indifference to Christina's profuse apologies for being so late. 'Carlotta, forgive me, please. I have never known the time to fly so fast.'

'Goodness, is that the time already?' Charlotte responded. 'I had no idea it was so late. I've been reading.'

Christina dropped gracefully on to the sofa and looked about her, to where her friend must have been sitting. The armchair with its squashed cushion was surrounded by a trail of late night snacking debris – an empty coffee cup, a plate with the remains of some crackers and an empty packet of crisps. No sign of a book.

'I was reading upstairs,' lied Charlotte, knowing the conclusion Christina must have reached. Then looking her friend in the eye, she said, 'What have you been up to all day and all evening?'

Christina laughed, eased off her shoes and stretched out her long painted toes, managing to make them perform a neat Mexican wave. Charlotte wondered whether those artful little piggies had just been caressed by Alex's hands. But the thought of Alex's hands, which she had so coveted caught her off guard and exposed the depth of her anger.

'So come on, Christina,' she demanded, 'what have you done to Alex?'

Again that light tinkling laugh. 'Carlotta, please, do you have to be so blunt?'

'Ah! That's rich coming from you. What was it you said yesterday in the garden and quite loud enough for Alex to hear – "Have you slept with him?" Well, if that wasn't being blunt, I don't know what is.'

Christina stretched back lazily on the sofa. The smile was still in place, but her eyes were not looking so kindly. 'Tell me, Carlotta,' she said, 'what exactly is it you want to know? Whether I have been making love to your adorable Mr Hamilton, the lovely Alex, with his so, *so* blue eyes? By the way, have you ever noticed his hands, he has the most creative hands?' She noticed Charlotte's face blanch. 'Well, Carlotta, is that it, is that what you want to know?'

'Yes,' cried Charlotte, pacing the room, 'yes it bloody well is!'

Christina sighed and got up from the sofa. Carrying her shoes, she made for the door. 'I think I shall go to bed now, I am so very tired . . . but Carlotta, I think you already know the answer to your question, don't you? Good night.'

33

Tiffany came into the kitchen brushing her long pink hair with a heavily matted brush that had never been near the salon sterilising unit. She took one look at Barry and whistled. 'You look a bit of all right. Shame you're my brother!'

'For God's sake!' rebuked Derek, coming in behind her. 'Do you have to be so vulgar? This is Bas's bloody confirmation, not an episode of *Blind Date*.' He turned to his son. 'She's right though, Bas. That suit looks great on you. Makes you look quite a chip off the old block.'

Tiffany cringed. 'Let's hope not.'

Barry ran his hand through his hair, nudged his glasses, then fiddled with the knot of his new tie. Picking up on his son's nervousness, Derek said, 'Where's your mum? It's about time to get this show on the road, isn't it?' He looked up at the kitchen clock and then at his wristwatch, remembering that this was how he had felt twenty-two years ago, standing in his parents' tiny kitchen, before driving off to the church in his father's light green Zephyr to marry Cindy. God, how he had wanted to get all the churchy business over and done with, so that he could get on to the reception afterwards and pour a beer down his throat. He began strumming his fingers on the worktop.

'For goodness' sake, Dad, calm down,' Tiffany said, tossing her hairbrush on to the table. She bent down to tie up a purple ribbon she had threaded through the lace-holes of one of her boots. The other boot wore an orange ribbon and both laces matched perfectly the tie-dye baby-doll smock she wore over aubergine-coloured Lycra leggings. Straightening up, she added, 'Mum was outside ordering the caterers about in the marquee the last time I saw her.'

'Well go and give her a shout, will you? Tell her it's time to hit Westminster Abbey.' He watched his daughter go clomping off, then called after her, 'And tell her nicely. I don't want you rattling her today. Nervous, Bas?' he said, when Tiffany had gone.

Barry smiled. 'A bit.'

'Jesus, so am I! Sorry, shouldn't have said that, should I?'

'What?'

'You know, the Jesus bit.'

Barry laughed. 'Relax, Dad, it's me who's getting con-firmed, not you.'

Derek looked hard at his son and felt real pride. Bas hadn't put the weight back on that he'd lost and his face still showed signs of fatigue, but despite this, Derek found himself having to admit that Bas was better looking than he himself had ever been. A damned sight smarter as well. Ever since that dreadful phone call, the day of the barbecue, he had felt differently towards Bas. Strange, too, that since that day he hadn't made any further attempts on Charlotte; he had left the gate to that particular field wide open for Alex. God, he hoped he wasn't going through some kind of mid-life crisis.

He glanced across the kitchen at Bas again, seeing him no longer as some young kid who embarrassed him, but as a man . . . as a friend even. He cleared his throat. 'Look, Bas,' he started to say, 'things haven't always been . . .' He paused, frightened of making a complete fool of himself.

'What, Dad, what's up?'

Derek paced over to the french doors and looked out at the garden where there seemed to be dozens of people milling about, some with chairs, some with covered trays and some with bottles of wine. He ran his tongue over his lips, wanting more than anything a drink.

'What's wrong, Dad?'

He turned round to face his son. 'I just wanted to say . . . well, the thing is . . . I don't want to let you down today.'

'You won't.'

'But I have already. I mean, all these years I've been a . . . I've been a right bastard to you, haven't I?'

'Dad . . .'

'You see, Bas, I've never really understood you . . . Jesus, Bas, I've always been scared of you.'

'Scared!' Barry repeated, taken aback at this revelation. 'How do you mean?'

'It's no good, I need a drink,' Derek said, striding across the kitchen and pulling open the fridge. He offered a can of lager to Barry.

'No thanks.'

Derek hesitated, his hand poised over the ring pull, his dry throat gasping to be satiated, but his brain calling for restraint. 'Perhaps you're right,' he said, 'perhaps I shouldn't either. Don't want the old biddies at St John's keeling over from the fumes of probably the best lager in the world, do we?'

Barry watched his father move away from the fridge. 'Why are you frightened of me, Dad?'

Derek swallowed hard and pushed his hands down into his trouser pockets. 'Because you're so bloody clever! You've always managed to make me feel such a prat.'

Barry looked shocked. 'I never meant to.'

Derek shook his head. 'I know, Bas, and let's face it, I don't need anyone's help to make me look an idiot. I do a pretty good job of it on my own.'

'Dad, I . . .'

'Yeah, well, keep it to yourself,' Derek said, his face breaking into a sudden smile as he heard the sound of his wife's voice coming towards the kitchen. 'Don't want everyone knowing I've been baring my soul to you, do we?'

Cindy stood still for a moment and stared at Barry. 'You look wonderful,' she said with a faint tremor to her voice.

Barry didn't know what to say; first a confession from his father and now, after all these years, for the first time in his life, he had pleased his mother.

Derek followed behind his family as they walked up the aisle towards their reserved pew. He tried not to look about him, tried hard to fix his eyes on the chequered floor ahead, but he found it impossible. He hadn't expected the church to be so full. He knew that Bas had invited a few friends, but he hadn't said half the school was coming. And wasn't that Mr Knox, the headmaster, sitting next to Louise Archer?

'Okay, Dad?' Barry whispered, as they sat down.

'Yes,' Derek rasped back, 'I'm fine.' No I'm not, he thought, panic stricken and looking anxiously about the church. He caught sight of Iris Braithwaite beneath a stern black hat and felt the comforting urge to crack a joke. He turned to nudge Bas and found he wasn't there. Oh God, he said under his breath, seeing his son on his knees beside him. Was that really necessary? He waited for what seemed for ever before Bas surfaced. 'That better?' he asked.

At the end of the service, Charlotte tried to bundle Christina out of the church as quickly as she could. She had no intention of letting her friend stir up as much interest at St John's as she had in the Spinner.

'Oh Carlotta, such a handsome young man, that Barry is,' Christina said, as they passed through the lych-gate. 'No wonder you wanted to come back to Hulme Welford. How is it that there are so many gorgeous men in such a tiny village?'

'Good grief, Christina!' Charlotte said bad temperedly. 'Isn't one conquest in the village enough for you?' She had barely opened her mouth to Christina all morning; breakfast had been distinctly chilly, just two cereal bowls and a jug of cold milk between them.

'Carlotta, you are very cross with me, aren't you?'

'Cross, me? Why on earth should I be cross with you?'

Christina laughed. 'Oh, there's Alex.'

Charlotte turned and saw Alex coming up behind them as they were about to cross the road. Her mood wasn't improved by the wide smile on his face. 'Saw you sitting at the back of the church,' he said, drawing level.

'We were lucky to get a seat,' Charlotte said tersely. 'Madam here was so exhausted from your exploits in the Italian Gardens yesterday that she overslept.'

Christina rolled her eyes at Alex. 'I think our poor Carlotta still has her headache, she is in such a bad mood.'

'Oh rubbish!' Charlotte said, stepping off the pavement and causing a Lycra-clad cyclist to swerve out into the middle of the road. He threw his fist at her along with a few choice expressions.

'Neville, have you gone completely mad?' Louise raised her voice above the sound of Abba's 'Dancing Queen'. 'There's more than a thousand calories on your plate.'

'Yes dear, I know,' Neville answered, licking his lips in eager anticipation of sinking his teeth into the chicken drumstick on his plate, along with the large dollop of avocado dip, a couple of miniature sausage rolls and a slice of salmon and cream cheese roulade, 'and that's nothing compared to the calories I shall be consuming when it's pud time,' he added with a glint in his eye. 'Tiffany told me there's trifle, crème brûlée and strawberries and cream.'

Louise raised her eyebrows. 'I don't know what's got into you. Ever since you won that prize yesterday you've been quite unbearable. It was only second prize. Anyone would think you'd won the wretched cup.'

Neville beamed, took a large bite out of his chicken drumstick and chewed with lip-smacking delight. 'Time to circulate, I think. I should get yourself some lunch. Derek and Cindy have done Barry proud.' Leaving his wife floundering – for the first time in their marriage – Neville saw Charlotte and her famous friend sunning themselves on a bright pink swinging seat. He pulled in his stomach and strolled over.

'Hello, Dad,' Charlotte said, helping herself to a sausage roll from his plate. 'Mum know you've got all that?'

'Indeed she does.'

Something in her father's voice made Charlotte look at him more closely. 'You're looking very pleased with yourself. What have you been up to?'

He smiled broadly and cleared his throat as though preparing to make an important announcement. 'I won second prize yesterday at the gooseberry show: thirty-five pennyweights and sixteen grains with my Edith Cavell.'

Charlotte's mouth fell open. She was mortified. 'Dad, I was going to be there.' She looked sideways at her friend. 'But I forgot all about it, what with Christina turning up so unexpectedly.'

With perfect timing, Christina held out her hand to Neville. 'My dear man, I am so sorry to have kept Carlotta from you, do forgive me.'

Neville chuckled like a schoolboy. 'Think nothing of it.'

Christina patted the space between herself and Charlotte. 'Now sit here with us and tell me about this wonderful prize you have won. But first, what is a gooseberry show and who is Edith Cavell?'

Charlotte got up from her seat. 'Go on, Dad,' she said, 'don't hold back. This is your big opportunity. Tell Christina all about it while I go and get us some wine.'

She wandered over to the yellow and white striped marquee and saw Barry coming towards her, carrying a tray of glasses. 'Hello,' he said. Behind him a small, attractive girl appeared. She had a mop of curly red hair, which gave her an Orphan Annie appearance. She too was carrying a tray of drinks. 'I'll go on ahead and give these to the others,' she said, offering Barry a dazzling smile.

'Okay. I'll be there in a moment.'

'Nice girl,' Charlotte said, watching Orphan Annie make her way to the bottom of the garden where all the younger members of the party were congregated.

Barry nudged his glasses. 'She is, isn't she? Going to Leeds as well.'

'Really,' she said with a smile. 'Medicine?'

'No. Theology.'

'You do surprise me.' She turned to look up at the house as the sound of 'Sultans of Swing' came to a finish and 'Like a Bat out of Hell' started up.

'Dad loves this,' Barry said.

'And so does Malcolm Jackson, by the looks of things,' Charlotte replied watching what was taking place on the patio.

Cindy's carefully placed tubs of pink geraniums had been moved out of the way and Malcolm – now in mufti – together with Derek, was giving Meatloaf a fair run for his money. They were each holding a stick of celery and singing into the leafy end as though it were a microphone, the volume of their voices matching that of the hi-fi system.

Charlotte and Barry looked at one another and began to laugh. Then Barry handed her the tray of drinks and, grabbing a baguette from a passing waitress, he went up to join his father and the vicar. But when Barry approached the patio Derek seemed to falter, losing his place. He watched his son take up the baguette and start to sing. He put his arm round Barry and they sang together.

Most of the guests started clapping and cheering, and Barry's schoolfriends, hearing the noise, came up from the bottom of the garden to see what was happening. They soon joined in with the cheering, and a few went on to the patio to give their voices an airing and to pluck a few imaginary guitars.

Coming out of the marquee with her hands full of dirty

plates, Cindy took in the scene. Charlotte watched her anxiously. Cindy's eyes filled with tears and she began to cry. Charlotte ditched Barry's tray of drinks on a nearby table, took the pile of crockery from Cindy and hugged her.

'Oh God,' Cindy cried, 'why has it taken eighteen years for this moment? Why are families so horrible to each other?' She sniffed loudly and then pulled away from Charlotte. 'I'm sorry,' she said, patting her perfect hair into place, 'this is absurd.'

Charlotte stiffened. Peter had said exactly the same the morning he had died, the morning he had revealed to Charlotte that he was emotionally fragile after all, just like any other human being. Poor Cindy. Why couldn't she just throw away that self-protective mask she wore and let people see her for what she really was? But of course it wasn't that easy, was it? Wasn't that what she herself had been doing all the time she had been back in Hulme Welford, hiding behind her precious mask of widowhood?

They watched the show on the patio come to an end and joined in with the applause.

'Muffin 'ell!' shouted Tiffany, coming towards them with Becky on her back. 'Were they embarrassing or what?'

'I thought they were good,' Cindy said, reaching for the pile of plates Charlotte had taken from her. 'I'll go and put these in the dishwasher.' She walked towards the house.

'What's up with Mum?' Tiffany shifted Becky to a more comfortable position on her back.

'I think she's happy.'

'Happy? Mum? Never. Come on, Becky, let's go and find you something to eat.'

Remembering she was supposed to have been fetching some drinks, Charlotte followed Tiffany into the marquee and was knocked back by the mélange of canvas-induced heat, the scent of crushed grass and the not-so-sweet smell of fifty-seven varieties of overstretched deodorant. On one side of the marquee tables covered in yellow cloths held an assortment of buffet food and on the other side stood white dressed tables laden with shining glasses and bottles of wine, mineral water and beer. Charlotte helped herself to three glasses of wine and, wanting to get out of the oppressive heat as fast as possible, she turned to go but crashed into another guest. She jerked at the splash of cold wine against her chest. She looked up to see Alex.

'I'm sorry, Charlotte,' he said.

She glared at him, and for a moment, neither seemed to know what to say next.

'Mrs Lawrence,' boomed Iris Braithwaite, who knew exactly what to say. 'Just look at the state of you. What kind of a confirmation party is this? First Reverend Jackson makes a fool of himself out there in the garden and now you, in here, revealing . . . revealing all!'

Charlotte followed Iris's pointed stare and saw to her horror that the top of her white shift dress was practically transparent. She wasn't wearing a bra and the material was clinging mercilessly to her breasts. She plucked frantically at the thin fabric, trying to pull it away from her nipples. Looking up, she saw that Alex was smiling.

'How dare you!' she shouted angrily. She crashed the now half-empty glasses on the table behind her and turned and slapped Alex hard on the cheek.

'Mrs Lawrence!' roared Iris. But she got no further as she watched in horror Alex seize Charlotte and kiss her full on the lips.

'Mr Hamilton!' Iris almost pleaded, looking about her for back-up. But none was in the offing and the only voice to be heard was, 'Ooh look, Mummy, Auntie Charlotte's bonking that man who lives next door to her.'

'How dare you!' Charlotte repeated as Alex dragged her out of the marquee and towards the bottom of the garden. 'How bloody dare you do this to me . . . and in front of everyone.'

'Oh, come on,' he said, rounding on her, 'that's not what this is all about.'

'And what's that supposed to mean?'

'You know perfectly well what I'm talking about. You're as angry as hell with me, aren't you?'

'Yes . . . I mean no. What am I supposed to be angry with you about, apart from drenching me and making me look a fool?'

'You're angry because you think I slept with Christina. Isn't that right?'

She gave a loud derisive laugh. 'What you get up to in the privacy of your own rented house has got nothing to do with me.'

'Admit it, you're jealous.'

'I am *not*!' she exclaimed contemptuously, raising her hand once more to slap him.

'Charlotte,' he said, catching hold of her wrist, 'do as you're told for once and listen to me, *please*.'

She snatched her arm away from him. 'Okay then, I'm listening.'

He placed his hand under her elbow and marched her to the seat they had shared once before, overlooking the small pond. The cherub was still spouting and the ornamental toad looked just as ugly.

'I'm sorry for what just happened, Charlotte. I shouldn't have done that. But haven't you any idea how incredible you looked, standing there . . .'

'Don't be ridiculous.' She crossed her arms in front of her.

'What in heaven's name do I have to do to make you understand what you mean to me? Tell me and I'll do it.'

She said nothing, her mouth tightly shut.

'Charlotte, I think you ought to know that I've simply no intention of letting you go. You should know me well enough by now to realise I don't give up easily. And as to last night . . .' He lifted his hand to stop her outburst. 'Please, just hear me out. I've asked you several times before if you trusted me, right?'

'Yes,' she said, heavy irony in her voice, 'you have.'

'Have I blown it now?'

'Well, what do you think? Christina's my friend.'

'Would it have been okay with Heather, then?'

'No! I mean yes . . . oh Alex. For God's sake stop it, please.'

'Charlotte,' he said, 'nothing happened last night. It was an idea I should never have agreed to.'

'Whose idea?'

'Christina's.'

'I might have known. And what was this *idea* supposed to achieve?'

'To make you jealous,' he said, shamefaced. 'I'm sorry. It was a rotten thing to do to you. I never wanted to hurt you. And now I have and I hate myself for it. You'd think at my age I'd be past playing juvenile games like that, wouldn't you?'

Charlotte thought for a moment, taking Alex's words in. Jealous. Of course she had been jealous. Christina's plan had worked perfectly. She had lain awake all last night picturing Christina and Alex in bed; the images of them together had tortured her hour after hour in the dark until finally dawn had filtered through the curtains, allowing her a couple of hours of precious sleep. 'Well, it worked, didn't it?' she said, looking straight ahead of her. 'I *was* jealous.'

Alex sighed. 'I've made a right bloody mess of things, haven't I?' He took her hand and raised it to his lips. 'Do you think you could forgive me?'

'You know, I told Christina the other night that I probably could fall in love with you . . .'

'Charlotte . . .'

'No, let me finish. It's just that I'm terrified of discovering that it's me . . . that I'm not capable of making a relationship work . . . I'm petrified of taking the risk, of hurting you.'

'Try me. I'm pretty tough.'

'There's something else I'm scared of: Lucy.'

'Lucy? My God, you don't think I'm still in love with . . .'

'It's possible, isn't it?'

He put his hands on her shoulders. She tried to turn away from him, but he held her firmly and forced her to meet his gaze. 'We all have a past,' he said slowly, 'and Lucy is mine. When she died I truly thought there'd never be anyone else in my life. But now there is. You. I just wish you could understand what that means to me.' He clasped her face in his hands and kissed her. 'Charlotte, I love *you*.'

She felt her throat tighten with emotion. She tried to swallow, but found she couldn't. 'Alex, I could never . . . I couldn't cope with being second best again.'

'Peter was a fool,' Alex said sharply. 'He didn't deserve you. And anyway, can't you see that I love you because you're not second best? Charlotte, you're special. You're bloody wonderful!' He kissed her again. 'If I had my way I'd spend the rest of my days making you feel unimaginably special.'

'Oh you sweet-talker,' she said, managing a smile.

'Don't look at me like that, Charlotte. I don't know which is more devastating, your smile or the sight of you in that wet dress.'

Charlotte cleared her throat and changed the subject. She said, 'If you weren't making mad passionate love with Christina till gone midnight, what were you doing?'

'Talking. She's a great listener, a vital ingredient in her line of work.'

'She told you what she does for a living?' Charlotte was shocked.

'Yes.'

'Were you surprised?'

'I don't know really.'

Charlotte laughed, kicked off her shoes and stretched out her toes in the warm sun. She closed her eyes. Suddenly she felt unbelievably happy.

'You have lovely feet.' He picked one up and manoeuvred it into his lap. He began to stroke her ankle.

'Alex,' she said warningly.

'A shame your dress has nearly dried out.'

Charlotte looked at him. 'You don't give up, do you?'

'No,' he said, 'I don't. And I won't.'

34

The airport was full of eager travellers brandishing pass-
ports and pushing overloaded trolleys of luggage or wheel-
ing tombstone-sized cases on small squeaky wheels. Standing in the departure hall waiting for Christina's plane to be
called, Charlotte felt reluctant to part with her friend. There
was so much to be said, especially since yesterday, when
Alex had told her the truth about the night before. She had
hoped they might have had a chance to talk after Barry's
party, but it hadn't broken up until nearly two in the
morning, with Derek and Malcolm Jackson forming a
cabaret act. Poor Iris was the only guest to leave early. She
went home to The White Cottage next door and pointedly
banged all her windows shut.

'Now Carlotta, my dearest friend,' Christina said, bringing Charlotte's thoughts back to the crowded airport,
'promise me one thing, that you will try to be honest with
yourself.'

'Are any of us?' Charlotte said, shaking her head.

Christina smiled. 'You know, it takes courage, real
courage to know another person, but it is a supreme act of
heroism to know oneself and one's own darkness –
remember that, Carlotta. Remember also that you are now
brave enough to stop being evasive with yourself or
anybody else. You must believe that.'

Charlotte reached out to her friend and hugged her. 'I
wish you weren't leaving today. Can't you stay a few more
days?'

'No, Carlotta, my plane will be called in a few moments, and anyway, I want to get back to my wonderful Henri. He will be waiting for me and I have a feeling that I do not want to keep him waiting for too long. He is quite a catch, you know, I think I may marry him.'

'Somehow I can't imagine you married.'

Christina feigned a look of shock. 'You want me to remain the old maid, as you call it?'

'You could never be that, Christina. But what does Henri think of your . . . your work, your profession?'

'He thinks it is a very good one. Why?' asked Christina, a mischievous smile on her lips.

'Oh,' Charlotte said. 'He won't want you to give it up, then, if you marry him?'

'I don't think so. Do you think I should?'

Charlotte wasn't sure what to say. This was an area of their friendship that had been discreetly tucked under the carpet, or perhaps under the bedclothes.

'Carlotta, you haven't answered my question.'

She felt she was being pushed into a corner. 'It's just that, well, you know, I wouldn't have thought that what you do – entertaining men, I mean – and being a diplomat's wife would be terribly compatible.'

Christina's beautiful eyes opened wide and she laughed. 'Oh my darling Carlotta, at last you have been honest with me.'

Charlotte looked confused.

'All this time,' continued Christina, 'you really did think I was a prostitute, or as Mr Carlotta called me, a high-class tart.'

'You mean . . .? But what about all those men who kept calling on you?'

'Of course I had men visiting me. I'm a sex therapist.'

'A what?'

'Surely I don't have to explain . . .'

'No. No, I didn't mean that.' Charlotte was stunned.

How could she have got it so wrong? 'I just meant . . . Oh, Christina, I made such an awful assumption. A sex therapist. You!'

'Yes, me,' Christina said. 'You know, there are a lot of sexual problems in Brussels, so many men who have the big work drive at the expense of the sex drive.'

'But there was no sign on your door, no office, no surgery, or whatever it is you need.' Part of Charlotte still needed convincing.

'One has to be discreet, my clients have to be treated with sensitivity. A large sign saying 'This way for all those who can't get it up' would not do.

'But even inside your apartment, it looked quite normal, not like . . .'

'Ah, you did not see the whole of my apartment, but then so often, we only scan the surface of life, only perceive what we are prepared to let ourselves see . . . for instance, you view Alex as another Peter.'

Charlotte frowned.

'There, I'm right, aren't I? You think Alex will hurt you in the same way Peter hurt you. But he really loves you, Carlotta, and for all the right reasons. Now they have called my plane, I must go, Henri awaits.'

They hugged each other again. Christina kissed Charlotte flamboyantly. 'Forgive me for trying to make you jealous, Carlotta,' she said. 'Forgive Alex too.' Then she walked towards the passport control booth and turned round for a final wave.

Ivy Cottage felt uncomfortably quiet when Charlotte got back from the airport. She wandered about the kitchen, absentmindedly picking things up, then putting them down. She made herself a drink, but left it untouched. She went into the conservatory and flicked through a magazine. Bored and restless, she tossed it on the table and went outside. She sat beneath the fig tree and looked up at the house. She saw Alex staring down at her from what she guessed was his bedroom window. She held his gaze. Her throat went dry and she felt her heart beat faster.

She walked purposefully across the lawn and pushed open the back door. She had never been inside Alex's part of Ivy Cottage before. She found him at the foot of the stairs, his hand on the banister. He looked as though he was waiting for her, as if he had known she would come. She went to him, and without speaking she kissed him. He covered her face with kisses and then her neck, whispering her name, over and over. Breathless with what she knew was relief, she moved away from him, to the first step of the stairs. He followed her up.

In the gathering twilight Hilary tugged at the weeds in amongst the fading nemesia in the front garden. The summer would soon be over, she reflected; new school uniforms to buy and label, and autumn term PTA functions to start thinking about.

From across the road she heard the sound of barking followed by laughter. She peeped over the low wall she was hidden behind. She saw Mabel first, then Charlotte and Alex, arm in arm. When they reached the end of the drive she saw Alex whisper something in Charlotte's ear and heard her sister laugh again. Hilary crouched a little lower behind the wall as she watched in fascinated delight Charlotte kiss Alex. Not just a peck, but a full-blown belter of a kiss, their hands and arms all over the place. Heavens! gawped Hilary, goggle eyed. And to think it was all down to her.

Iris Braithwaite stood poised over her tomato plants, a green plastic watering can in her hand. In the dwindling light she peered through the privet hedge, hearing the sound of voices coming towards her along the footpath.

'If you ask me,' she said in a loud voice, 'it's time you got yourselves married. At least that way we'd all be spared scenes of depravity such as we witnessed yesterday after-noon.'

'I beg your pardon, Mrs Braithwaite,' said Charlotte, facing Iris through the hedge.

'It's what I should have done after Sidney died. I've regretted it ever since.' Her voice sounded out of character; wistfully pensive. 'Of course now I've left it too late. Who would want an old thing like me?'

'I'm so sorry, Iris,' Charlotte said, risking the uncustom-ary familiarity of using Mrs Braithwaite's christian name, albeit through the safety of the hedge. 'I had no idea. You've always given the impression . . .'

'That's as may be, but don't ever quote me as having said it. I shall deny it of course. Goodnight, Mrs Lawrence, you too, Mr Hamilton.'

With the smooth, darkening water of the mere behind them Charlotte rested her head against Alex's chest, his arms around her shoulders.

'I'm exhausted,' she said.

'Me too.'

She gave him a playful punch. 'I wasn't talking about this afternoon.'

'Oh,' he said.

'It's been an exhausting summer.'

'That's because you spent most of it fighting me.'

'Only because . . .'

He kissed her. 'I think I've found the only way to keep you quiet.'

'No. There is another way.'

He caught the look in her eye and laughed. 'You do realise, don't you, that I won't let you end up like Iris Braithwaite, blue rinse and sensible lace-up shoes?'

'Well, that's a relief.'

'Charlotte?'

'Be quiet, Alex, and take me home, please.'
'Your place or mine?'
'Alex!'

Time for a Change

To Edward and Samuel
who said it would be all right

Thanks to everyone who helped me through *Time for A Change*. To Big G for making it happen. To Helena for the gossip and inspiration. To Maureen for the laughs and kind words of encouragement. To Miranda and Adrian for the quality bed and breakfast facilities. To John and Eirian for the long, long phone calls. To Jonathan and Victoria at Curtis Brown.

And lastly, but by no means least, thanks to Jane and Sarah at Orion who know how to make a girl feel great.

'Change is not made without inconvenience,
even from worse to better.'

Richard Hooker 1554–1600

'The mind is its own place, and in itself
Can make a heav'n of hell, a hell of heav'n.'

Paradise Lost
John Milton 1608–74

Chapter One

Hilary Parker was a Monday-morning kind of person, but there was something not quite right about this particular Monday morning.

Usually she liked nothing better than to answer Terry Wogan back while bustling about her large cluttered kitchen, organising breakfast with one hand and sorting out her daughter's lunch-box and her son's chaotically filled sports bag with the other. She believed in taking the start of any day firmly by the horns and meeting it head on. Today, though, Hilary had the uneasy feeling that something was wrong.

She popped a couple of tea-bags into the Welsh-dresser-shaped teapot and swept aside the thought that a potential disaster was hanging over her.

Breakfast dealt with, she watched David make his escape to his estate-agency office in the centre of the village and then she began the ritual of shouting at the children to make them get a move on while she filled the washing machine and added a few last-minute thoughts to her shopping list. Eventually, when Becky had found her gloves – not the plain blue hand-me-downs from Philip, but the cream pair with the fluffy bits at the wrists – they set off to wait for the bus to take Philip to his new school. One child down and one to go, Hilary took her seven-year-old daughter's hand and crossed the road to join the posse of frazzled mothers heading for the local primary school.

It wasn't until Hilary had reached home and drawn breath

as she stood over the washing machine waiting for it to finish its last spin cycle that she could no longer avoid the unconscious thought that was battling its way through the Monday-morning rush-hour traffic of her mind. Had she forgotten to do something?

She bent down to the machine and looked through the glass port-hole. She caught strobe-like flashes of Becky's pink pyjamas being chased by a pair of Philip's rugby shorts. The machine finally shuddered to a halt and she waited impatiently before the door-release button would work. She debated whether to go and clear the breakfast things from the kitchen table but the nagging worry wouldn't leave her. Was she supposed to have telephoned somebody? Was it some PTA matter? Georgia D'Arcy could be quite sharp if she felt people weren't pulling their weight.

She pressed the button and started hauling out the clothes. First came Philip's determined shorts, followed by a tangled ball of leggings, socks and pyjamas. She tugged hard at the bulky mound until it finally burst free – pulling washing out through that black rubber ring always reminded Hilary of childbirth, especially Philip's difficult breech birth.

No. It wasn't something she hadn't done. It was David. Something *he* had done.

She moved the basket of wet clothes to one side and refilled the machine, pushing David's work shirts into the gaping hole; something that never failed to give her pleasure. Ever since they had been married and she had washed and ironed David's shirts she had enjoyed the smell of maleness from his clothes. She picked up the last of the shirts, the one he had worn last night for a Rotary Club dinner.

Last night. That was it. David had been talking in his sleep.

Then suddenly there it was: the nagging subconscious knowledge that had been with her throughout the darkness of night to the break of day was finally free and she heard David's words as clearly as if he were crouched on the floor next to her and reciting them: 'Catherine ... Hilary must never find out ... she'd never forgive me ... the children.'

She gasped and crushed the shirt to her face, but something hard in the folds of the fabric scraped against her cheek. She pulled out a small restaurant card together with a bill. The strip of paper had yesterday's date on it and showed it was a meal for two.

But David had said he was going to a specially arranged Rotary Club dinner ... 'Catherine ... Hilary must never find out.'

Well, she had. She bloody well had!

Hilary turned the key in the ignition of her car. 'It can't be true, it just can't be. Not David!' She pressed hard on the accelerator and launched her Renault Clio out of the drive. She hurtled noisily down Acacia Lane, ignoring the look of outrage on the face of Iris Braithwaite, who was already hard at work sweeping the autumn leaves from the baize-green lawn of the White Cottage, and drove through the village, past the row of shops including David's black and white half-timbered office and reached the supermarket in less than ten minutes. She bolted into the first available space in the car park.

Inside the store and propped up by a trolley, Hilary gripped her shopping list. Fruit, vegetables, she muttered. Fruit, vegetables. How could he? How could he have an— She scrunched up her shopping list unable to utter, even in her head, the unthinkable. Anger and bewilderment threatened to overwhelm her and she made for the neatly constructed pyramids of fruit, which normally appealed to her sense of everything being well ordered and exactly placed. 'A home for everything,' she always told the children. David wasn't tidy, though. Ties strewn all over the bedroom, trousers left on the ... Her throat tightened and her legs went wobbly. She felt sick.

Concentrate, she told herself. The shopping. She ripped off a plastic bag and with shaking hands she picked an apple from the top of the pyramid of Granny Smiths. She carefully selected another three but as she reached for a fifth her hand knocked against the pile and she watched in helpless horror as she set off a shiny green avalanche; apples cascaded onto the floor, bumping against her legs as they fell.

'No!' she cried out. 'No. Stop it.' Tears streaming down her cheeks she fled, aware of people staring at her as she skittered up the next aisle. She raced alongside the shelves throwing things into the trolley: baked beans, sweetcorn, flour, rice.

Why had she come? What was she doing here in the supermarket? She had just discovered her husband was having an affair and she was doing the weekly shop. Was she mad?

On autopilot she reached the aisles of frozen food. Pizzas, garlic bread, peas. Stir-fry vegetables, where were they? It was Monday. She always did stir-fry vegetables for David on a Monday evening. She leaned over the freezer, pushing the packets of frozen broccoli and cauliflower aside in her determination to find what she was looking for. 'Where are they? They must be here.'

'Hilary?'

She jerked upright and found herself face to face with her neighbour Cindy Rogers, who together with her husband Derek ran In the Pink, the thriving health and beauty centre in Acacia Lane. As ever Cindy's hair and make-up were immaculate. Hilary felt Cindy's critical eyes sweep over her. 'Hello, Cindy,' she said. Her voice sounded breathless and overly cheery.

'You okay?'

'Of course I am ...' *Catherine ... Hilary must never find out ...* 'I'm fine, why wouldn't I be?'

Cindy was convinced Hilary looked far from well. It was obvious that the Princess of Hulme Welford – as Derek called

4

their neighbour – had been crying. She said nothing and reached into the freezer for a packet of peas. If Hilary was upset and didn't want to share it, then that was her business and Cindy certainly wasn't going to get involved in someone else's problems if she could help it.

'I'm fine, really,' Hilary repeated, 'just a bit of a cold, that's all. It's always the same – soon as the children go back to school after the summer holidays it's an endless stream of colds and runny noses' ... *she'd never forgive me* ... 'run down a bit I suppose if I'm honest.' The flow of words came to an end and she stood staring blankly at Cindy.

'How's David?' Cindy asked. It was all she could think of to say.

'David? Oh, he's fine. Busy, working all hours, you know what it's like.' He had, hadn't he? He'd been coming home later and later just recently. And there'd been all those phone calls in his study with the door shut. Oh, it was all so obvious! How could she have been so blind and not seen the signs? Her lip trembled.

Cindy didn't know what to do. She hated being confronted with emotion of any kind. She'd spent a lifetime keeping hers in check and she expected others to do the same. 'I must get a move on,' she said. 'I only slipped out for some—'

'Yes, of course, don't let me keep you, I know how busy you are.'

'I'll see you, then, Hilary. Why don't you call me some time? Treat yourself to a facial.' Heaven only knows she could do with it.

'Yes, perhaps I will.' What, at their prices? Hilary watched Cindy push her trolley further up the line of freezer compartments. But suddenly she felt frightened at being left alone. Cindy might be an ice maiden but her company right now seemed infinitely better than her own. 'Cindy,' she called out. 'I just wondered ...'

'Yes?'

Something in Cindy's manner was so cold, so matter-of-fact, it prompted a mirrored reaction from herself. 'I've just discovered David's having an affair,' she said. She saw Cindy's hand tighten on her trolley, her long pearly pink nails curling round the metal handle. 'I ... I don't know what to do,' she added, her voice now wavering and not at all stoic as she had intended.

'Come on,' Cindy said, 'I'll take you home.'

They abandoned their shopping, left Hilary's car in the car park and drove back to The Gables in Cindy's brand new Celica.

'I'm all right. Really I am,' Hilary said, sniffing loudly as they got out of the car.

'Don't be ridiculous,' Cindy threw at her. 'You feel awful. You feel like your world's just come to an end. I should know.' She glanced over the road towards In the Pink. 'Just remember who I'm married to.'

Cindy made Hilary sit in a chair next to the Aga. She filled the kettle and to her shame found herself cringing at the state of Hilary's kitchen. While her own kitchen was spotless and devoid of clutter, Hilary's worktops were lined with rows of brightly coloured tins, above which were intricately carved shelves weighed down with a hundred and one cookery books. Did anyone really cook that much? She herself ate little more than a lightly dressed salad each night. She reached out for one of the brightly coloured tins, hoping it contained coffee. It was tea and behind it was a faint tidemark of dust. She pulled a face, wondering how long it was since there had been the merest hint of Jif behind the tins. Weeks possibly. Months more like it. But whatever else had been going on at The Gables just recently it certainly wasn't any cleaning, not to her way of thinking anyway.

She poured out the tea into two mugs with pictures of huge pigs on tiny legs. 'Here you are,' she said to Hilary, who was now sitting at the kitchen table, her elbows resting amongst the breakfast things. There were toast crumbs and splashes of milk everywhere. A blob of orange marmalade was clinging to the side of the jar. Cindy had to fight the urge to gather up all the offending mess and put the kitchen straight. It would be a far easier task than trying to reassure Hilary that everything would be all right. In her experience, once a man had one affair it didn't stop there.

Hilary sniffed. Cindy glanced round the kitchen for a box of tissues. All she could see was some kitchen roll on one of those green cast-iron posts. She tore off a square and handed it to Hilary.

'Cindy, I'm so sorry to land you with all this ... I didn't mean for you to ...' She sniffed again.

Blow it, for goodness' sake, Cindy thought.

'Look,' Hilary said. She pushed a small piece of paper across the table towards Cindy.

Cindy read the restaurant bill. It was familiar enough. 'Could it have been an ordinary business dinner?' she responded. She had asked herself the same question twenty-two years ago, a year after her first wedding anniversary.

'No,' Hilary whispered. 'He told me he was going to a Rotary Club dinner. He lied to me, Cindy. He's been coming home so late these past few weeks, and he talked in his sleep last night. Her name's Catherine ... How could he, how—' She began to cry.

Cindy didn't want Hilary to cry but she had no idea how to stop her. She sipped her tea and tried hard not to think of the grotesque pig in her hand. Instead she thought of herself twenty-two years ago: first she had found a restaurant receipt, then a letter and then the phone calls had started. She had tried to ignore it, just as her mother had advised her. 'Let him get it out of his system. It'll blow over.' And it had. Until the next gust of wind had brought with it another black cloud almost a year later.

Another sniff from Hilary made Cindy put down her mug

with a bang. 'So what do you want to do, Hilary?'

'Do? What do you mean?'

'You either confront David with this,' she waved the small piece of paper in the air, 'and risk losing everything, or you pretend you never found it.'

'Pretend I never found it!' Hilary shouted, her bloodshot eyes wide in bewilderment. 'How can I do that? I mean, he's been ... he's been ...' Her voice trailed away.

Cindy leaned forward. 'It just happens in some marriages. Particularly in mine.'

'Oh, God, Cindy. I'm sorry. I've been so insensitive to you, haven't I?'

Cindy nearly smiled. She knew only too well that in the nineteen months they'd been living in the village of Hulme Welford it had become common knowledge what sort of a man Derek Rogers was. It was also generally accepted that Cindy knew exactly what was going on but chose to turn a blind eye to his infidelity and, more importantly, nobody spoke to her about it. Though recently she had become increasingly concerned about Derek's behaviour, but for the life of her she could not work out exactly what was wrong. It was odd that he had taken to reading all those strange books – that really was out of character. It was the first time she had known him to sit still long enough to get through anything more detailed than the front page of the *Daily Mail*. She was concerned that Derek was dissatisfied with his life. Perhaps even the affairs had begun to pall for him. So what was next?

'You have to decide what it is you want, Hilary,' she said at last. 'I presume you do love David.'

'How could you ask such a question?'

'I'm sorry, but it would make things easier if you didn't.'

'Don't you love Derek, then?' Hilary asked, hardly daring to ask Cindy such a personal question. Before today their conversations had always been impersonal and along the lines of 'Tea or coffee?' and now here they were

8

discussing adultery and whether or not they loved their husbands.

'Goodness knows why, but yes, I do love Derek,' Cindy said simply. 'That's why I know it would be a lot easier if love didn't come into it. It's easier to be objective then.'

Hilary raised her tea to her lips. It was cold. She put it down. 'I can't believe we're sitting here and being so rational. I mean, aren't you at all shocked by what David's doing?'

'That's hardly the point, is it? The point is, what are *you* going to do?'

Hilary started to cry again. 'I don't know,' she squalled. 'I just don't know.'

'Do you want me to make a suggestion?'

'Please,' Hilary said, lifting her eyes from the screwed-up piece of kitchen roll in her hands. 'I need all the help I can get. I don't want to lose him, Cindy. He's the only man I've ever loved.'

'Right, then. The first thing is that you mustn't tell anyone. The fewer the people who know the better. From now on you've got to pretend, just as I said earlier, that you never found that receipt or heard David talking in his sleep. Hilary, you're going to have to fight for your husband.'

'Like you have for Derek?'

'Yes,' Cindy said grimly. 'Like I have for Derek.' She got up from her chair and took the mugs to the sink. 'By the way. Do you know who this Catherine might be?'

'Yes,' Hilary said softly. 'She's his new secretary.' Her body shook and she covered her face with her hands and sobbed.

Men, thought Cindy. Consistent if nothing else.

Chapter Two

'Okay, folks. Let's cut the waffle and get straight on. We've got a hell of a lot to cover tonight and I don't know about you but I'm knackered.'

Hilary saw the raised eyebrows along the front row of chairs which testified to the fact that this was not the usual way to open a St John's Infant and Junior School PTA meeting. There had been murmurs and more vocal expressions of dissent at the start of term when the outgoing chairwoman Patricia Longton had been replaced by Georgia D'Arcy, whose eager supporters were presently occupying the back row of seats in 2A's classroom, while Patricia and company were at the front where they felt they could be most intimidating. They had no idea what the members of the opposing camp were mouthing behind their backs.

Hilary did a quick head-count. Numbers were abnormally high. She suspected it had something to do with the free drinks on offer that evening – another change from the norm. She jotted the number down, disappointed that yet again she had been asked to remain as secretary – it was always the job nobody else wanted. She had hoped to step into Patricia's shoes herself but had withdrawn her name from the selection procedure when she found out she was up against the for-midable Ms Georgia D'Arcy who had been well backed by the hairy-armpit brigade, as David called the more maverick and Bohemian inclined mothers of the school – 'Hippie by nature and hippy in size,' he would laugh.

'First on the agenda,' Georgia D'Arcy announced, 'is to

thank all those present and note those absent.' She gave a deep laugh, which belied her bone thin appearance and put paid to David's hip theory. 'Jobs will, of course, be allocated to those not here to defend themselves.' There was raucous laughter from the back row, while Patricia and Co., scandalised, exchanged sideways glances, uncrossed and recrossed their legs, knowing that this jibe was aimed at one of their number – Kate Hampton, the PTA treasurer.

Hilary wrote down 'thanks' and wished she was at home. She was exhausted. It had been a long day since her discovery that morning that David was having an affair. She hadn't eaten a thing, had felt too sick even to consider food. It was as though a pneumatic drill was at work inside her and one minute she was hot, the next cold.

Cindy had told her to expect this. 'You'll lose weight as well,' she had gone on to say. So that was the secret to Cindy's enviable sylph-like figure, Hilary had thought cynically. 'You must keep yourself busy,' Cindy had instructed, as they drove back to the supermarket to pick up her car. 'Or otherwise you'll find yourself thinking of *them*.'

'But what else can I think of?' Hilary had wailed in return.

'Your children, for a start.'

After Cindy had left her she had tried to keep herself busy. But it was hopeless. All she could think of was David's betrayal. So wantonly had he destroyed all that was important to her. She had tried to occupy herself by switching on the television but had ended up mindlessly channel-hopping between *The Rockford Files*, a programme on flamenco dancing, an old movie with Bette Davis and horse-racing from Newmarket until it was time to go and collect Becky. They had walked back from school and, turning into the tree-lined cul-de-sac of Acacia Lane, they had made slow progress as Becky kicked her way through the drifts of fallen leaves in the gutter. 'Ooh, what's this?' she had said, her voice ringing with seven-year-old delight as she bent down. It was a dead mouse. 'Why's it so flat?'

'Because it's dead.'

'Will I be flat like that when I'm dead?'

'No, dear,' Hilary said, taking hold of Becky's hand.

'But why—?'

'Because it's been run over lots of times,' Hilary answered, feeling a bit flat herself.

She had been looking forward to Becky's company, hoping that her daughter's usual demanding behaviour would occupy her. It hadn't. Instead she found she was irritated by Becky's incessant chatter.

'Are you listening to me, Mummy?' Becky had asked in the kitchen where they usually sat with a cup of tea and a biscuit discussing what kind of day Becky had been subjected to.

'Of course, darling,' Hilary had replied.

'Fibber.'

'I'm not lying.'

'Yes, you are. I can tell.'

'Well, what were you saying? Tell me again.'

Becky pouted. 'No.'

Hilary had wanted to cry then. Had wanted to put her arms around her small daughter and talk woman to woman with her. But she couldn't. She'd have to wait at least ten years before she could do that.

Philip's first words when they went to pick him up from school after his rugby practice were: 'You been crying, Mum?'

Strange that her eleven-year-old son should have noticed her red eyes and not Becky. But that was Becky all over.

Tea-time had passed without event, until David had telephoned. Philip took the call. 'Dad'll be late,' he had shouted from the hall. 'He's got an appointment to keep.'

She had cried again, upstairs and alone. Then she had phoned Cindy's daughter Tiffany to see if she could babysit that evening. 'Sorry it's such short notice, I just can't keep up with David,' she had said brightly to Tiffany when she arrived to take charge of the children . . .

'I'd like that going on record.'

'Hilary, you are getting all this down, aren't you?'

Hilary lifted her head and wondered what on earth she was doing at a PTA meeting when her life was falling apart. 'Carry on as normal,' Cindy had told her. But not a word had she said about how one went about acting normally when all Hilary felt like doing was throwing herself on the floor and screaming like a baby.

'Hilary?' Georgia D'Arcy was frowning at her, one eyebrow quizzically arched beneath an urchin short fringe which had the colour and shine of a perfectly plump aubergine. Two fob-watch-sized ear-rings dangled either side of her sharp little face. She wore no make-up but her complexion was nut-brown, corroborating the fact that she worked outside each and every day. Since her husband Rory had left her two years ago the inhabitants of Hulme Welford had watched Georgia singlehandedly build up and run Hulme View Nursery on the edge of the village. She was not a woman who suffered fools and Hilary was a little in awe of her. 'I'm sorry,' Hilary said, 'what did you say?'

Georgia caught sight of Hilary's blank note-pad. She cleared her throat and waved to one of the mothers in the back row. 'Crack open those bottles of wine, will you, Cas, and pass some cups round while I have a chat with Hilary.'

Hilary heard muttering from the front row. 'Wine? We've never had wine before.'

'Right, chuck,' Georgia said, turning back to Hilary. 'What's up?'

Hilary's mouth opened but no words came out. She shut her mouth and tried hard to keep her lips from trembling.

'Come on, Hilary. I've watched you do this job standing on your head for the past three years. Granted I've seen you get flustered, but never incapable. Is it me? Can't you work with me? Because if so—'

'No. I mean, no, it's not that.'

Georgia smiled. 'Good. I know I put certain backs up, like

the frosty five there,' she inclined her head towards Patricia and company, 'but I'd hate to think I was that bloody obnoxious. I had hoped that you and I could get along. Perhaps some wine will help.' She got up from her chair and went across to where Cas Mitchell and Jo Shaughnessy were handing out plastic cups. Hilary noticed that the 'frosty five' were huddled together and guzzling their wine enthusiastically.

'Here,' Georgia said, coming back. 'Take a big mouthful. I'm not going to pry. It's none of my business what's given you a face like an empty coal scuttle, but I guarantee there's a man in there somewhere prodding you where it hurts.'

Hilary tried to protest but Georgia ignored her. 'Sod the lot of them, I say. If it'll help I'll take notes as we go along.' She drained her plastic cup, faced everyone and instantly called the meeting back to order.

Hilary felt herself relax for the first time that day. How good it was for somebody else to take charge. She had been grateful to Cindy earlier that morning for being there when she needed somebody in whom to confide, especially with her own experiences to tell, but she hadn't made Hilary feel any better. In fact, she had made her feel worse. Listening to Cindy had filled her with fear, as if all that lay in store for Hilary was a life stretching ahead as dauntingly as a life prison sentence. But Georgia was different. Somehow, in those few no-nonsense words Georgia had just uttered she had lifted some of the awful responsibility of the day off Hilary's shoulders. She felt enormously grateful to Georgia.

Chapter Three

Cindy came out of the *en suite* bathroom, a thick peach towel swathed around her slender body. She was surprised to see Derek sitting up in bed reading. He slapped the book shut when he saw she was there.

Just over an hour ago she had left him downstairs in the office. 'Paperwork,' he had said to her when she had looked in on him before coming upstairs for a bath.

'Everything's all right, isn't it?' she had asked. It was more by way of making conversation than worrying about the state of the business. All their married life Cindy had kept a firm hand and a weather eye on all the financial elements of the six salons they owned, as well as In the Pink. There was nothing that could get past her. But the persistent thought that had kept running through her mind these past few weeks was the possibility that Derek was sorting out their finances before leaving her. Since this morning when she had witnessed Hilary's shock she had felt it was an omen that she, too, was about to discover something unpleasant.

'Good book?' she asked, pulling a silk nightgown out of the stencilled chest of drawers by her side of the bed.

'Not bad,' he answered, his face noncommittal. He dropped the book face down onto the floor.

'You've been doing a lot of that lately,' Cindy said, her back to Derek. She let the towel fall away from her and slipped the nightgown over her head.

'A lot of what?'

She caught the defensiveness in his voice, and to avoid any

kind of confrontation that might lead to him declaring his hand, she said, 'Have you seen much of David recently?'

'Are you going to stand there all night giving me the third degree or are you getting in?' He pulled back her corner of the duvet and patted the bed.

She climbed in and sat stiffly beside him, taken aback by this simple act of courtesy . . . Helping her into bed? What was it she had heard once? A man about to leave his wife behaves out of character, starts doing all he can to please her before dealing the final blow. Scared, she said, 'Well, have you?'

'Have I what?'

'Seen much of David recently.'

He shook his head. 'Same as usual, I suppose.' He took off his paper-thin wristwatch and gold bracelet and placed them by the bedside lamp. 'What's all this anyway? What's the sudden interest in David?'

'Oh, nothing,' Cindy said, turning out her light. She lay back and waited for Derek to do the same. She had the feeling, though, that he wasn't about to. She was right.

'Cindy?'

'I'm tired, Derek. Can it wait?'

'I'm tired as well.'

'Then switch off your light.'

'Not that kind of tired.'

She sat up. Well, if this was it, if he was about to tell her he wanted a divorce, she might just as well pay attention and listen to him.

'Are you happy, Cindy?'

'Happy?' This was new. He'd never asked her that before.

'Because,' Derek said, facing her, 'I'm not.' He smiled.

Oh, God. How could he? How could he smile like that? Was it supposed to soften the blow? She clenched her fists under the duvet and braced herself for what she had feared all her married life.

'I've been thinking about us.'

'Yes.'

'I think it's time for a change.' He kicked back the duvet and suddenly leapt to his feet. He pulled on his towelling robe and started to pace the bedroom floor, backwards and forwards at the end of the brass bed.

'What kind of change?' she asked.

'Life-enhancing!' he shouted, throwing his arms up in the air. He stared at her, wide-eyed. 'Tell me, Cindy, how long have we been in the beauty business?' He didn't wait for her reply. 'Too long is the answer.' He came round to her side of the bed and sat down. She moved her legs away from him.

He grabbed her hands and held them tightly. 'I've had this idea. I've been working on it for weeks now. I want to turn In the Pink into a sanctuary of spiritual exploration, where the hopeless can find hope, where ...' He looked about him as though seeking inspiration from the walls of their bedroom. 'Where the unsure can find themselves. And let's face it, there's plenty of people like that here in Hulme Welford. What do you think?'

'You're hurting my hands,' Cindy whispered.

'I'm sorry,' he said, letting go. 'Don't know my own strength. But what do you say to my idea?'

Cindy was speechless. She was so relieved that Derek wasn't about to leave her that she knew at that precise moment she would agree to anything he wanted to do. She hadn't been so relieved since the day just over a year ago when she had realised that Hilary's sister Charlotte Lawrence was in love with her tenant Alex Hamilton. Prior to that day she had been convinced that Charlotte would be yet another woman to come between Derek and herself. But it was clear to Cindy, as it was to everyone in the village, that Charlotte and Alex were very much in love, and even Derek himself had made it obvious that he was no longer interested and had backed off.

'I don't know what to think, Derek,' she said finally.

He kissed her, excitedly. 'That's the whole point. Too many

people out there don't know how or what to think. We're going to help change all that.'

'A sanctuary of what did you say?'

'We'll run courses on inner healing, assertiveness, there'll be journeys of self-discovery—'

'There won't be any chanting, will there?'

'Chanting?'

'I've seen things like that on the television. People sitting on cushions, their eyes rolling and rubbish coming out of their mouths. It's so embarrassing.'

He laughed. 'Cindy, Cindy, this is me, Derek. Would I be that stupid?' He mentally ruled out that particular course he'd been reading up on. 'Come on, I feel like celebrating. Let's go down and open a bottle.' He kissed her again and ran his hand the length of her arm. 'Then we'll come back up and I'll take you on a journey of self-discovery.'

'I haven't said yes yet,' Cindy said, getting out of bed.

'You will, though. I just know it.'

Cindy had a feeling he was right.

Chapter Four

Becky looked pleased with herself, which Hilary knew meant one thing and one thing only: Becky had got one over her brother. For most of her young daughter's life Hilary had generally taken her side in any sibling fracas, but more recently her loyalty had been pushed to its limits and Philip had started to gain more of her respect and sympathy.

She handed Becky the packet of breakfast cereal and scanned her daughter's face for any tell-tale signs of guilt. She found none, only a look of undisguised glee.

She lifted the kettle from the Aga and made the tea, setting the pot down on the table. She then switched on the radio. 'Are we downhearted?' asked Terry Wogan from beside the bread bin. Yesterday the self-effacing Irishman had posed the same question and she had smiled back at him. Today she had nothing to smile about. She *was* downhearted.

When she had got home last night after the PTA meeting she had gone straight upstairs, calling to David in the sitting room that she had a headache and was going to bed.

She had pretended to be asleep when he had joined her. She had lain silently beside him, her body tense with fear and anger, trying hard not to think of him as he lay on the other side of the bed; a chasm of duplicity between them. And as the night hours had slowly passed she had punished herself again and again wondering how many times David had done *it* with *her*? And was *it* better with Catherine? Of course it was, she had told herself angrily while tiptoeing to the toilet at three in the morning, why else would he be

19

having an affair? Illicit sex early in the evening was always more fun than a tired ten-minute domestic session slotted in between Jeremy Paxman's *Newsnight* and setting the alarm clock.

Eventually, worn down by such torturous thoughts, she had given up the fight and had slept, but now it was breakfast time and any minute David would be out of the shower and downstairs. How would she cope? She would have to look at him, speak, even. She could avoid him no longer. There could be no escape.

'Mummy?'

'Mm . . .'

'What do you get if you hang—?'

'Please, Becky, not now.' Hilary could hear footsteps on the stairs. She pushed four slices of bread into the toaster.

'Daddy, what do you get if you hang Pamela Anderson upside down?'

'Shut up, Becky,' Philip said, coming into the kitchen behind his father. He knew he shouldn't have told his sister that joke. She was always getting him into trouble with her big mouth. 'Mum, these pants you got me, they're too small.'

Hilary looked at Philip. She could see David out of the corner of her eye. He was pouring himself a mug of tea. 'I only bought them at the start of term,' she said. 'They can't be too small.'

'Well, they are,' Philip said sullenly. He sat down. Hilary noticed him wriggling. She noticed too that David seemed to be moving uncomfortably in his chair. He looked shifty. Guilty. How long had he been doing that?

'Any toast?' he asked, barely lifting his eyes from the level of his mug.

'Coming,' she replied. She filled the toast rack and sat down.

'Flora?'

She looked up at David and moved towards the fridge. 'Flora,' she repeated slowly, taking off the lid and dropping the plastic tub onto the table. The china and cutlery rattled and a small yellow dollop of sunflower spread leapt out of the carton and landed on David's forehead. For a few moments nobody spoke, then Becky's shrill laughter, accompanied by the eight o'clock pips on the radio, filled the kitchen. Hilary didn't know what to do. The atmosphere was awful. She watched David take out his handkerchief from his trouser pocket and wipe his forehead. He didn't look at her and he wasn't smiling. 'Here,' she said, offering him the dishcloth. 'Wipe up your tea.' Then, sensing Philip wriggling next to her, she vented her anger on him. 'For goodness' sake, keep still!' she shouted.

Philip sprang from his seat. 'I can't,' he shouted back. 'It's these pants. I told you, they're too small.'

'And I told you they can't be.'

'Mummy's right,' Becky said slyly, her mouth a dark cavernous hole of Coco Pops. She started to laugh again and getting up from her chair she began pirouetting about the kitchen. 'Itchy bum, itchy bum!' she chanted delightedly.

Hilary looked from Philip to Becky. 'What have you done?' she demanded.

Philip's face darkened and he rushed from the room. 'Itchy bum!' Becky yelled one more time after him.

'Becky!'

Becky came to a balletic stop, her feet in a perfect first position. She looked like a penguin. 'I put itching powder in his pants,' she confessed with a giggle. Her words were said with immense pride and satisfaction. She looked like a smug penguin now.

For the first time ever, Hilary slapped her daughter, hard, on the legs and then she too left the kitchen.

Hilary couldn't bear to see the expression of humiliation on Philip's face as he climbed onto the school bus. His sister's antics would be with him for the rest of the day, a day that Hilary knew would be bad enough for him anyway. The transition from the village primary to senior school had not been an easy one for him. He had won a scholarship to the same school Tiffany attended and which her brother Barry had recently left with his string of grade A A-levels. He was now studying medicine at Leeds, and while Derek was vocally proud of his son, Cindy was more reluctant to sing his praises. It never ceased to amaze Hilary that Derek and Cindy could have produced two such unlikely children – Tiffany, possibly every mother's nightmare and Barry, every mother's dream son-in-law. On the other hand, she herself had produced Becky.

'Come on, Mummy. We'll be late. I want to get to school before Sarah Jenkins today.'

There was no contrition in Becky. No sense of remorse for what she had done to her brother. Not even any hurt pride or anger for having had her legs smacked. Life was just one series of practical jokes as far as Becky was concerned. It made Hilary even angrier, this blatant cavalier attitude to life that Becky had. It made her want to lash out at her daughter. Life wasn't one big bloody joke. Life was hard, tough, and just now hers was tumbling down around her. She stuffed her fists inside her coat pocket. She had always prided herself that while most of her friends gaily slapped their children for their wrong-doings, she had not. 'A mother who resorts to violence has lost the respect of her children and the right to their love,' she had said, on so many occasions. She could remember telling her own mother this after she had caught Louise smacking Becky for smashing a small china dog in her antique shop. Her mother had responded with, 'Don't you know anything, Hilary? You slap the respect into them.' And now here she was, twice in one day wanting to unleash an extraordinary amount of violence on her young daughter. She knew, though, that it had nothing to do with disciplining Becky and all to do with her anger and frustration at what David was doing to her and what he was apparently prepared to keep on doing.

They walked away from the bus stop and crossed the road towards the church. At the school gate Becky skipped away, leaving Hilary standing empty-handed. She felt relieved, rid of Becky and the threat of causing her any real physical harm. She turned to hurry off, not wanting to get caught by Patricia or any of the other mothers and be sucked into the early-morning school-gate gossiping session.

'Hilary, I was hoping I'd catch you.' It was Georgia D'Arcy striding purposefully behind her. She was wearing a mustard-coloured beret pulled down over her head and a bulky scarf wrapped loosely around her thin neck. She wore no coat, despite the sharp October wind that morning, just a striped woollen jumper and a pair of khaki dungarees.

'I'm sorry,' Hilary said automatically, 'I haven't had a chance to write up the minutes yet.'

'To hell with those. The meeting was only last night.'

Only last night. It felt an age away.

'Why don't you come for lunch? I usually break about twelve thirty. The nursery's as dead as the grave then.'

'Oh, I couldn't. I've got—'

'Suit yourself,' Georgia said, already moving towards her mud-splattered Jeep. She looked back over her shoulder. 'But if you change your mind, you know where I am.'

While Hilary cleared up the debris of breakfast she had the strongest of desires to smash everything within sight. She was shocked. She was not a violent woman, not one of those drama queens given over to fits of plate-smashing pique. But now she crashed and slammed her way about the kitchen until at last everything was put away. Then she found one of David's whisky tumblers in the sink. He usually had a glass of whisky when he came in from work each evening and never once did he wash the glass or put it in the dishwasher, he just dumped it in the sink each night. She picked it up and turned it round in her hand. She wanted to smash the glass, wanted the satisfaction of throwing it hard against the wall. But she thought of the shards all over the kitchen and knew she couldn't do it. How about outside? Against the garage wall, perhaps? No. There would still be all that mess to clear up afterwards; slivers of lethal glass everywhere. Surely there had to be some way of satisfying her craving to destroy something of David's that wouldn't involve her in clearing up any mess.

Yes, of course there was. She laughed. My God! She could laugh at a time like this. Was she going completely round the bend? She opened the glass display cupboard above the worktop at the far end of the kitchen. There were twelve tumblers in it, all expensive cut glass, which David's mother had given him over the years. In the drawer below Hilary found a plastic carrier bag and started filling it.

She drove to the local council tip, negotiating the bumps and bends in the road with infinite care – she didn't want to waste her precious cargo and be cheated out of her moment of revenge.

She drew up alongside one of the huge metal containers and put on her sunglasses from the glove compartment. On the back seat she saw one of Philip's old Manchester City caps. She grabbed it and forced it on her head.

She carried the glass-filled bag under one arm and made her way up the metal steps to the container. After a quick surreptitious glance to check that she was completely alone, she pulled one of the tumblers out of the bag and threw it. It was a lousy shot. A timorous effort that had the glass landing comfortably on a discarded piece of Axminster. It hadn't even broken. She felt no satisfaction. She picked out another tumbler and this time extended her arm for greater leverage. The tumbler crashed noisily against the sides of the container and Hilary felt the smash deep inside her. Thoughts of a broken heart flickered through her mind, but she dispelled this poetic image instantly by reaching into the bag for another glass. She threw it, followed by a fourth and a fifth. She was well into her stride now, remembering how at school she had been rather good at rounders; the best fielder, she had been called, noted for the quality of her over-arm throw; she had even won a small medal. 'Bastard!' she shouted, as the sixth glass shot into the air.

'Deceitful bastard!' she hurled after the seventh.

'Having fun?'

Shocked, she spun round and nearly toppled off the narrow gangplank and into the container. A strong arm caught her and held her firmly. 'Steady on. You don't look ready for the rubbish heap yet.'

'Somebody obviously thinks I am,' she muttered, without looking up. She clutched the half-empty bag to her, rigid with embarrassment and the realisation that she had been so engrossed in exacting what now seemed her petty revenge on David that she had been oblivious to everything around her, even the sound of an approaching car.

She moved to get past the man but found his hand was still on her arm. She slowly lifted her head, mortified that he must have heard all the terrible expletives she'd just uttered.

He released her and bent down to a cardboard box of junk at his feet and because there wasn't room on the gangplank for Hilary to squeeze past she was forced to stay where she was. She watched him drop his box into the container. A gust of wind snatched at a small wodge of photographs and they flew up into the air then fluttered momentarily in the breeze before settling like butterflies on an old mattress, its springs bursting through the stained and ripped fabric.

'No point in hanging onto the past,' he said, as though addressing the mattress. 'It only makes us cling onto what we once thought was important.' He turned and gave her an uncomfortably direct stare.

Hilary was glad of the sunglasses she was wearing, but not of the hat – it probably made her look like an eccentric old bat.

'Go on, then, throw the rest of them away, don't mind me.'

She suddenly remembered the bag in her hands. 'I don't need to,' she said, knowing that her voice didn't ring true.

'Perhaps you should, though.' And without another word he left her and walked back to where his car was parked just behind hers.

She watched him go. His hair was dark and slightly curly, streaked with grey and much too long, she decided. His plum-coloured jacket and black polo-neck struck her as being of good quality and quite fashionable but his moss green trousers were rumpled and baggy with creases at the knees. He looked vaguely arty or perhaps academic, or how those types were so often portrayed on the telly.

He drove away leaving her alone with her bag of whisky tumblers. She tried throwing the eighth glass, but she felt no anger, no excitement at what she was doing. She had run out of adrenaline and the moment had passed. She dropped the carrier bag on top of the mattress displacing the rubbish the man had just left behind him. A wedding photograph showed itself fleetingly before it coyly slipped under cover beneath an unwanted pushchair.

Hilary got into her car and drove home, disappointed and annoyed that the interfering man with his direct stare and untidy trousers had spoilt things for her.

Chapter Five

'Good God, Hilary, you look awful!'

'And what, in the name of all that is wonderful, is that disgusting smell?'

Hilary looked first at her mother then at Iris Braithwaite, whose nose was twitching like that of a cartoon mouse catching a whiff of cheese on the air. 'Must be *eau de* tip,' Hilary said, surprising herself with the unexpected sharpness of her wit. She tried to squeeze past Iris and her mother who was scrutinising her so intently that she was inadvertently blocking the path of a man behind her, pinning him against the racks of greeting cards with her shopping basket.

'Oh-the-what?' Iris demanded, her nose still taking in the air.

'I think my daughter was trying, in her oh-so-clever way, to tell us she's just been to the council tip,' Louise Archer said, shifting her basket from one hand to the other. Seizing his moment, the man behind her made his escape.

'Never go there myself,' Iris said. 'I have a perfectly good working compost heap at the end of my garden. Grass cuttings in one, peelings in another and leaves ... Hold it right there, young man.'

The escapee froze, his hand hovering over the door handle.

'It's you, isn't it?'

He looked at Iris. 'Sorry?'

'Dog mess. Check your shoes, young man, and watch where you're walking in future.'

He fled.

'Now, as I was saying, I always put my leaves in a separate area. Laurel leaves never rot down. Remember that.'

Oh, shove your leaves, Louise thought, as Iris moved away. I want to know why Hilary's looking as threadbare as an old rug. 'Join you for lunch, Hilary?' she said, curious rather than concerned, because nothing ever went wrong in her younger daughter's life. She watched Hilary straightening the magazines; a crooked *Bella* here and a slipped *Hello!* there. You always were a fidgety little madam, Louise reflected. 'Lunch, then – what do you say?'

'*Orgasms for the Woman in a Hurry*', Hilary read to herself from the cover of *Cosmopolitan* as she jerked it upright, trying hard to concentrate on anything but her mother. She couldn't bear the thought of Louise knowing that she had failed in her marriage. Oh, God. It was such basic stuff. She was ashamed that she had failed to please her man. She pulled out the magazine and pretended to flick through it, while all the time thinking of a way in which she could avoid having lunch with her mother and end up spilling the beans.

'Hilary, in my opinion if you haven't learned about multiple orgasms by now it's much too late. Now do you or do you not want me to join you for lunch?'

'Multiple what?' exploded Iris Braithwaite, from the revolving rack of tights.

'Multiple orgasms, Mrs Braithwaite,' called out Ted the Toup helpfully from behind his counter. His hands covered in newspaper print, he was putting the finishing touches to his display of confectionery.

Iris gripped the ends of her headscarf as though protecting herself from a high wind. 'All I came in for was a pair of tights. I did not think I would be subjected to the smell and language of the gutter.' She slapped a packet of tights on the counter.

Ted the Toup's face cracked into a nicotine-tinted smile. 'Three pounds fifty, love.'

'Don't you love me anything, you charlatan!' Iris roared. 'Three pounds fifty, indeed. Last week I only paid—'

'Ah, well, these ones you've picked out are special, like.'

'I should say they are at that price. Explain yourself.'

Ted leaned forward, his patched elbows resting on the counter. 'Peephole gusset,' he said confidentially.

Iris gasped and shrank back from Ted's leering face.

He picked up the packet of tights and began reading from the label, curling his tongue round the words as though giving them extra meaning, ' "Glamorous and fashionably hygienic, to leave you cool and sensual—" '

'Stop!'

'You haven't heard the best bit. It says here—'

'Outrageous,' fired back Iris, breathless with shock. 'Absolutely outrageous.' She turned on her heel and pushed past Hilary and Louise. She gave Ted one last look of disgust before slamming the shop door behind her.

'What about you, ladies?' Ted tried gamely.

'Not now, Ted,' Louise said, amused. She had other fish to fry. She took Hilary by the arm and led her outside.

In the chill, leaf-swirling wind Hilary felt like a small child who had just been dragged out of a sweetshop before having the chance to spend her pocket money. She said, 'But I didn't get my magazine, Mother.'

'Never mind your magazine, Hilary. Just what the heck is going on? You look dreadful. Come on, out with it.' Stern words had always worked with Hilary when she was little; they would have her trembling into submission in no time at all.

'Why aren't you at your shop, Mother?'

Louise frowned, annoyed that she didn't seem to be getting through to Hilary. Normally her daughter was a giver of information, painfully honest and unable to avoid answering a direct question, and here she was parrying with all the ease of a well-seasoned, tabloid-hounded politician. 'It's Tuesday, Hilary,' she said. 'I never open the shop on a Tuesday. It's my day off, you know that. Would you like to join me for lunch?'

'Lunch?' Hilary tried to appear thoughtful, as though giving the invitation all her consideration. Inside she was panicking. If her mother got her round the lunch table she would never be able to withstand her lightbulb-in-the-eye interrogation tactics. 'Oh, yes,' she suddenly said, inspiration dawning.

'Krakatoa erupts,' Louise said scornfully. 'I'm getting through at last. Shall I come to you, or shall—'

'Sorry,' Hilary said, sounding as genuine as she could, 'but I'm having lunch with Georgia D'Arcy.' She edged towards the door of the newsagent. 'I really must get her a box of chocolates.' And before her mother could say another word she shot back inside the shop.

Louise was put out. She decided to pay a call on her elder daughter, Charlotte, to see if she knew what was going on. She wheeled her bicycle along the pavement, passing the row of shops until she came to the end of the road where the expensive kitchen and bathroom shop had been in business, selling Jacuzzi baths and rainforest-free mahogany units at vastly over-inflated prices – until last winter, that was, when the market for conscience-clear goods at unrealistic prices had slipped down the plug-hole, as David had joked when he'd put the leasehold of the premises on the market. 'It's impossible to be truly environmentally friendly and make money,' he'd said. A few days later they had all been surprised when Charlotte had pulled out her cheque book and announced she would like to take on the lease and run her own business again. 'Another attempt at turning back the clock, Charlotte?' Louise had said to her daughter.

Charlotte had had her own shop years ago, before her marriage to Peter. As sons-in-law went Peter hadn't been a bad effort; not the worst but certainly not the best. Louise herself didn't like men who had too high an opinion of themselves and Peter had definitely thought a little too well of himself for her liking, though since his death she was conscious that he had gone up in her estimation. Death did that, she supposed, softened and smoothed the bits that had previously irritated and snagged on one's nerves.

She propped her bicycle against the plate-glass window of Charlotte's shop and thought of Alex, who was shaping up into a much better proposition. She opened the door.

'Hello, Mother.'

'Surprised you've not got yourself one of those twee tinkly little bells for the door.'

'What, and go completely round the bend?' Charlotte replied, wanting to add, *like you*.

'Of course, you wouldn't catch me dead with one,' Louise continued, coming further into the shop. 'I've come in for some of those dried flowers,' she said, deciding to take the devious route for what she really wanted, 'the dusky pink ones that look like they were used in Miss Havisham's wedding bouquet.'

'Sorry, I've sold out of those. And, anyway, I told you last week I wasn't going to let you have any more, not after Mrs Braithwaite told me you were selling them on at double the price.'

Louise smiled. 'That's the antique trade for you.' She rested her heavy basket on the corner of the stripped pine table which Charlotte used as a counter. She watched her daughter arranging some large china ducks, their long necks straining over the wooden shelf, black beady eyes staring dumbly at the floor. She was reminded of Hilary's expression just now at Ted the Toup's.

'Anything else I can help you with, Mother?'

Louise wasn't going to be rushed. 'Set a date for the wedding yet?' She knew that would annoy Charlotte and set up a suitable smoke-screen for the real question she wanted to ask. If Charlotte did know what was wrong with her sister and was under orders to keep quiet, Louise knew it would be a waste of time coming out directly with 'What do you know about Hilary?' Charlotte would only dig in her heels and refuse to tell her. Her elder daughter had always played it close to the chest and it had irritated the hell out of her.

Charlotte swung round. 'No, not yet, but I'll stick an invitation in the post for you, just as soon as we know ourselves.'

'You've lost one husband, Charlotte, you don't want to let Alex slip through your hands. Husbands aren't like buses, they don't come along in threes.'

Charlotte returned her attention to the necky ducks. 'If he's that slippery a customer, I'm not so sure he's worth keeping.'

'And if you're going to bore me with your enigmatic routine, Charlotte, I'll be off.' She picked up her shopping basket and said casually, 'Seen much of Hilary recently?'

'No. Why?'

Louise decided to offer a snippet of information. 'I've just seen her in Ted's. She really doesn't look at all well.'

Charlotte was suspicious. Her mother rarely noticed what was wrong with anyone, and if she did, she never commented on it. 'Perhaps she's got a cold. You know what a terror Becky is for bringing germs home from school.'

Louise knew only too well what a terror her granddaughter was, and not just where germs were concerned. She said goodbye and left.

Charlotte stood in the window and watched her mother cycle across the main road, past the church and towards Pippin Rise, the new development which had been built almost on the doorstep of her parents' black and white thatched cottage.

Even when Louise had disappeared out of sight, Charlotte remained where she was. Why had her mother asked about Hilary? And why did she have to keep bringing up the subject of marriage? That was the third time in as many weeks. It really was none of her business, but all the same, she hugged the thought to herself that only that morning before she'd left to open up the shop she and Alex had been discussing what they were going to do.

He had been Charlotte's tenant, and technically he still was, but now he used the granny annexe of Ivy Cottage solely as his office. Since last Christmas when he had moved in with her, Charlotte had lost count of the number of times he had proposed. He had been so patient, never once giving her an ultimatum, and not once had he made her feel guilty for her indecision. But last week she had finally said yes to the idea of marriage. He had been delighted, had wanted to rush her down to St John's there and then. 'No!' she had cried, as he'd swung her round.

'Now don't give me any of that,' he'd shouted. 'You can't change your mind. I clearly heard you say yes.'

'I mean yes, I'll marry you, but no, not straight away. Let me get used to the idea.'

He had bought her a ring the very next day. It was beautiful and, looking at it now on her finger, she felt so sure she was doing the right thing. Her hesitation in marrying Alex was nothing to do with him, but all to do with herself. The latter years of her seven-year marriage to Peter had had a disastrous effect on her self-confidence, and the circumstances surrounding his sudden death in a car crash had compounded her already low sense of self-worth to the extent of making her think she wasn't capable of making a relationship work.

A cold draught blew in at her feet through the badly fitting door and she moved over to the counter where Mabel, her West Highland White terrier, was curled up in her basket in front of a small fan heater which was gently humming to itself. She smiled, reminded of Alex. He had been humming this morning in the shower and she had thrown a wet sponge at him for his choice of song – 'I'm Getting Married in the Morning'.

'Don't waste your breath,' she had said, laughing at him, loving him for his ability always to make her feel *something*. But to surprise him, just as she was leaving the house she had promised she would make up her mind by that evening as to when they would get married. He had telephoned her three times already that morning. She shook her head and suddenly thought how happy it would make not just herself but her sister to see her and Alex married. How busily Hilary had schemed all last summer to get the pair of them together but, then, she always had been such a shocking schemer.

Charlotte's thoughts strayed from her sister to their mother. It was so unlike Louise to notice anything amiss with either Hilary or herself, and yet she had been very specific: 'She really doesn't look at all well.'

Charlotte bent down to a box under the pine table and opened it up. It was full of the dusky pink roses Louise had asked for. She filled a large wicker basket with them and decided to call in at The Gables on her way home later that afternoon.

Chapter Six

Hilary parked in the gravelled area alongside a row of large greenhouses; they were constructed of plastic sheeting and as she got out of her car a gust of wind rippled their sagging sides, making them flap and snap like sails in a boatyard.

She was nervous. It had been all very well using Georgia D'Arcy as an excuse for avoiding her mother but the trouble was, as she'd known the moment she'd uttered the words, she was then committed to following through. She had never been able to lie to her mother and, having told Louise she was seeing Georgia, there was nothing else for it but to do exactly that or the inevitable would happen – her mother would find out she had lied.

She had fibbed once to her mother when she was ten years old. It had been her birthday, and while Louise had been busy in the kitchen preparing for the party and putting the finishing touches to her birthday cake Hilary had been in the sitting room, playing with one of her presents, a plastic dolls' house, which for months she had longed for and had been promised. She had been delighted with the gift, so much so that she had hopped and skipped around it. But disaster had struck. She had slipped and kicked it with her black patent-leather party shoe. Quick as a flash she had carried the dolls' house to her mother in the kitchen and said – with real tears welling up in her eyes – 'Mummy, look, there's a crack in one of the walls. It must have been like this when you bought it.' The next day, she and the dolls' house were taken to the toy shop in Macclesfield where Louise had made the purchase. Hilary had stood there, mortified, in front of the little bald man who, from behind his counter, was being pebble-dashed with a vitriolic attack on shoddy shop practice. When the man tried to defend himself, Louise, with a curious smile on her lips, had said very quietly, 'On one side of this counter stands a liar.' Unable to cope with ten-year-old guilt and feeling sorry for the poor pink-headed man, Hilary had piped up with, 'It's me. I'm the liar.'

In the car going home she had cried and her mother had said, 'I knew all along you were lying, Hilary. I hope I've taught you a valuable lesson today. Lies always have reper-cussions.'

She glanced at her watch, it was just before twelve thirty. Probably Georgia wouldn't be over at her bungalow yet. Through the smeared window of a small battered caravan beneath an oak tree Hilary saw Georgia's bereted head bobbing to and fro as she talked into a mobile phone. When Georgia caught sight of Hilary she beckoned her over.

It was three years now since Georgia and Rory had moved into the village with their young daughter Chloe. Shortly before this Rory had lost his job with a local pharmaceutical company and had decided to use his redundancy money to start up his own landscaping business, but within a short space of time things started going wrong and gossip began flying round Hulme Welford. The most credible rumour Hilary heard was that Rory had started to drink more than was good for him and the offers of work had dwindled away to nothing. Not long after this Georgia had thrown out her husband and instigated divorce proceedings. Rory had been a good-looking man, full of bonhomie, and had been generally well liked in the village, so not surprisingly Georgia was cast as the villain of the piece. 'A woman should stand by her man,' was the commonly shared view and voiced principally by Patricia Longton. And Georgia had not. She had kicked a man when he was down.

Before yesterday Hilary would have agreed with these smug sentiments. But now she wasn't so sure. Based on what she had unearthed in her own marriage in the past twenty-four hours, what did any of them know of Georgia's and what had gone on before? How easily they had taken sides, because they had all been fortunate enough to have the safety net of a trouble-free marriage.

But that had all changed now.

She remembered how David had come home one evening and said, 'Poor old Rory's ended up with nothing and that hard piece of an ex-wife of his has just been into the office today and bought a two-acre parcel of land up at Hulme View.' Even Hilary had known that Rory had ended up with a whole load more than nothing – namely, most of their savings, what was left of them. In order to buy the land for the nursery Georgia had sold the house, which she'd been awarded as part of her settlement, and she and Chloe had lived in a draughty old caravan while she got the nursery business up and running, working and saving like mad to have a small bungalow built for the two of them.

'Come in,' Georgia mouthed as Hilary peered into the caravan. She stood awkwardly amongst the piles of paper-work, seed catalogues and ripped-open bags of potting compost and bone meal. Georgia pointed to a bench seat and after Hilary had brushed off a sprinkling of white powder, which she then identified as mildew, she sat down and tried her best to pretend she wasn't listening to Georgia's one-sided conversation.

'I don't give a damn about your mother's plastic hip. I ordered that forest bark two months ago ... Well, don't complain to me. I didn't vote this bloody government in ... I'll expect you tomorrow, or I'll come over and do your mother's hip for her.

'Hi,' Georgia said, facing Hilary and slipping the phone into the pocket on the front of her dungarees. 'Come on, let's go over to the house. It's freezing in here.'

Hilary was glad to get out of the caravan. The confined space, together with its damp coldness, was having a depressing effect on her. How on earth had Georgia and Chloe stuck living in it? She followed Georgia down the rusting metal steps, across the gravel car park to a muddy path that led to the recently built bungalow, which in Hilary's mind sparkled like an oasis in this jumbled mess of dirt and toil. She imagined the house to be warm, clean and inviting.

Georgia unlocked the front door and kicked off her mud-caked boots. 'I didn't think you'd come,' she said. 'Throw your coat over the back of that chair and come on through to the kitchen.'

Hilary's oasis image was fast disappearing as she watched Georgia washing her hands at the sink amongst an enormous pile of dirty pots and pans. The kitchen was almost as untidy as the caravan, but at least it was warm and there was the tantalising smell of garlic and herbs, which certainly had the edge on bone meal.

'I'm not going to apologise for the state of the place,' Georgia said, as she bent down to open the oven. 'I know it's a mess, but Chloe comes first, the nursery next and the dust and mess a poor last.'

'It's not a mess at all,' Hilary said, politely turning away from the sight of Georgia's and Chloe's underwear drying on the radiator. To her shame she found herself thinking how much more acceptable washing was hanging from the ceiling on one of those smart Edwardian clothes-dryers.

'That's a load of crap, Hilary, and you know it.' Georgia slammed the oven door shut. 'Now what have you got there?'

Hilary looked down at her hands, suddenly remembering what she was holding. 'They're for you. Chocolates. I thought you'd like them.' She offered them to Georgia and found herself holding her breath. *Déjà vu*. She breathed out. No, it wasn't *déjà vu* at all. It was the past, something that had happened a long time ago, when she had moved on to grammar school, joining Charlotte who was already there in her third year. In her first term she had developed a monumental crush on a girl in the fifth form and after days of plucking up courage she had approached Naomi Scott with a box of chocolates that had cost her several weeks' pocket money. 'I thought you'd like them,' she had said. Naomi, beautiful as well as clever, had taken the box and walked away without even thanking her. Later that day Hilary heard Naomi laughing about her with her friends. She had cried that night in bed, trying to come to terms with her first lesson in rejection.

And now something very real and intense inside her was making her hope that Georgia might be her friend, that she wouldn't reject her.

'How bloody daft and lovely of you,' Georgia said, taking the box and placing it beside a pile of ironing. 'I can't remember the last time anyone gave me chocolates.'

Lunch was better than Hilary had expected. She hadn't thought a radical like Georgia would be able to do anything creative in the kitchen. She didn't know which most surprised her, that there was meat on the table and not beans and pulses, or that she had actually managed to eat any of it. It was her first meal since yesterday morning.

'We must leave enough for Chloe's tea,' Georgia instructed, scooping out a second portion for Hilary, 'or I'll be in the doghouse for days.'

Hilary could think of nothing more unlikely.

'So, Hilary, what gives in Acacia Lane?'

'Gives?'

Georgia smiled. 'What's going on at The Gables that's made you take up a wild invitation for lunch with a heretic like me?' Georgia watched Hilary closely as she finished chewing what was in her mouth. She was aware she had just put Hilary on the spot, and even more aware that she was making her guest nervous. She was often told she made people feel uncomfortable. It was her honesty, she supposed.

People didn't usually appreciate such directness. But life was too short to waste time beating about the bush.

'Nothing,' Hilary said at last. 'Why ever would you think there was?'

'In my experience, there's always something going on at home. When there isn't, that's the time to worry.'

Hilary felt torn. Something made her want to confide in Georgia, but Cindy's words telling her to keep quiet were rattling around inside her head. 'How long is it since you've been on your own?' she asked, already knowing the answer, but finding herself wanting to hear it from Georgia herself.

So that's it, thought Georgia. Our old friend matrimonial trouble giving Hilary grief. Wasn't it always?

'Two marvellous years,' she answered, resting her elbows on the table and her chin on her roughened and scratched knuckles. A moment passed, then she threw back her head and laughed, her long ear-rings dancing against her slender neck. 'Okay, then, I admit it. One exhausting year preceded by one year of sheer hell.'

'Why did—?'

'Why did I throw him out? Is that what you want to know?'

Hilary nodded and lowered her eyes, unable to meet Georgia's gaze.

'Ever since Rory had been made redundant he'd been knocking about with another woman. Coming here to Hulme Welford was supposed to have been a new start but I soon found out that he was still seeing her. And why did our marriage go wrong in the first place, is probably your next question. The answer to that is easy. Like so many men, Rory couldn't handle the dent that redundancy had made in his self-esteem. And yeah, sure, I'm fully aware that Rory is by no means the first man to seek out somebody else to bolster up his deflated ego.'

'So where is he now?'

'God knows. We've not seen hide nor hair of him for over

six months. But Chloe and I are just fine without him. At least now I don't have to spend half my time mothering an overgrown schoolkid who still needs to be told what a good boy he is. Men just never grow out of needing a mother figure to tell little Johnny, or little Rory ...' she hesitated before adding one other name '... or little David, what a good boy he is. When they come home from work, their briefcases bulging with the flimsy achievements of the day, they're only after one thing, and that's to be told what clever boys they are. Do you see what I mean?'

'I think so, but—'

'It's all sick. If they think they're not getting enough praise at home they simply look elsewhere.'

'Why did you mention David's name just now?' Hilary said quietly. 'He isn't like that.'

'You sure?'

Hilary thought for a moment. She tried to think of an average evening spent at The Gables: David would come home from work, pour himself a glass of whisky and stand in front of the Aga – getting in her way – and proceed to tell her about the latest house he'd sold or been offered to sell. And she, while getting the supper ready and supervising Philip's homework, would nod and say things like, 'That's nice, dear.' She swallowed hard. Maybe Georgia was right: perhaps David had simply found somebody who would listen more attentively; somebody who would ask all the pertinent questions that she was too tired or bored even to consider.

She put down her knife and fork and looked up at Georgia. For a split second Cindy's words from yesterday went quiet inside her head and she seized her opportunity, wanting Georgia to know ... wanting Georgia to help her. 'David's having an affair,' she heard herself say. 'Oh, God. This is like something out of a Joanna Trollope novel.'

'Get out of here. This is an Aga-free zone, I'll have you know.'

'Please don't joke with me,' Hilary said, her stomach

beginning to churn, her throat tightening with the effort of holding back the tears.

'I'm sorry. So what are we going to do about it?'

'*We?*'

'Good grief, Hilary. You don't think I'm going to let you go through this alone, do you? Hey, come on. Don't go all trembly on me.'

'I can't help it,' Hilary whispered, tears filling her eyes and trickling down her pale cheeks. 'I can't help it. You're so much nicer than Naomi Scott.'

Georgia didn't have a clue what Hilary was talking about, but she got up from her chair and went to her. She knelt down and put her arms round Hilary's shaking shoulders.

The comfort of Georgia's slight body against her own made Hilary lean into her and she cried all the more.

Chapter Seven

'So, Dad, let me get this straight. You want to give up the world of curling tongs and mud packs for the world of emotional cripples looking up their bums?' Tiffany let out a loud laugh. 'This I have to see!'

Derek looked across the office desk at his seventeen-year-old daughter. He had just told Tiffany about his plans for changing In the Pink into a centre of self-discovery and he knew, as any parent knows, that his teenage daughter was probably his biggest critic. Part of him, the old Derek, wanted to shout at Tiffany for her insolence and tell her not to be so bloody rude, but the new Derek was struggling to remain a paragon of selfless patience and understanding. There was no room for outbursts of indignation and anger in the new world he wanted to create. 'Prejudice against any new idea does, of course, betray an underlying sense of inadequacy and inferiority,' he said smoothly, pleased with himself for being able to quote so easily from the book he'd been reading earlier in the salon while Mrs Jeffs was at the back wash.

Tiffany laughed again. 'Muffin 'ell, Dad. What's got into you? You've not been the same since Barry had his born-again experience.'

Derek shuffled some papers in front of him. He kept his eyes down, finding Tiffany's words uncomfortably near the truth, but he'd be damned if he ever let on. All that talk from Bas of a living Christ had brought him up short and left him feeling embarrassed but strangely curious. Sure, it was all gobbledegook, but for the life of him he couldn't work out how a smart bloke like Bas could get caught up in it. But that wasn't really what had got to him. What had was Bas being flown home from Romania with meningitis. That was when things had got to him. He'd always kept his distance with Bas because secretly he'd been afraid of him. Bas was so effortlessly more intelligent than he was, but seeing his son helpless in that hospital bed, not knowing whether he was going to live or die, had made him feel so useless, had made him face up to how badly he'd let his son down. That was the moment when something – something he didn't really understand – had touched him on the shoulder and said, 'Get a grip, Derek old mate. There's more to life than touching up Mrs Jeffs' roots every three weeks.'

But it wasn't until he'd been listening to some of his customers discussing how they had to get home early that afternoon because they wanted to catch the latest daytime discussion show on the telly that an inkling of an idea had begun to take root in his mind.

The following day he'd set the video to record the pro-gramme and later that night, when both Cindy and Tiffany were asleep in bed, he'd secretly watched a dozen or so Americans laying out their neuroses in front of a live audience along with countless numbers of viewers. An expert in an absurd waistcoat with an equally absurd name – Dr L. S. Nutter III – was there on hand to help these troubled people work through their phobias and self-doubts. He'd been gobsmacked. It was incredible. And rewinding the tape he'd watched the bit again where a grossly overweight man had stood up and said, 'Help me! I'm terrified of my left hand.' He had gone on to explain in detail that ever since the age of thirteen he'd been unable to bring himself to use it. Dr L. S. Nutter III had suggested that the man was, in fact, lying and that what he was really saying was, 'Hey, look at me, I'm into self-abuse and what about it?' The fat man had leapt out of his chair and grabbed Nutter by the throat, but the doctor, cool as you like, had merely said, 'The truth has cured you. You see that hand you're about to hit me with? It's your left one!' The fat man had broken down and cried like a baby and the audience had gone wild, clapping and stamping their feet. They'd witnessed not only real live drama but a miracle. It was heady stuff.

'Just wait till I tell Barry.'

Derek dropped the papers he'd been shifting around on the desk. 'No. I'd rather you didn't.'

Tiffany stared at him, her eyes dark and critical – a reflection of her mother's. He had a pretty good idea what she was thinking and he didn't want to hear it. He got up from his chair and went over to the filing cabinet behind the desk. He opened one of the drawers. 'I want to be the one to tell Bas,' he said casually, his back to Tiffany.

'Suit yourself.'

He heard her open the door and when he turned round she was gone. Well, that wasn't so bad, he told himself.

'Classic mid-life crisis behaviour, I reckon,' Tiffany said, her head suddenly appearing round the door. She was grinning at him.

'Out!' he shouted.

Damn silly thing to say. Of course he wasn't going through a mid-life crisis. Good God, anyone would think he was behaving like those stressed-out executives you read about, who for no apparent reason give up their smart company cars and take to growing turnips in Wales. He wasn't like that. All he was doing was reviewing the schedule. It was time for a change. Surely that wasn't such a big deal. And there were market trends to take into account. It didn't pay to play the same game for too long, not when there were so many other opportunities out there to grab hold of.

There was still the question as to how he was going to tell Bas. The last thing he wanted was Tiffany running off to the phone and smirking into it that their father was going doo-lally. He hoped Bas would be pleased, even proud of him. It was important to him now that he had his son's approval.

'Life. Bloody old life,' he said out loud. 'What's a simple guy supposed to make of it?'

Tiffany gave a quick knock on the conservatory door. There was no response so she knocked again. She hoped Charlotte and Alex were in. She liked coming next door to Ivy Cottage where she was never treated as an awkward teenager. Instead Charlotte and Alex treated her as an awkward adult. She often came round to them when she wanted to get away from In the Pink – at least here she could escape the sight of all those gullible over-dressed women pandering to their vanity. Sad. Woefully sad the whole lot of them. Didn't they know that there were millions starving all over the world while they tried to sweat a few pounds off their wobbly bums and chins? Disgusting.

She knocked at the door again then turned the handle. 'Charlotte,' she called out. 'It's me, Tiffany.'

'Hello, you Tiffany,' said Alex, from the kitchen. 'Charlotte's upstairs having a bath. Anything I can help you with?'

Tiffany rolled her eyes and pouted. 'I need some help with my biology homework,' she said, sounding and wiggling her hips like Marilyn Monroe. It was a ritual she and Alex went through occasionally – she parodying the dumb blonde and he the lecherous older man.

'Ah-ah! And would I be right in thinking it was to do with the reproductive organs?'

She rolled her eyes again. 'You've found me out. How about we try psychology, then?'

Alex sidled up to Tiffany. 'Miss Vogers,' he said, 'I know your problems only too vell. You are mad for zee right man in your life. Am I correct?'

'Oh, oh,' squeaked Tiffany, sounding more like Betty Boop. 'Take me, Doctor, take—'

'Just watch yourself, Dr Kildare!'

It was Charlotte, standing in the doorway wearing Alex's bathrobe and a towel round her head. She was smiling.

'Honestly, I leave you to tidy up the kitchen and then find you seducing our next-door neighbour's daughter. Is it your age? Or am I making your tea too strong?'

Alex put his arm round Charlotte and kissed her.

Tiffany coughed loudly. 'If you could stop thinking about sex for a few moments, you two, I've got some news.'

Alex could feel the warmth of Charlotte's naked body through the towelling robe and suddenly sex was very much on his mind. 'Well, don't let us keep you, Tiffany,' he said.

'Don't be so rude,' Charlotte said, pushing him away.

'That's all right. I've heard about men like him. Anyway, do you want to hear my news, or what? Dad's having a mid-life crisis. The full works. He's chucking in exploiting women under the guise of health and beauty and setting himself up as a manager of some kind of therapy clinic. Never mind In the Pink, this'll be In the Stink if you ask me.'

'You mean no more Don Juan of the curlers?' Alex laughed.

'No more Lothario wielding his scissors?' Charlotte said, amazed.

'He's not been the same since Barry was ill. I've seen him mooching about the salon. He's obviously bored with the whole scene.'

'Perhaps he thinks he'll make more money out of therapy. Your dad's no fool.'

'You could be right, Charlotte,' Tiffany said. 'On the other hand, maybe he's worked out he can get to women more successfully by curing their emotional problems.'

'Talking of which,' Alex said, 'time you were going. I want to talk to my future wife about her emotional problems.'

'Future wife, eh? When, how and why?'

'That's what I want to talk to her about, little Miss Nosy Parker. So on your way.'

'I'm going, I'm going,' Tiffany said good-humouredly. 'I'm due at Hilary's in a few minutes to babysit.'

As Tiffany closed the door behind her, Charlotte frowned.

'Oh no you don't,' Alex said. 'Don't go pretending you're suddenly ill in an attempt to get out of our conversation.' He picked her up and carried her through to the sitting room where earlier he'd lit a fire. Mabel was stretched out in front of it on the rug. He set Charlotte down on the sofa and knelt beside her.

'What a suspicious nature you have, Alex. As a matter of fact I've just remembered I was supposed to go and see Hilary myself.'

'Hilary can wait. I can't.'

She raised an eyebrow and reached out to him.

'No,' he said firmly. 'I'm withholding my body until you've given me a date, time and place.'

She laughed. 'Ssh, you're embarrassing Mabel.'

He kissed her, then stood up. 'I'll get you a glass of wine, then I'll have your answer.'

When he came back into the room, Charlotte was sitting in front of the log fire; she'd removed the towel from her head and was running a hand through her long dark hair. She looked up as he stood over her.

'What do you think about Christmas?' she said.

'I rather thought we'd have it here again, like last year.' He put another log on the fire and nudged it into place with his foot.

'I didn't mean that.'

'You mean . . .'

'Christmas Eve falls on a Saturday this year. I've phoned Malcolm and he says he can fit us in. What do you think?'

'I think I've just stopped withholding my body.'

'Où est Paul?'

How should I know? Hilary thought angrily to herself. Carry on as normal had been Cindy's advice and, God help her, she was doing her best. Tuesday night was David's squash night and her French evening class at Becky's school,

48

and unbelievably, here she was – but was David really playing squash?

'Hilary, où est Paul?'

She looked down at her textbook and studied the drawings. 'Il est encore au lit,' she answered. Typical. Half past eleven in the morning and the stupid man was still in bed.

'Pourquoi?'

The classroom door opened.

'Bonsoir! Sorry I'm late.'

Everyone looked up, including Martina their French teacher. 'Hello,' she said, from the desk on which she was perched and uncrossing her legs. 'Are you sure you've got the right room?'

'I hope so. French, intermediate? My name's Nick Bradshaw. I should be on your list.'

While Martina flicked through the names on her register, Hilary bent her head and tried to sink as low as she could into the small primary-school chair. Her only hope was that he wouldn't recognise her without her sunglasses and ridiculous hat.

'You *are* late, aren't you?' Martina said, looking up from her file.

'About three weeks late, I make it.'

She laughed. 'Find a seat and we'll chat at the end of the session. If you sit at the back with Hilary you can partner her in the conversational work in a moment. Hilary, would you mind sharing your book?'

Hilary mumbled a yes and without looking up she slid it across the small desk.

'D'accord. Paul, il est encore au lit. Pourquoi? Patricia?'

'Parce qu'il est fatigué.' Hilary heard Patricia's reply, quick as a flash.

'Hi,' Nick Bradshaw said, squeezing himself into the chair next to her.

She managed a nod.

'Et Maman, où est-ce qu'elle est?'

49

'Where all good mothers are,' Nick Bradshaw whispered, 'at the tip throwing away expensive cut glass.'

Hilary froze. Out of the corner of her eye she could see he was smiling at her. He was making fun of her.

At the front of the classroom Martina closed her textbook. 'Okay,' she said, 'conversation work now. Pair off and choose one of the following subjects.' She started writing on the blackboard: Shopping, Gardening or Discussing a Book or a Film.

'What shall we pick?'

'You choose,' Hilary murmured, her head still bent over the textbook.

'How about some small-talk instead?'

Oh, please, the smaller the better. 'Oui,' she said.

He laughed. 'Très bien. Bonsoir, je m'appelle Nick.'

At last she looked him full in the face and flinched slightly under the same direct stare he'd offered her at the tip. He seemed older than she'd remembered him; somewhere in his early forties. His face had that rumpled kind of look that she supposed some women found attractive. She decided it matched his trousers – a quick glance downwards told her he was wearing the same pair as this morning. When she didn't say anything, he said, 'Hilary *qui*?'

'Hilary Parker,' she said reluctantly.

'Et qui est le bâtard?'

Who is the bastard? Oh my God! He *had* heard her this morning. She turned away, the colour instantly draining from her face.

'Votre mari peut-être?'

What was he, some kind of mind-reader? 'My husband? Of course not,' she said loudly.

'En français, Hilary.'

'I'm sorry, Martina,' Hilary said, suddenly gathering up her book and getting to her feet. 'I'm not feeling well. I'd better get off home.'

'Okay, everyone. Time's up anyway. Now remember,

there's no lesson next week, it's half-term break, so that means you have two weeks in which to do your homework. I want you to prepare a talk on your last holiday. Hilary, you do look rather pale, do you want me to give you a lift home?'

'No. I'll be fine once I'm outside. It must be the heating in here.' She struggled into her coat.

'What, no hat?'

Hilary flashed an angry look at Nick. 'Why don't you mind your own business?' she said. Then, astonished at what she'd just said, she hurried out of the classroom. But Patricia was there, barring her way at the door.

'Martina's right, Hilary, you do look pale. You do know there's diarrhoea doing the rounds at school, don't you?'

'Then you'd best get out of my way,' Hilary snapped.

Outside in the corridor as she hurried past the frieze of autumn artwork displayed on the walls, Hilary wondered what was happening to her. She was never bad-tempered with other people. Patience was her middle name and here she was sounding off at anyone who spoke to her. Bloody David! It was all his fault. Because he had changed, she was changing. She didn't like it. She wanted him to be the same old David and her to be the same old Hilary.

She scurried across the floodlit playground and paused at the school gate to catch her breath. How long was she supposed to keep this charade going? How had Cindy managed it all these years? From behind her she heard the sound of footsteps.

'I'm sorry about that, back there,' a voice called out. And before she was able to push open the gate Nick Bradshaw was next to her standing in the light cast from the street-lamp above them. 'I have a habit of wading in, I can't be bothered with mincing about. Getting to the nub of things is what I like to do, it's what I'm paid to do.'

'I'm sorry too,' she responded, deciding that David wouldn't change her completely. She would still remember her manners. 'I shouldn't have bitten your head off like that.'

'I probably deserved it. Fancy a drink?'

The rest of the group were now coming towards them across the Tarmac. Hilary could see Patricia walking alongside Martina. Bet she was teacher's pet at school, she thought. 'A drink?' she repeated, suddenly registering what this practically unknown man had asked her. How ridiculous. She was a married woman, a mother of two young children being asked out for a drink! The very idea.

'From the look on your face I'll take that as a no.'

'I really must be going,' she said, flustered. 'I've a babysitter waiting, PTA minutes to type up and—'

'And a husband.' He smiled. 'No worries. I'll see you in two weeks.' He held the gate for her. 'Don't forget your homework.'

Chapter Eight

When Hilary let herself in there was no sign of David, or of the children. Tiffany was lying on the sofa reading a book. She moved her long legs and made room for Hilary.

'I hope that's homework,' Hilary said, betraying her years as a teacher. She knew that Tiffany's mock exams were fast approaching, and although it was obvious that Tiffany was a bright and able student, she was also aware how easy it was for her to get sidetracked. In the short time that the Rogers family had been living in Acacia Lane Hilary had not only witnessed Tiffany trying to come through her adolescence by battling with her parents over her individuality – whether it was dressing herself from top to toe in black or dyeing her hair bright pink – she had also watched her go through her vegetarian phase, her custodians-of-the-earth phase and more recently her singlehanded attempt at shaming the residents of Hulme Welford into donating money for the homeless by sitting in a cardboard box outside Ted the Toup's shop one wet Saturday afternoon. Cindy and Derek had been away that particular weekend, had been blissfully ignorant of Tiffany's plan and had missed the sight of their daughter drenched and shivering, her hand outstretched, and the opportunity to try to stop her. But Hilary suspected that even if they had known about the collapsible cardboard box Tiffany had stashed away under her bed, Cindy and Derek would have been powerless to prevent their daughter's protest – like herself, they must have long since arrived at the unpalatable truth that there was nothing they could do to dissuade their youngest child from pursuing her chosen line of action.

'Background reading for Jane Austen,' Tiffany replied, waving the cover of *Emma* in front of Hilary. 'Bit of a spoilt madam, isn't she? Always poking her nose into everybody else's business and all the time she hasn't got a clue what's going on right under her own smug nose.'

'I think you'll find things change for her later,' Hilary said thoughtfully, struggling to recall her own A-level studies.

'Yea, well, she deserves the fall that's coming to her, if you ask me.'

'Children okay?' Hilary asked, suddenly feeling uncomfortable with the conversation.

'Philip was his usual quiet self and Becky got worked up over something and nothing.'

'Mm ...' Hilary said, distracted. Her mind was still on *Emma*. At the door she paid Tiffany and said goodbye, then went back into the sitting room where she looked along the shelves of the bookcase to the right of the fireplace. There, on the highest shelf, she found what she was looking for. She blew away the dust and opened the book at chapter one.

Emma Woodhouse, handsome, clever, and rich, with a comfortable home and happy disposition, seemed to unite some of the best blessings of existence, and had lived nearly twenty-one years in the world with very little to distress or vex her.

Apart from the age and perhaps the *handsome* and *clever* references it could be herself. Hadn't she always thought she'd lived a charmed life with David? All these years she had been so complacently happy with her lot ... and now there was the risk that she was about to lose everything.

She put the book back in its place on the top shelf then caught her reflection in the mirror above the fireplace. She looked tired, dull even, but surely not so awful that David had stopped loving her? When had it all gone wrong? She thought back over the past year or so, searching her mind for some tell-tale sign that would explain David's indifference to her. She could find none, but she could hear Charlotte's voice telling her how bossy she was. And, yes, deep down she knew her sister was right, but that wasn't such a crime, it was just her way, and anyway everybody had their little foibles. But Charlotte had also implied that she had a habit of interfering and David himself had accused her of the same thing last year. 'Stop meddling in other people's lives,' he'd said, 'especially your sister's.' She had been stung by his words – after all, she'd only been helping Charlotte to get over Peter's death by nudging her in Alex's direction. What harm had she done? And were these crimes justification for a husband to cause untold harm to his family by having an affair? Tiffany had just condemned *Emma* by saying she deserved the fall that was coming to her – would people say that about herself, she wondered.

The phone rang.

'It's me.'

'Where are you?'

'Still at the squash club.'

Hilary pushed the receiver closer to her ear, trying to make out the sound of squash balls being whacked against a wall – she wanted to believe David, truly she did.

'I'll be a bit later than usual. There's a free court so I'm having another game ... Hilary, you still there?'

She slammed down the phone and was still crying when she heard somebody at the front door.

'Cindy!' She had never known Cindy to go calling, not even during the day, let alone at night.

'When Tiffany came home, I thought I'd see how you were.'

'As you can see, not very well,' Hilary answered, making no attempt to wipe away her tears.

'Would you rather I left you alone?' Cindy said awkwardly.

'No, no. Please come in, I was just going to make myself a drink.'

Cindy followed Hilary into the kitchen and while Hilary made some coffee, she took off her coat and started to clear away what was obviously the remains of tea. 'You should get Tiffany to tidy up for you while she babysits,' she said.

'I couldn't do that,' Hilary snivelled, 'she's got her homework to do.' She blew her nose, loudly and messily, knowing she looked awful; she always did whenever she cried. At the first sign of a tear her eyes would swell and redden, almost to the same shade as the rubber gloves Cindy was now pulling on. What on earth was Cindy doing? She sensed Cindy didn't approve of tears, which made her want to cry even more. Disapproval was almost as bad as rejection.

As she watched Cindy wring out the dishcloth she realised that the other woman made her feel ashamed and inadequate. Georgia hadn't made her feel like that. Georgia had been warm and comforting, which had surprised Hilary. She hadn't expected kindness from such a tough woman.

Cindy had now moved on to wiping the work surfaces. Hilary felt a stab of anger towards this woman who was so calm, so cool, and who had probably never cried in her life. 'Cindy,' she said, trying to sound assertive, 'you don't have to do that. Come and have your coffee.'

'It's no trouble,' Cindy answered, moving back to the sink and spraying some Mr Muscle behind the mixer taps. She rubbed hard then, satisfied that the worst of the tears were over, she peeled off the gloves, sat opposite Hilary and thought, Thank God I never fell apart like this. She felt proud of herself that during all the years of putting up with Derek's dalliances she had held herself together as well as their family.

She had called on Hilary to see how she was and to escape Derek's endless talk of his latest brainchild. She was finding it hard to be as motivated as he was about the whole idea, but in a funny kind of way it pleased her to see Derek so enthusiastic about something. Just after Barry's confirmation last summer Derek had seemed more content than she'd ever known him, but more recently he had become distant and distracted. She hoped that the transformation of their business would be the answer to whatever had been causing him to wander listlessly about the salon. Perhaps, finally, he was about to find his true vocation. It might even stop him from straying, give him a sense of fulfilment. She was beginning to sound like him now, as though quoting from one of his wretched books.

A sniff from the other side of the table reminded her of Hilary.

'I don't think I can carry on much longer pretending nothing's happened,' Hilary said flatly.

'Why don't you come over to me tomorrow and I'll give you a facial?'

'Georgia D'Arcy says I should confront David.' She paused. 'Actually, Georgia said I should confront the sodding bastard.' She gave a queer little laugh. 'I don't normally go in for profanity, but since yesterday I seem to have done little else.'

Cindy examined one of her long, varnished nails. It was chipped. She must have knocked it just now. She said coolly, 'Well, Georgia D'Arcy would say that, wouldn't she?'

Hilary looked up sharply. 'What do you mean?'

'And just where did it get her when she confronted her husband? Living in a caravan and working all hours just to scratch a living together. Is that what you want, Hilary?' She cast her eyes round the cluttered but comfortable Aga-warmed kitchen. 'You'd lose all this. You know that, don't you?'

Hilary began to cry again. 'She doesn't live in a caravan any more and at least she has her dignity.'

'And I haven't?' suggested Cindy.

'I . . . I didn't say that. All I meant was—'

'I know what you meant, Hilary, but are you strong enough to do what Georgia did?'

'Georgia says that a woman is like a tea-bag and it's only when she's in hot water that she knows how strong she is.'

57

Cindy's usually brittle features softened. 'I like that,' she said, smiling.

'I don't think I have the same kind of strength you have, Cindy. I'm not at all stoic like you.'

Stoic? Strength? Cindy had never thought of it like that. She had merely taken it for granted that she would hold things together.

Hilary sniffed. 'Georgia says—'

Cindy raised her hand. 'Okay. I think I've heard enough from Ms D'Arcy. As far as I can see, you've a choice to make, Hilary. Either you play it my way and hope David tires of this one-off thing—'

'If it is a one-off—'

'Or you confront him and risk losing your husband because you've forced him into making the wrong choice. It's up to you.'

Not long after Cindy had left, Hilary went upstairs to check on the children. She stood in Philip's bedroom at the end of his bed. She watched him turn over in his sleep. He was restless, the duvet tossed aside, his pillow hanging over the edge of the bed. She moved forward and stooped to rearrange the duvet, remembering how when Philip had been a baby she would put him in his cot on his side at bedtime and in the morning he'd be in exactly the same position – the sheets barely wrinkled, the blanket undisturbed. So when had he changed? And when had he started biting his fingernails, she wondered, catching sight of one of his hands in the strip of light from the landing as it streaked through the doorway and across his bed? Poor Philip, she suddenly thought, what was troubling him?

And how on earth could she confront David when it might threaten her children's security?

Chapter Nine

It was Saturday morning when Charlotte remembered she still hadn't called on her sister to see how she was. But as she unlocked the door of her shop she decided that if anything had been seriously wrong, Hilary would have come to see her.

Not so long ago Hilary had practically been a permanent resident at Ivy Cottage, continually popping over the road with some spurious reason for visiting when all the time she had been checking up on Charlotte and Alex.

Their relationship had been what Charlotte had supposed was a fairly typical one between sisters. As children they had been the best of friends one moment and sworn enemies the next. Best friends had consisted of sleeping together in the same bedroom, playing T. Rex records until gone midnight and then tuning in to Radio Luxembourg. Enemies had consisted of Charlotte defacing one of Hilary's treasured David Cassidy posters and Hilary jamming her up against the wall and beating her about the head with the lid of a biscuit tin. Thinking about it, it was the only time Charlotte could recall her sister losing control. On the whole, and especially so nowadays, Hilary had always been a control freak; worrying and herding those around her like the most persistent of sheepdogs.

There had, of course, been the one-way rivalry between them. Hilary had desperately wanted to be the older sister and had fought sneakily as well as blatantly to usurp Charlotte's role; a role for which Charlotte had never given tuppence. She knew that, after Peter's death, Hilary had relished her role as sister of mercy to the rescue and had played the part with supreme heavy-handedness.

Charlotte opened the small safe at the back of the shop and then put the float into the till. At nine o'clock she switched on the lights and waited for her first customer of the day, knowing that trade wouldn't really get going until gone nine thirty, and now that the weather was turning nasty perhaps it would be even later. She was enjoying running her own business again, even if her mother had greeted her decision to take on the lease with her usual scorn. 'Just don't be muscling in on my patch,' Louise had said. 'Only room for one antique shop in the village.' Charlotte knew that her mother was as mad as hell that by somebody else's bad luck she had acquired one of the largest shops in the village with its spacious double frontage – Louise had only the one cramped window. Dad had been great and helped her and Alex redecorate the place after Jim Lloyd had cleared the last of his bathroom fittings from the shop.

She had decided against going back into clothes retailing, which she had done in London, all those years ago, before Peter had forced her to sell up and move abroad. What Hulme Welford needed, she had concluded, was a shop selling quality gifts, along with a cheaper line in Third-World goods for the caring nineties consumer.

Filling a basket with a new batch of friendship bands – ready for the pocket-money spenders – Charlotte thought of the look that she would put on Hilary's face when she told her she and Alex had at last fixed a date for the wedding. The only downside was that Hilary might dive in, take over and organise a monumental bunfight. The last thing Charlotte wanted was her sister hijacking her wedding.

The shop door opened and Charlotte lifted her head to greet her first customer. It was Hilary with the niece from hell, Becky. 'Hello,' Charlotte said, trying to keep the shock out of her voice. Her sister looked dreadful. She was so pale.

'Hello, Auntie Charlotte,' piped up Becky, making a bee-line for the shelves of china candlesticks.

Charlotte watched Becky start to move the expensive pieces of Italian chinaware as though she were playing chess, while at the same time she was conscious of Hilary drifting towards the counter, her hands playing nervously over the pile of paper bags next to the till.

'You're out and about early,' Charlotte said, troubled that for the first time in her life she was experiencing the sensation of feeling sorry for her sister.

'I'm selling tickets for the school firework party. Do you want some for you and Alex?' Hilary replied, without looking at Charlotte. Her voice was flat and mechanical, and unmistakably wrong to Charlotte's well-trained ear. Even though Hilary believed herself the most circumspect woman alive, Charlotte knew otherwise. Her sister had never been able to hide anything – secrets had always burst out of her with rocket-like propulsion and her face was as easy to read as a book.

'I'll get my bag,' Charlotte said.

When she returned from the small back office, she found her sister looking at a handmade Advent calendar. Charlotte noticed that Hilary's hands were shaking. 'What is it, Hilary?'

Without turning round, Hilary said, 'I was just thinking of Christmases when we were little. It was always Dad who made it happen, wasn't it? I'd never thought of that before.'

'Dad did the presents, but it was you who made everything else happen, bossing everybody about like a good 'un.'

'I wasn't that bossy,' Hilary retaliated.

Charlotte frowned. Hilary, bossy – the two were synonymous, everybody knew that. 'How much are the tickets?' she asked, moving onto safer ground.

'Two pounds fifty each. There's a free drink thrown in.'

A sudden crash from Becky made them both turn.

'I haven't broken anything,' Becky said brightly.

'For heaven's sake,' shouted Hilary, 'can't you be more careful?'

Charlotte was taken aback. She'd never heard Hilary admonish her daughter like this before. It had always been Charlotte's privately held opinion that if Hilary had been firmer with Becky from the word go, she wouldn't be such a pain now. 'Hilary,' Charlotte said, quietly, 'what's up?'

Hilary glanced away, but not before Charlotte had seen her lips trembling and her eyes filling with tears.

'Has something happened?'

Hilary shook her head.

'Please, Hilary. If I can help.' She placed a tentative hand on her sister's arm. 'What is it?'

'I'm not supposed to tell anyone,' Hilary blurted out. It sounded ridiculous.

'For God's sake, why?'

'I . . .' Hilary finally met her sister's gaze and disintegrated beneath it. 'It's David . . .' She looked over to where Becky was still playing chess. 'An affair,' she whispered, 'he's having an affair.'

'No! Not David, I don't believe it.'

The door flew open, followed by a dramatic blast of wind which brought with it a flurry of leaves and Iris Braithwaite.

'Mrs Lawrence, a word, if you please.'

'Can it wait, Mrs Braithwaite?' Charlotte asked, her eyes never once leaving her sister's face.

Iris rattled the door shut and approached Charlotte and Hilary. She had with her a pen on a long piece of string attached to a black clipboard. 'I'm on a mission of merchandise cleansing,' she boomed, 'so no, it cannot wait. And waiting, I might say, Mrs Lawrence, is the very kind of attitude that has got us where we are. The day has come—'

'Mrs Braithwaite—'

'I haven't finished, Mrs Lawrence. The day has come for us to rid Hulme Welford of everything unsavoury and of an ambiguous nature.' Her eyes swept accusingly round the shelves of Charlotte's shop.

'What on earth are you talking about, Mrs Braithwaite?' Charlotte asked.

'A smut-free zone is what I'm talking about and I'm not at all sure I like your tone of—'

'A what zone?' Hilary interrupted, speaking for the first time.

Iris approached the counter and banged down her clipboard. She gave Charlotte a handwritten poster. 'Make Hulme Welford a Smut-free Zone' it declared in large letters. 'In the window, if you please, Mrs Lawrence, and if you'd like to sign my petition I'll be on my way. You too, Mrs Parker.'

Charlotte read aloud from the piece of paper: ' "I the undersigned agree to the closure of Ted Cooper's newsagent's and will not tolerate the selling of undesirable items in any other retail establishment in Hulme Welford." '

'Undesirable items?' Charlotte repeated.

'Pornographic!' exclaimed Iris, so vigorously that her brown cowpat of a hat with a little stalk sticking up from it nearly slipped off her head.

'But he's always sold smutty magazines.'

'I'm not referring to those.' Iris shuddered. 'It's pornographic items of clothing he's moved on to. He'll be turning the premises into a sex shop next. Hulme Welford will soon become the Soho of the North if we don't stop him.'

Charlotte wanted to laugh, but Iris's highly censorious manner was verging on the manic and it was possible that an unchecked snigger might tip the old woman over the edge.

'What exactly is Ted selling?' she asked patiently.

'Tights with . . . tights without a . . .' Iris cleared her throat and began again. 'No gusset,' she hissed. ' "Peephole", he called them.'

'Peep-bo!' sang out Becky, her head appearing over the top of a display rack of cotton throw-overs. 'What's a sex shop?'

*

It was complete chaos. They would never be ready in time, and just how on earth had she let Derek talk her into this?

Cindy looked at what, until a few days ago, had been the reception desk in the foyer – it was now pushed against the door waiting to be thrown away. According to Derek they weren't going to have a desk. Apparently such a solid block would act as both a mental and physical barrier, making a them-and-us situation. 'We are to meld as one,' he had explained last night, while watching Cindy stack the dish-washer after she'd got back from seeing Hilary. Tiffany had walked in at that point looking for food and had muttered something about melding her father together.

'And what exactly are we calling ourselves?' Cindy had asked.

'Don't tempt me,' Tiffany had sniggered, her head inside the fridge.

Derek had looked pleased with himself. 'All in the Mind. What do you reckon?'

'I should think it bloody well is all in your mind!' Tiffany had shrieked, her raucous laughter telling Derek exactly what she thought. Cindy had wanted to laugh, too, but had refrained from joining in with her daughter's ridicule.

Cindy was struck now as she had been last night that this was a new and strange phenomenon – Tiffany and herself in agreement. For years it had been open warfare between the two and over the slightest of issues, mainly her daughter's appearance. But recently the friction had eased. It was as if all Tiffany's energy was being channelled into the superhuman feat of her becoming a woman, leaving her little or no strength to be so antagonistic – though there had been that recent incident with the cardboard box outside Ted Cooper's.

Earlier in the year, she and Derek had breathed a sigh of relief when Tiffany had at last thrown away her wrung-out dishcloth look in favour of the more stylish and flattering clothes she spent her Saturday afternoons unearthing in the charity shops in Congleton. She still wore predominantly black but gone were the heavy eye make-up and dyed black hair: instead she'd let her own sandy colour grow through and had actually allowed her father to restyle it, asking him to cut ten inches off the length, keeping it bulky on the top but graduated into the nape of her neck. It made her look older but at the same time more vulnerable.

Tiffany's appearance might have softened over the last year but Cindy knew, better than anyone, that her tongue had not. That was still as sharp as ever, but instead of being directed at her, it was now aimed mostly at Derek.

Funny thing was, Derek seemed reluctant or perhaps unable to fight back with his daughter. Was this because he no longer saw Tiffany as a child, but more as a woman? Derek had never been able to resist the charm of any woman, no matter what kind of charm she exuded. In many ways Tiffany was just as much a challenge to win over as any of his past conquests. It was also true that since Barry had gone to university the atmosphere in the house had changed. Derek as the sole man was up against two women, who were showing all the signs of joining forces.

Cindy smiled to herself as she heard the sound of a radio playing loudly from somewhere in the salon. Bob Dylan was singing 'The Times They Are A-Changin''. And weren't they just?

She looked out of the large window onto the front garden and the parking area filled with builders' and decorators' vans. At the end of the drive two men were hard at work removing the old In the Pink sign and replacing it with a new one. She supposed that it was only a matter of time before the colour of the house was changed. Cindy had been well aware that when the first coat of pink paint had been brushed onto the walls there had been shock waves of disapproval in the village. She had asked Derek to show restraint but he had ignored her. 'Cindy,' he'd said, 'this is to be the pinnacle of our career in the health and beauty industry, we've got to go for it.'

So, Cindy thought wryly, as she watched the two men at the end of the drive, if the pinnacle of their career was in the process of being dismantled, what was next? Her life before had been predictably unsure, but she had successfully walked the tightrope of their precarious marriage in the knowledge that beneath her was the safety of the business. It had been the one certainty in her life and had provided the reassurance – the only tangible reassurance – upon which she had been able to rely. But what was she sure of now? What was her role to be at All in the Mind? Not so long ago, Tiffany, in one of her bitchier pre-menstrual moods, had described her as being good only for plucking and pruning. Had her daughter been right? After all, she was no counsellor, no mind-bender, as Tiffany described the people who were going to be taking the places of Tracy and Lorraine, along with all the other members of staff who had grumbled to hell and back at being made redundant. Their grievances had soon been mollified by the generous financial packages Cindy had offered.

Last night she had asked Derek what her role was to be. Plumping up the cushion in his armchair he had said, 'We'll all find our own niche, given time.'

'Niche?' she had repeated. 'I'm not sure I want a niche, Derek. I want something I know I can do. Something real.'

He'd smiled. 'Finding our own personal niche is the challenge we're all seeking in this life.'

She'd switched on the television at that point and settled down to watch a videoed episode of *Coronation Street* – something she could understand. Her husband was now communicating in a language she didn't recognise, but at least the goings-on of the Street were familiar territory.

'Cindy! There you are, I've been looking all over for you. I'd like you to meet Rosie Williams. She's to be our marriage guidance expert.'

A bit late for that, thought Cindy, as she turned round to face a statuesque young woman at Derek's side. She took in the soft brown eyes flecked with green, the smart suit and the long, long legs encased in the sheerest of tights. One hand held a briefcase and the other was extended towards her.

'Your husband has just confirmed my position.'

'Has he, indeed?' Cindy was nettled, not just by this woman with her smooth poise and well educated voice but by Derek. 'I had no idea he was interviewing this morning. I thought *we* were doing that *together*, this afternoon.'

Derek laughed awkwardly and Rosie raised a surprisingly large hand in the air. 'And there we have it,' she said, in a tone of voice that smacked of teacher-knows-best. 'Communication. That's the name of the game, isn't it? It's the basis of every sound, rock-solid marriage.' She put down her case and drew a square in the air with her two forefingers. 'See?' she said. 'The lines meet head on. There are no crossed wires.'

'That's the stuff,' Derek said enthusiastically.

God help us, thought Cindy.

'I'll see you to your car,' Derek said, filling in Cindy's obvious silence. He steered Rosie Williams towards the door. 'Mind how you go, don't want you breaking your neck on all this rubbish before you've even started work with us.' He picked his way over a large blue tool-box and a coil of electric cable with a drill attached at one end.

'Nothing is rubbish,' Rosie said meaningfully. 'Everything and everyone has a purpose. Thrilled to have met you, Cindy. Byee.'

'Goodbye, Miss Williams, or is it Mrs?' Cindy asked, her voice just as meaningful.

'Oh, definitely Miss.'

Perfectly qualified, then, to guide others through the misfortunes of marriage. Cindy watched their first recruit follow Derek out of the door and down the steps to the parking area. 'Late twenties perhaps, and about as many brain cells,' she muttered. She turned away and tried hard not to think of leopards and spots.

Chapter Ten

Thank God, Hilary thought from her front pew.

Thank God it wasn't her turn on the Sunday School rota. And thank God Malcolm Jackson was a devil for rambling sermons and she could sit here in peace for a whole hour and thirty minutes. No Becky – she was tormenting some other unfortunate volunteer. And no Philip either – he was playing in a school rugby match with David standing on the touchline ... Please, God, let David freeze to death.

She could hardly believe it was a whole week since she'd discovered David's affair and it was a reflection on her own life that up until now she'd had no idea what despair and misery were really about. How glib adultery was made to look on television. How poignant it was in novels, and how glamorously sensational in the tabloids. Never was it portrayed as it was. It was terrifying. Terrifying and bewildering, so much so you could barely eat, sleep or even think properly.

Yesterday Charlotte had suggested she go to the doctor. 'You're obviously worn out, Hilary,' she'd said, when Iris Braithwaite had finally left them in the shop. 'Are you eating? And what about sleep?'

Sleeping and eating were the least of her concerns right now. Coping was uppermost in her mind and it seemed to her that that alone was taking up all her energy. David, blast him, had even had the nerve to say, 'What's wrong, Hilary? You don't look right.' She had nearly confronted him then, had so very nearly thrown the whole damn thing at him and shouted, 'Of course I'm not looking right, and is it any wonder knowing that your every spare moment is spent with that ...?' But she hadn't. She had kept quiet and carried on ironing his shirt, banging the iron down on the cuff, wishing his arm was still in it.

And each day it took all her powers of self-restraint not to march straight into David's office in the village and have it out with that wretched Catherine. How could she do it? How could one woman treat another so badly? It was beyond her. A part of her didn't want to confront Catherine. It was almost as though her subconscious was saying, 'If you leave well alone, then it's more likely that none of this is really happening.'

Like Cindy, Charlotte had urged her not to have it out with Catherine. 'You're blameless in all of this, Hilary,' she had said. 'Keep it that way. If you see her you'll lose your temper. Just don't do anything you'll regret. Would you like Alex to talk to David?'

'No!'

'But he might be able to get David to see what he's doing, what he's risking.'

'I don't want David to find out that I know—'

'Why in heaven's name not?'

'Oh, Charlotte, you just don't understand. Just think yourself lucky that Peter died.'

Their conversation had ended at that point with a sudden rush of customers coming into the shop and Hilary and Becky setting off for home.

Now, in St John's, Hilary felt appalled at what she'd said to her sister: ... *think yourself lucky that Peter died*. What a dreadful thing to say. She tried to concentrate on the sound of Malcolm Jackson's voice telling her, along with all the other sinners assembled in St John's that morning, that she was saved, and wasn't that wonderful.

But all Hilary could think of was how wonderful it would be to be saved from having to go back to The Gables when this service came to an end, and how wonderful it would be to be saved from pretending that everything was fine. Everything was not fine. Far from it. David, her husband, a man whom she had trusted with her life all their marriage, had betrayed her in the worst possible way, and what, she demanded, looking up at the stained-glass window above the altar, was God doing about it? Never mind all this stuff about saving sinners. How about some old-fashioned retribution? In her opinion a dose of Old Testament wrath was called for. A thunderbolt or two wouldn't go amiss, especially in the direction of the trollop who had thrown herself at David.

Aware that all behind her were now on their feet, hymn books open, Hilary stood up. Still thinking of this other woman in David's life she clenched her hymn book as though she were grasping Catherine bloody Renshaw around the neck while she sang with the rest of the congregation, ' "Your hands swift to welcome, your arms to embrace." '

As usual coffee was being served at the back of the church by Iris Braithwaite along with Mrs Bradley and Mrs Haslip. Alex nudged Charlotte. 'There go the Golden Girls,' he whispered.

'Why don't you make Mrs Bradley's day by chatting her up over the coffee urn?' Charlotte replied. 'You love it when she goes all breathless over you.'

'I'd rather you were breathless—'

'That's as may be but I need a word with Hilary.'

Charlotte found Hilary at the foot of the altar, not deep in supplication, as her position suggested, but fiddling with the large arrangement of autumn flowers. Since yesterday morning Charlotte hadn't had an opportunity to talk to Hilary about what she'd told her in the shop – after all, she could hardly have gone over to The Gables with David there. She still couldn't come to terms with what her brother-in-law was up to. She bent down and touched her sister lightly on the shoulder. Hilary almost leapt in response, pushing Charlotte up against the altar and sending the eucharistic tackle crashing.

'Charlotte! I'm so sorry, I had no idea you were there.' Hilary was flustered.

Charlotte tidied up the mess and led her sister to a pew.

'Please don't be nice to me,' Hilary suddenly said. 'I ... I really couldn't bear that.'

'Okay,' Charlotte agreed, remembering how difficult she had found coping with sympathy offered to her after Peter's death. 'I'll do my normal horrid-sister routine, shall I?' She was conscious that, whether Hilary liked it or not, she was going to have to let her, Charlotte, be the older sister for once.

Hilary sniffed. 'All right,' she said, staring straight ahead of her, her hands twisting the stalk of a dying chrysanthemum she had just pulled out of the altar flowers. She suddenly faced Charlotte. 'You haven't told anyone, have you?'

Charlotte shook her head. 'Nobody.'

'What about Alex?'

'Hilary, you made me promise not to tell anyone. Now stop worrying about that and tell me when you found out about David.'

'On Monday.'

All that time ago and her sister hadn't come to her. 'How? How did you find out?'

Hilary told her.

'But are you sure? I mean—'

'Good God, Charlotte, of course I'm sure. You always did treat me like a fool. I never could—'

'Shut up, Hilary,' Charlotte said sternly. 'This is no time for one of our squabbles.'

'I wasn't squabbling, I was merely—'

'Never mind that. What are you going to do?'

'Cindy says I should pretend it isn't happening and Georgia D'Arcy says I should confront David.'

'Who else knows about this?' Charlotte asked, surprised at how hurt she felt that Hilary hadn't come to her for help. But then she herself, when her own marriage had been falling apart, hadn't turned to her sister or any member of her family for advice and support. Even now Hilary had no idea that she had asked Peter for a divorce the morning he had died.

'Nobody else,' Hilary replied, 'just Cindy and Georgia.'

'So you've told me what they think you should do, but not what you want to do.'

'It's obvious, isn't it? I've got to try and ignore what's happening.'

After a moment's quiet Charlotte said, 'If it's worth anything I agree with Georgia. Until you and David talk this through you're not going to be able to—'

'But don't you see? I could risk losing him if I do that.'

'You risk losing him anyway,' Charlotte said softly.

Hilary swallowed. 'There's less danger this way.'

'But, Hilary, you never could keep a secret, or lie convincingly. You've got to say something to David, or you'll end up making yourself ill.'

'I've got Philip and Becky to think of, they need their father. I'll do it for them.'

'And you truly believe staying silent will—'

'It's worked for Cindy. Why not for me?'

Charlotte covered her sister's hands. Poor Hilary. Poor Hilary trying to be so brave. 'Because you're not Cindy and you're not used to living with all this bloody chaos.'

'Auntie Charlotte, that's not nice,' Becky said, squeezing into the pew. 'Jesus won't have you in heaven if you go round saying bloody all the time. Ooh!' she squeaked, and quickly slapped a hand over her mouth. 'Now Jesus won't want me to sit by his throne either.' Her eyes swivelled in their sockets as though expecting to see the Messiah himself lurking behind one of the pillars.

Charlotte watched Hilary hug her daughter to her. What

a mess indeed, she thought, raising her eyes to the vaulted ceiling above. Sorry, Jesus, but throne or no throne, it's a bloody fine old mess down here.

Chapter Eleven

Monday morning, the first day of half-term. David had already left for work, the children were downstairs, plugged into the cartoons so thoughtfully programmed for the school holidays, and Hilary was in the shower. She was crying and washing away David's semen. How could he have made love to her? How could she have let him?

The questions had ricocheted around inside her head all night. She had no answer for why David should want to have sex with her, when he was obviously satisfying himself elsewhere, but she knew well enough why she had offered herself to him. It was all part of the charade: letting him, encouraging him even to make love with her might make everything all right. Allowing him to join their bodies as one would perhaps magically hold their marriage together – might even make him give Catherine up. In the moment he had reached out to Hilary in bed last night she had known that her decision to follow Cindy's example was the right one. She would do exactly as Cindy had done all these years. It was a small sacrifice to ensure their family stayed together.

She turned off the shower and reached for a towel. She wrapped it round her and walked over to the basin. Wiping the steam away from the mirror she looked at her wet face. Tears or shower water? Who would know? Who would even care? She felt herself succumbing to that one single emotion she despised in others – self-pity. She had never once pitied herself and something deep within her was telling her to pull herself together. 'Right,' she said aloud, 'you may cry in the shower, but nowhere else. You are going to be strong. You are going to smarten yourself up and show David you're worth a hundred Catherines – bet she can't make flapjacks like you!' She gave a brave little laugh, but immediately felt the onset of tears again. She quickly leapt back into the shower so as not to break her first resolve of the day.

At half past ten Hilary left Philip in charge of Becky while they watched a video and she went across the road to see Cindy. Cindy, Hilary had decided, was going to be instrumental in her plan to win back her husband.

She stood for a moment at the end of the drive of In the Pink, except it wasn't any more. Gone was the puce board and in its place was a discreet dark blue sign with stylish Gothic letters in gold: All in the Mind, it read. How long had that been there? Was she in such a state that she'd lost touch with what was going on around her? She walked past the caravan of builders' and decorators' vehicles and found the front door wide open. Loud music, accompanied by the sound of an electric drill, blasted out at her, along with the smell of paint. A man in overalls with a woolly hat pulled down over his head was kneeling on the floor painting a skirting board.

'They're busy,' he shouted at her, pausing briefly with his paintbrush, 'interviewing.'

'Oh,' Hilary said, her disappointment obvious.

''Bout another ten minutes, I should think. They said they'd be free at quarter to.'

'I'll wait, then,' she said, knowing that if she went back to The Gables now, she might never pluck up the courage to come back to see Cindy.

'Suit yourself. There's a chair in one of them back rooms.'

She picked her way carefully over the dust sheets, minding the haphazardly placed tools and off-cuts of wood. The hair salon had undergone a dramatic change. The back washes and mirrors had all gone, so had the chairs and shiny floor. Now all there was was a large empty room with an oatmeal-coloured carpet, the smell of which testified to it being new and only recently laid. Behind the door was a small stool and on this was a stack of glossy pamphlets. Hilary helped herself to one. On the front cover was a picture of Derek and Cindy with the words All in the Mind emblazoned above them. She turned the first page and started to read about Derek and Cindy's new venture:

Join us at our sanctuary of inner spiritual exploration and hope. Come on a voyage of discovery to experience your hidden depths. Let us help you to find the real you so that you can reach your full potential. Marital problems a speciality at All in the Mind.

In the background all went quiet as the sound of the drill stopped. 'Brew up,' shouted a man's voice. Then Hilary heard Derek. She replaced the pamphlet on top of the pile and went out to the reception area.

'Hello, Hilary,' said Derek, 'you anxious to get your name down for one of our classes? Positive thinking, assertiveness or how to pep up your marriage? Take your pick.'

'Goodness. What would I want with all that?' Hilary said, her cheeks reddening. 'I've only come over to see Cindy.'

'She'll be out in a moment. She's just showing one of our new members of staff round the place.' He looked about him. 'What do you reckon, then? Bit of a change, isn't it? Might even put sleepy old Hulme Welford on the map.'

'Lovely,' she responded, trying her best to sound enthusiastic.

'Marriage will be the thing, mark my words,' Derek continued, rubbing his hands together. 'Always marital problems going on, especially in a place like this.'

'Really,' Hilary said quietly. 'What makes you think that?'

He grinned and slipped his arm round Hilary's waist. 'Now I know what you're thinking. That's rich coming from old Derek, but believe me, I'm a reformed character. I—'

'And what could that possibly mean, I wonder?'

'Ah, Cindy my pet,' Derek said, swinging round to face his wife.

Hilary tried to manoeuvre herself away from Derek's arm, but he didn't seem at all inclined to let her go. At Cindy's side stood someone she recognised only too well. Nick Bradshaw. He smiled at her and she wished even more that Derek would remove his arm.

'What do you make of the set-up, Nick?' asked Derek. 'Glad to be in on the ground floor, I should think.'

'I'm impressed. You've thought it all out very well.' His words were aimed at Derek but his eyes were on Hilary. She felt uncomfortable beneath his now familiar gaze and wanted very much to wriggle out of Derek's grasp and away from this man's direct way of looking at her.

'Sorry,' Derek said suddenly. 'Forgetting my manners. Let me introduce Hilary Parker, she lives over the road and is one of our most industrious neighbours, organises us all like you'd never believe.'

'We've met already . . .'

Oh, please don't mention the tip, thought Hilary, not that.

'. . . at, of all places, the local tip,' Nick said, with a light, easy laugh.

Derek gave Hilary a squeeze with his arm. 'Well, you are a dark horse, Hilary,' he said, 'but I can think of more salubrious venues for a secret assignation.'

'Don't judge everyone by your own standards, Derek,' Cindy said coolly.

'I was only throwing away some rubbish, that was all,' Hilary said, flustered.

'Aha,' Derek said, remembering Rosie's words of a few days ago. 'There's no such thing as rubbish. Everything and everyone has a purpose.'

Cindy shook her head and Nick Bradshaw gave his new employer a polite smile.

'Nick's going to be head of stress and positive thinking here at All in the Mind,' Derek went on. 'Perhaps you should book your David in for a course. He's looking a bit frazzled these days. Been burning the candle at both ends, has he?'

'Derek!' snapped Cindy. 'I'm sure that what David is or is not doing is none of our concern. Mr Bradshaw, I'll show you out. Hilary, I presume it was me you wanted to see. I'll be back in a few minutes. Derek, go and put the kettle on.'

'Ja, mein Kapitän!' Derek said, letting go of Hilary and clicking his heels together.

Chapter Twelve

It was nearly half past three when Neville Archer remembered he hadn't been out to the shops. He threw a last handful of leaves onto the bonfire, picked up his rake and lumbered up the path to the back porch of the black and white timbered cottage.

He slipped off his gardening boots and padded through to the kitchen where he'd left his shoes over an hour ago. From the window he could see a thin trail of smoke threading its way upwards in the still, damp afternoon air. He knew he shouldn't leave the bonfire unattended but Louise would play up worse than a child if she came back from the shop and found no supper to eat, which right now far outweighed the potential risk of their thatch catching fire. But gradually the thought of explaining the remains of their burnt-out cottage to Louise took root in his mind and had him reaching under the sink for a plastic bucket. He carried it, slopping, down the garden path and doused the fire.

Back inside he grabbed his keys from the hook above the boiler, put on his overcoat and banged the front door shut after him. He left his Volvo in the car park behind the doctors' surgery, where he hoped that neither his wife nor Hilary would catch sight of it. 'Not too old to learn to ride a bike,' Louise would, no doubt, jibe at him for his laziness. He crossed the road and delved in his coat pocket for his shopping list. He tutted. He'd left it behind on the kitchen table. With a surge of regret he remembered how easy and straightforward his days as a GP had been – diagnosing and prescribing had been simplicity itself compared to the haphazard way he led his life now.

Now that he had been retired for some time the tasks of cooking and shopping had fallen into his lap. Not that he minded. But Louise seemed to take great delight in making things more complicated than they needed to be. Instead of writing a clear and easy-to-read message on the wipe-board on the kitchen wall as a reminder of something they had run out of, she would leave him cryptic notes lying about the house, yellow rectangles of paper with messages such as, 'We need some cuts grease to the squeak' – that was washing-up liquid – and 'some squeezably soft', toilet paper.

She was going through a phase of avid television viewing and she plundered the adverts each evening not only for new slogans to add to her collection of obscure names for household products, but for new and faster ways of eating. No longer was she obsessed with trimming him down to what she felt was a better weight. Now she had a thing about convenience foods. 'That looks easy enough,' she'd say, in response to a parsley-garnished meal-for-two emerging from a gleaming microwave. 'Even you could manage that, Neville.'

In defiance he'd taken to watching a cookery programme just before the lunch-time news. Last week he'd jotted down the recipe and served up beef and orange stir-fry for supper the following evening. He had thought it a culinary triumph and later that night had caught Louise hunting in the kitchen bin for the packaging.

Today on the television that nice blonde girl with the lisp had been making carrot soup. It had looked easy enough to him, just a matter of putting all the ingredients into a blender and Bob's your uncle – if only he could remember all the ingredients.

There was nobody in the grocer's when he pushed open the door. Joan Carter, whom he'd diagnosed three years ago as having angina, served him.

'Carrot soup? Well, you'll be wanting some carrots, then, won't you?' she said, putting some muddy ones onto the scales. 'A couple of pounds should do it.'

'I need an onion as well.'

'Spanish or home-grown?'

'You've got me there,' Neville said, trying to remember what the girl with the lisp had said above the noise of the blender.

'I've no truck with all this Euro nonsense,' Joan said. 'Have home-grown. How about some coriander?'

'Curry what?'

'Coriander. It's a herb. Here.' She handed him a bunch. 'You chop it up and sprinkle it over the food. It's all the rage, but give it a while and we'll soon be back to parsley. Probably them that knows best will find coriander's bad for you and say it's poisonous.'

Neville thought of Louise and nearly asked for two bunches.

Outside on the street again, he walked along the row of shops until he came to Charlotte's. She was busy stacking a set of shelves with Christmas ornaments. It didn't feel two minutes since Charlotte had stood on a chair helping him to decorate the Christmas tree each year; he passing the glass ornaments up to her while she, with infinite care, placed things in order of colour and size. 'No, not there,' she would say to herself, 'that bauble needs more space.'

'Hello, Dad,' she said, turning round to face him, 'and, yes, before you say anything I know I'm early with the decorations, but what the heck? Can you pass me that box from the counter?'

He handed it to her. 'I can't stop for long. I just thought I'd call in to see how you are.'

'I'm fine.'

'And Alex?'

Charlotte smiled. 'He's fine as well. How about you?'

'Fine.'

'Good,' Charlotte said mischievously, 'it's good that we're all fine.'

Neville picked up one of the large glass ornaments and turned it round in his hand. He could see his face looking back at him, all bulging eyes and bulbous nose. 'Any sign of ... well, you know?'

'Oh, Dad. Stop beating about the bush. Come right out and ask me.'

'Ask you what?' Neville said, putting the ornament back on the shelf.

'When Alex and I are getting married.'

Neville looked away, embarrassed. 'I'm not being nosy, Charlotte.'

She gave him a hug and breathed in the smoky smell of burning leaves from his clothes. 'I know you're not and as a matter of fact I'd like you to do something for me. Are you free on Christmas Eve?'

'I should think so. You know me, more time on my hands than I know what to do with.'

'Well, put it in your diary. You're coming on a walk with me.'

'I am? Not some ghastly rambling event, is it? That's more your mother's line of country.'

'Up the aisle of St John's. Let's see if we can get it right this time, shall we?'

Neville looked affectionately at his favourite daughter. Last year Charlotte had told him the truth about her marriage to Peter. At first he had been shocked, not so much because Charlotte's life with Peter had worked out the way it had but for the pain she had gone through alone after Peter's death – until, that was, Alex had come on the scene.

'I've a feeling Alex will make you a good husband,' he said simply. 'Peter was all right, but he wasn't really ...'

'He just wasn't the right man for me, Dad.'

'And you're absolutely sure Alex is?'

'I'm as sure as I can be.'

'Shall I tell you mother you've set a date?'

'Why not? She'll have to be told sooner or later.'

'You'll be making Hilary's day. She's convinced it's down to her that the two of you got together. Flushed with this victory under her belt, who knows who else will come in for her Cupid's arrow?'

Poor Hilary, thought Charlotte. The last thing she needed to think about at the moment was a wedding, never mind Cupid's arrow. She was wondering whether she ought to say anything to her father when the door opened and in walked David's secretary, Catherine Renshaw.

Too thin, was the first thought that came into Charlotte's head. Too thin, with much too much of the little-girl-lost look about her.

David's previous secretary had left to have a baby last year and Catherine had been the replacement. Then, a little over five months ago, David had reported to them all one night over dinner at The Gables that Catherine had been in tears in the office that day. 'That wretch of a husband has simply upped sticks and walked out. What kind of a man does that? Of course I've said I'll help all I can. Probably a pay rise would be a good idea.'

A pity David couldn't have stuck with just adding a few extra pounds to his secretary's salary, Charlotte thought angrily, watching Catherine in her smart woollen jacket move about the shop. She came to a stop at the shelf of silver frames and took off her leather gloves. Must have been a damn good pay rise, Charlotte thought bitterly, thinking how simple it was for a man like David to fall so helplessly for the oldest trick in the book, that of providing his strong manly shoulder to the tearful woman who seemingly has no one else to turn to.

'I'd better be off,' Neville said. 'I'm making carrot soup for your mother's tea.'

'Lucky old Mum,' Charlotte said, opening the door for her father.

She returned to displaying and pricing yet more Christmas decorations, while all the time keeping a watchful eye on her only customer. She felt fiercely protective towards her sister and wanted very much to lay into this smart piece of work who was doing her best to destroy another person's life.

'Do you have this in a smaller size?'

What, to match your brain? 'No, that's the smallest I have.' Charlotte kept her eyes on the frame in Catherine Renshaw's hands, not trusting herself to look her in the eye without revealing her anger. She was only too thankful that although this woman worked for her brother-in-law, there had been no previous social contact between them in the village, so no bright chit-chat was expected of her. She could remain aloof and sacrifice a sale if need be.

'Oh, that's a real shame. I suppose I could always have this one and put a mount in.'

'You could,' Charlotte replied airily.

'Except I don't really like mounted photographs.'

And I don't like you, so why don't you push off and leave my brother-in-law alone? 'Not working today?'

'Yes, but I've just slipped out. It's so quiet at the moment. No one likes to put their house on the market at this time of the year.'

'That's funny. David seems to have been pretty busy just recently. Hilary was only telling me the other day how he's always so late coming home these days.' She gave Catherine a long, hard stare, deciding to make her understand that nobody messed with the Archer sisters.

'I don't think I'll bother today.'

'Bother?'

'With the frame. I think I'll sleep on it.'

'Okay.' And make sure it's alone!

Chapter Thirteen

'What do you think?'

Cindy didn't answer. All her working life she'd been asked to transform women into something they weren't meant to be. She had lost count of how many women had asked her to turn them into the Princess of Wales – with or without the marriage problems. Years ago, of course, there had been a run on young girls wanting the Kylie Minogue or Madonna look, but the older women usually went for television presenters. Jill Dando was popular at the moment with the every-hair-in-place look, along with that wine expert now turned antiques buff. Judy Finnigan and Anne Diamond continued to have a steady following for the stay-at-home-mum look, but Gaby Roslin and Anthea Turner, with the more tousled appearance, were definitely number one for the wannabes.

'Well?'

'Hilary, are you sure this is a good idea?'

'I wouldn't be here if I didn't think it was,' Hilary answered with more assurance than she felt. She'd have preferred to be at home in the kitchen baking parkin and wrapping potatoes in foil ready for tonight's PTA bonfire party as in previous years, not sitting here in Cindy's pristine bathroom. It had seemed such a good idea on Monday when she'd called in and asked Cindy to do her hair later in the week for her – but, then, she hadn't let on to what she had in mind.

Cindy looked again at the picture Hilary had given her. It

was a cutting from the *Radio Times* and Anthea Turner stared back, eyes twinkling, mouth grinning, skin perfection itself. Cindy gave Hilary's face in the mirror a professional appraisal: eyes red, mouth sloping, complexion mottled. She would have to lie, she decided, like she had to all those other women. So why, then, was she hesitating? Because ... because Hilary was depending on her. Poor Hilary was hoping that this was all it would take to save her marriage. And it wasn't the first time she'd been asked to perform this miracle.

'Wouldn't you rather stick to your own hair colour?' Cindy suggested. 'This will be such a dramatic change.'

'I want it just like that,' Hilary replied, pointing at the picture in Cindy's hand. Her voice was raised and bordering on the petulant. 'I want my hair and make-up exactly like that. David likes Anthea Turner. He never used to miss her on a Saturday night. He once said he'd rather win a night out with Anthea than the lottery.' Hilary almost snatched the piece of paper out of Cindy's hands. She looked at it closely. When she'd been younger she'd always had her hair lightened, but since she'd had the children she hadn't bothered. At odd times over the years David had hinted at her having her hair like she'd worn it when they'd first met. 'Why?' she'd once asked him. 'Don't you like me as I am now?'

'Please, Cindy,' she said, 'can't we try it? What have I got to lose? It shouldn't be that difficult. After all, she's about my age, isn't she?'

True, thought Cindy, but sadly that's the only similarity. 'I'm sorry, Hilary, but I'm not a miracle worker.'

'Then I'm sorry to have taken up so much of your time,' Hilary said, getting up from the chair and mustering what little dignity she had left.

Years of professionalism hit Cindy smack in the face – she'd never yet lost a customer. 'I'm sorry, Hilary. I didn't mean that the way it sounded. Sit down and I'll explain.'

Under the slight persuasive pressure of Cindy's hands on her shoulders, Hilary sat down.

'I was going to say that I'm not a miracle worker in as much as I can't turn you into a replica of Anthea Turner. Your bone structure's completely different for a start and your hair—'

'How about as near as you can?'

Cindy smiled. 'So long as you accept the limitations I'm working with.'

Hilary nodded.

'Okay. Let's get started. It's going to take a few hours. I'll do the cut first, then put the highlights through and after I've blow-dried your hair and done your make-up we're going into Manchester.'

'Manchester?'

'Clothes, Hilary. We're going shopping.'

'But I can't, the children—'

'Tiffany won't mind babysitting for a few more hours. She needs the money.'

Manchester was busier than they had expected and when they had managed to find a space on the third level of the multi-storey car park Hilary and Cindy joined the warm buzz of shoppers inside Kendal's.

'These are much too expensive,' Hilary protested, after Cindy had guided her towards an area of spaciously displayed suits and separates. 'I can't possibly afford these prices.'

'It's your marriage we're trying to save, not your money,' Cindy said impatiently.

'But you know how stingy David is. He's only one step away from recycling the toilet paper. It won't just be my marriage I'm trying to save when he sees the bank statement, it'll be my neck. Can't we go downstairs? The clothes are cheaper – I mean, more reasonable – there.'

Resigned, Cindy headed towards the escalator. Hilary

followed quickly behind and they climbed aboard. Half-way down Hilary caught sight of herself in the mirror that lined the wall to her right. She felt a slight quickening in her stomach at the thought of surprising David when he came home from work that night. She felt so sure that her new hairstyle and make-over would bring him to his senses, would make him appreciate what he already had.

When Cindy had turned the chair round and Hilary had seen her hair for the first time, several shades lighter than her own natural mouse, it had been a shock. It certainly was a startling transformation, that and the effect of Cindy's cleverly applied make-up techniques. The initial shock now dealt with, Hilary was delighted with her new look and she smiled back at her reflection, confident that she had found the answer. *She would have her man.*

They stepped off the escalator and made for the racks of colour co-ordinated clothes. Hilary's eyes lit up at the sight of a display of red polo-neck sweaters. On the front of each jumper was a Scottie dog wearing a large tartan bow.

'No!' Cindy said adamantly.

'What do you mean?' Hilary said, already searching the rail for a size twelve.

'Tat!'

Hilary looked hurt. 'But they're so cute.'

'Look, Hilary. Cute is not going to woo David away from what's keeping him late at the office.'

'But I've always worn—'

'They're awful and I'm not letting you buy one. Not after all the trouble I've gone to. Believe me, Anthea wouldn't be seen dead in one. Now come on.'

Hilary raised her eyebrows. She'd had no idea Cindy could be like this – and Charlotte thought *she* was bossy!

An hour and a half later Cindy sank gratefully into a chair in the Venetian Restaurant on the fourth floor of the department store. She slipped her heels out of her shoes and moved her feet around, easing away the strain of supervising

Hilary's new wardrobe. She poured out two cups of tea and saw Hilary coming towards her, squeezing her way through the crowded restaurant. She looked hot and flustered, her hair showing signs of beginning to flop. More mousse needed, Cindy told herself. She would have to tell Hilary.

'Sorry I've been so long. The queue for the loo was horrendous. I thought I'd never get in.' She plonked herself down and stowed all her carrier bags on a ledge behind her. 'Oh, lovely, a cup of tea.'

'I got you a cake as well.' Cindy pushed the plate towards Hilary.

Hilary was touched. 'Thank you,' she said. 'And thanks also for, well, you know ... I'm sure it's going to work.' She looked at Cindy expectantly, hoping for her agreement.

Cindy didn't say anything. She opened her napkin and placed it on her lap. She knew the words Hilary wanted to hear – *Don't worry, this will put an end to David's adultery* – but she couldn't say them. She sipped her tea, feeling surprisingly sorry for Hilary and remembering how years ago when she had stumbled on Derek's second affair she had confided in Angela, her closest friend. Angela had been so helpful, had let Cindy cry on her shoulder and had even said all the right things, that everything would be all right. A week later she had discovered that it was Angela with whom Derek was sleeping. She had never trusted another woman since, which was, perhaps, why she had relied so heavily on the potential Tiffany had offered. She had hoped that Tiffany would become the close female confidante that she had so badly needed, someone who would never betray her. Poor Tiffany, Cindy thought, no wonder she had bucked from such an early age at her attempts to make her an ally. She had probably felt used and put upon.

But, now, here she was, helping another woman to cope with her husband's adultery. Why? What did she feel towards Hilary, with whom she had nothing in common, other than their unfaithful husbands?

Cindy's silence was making Hilary feel uncomfortable. She could sense some of her new-found hope slipping away from her. 'Cindy, you don't think I look like mutton dressed . . .?'

Cindy placed her cup on the saucer and, meeting Hilary's anxious eyes, it came to her that it wasn't just pity she felt towards Hilary, she actually quite liked her. Since living in Hulme Welford she had viewed Hilary as nothing more than a neighbour – a rather interfering neighbour at times – but more importantly she had seen her as safe, someone who wouldn't interest Derek and pose a threat. Now she saw her not only as neutral territory but as someone she could trust. Suddenly she wanted Hilary to be able to trust her.

'I'm not going to lie to you,' Cindy said, 'but I really do believe that what you've done today will make you feel better about yourself. It'll give you more confidence, which in my opinion is the most important aspect of trying out a new image.'

'You're right,' Hilary said, stirring her tea thoughtfully. 'You're absolutely right. And I'm going to go home and show David that I'm the best thing since sliced bread.' She took a long sip of her tea, then said, 'Cindy, can I say something?'

'Go on,' Cindy said warily.

'Since you've lived in the village you've always kept yourself to yourself and I think that's a waste, because until today I hadn't appreciated what a strong and considerate person you are. You don't mind me saying that, do you?'

Cindy slipped her shoes back onto her feet. For the first time since Angela's betrayal, she had allowed herself to make a friend. 'No,' she said quietly, 'I don't mind at all.'

Hilary sensed Cindy wasn't going to say any more on the subject and because she never felt comfortable with pregnant pauses in conversations she said the first thing that came into her head. 'That Nick Bradshaw character you've just taken on, what's he like?'

'That remains to be seen,' Cindy answered, forever cautious. 'He's certainly got all the right credentials and at least he . . .' Her voice trailed away.

'At least he's what?' Hilary asked, curious.

'I was going to say at least he's a man and not another woman roaming around the place.'

'Oh,' Hilary said, disappointed. For some reason she had hoped Cindy was going to embark on some long, elaborate story about this man, who from nowhere had suddenly appeared in Hulme Welford. 'Is he married?' she found herself asking.

'Has been, I think.'

Come on, Hilary thought, what kind of an interview session was it? 'How old is he and where does he live, in Hulme Welford?'

'Forty-four, I think, and not in the village, though offhand I can't remember exactly where. Why all the questions?'

'No reason,' Hilary answered, annoyed with herself for having even thought of the wretched man. But then he had, in fact, provided her with a few short moments during which she had thought of something other than the pain David was inflicting on her. Maybe he wasn't all bad.

Chapter Fourteen

'Bloody hell!' David stood in the kitchen doorway, his brief-case in one hand, the evening paper in the other, his mouth wide open. 'What have you done?'

'Don't you like it?' Hilary asked, as she passed him a glass of whisky and offered him a smile, both of which she'd prepared in advance.

'It's ... so different.' He took a gulp of whisky and con-tinued to stare.

'Cindy did it for me. I fancied a change,' Hilary said, as casually as she could manage. Earlier, in the bedroom, she had stood in front of the mirror and practised what she was going to say to David. *I fancied a change* was supposed to have been accompanied by a sultry stare and a nonchalant flick of her hair while leaning back against the worktop, a vision of sexual enticement. But, from the way David was staring at her, she had the feeling that she looked about as alluring as one of those models from a fifties knitting pattern.

'You remind me of someone,' David said, putting down his briefcase and loosening his tie.

Self-conscious, Hilary turned her back on him and straigh-tened the tea towel on the Aga rail.

'Damned if I can think who.'

'But you like it, don't you?' Oh, God, she was almost pleading with him. It wasn't supposed to have been like this at all. Why couldn't she be more confident?

'Hope Cindy gave you a bargain rate.'

Hilary whipped the towel off the rail and twisted it in her

hands. 'No, she didn't,' she almost shouted, turning round and facing him. 'Cindy did it for free, if you must know, as a friend.'

David smiled. 'Clever old you. What do the children think?'

Bugger the children! Hilary wanted to scream, I haven't gone to all this trouble to please Philip and Becky. When she'd arrived home from Manchester their reaction had been predictably derisive, with Becky shouting out the most painful comments. 'Mum looks like that woman on the telly.'

'Which one?' Hilary had asked hopefully.

'That one in the film we saw. Mrs Doubtfire!' She had then collapsed in exaggerated laughter on the floor in Philip's bedroom.

Philip had been comparatively less hurtful in his condemnation. 'It makes you look . . . well . . . kind of too young.'

'Too young?' she had repeated. 'What's wrong with that?'

Barely taking his eyes off the computer screen, he had gone on to say, 'Well, you're old, Mum, aren't you? And now you don't look right. You look wrong. I can't explain it any better.'

Tiffany had been sweet, though, but then Hilary had just been handing over her babysitting money. 'You look great,' she had said, eyeing Hilary up and down, taking in the new clothes Cindy had insisted she change into before dropping her off at The Gables. 'You've got less of the Marks and Spencer about you now.'

Under David's critical eye Hilary could feel her cheeks reddening despite the foundation and blusher Cindy had applied. 'Becky laughed, if you must know,' she said.

David gave a loud snort of appreciative laughter.

Hilary glared at him, knowing that all the anger she had been working so hard to keep in check since she had discovered David's unfaithfulness was no longer in check. She took the glass from David's hand and tipped the last quarter of an inch of whisky over his head, then calmly handed it back to him.

'What the hell—?'

'Yes, David,' she said, over her shoulder, as she walked away from him. 'What the hell indeed?'

'The flames of hell will be hotter still for some of those in this village,' declared Iris Braithwaite, as she and Charlotte backed away from the twenty-foot-high bonfire – all that was left of poor old Guy Fawkes was a pair of charred safety shoes, which were more than living up to the manufacturer's claims.

In the darkness and flickering orange light Iris's face had taken on the guise of a luminous Hallowe'en pumpkin. She looked dangerously menacing and, assuming that the older woman was referring to Charlotte and Alex's impure state, Charlotte prepared herself for the onslaught of a homily on the avoidance of sin. Instead, and above the crackle of burning garden refuse and wooden pallets, Iris hissed just two words, 'Ted Cooper.'

Charlotte relaxed and unclenched her gloved hands. At least she was off the hook. 'Ted Cooper?' she asked innocently. 'What's he been up to?'

'Been up to?' repeated Iris. 'Been up to, Mrs Lawrence? The man's a monster. A sexual fiend, peddling . . .' She paused for breath.

'Peddling what, Mrs Braithwaite?' Charlotte said, hoping the laughter rising within her could be staved off just a few minutes longer.

Iris fixed her with a long, hard stare. 'I notice you did not put my poster in your window as I asked.'

Charlotte stamped her feet on the iron hard ground; her face was hot and flushed from the heat of the bonfire, but her feet were frozen. 'I can't see what Ted's done wrong,' she said. 'You can buy those sorts of tights in most department stores. They're quite respectable, in fact women who suffer from thrush wear—'

'I'll thank you not to go into details, Mrs Lawrence. But I

take it, then, that you have not been in for a newspaper today?'

'No. No, I haven't.'

'I suggest you get down from your high and mighty position on the fence, Mrs Lawrence, and see for yourself what's going on here in Hulme Welford. It's quite apparent that Ted Cooper is not going to stop at the one lewd item of merchandise in his shop. He's added to his stock and it's the fault of people like you who don't care a fig. I hope your conscience allows you to enjoy yourself here tonight. Good night.'

Charlotte watched Iris Braithwaite disappear into the crowd. Added to his stock, she reflected. What on earth had Ted the Toup placed on his shelves that was giving Iris such apoplexy?

From the other side of the bonfire she saw Derek Rogers in a smart blue and cream skiing jacket and matching band round his head. He was waving to her through the smoke and flames. She waved back and he started making his way through the throng of over-excited children waving sparklers in the air and overwrought parents trying to prevent a replay of last night's television programme, 999.

Derek would be bound to know of any dodgy goings-on in the village, Charlotte decided. After all, he had been the main perpetrator of most things newsworthy since his arrival in Acacia Lane.

'Charlotte, where's that man of yours?' Derek greeted her, kissing her on the cheek. 'Abandoned you already, has he?'

'He's gone for some mulled wine.'

'Now, what's this I hear about you finally succumbing to his charms? I hope I'm invited. I'd love to be the one at the back of St John's with a just cause or impediment.'

'Well, you've certainly got an impediment,' Charlotte said, with a laugh.

'Oh, Charlotte, how did I ever let you slip through my fingers?'

'Derek,' Charlotte said firmly, 'I was never even there in your hands.'

He grinned. 'I distinctly recall a moment when I had you up against the kitchen sink in what the romantic novelist would describe as a passionate embrace.'

'Rubbish. You kissed me and tried to stick your hand down my blouse, in what a pubescent *Just Seventeen* reader would describe as a grope.'

'Yeah, well, call it what you want, but the old Derek Rogers School of Charm never fails. I still got you to kiss me.' And, as though to prove his point, he leaned into her and kissed her on the lips.

'Having trouble with your balance?' asked Alex, coming up behind Derek. 'Or are you still testing the water?' He handed Charlotte a polystyrene cup of mulled wine and placed a proprietorial arm around her shoulder. 'Oh and, Derek, if you're going to make a habit of kissing Charlotte, perhaps you could go easy on the aftershave. Less obvious that way.'

'Hey, you've got me all wrong,' Derek said, putting up his hands in a gesture of innocence. 'I was merely congratulating Charlotte on her good fortune. The best man obviously won.'

'Oh, shut up, Derek,' Charlotte laughed, 'and tell us how All in the Mind is shaping up.'

For a few minutes Derek had wandered back into the territory of his old self. He hastily switched to the new-style Derek – this New Man thing was going to be harder work than he'd supposed. 'We open next week,' he said, adopting what was fast becoming his welcome-to-the-fold voice. ' "Spiritual Journey" is fully booked. So is "Reaching Your Full Potential".'

'How about the marriage seminars you were advertising in the *Chronicle* this week?' asked Alex. 'Many takers?'

'Little disappointing there. I feel people are reluctant to step forward to the altar on that particular subject. They're frightened to admit to problems going on in the jolly-rogering department. So often marital problems are caused by sexual inadequacy and people just don't want to admit to it. But you, Alex, you wouldn't have any qualms about coming to our "Screw Your Inhibitions to the Bedpost" seminars if you weren't all that our lovely Charlotte was in need of, would you now?'

Alex smiled. 'Maybe people just can't equate All in the Mind with the man who probably thinks *The Man Who Mistook His Wife For a Hat* is a Les Dawson joke book.'

Charlotte gave Alex a dig in the ribs, but Derek looked at him as if he'd just flown in from Mars.

'Ever thought of some kind of therapy, Alex? Perhaps you should book in to see our Nick Bradshaw. He's head of stress and would be great at getting to the bottom of all your funny little quirks. He's here tonight as my guest with Rosie Williams. I'll introduce you. He'll have you sorted out in no time.'

'If Alex has got any funny little quirks, I'll be the one to minister to him.' Charlotte laughed, then changed the subject. 'Tell me what you know about Ted the Toup. What's he doing to give Iris such palpitations?'

'Come off it! The Pope would give old Ma Braithwaite palpitations, never mind Ted's range of intimate items of clothing.'

'His what?'

Derek gave Charlotte a wink. 'Best get yourself down there and order your trousseau. You might even pick up a little something in the way of posing accessories for your man here.'

'For goodness' sake, talk sense. What exactly is he selling?'

'It's perfectly harmless stuff, just a little erotica to pick up with your daily tabloid – you know the kind of thing.'

Charlotte and Alex waited expectantly. 'Come on then, what?' Alex said at last.

'Well, he's moved up the body, doing a line in lingerie. Basic kind of things, mostly cheap imports from the sweatshops of our Far Eastern friends – nothing that I would buy for Cindy, of course.'

'But why?'

'Cindy prefers pure silk, not—'

'No,' Charlotte said, exasperated. 'Why's Ted doing this?'

'You can't knock a man for extending his business, Charlotte.'

'Cods!' she retorted. 'Why smutty underwear? Why not birdseed?'

'Obvious, I suppose,' Alex said. 'After Mrs Braithwaite's petition he's coming back guns blazing.'

Charlotte shook her head and, as the first of the rockets was let off on the far side of the school playing field, she thought of the fireworks about to explode in the village, and of Iris Braithwaite putting on her boxing gloves for possibly the fight of her life.

As the fireworks exploded high above her head, Hilary caught sight of David and Catherine Renshaw standing together. Catherine's face was turned upwards, her lips parted in the obligatory *aah* position as diamonds of white magnesium light speckled the windless night sky forming, for a few magical seconds, a perfectly shaped dandelion.

Hilary's first thought was to run; to run all the way back to the safety of The Gables. Her second inclination was to ram the hot dog in her hand down that *aah*-shaped mouth.

She did neither, hearing the sound of her name spoken at her side.

'*Bonsoir*, Hilary.' It was Nick Renshaw. 'Go easy on that hot dog – you're squeezing the life out of it.'

Hilary grimaced at the sight of mustard and ketchup oozing all over her hands. The twisted bread roll and sausage looked disgusting. She threw it on the grass.

'Here.' Nick offered her a tissue from his coat pocket.

'Thank you,' she mumbled.

'I nearly didn't recognise you.'

She looked puzzled.

'Your hair. You've changed the colour and the style. It looks good.'

She turned away self-consciously.

'Ah,' he said.

'What do you mean, *ah*?' she said, meeting his gaze.

'You've forgotten how to receive a compliment, haven't you? Especially from a man you hardly know, whose motives could be considered at best dubious and at worst manipulative.'

'Good Lord. How ridiculous.'

Overhead another firework illuminated the smoke-filled sky and Nick's face suddenly seemed much too close. She took a small step away from him.

'Do I make you feel uneasy, Hilary?'

'You say the most absurd things. Or is that what you're paid to do?'

He laughed. 'More or less, but if it makes people understand that bit more about themselves then I can justify it. That throttled frankfurter, anyone I know?'

Hilary caught her breath. 'I shouldn't think so. And, anyway, why should it be *anyone*?'

'Just wondered whether it had anything to do with those glasses you were smashing the other day and the rich vocabulary you were trying out.'

Hilary had had enough. Everything was going wrong. Her new image had done nothing to bring David to his senses, in fact almost the reverse. On the way here he'd even questioned her on how much money she'd spent in Manchester with Cindy and then he'd gone on to ask her where she'd put his special whisky tumblers – without looking at him she'd made up some stupid story about having an accident when cleaning out the cupboard – and now here he was enjoying the fireworks with his mistress. And here she was, stuck with this wretched man and his smart-alec questions, poking his nose in where it just wasn't wanted. 'Why can't you mind your own business?' she responded hotly.

'Ouch!' Nick said. 'That's the second time you've said that. But well done. Keep going and I might eventually get the message that you don't like me.'

Hilary turned her back on him and watched Patricia Longton's husband light the fuse for the mounted display of fireworks. The first to go was a Catherine wheel. In the hushed, expectant silence Hilary suddenly laughed.

'Want to share the joke?' Nick whispered in her ear.

'Definitely not,' she said, trying to stifle yet more laughter at the image so clearly forming in her mind's eye – that of David's mistress impaled on a spike and spinning round and round before being tossed into orbit, never to be seen again.

'Enjoying yourself, Hilary?'

'David!' She decided to test him. 'Where have you been?'

'Just over there.' He pointed to where Catherine was talking to someone Hilary didn't recognise. 'I'm surprised you didn't see me.'

How brazen he was!

'I'm afraid I'm probably to blame,' Nick said, 'I've been talking too much.'

'This is Nick Bradshaw, David. He's starting at All in the Mind next week.'

David gave a short, loud laugh. 'You need your own head tested getting in with Derek on this latest harebrained scheme of his.'

'David!'

'It's all a load of tosh, isn't it?' David carried on, ignoring Hilary's admonishment. 'Just another way to exploit bored housewives. I guarantee you won't find any decent hard-working bloke skulking there on a couch having his inner-most thoughts paraded in front of him. What do you call it? Ah, yes, getting in touch with oneself.'

'That's quite a commonly held view. But usually voiced by

those with something to hide. Tell me, David, what are you most afraid of?'

'What's this? A free therapy session?' David said aggressively. 'I'm not that stupid. Next you'll be pulling out the ink blots and trying to draw out the feminine side of me.'

'David, stop being so rude.'

A firework screeched overhead, zigzagging its way high into the sky. In the sudden burst of silvery light Hilary saw both men clearly illuminated in front of her. In David's face she was struck by the hardness of his features, lips tightly drawn in a rigid line, which seemed to her in that moment to betray his dislike of their marriage. If there had been any trace of doubt in her mind that David was innocent of the crime he had allegedly committed, his face now confirmed his guilt. She felt sick, consumed with pain, as if her insides had just been ripped out. She turned to Nick and in his face saw all that she so badly wanted to see in David's face – warmth and understanding, kindness and humour. It was all there . . . *but in the wrong man.*

'I apologise for my apparent rudeness, which my wife has been only too quick to point out,' David said stiffly, when the sky darkened once more. 'I just wanted you to know that you're banging on the wrong door as far as I'm concerned.'

'You're probably right,' Nick said lightly. 'But at some time in our lives we all need a guiding hand. When we're up against the wall there's no better time to explore the dark nooks and crannies of our minds.'

'And what's that supposed to mean? Are you trying to tell me—'

'All I'm saying is that by having the opportunity to examine ourselves we can so often change our attitude or improve on our situation, not just for the benefit of ourselves but more importantly for those around us.'

'Mm . . .' David said. 'I suppose there could be an element of truth in what you say.' He turned to Hilary. 'You've got no complaints with me, though, have you?'

Hilary wanted to pick up the squashed hot dog from the grass beneath her feet and shove it down David's throat. No complaints! Not much she hadn't. She was only having to share her husband with another woman. 'Well, David, there are times when I feel you could—'

'There you are!' David rounded on Nick. 'You see what you've done. You've filled her head with silly nonsense about me not making the grade in some way.'

'And is that what you're afraid of, David?' Nick said quietly. 'Not making the grade?'

For a moment David seemed unable to speak. His anger was almost palpable. Then, as though fighting the urge to take Nick by the throat, he said, 'That's a load of crap. And if you want somebody to analyse try Hilary. Ask her why the new hairdo and why earlier this evening she poured whisky over me.' He walked away, his shoulders hunched, his hands thrust deep inside his coat pockets.

Hilary gasped.

'Interesting man, your husband.'

'Oh, shut up, can't you!'

Chapter Fifteen

'Bloody marvellous!' Georgia shouted at the top of her voice as she threw down the *Chronicle* on top of the paperwork spread over the small table in the caravan. Gordon, who was leaning on a broom outside, gave her a quizzical look. She went to the door and called him over. 'Come and see this.'

Gordon left his broom propped against a greenhouse, grateful for the opportunity to get out of the cold for a few minutes. He pulled off his gloves and climbed into the caravan. 'What's up? Not that git of an ex-husband of yours making a nuisance of himself again, is it?'

Georgia shook her head. Ever since she'd taken Gordon on as her right-hand boot – as he described himself – he had referred to Rory in this way, which was how he also referred to his previous employer. Several years ago, and at the age of sixty, local cutbacks in the National Health Service had forced him out of his post as a hospital porter. Then, having watched the work going on over the road from his cottage, he had called in one morning to ask Georgia if there were any jobs going. At first she'd turned him down for the simple reason that she didn't have the money to pay any wages. But within four months she was knocking on his door in a position to offer him part-time work. 'It's not much,' she'd told him.

'He'll take it,' his wife Winnie had said. 'I want him out from under my feet. He's always talking through Jimmy Young's programme on the radio. It's the medical bits he hates, embarrasses him summat rotten. If he starts giving you any nonsense just start talking prostate trouble. Lord knows how he lasted all those years in the hospital.'

Georgia had taken an instant liking to Winnie – who turned out to be a willing babysitter for Chloe – and Gordon, who more than proved his worth around the nursery.

She showed him the paper. He let out a long whistle. 'Skin and hair'll soon be flying, then, won't it?'

A black and white picture of fury stared back at them from the front page. Iris Braithwaite was photographed outside Ted the Toup's and the headline read, 'Hulme Welford's very own Mary Whitehouse'. The journalist had then gone on to report on Mrs Braithwaite's campaign to clean up the village of Hulme Welford. 'We must all fight this evil sin and do our public duty,' she was quoted as saying. The paper's editor had added to the article by inviting readers to write in with their comments on the debate 'To Censor or Not to Censor' – a debate which no doubt he clearly hoped would run and run and increase his circulation figures.

'I've said it once and I'll say it again,' Georgia said. 'It's bloody marvellous. Good for old Ma Braithwaite.'

'That's as may be,' Gordon said, pulling on his gloves to go back out into the cold. 'But, like as not, she'll bring trouble on herself and others.'

'How very profound of you, Gordon. You been listening to *Thought for the Day* again?'

From the doorway of the caravan she watched Gordon pick up his broom and start sweeping the leaves covering the path leading to one of the greenhouses. The newspaper was still in her hands and, catching sight of Mrs Braithwaite again, she made up her mind to go and see her.

'Gordon,' she called out, 'I'm going early to pick up Chloe, there's something I need to do. Hold the fort, will you?'

Georgia parked outside the White Cottage in Acacia Lane and as she walked up the garden path she tried hard not to be too disdainful of the overly ordered front garden. There was not a stray leaf in sight, not an overlooked bedding plant left there by chance from the summer. All was crisp and dreadfully bare.

She banged the brass knocker, loudly and eagerly: she had much to say to Mrs Braithwaite. She knew that most people in the village were scared of her, intimidated by her over-bearing manner. Georgia had always privately admired the way she handled herself. Before she'd encountered the older woman she had never come across anyone more single-minded than herself – a criticism Rory had levelled at her on more than one occasion.

But she was used to criticism, having put up with a bellyful since she'd got rid of Rory and his endless stream of excuses. She knew only too well what people like Patricia Longton had to say about her: What kind of a woman kicks out her daughter's father? She could have retaliated with the truth – which was, quite simply, that Rory couldn't be trusted to part his own hair, never mind run a business – but she'd chosen instead to thumb her nose at anyone who dared to point the finger of accusation in her direction. She knew, though, that despite themselves people had come to respect her for having got the nursery up and running. Where Rory had failed, she had succeeded. In her opinion people generally preferred success stories to depressing tales of failure.

She rapped the door knocker again.

'Whoever it is out there, kindly show some manners and have the goodness to wait a few moments.'

Georgia smiled and listened to the lock being turned.

'Oh, it's you, Mrs D'Arcy,' Iris said, surprised. 'What can I do for you?'

'It's *Ms* D'Arcy,' Georgia said firmly. 'I've come to see you about Ted Cooper.' Georgia felt the older woman's suspicious eyes weighing her up. She decided to take the initiative. 'May I come in?'

Iris pursed her lips at such forwardness. 'I'm a busy woman, Mrs D'Arcy.' She began to nudge the door closed.

'And so am I,' Georgia parried. 'I don't have much free

time but I've come especially to see you.'

The older woman seemed to consider this for a few seconds before saying, 'I can spare you a few minutes, no more,' holding the door fully open, and grudgingly allowing Georgia over the threshold. But almost immediately she shouted, 'Boots! Off with those muddy boots, if you please. I've had this carpet twenty-two years and I'm not about to have it ruined.'

She left Georgia to take off the offending articles and went through to the kitchen. 'I presume you do drink tea, Mrs D'Arcy,' she called out, 'or is that too conventional for you?'

'Tea will be fine and it's Ms D'Arcy. I was Mrs Maddox, but now that I'm divorced I've reverted back to my maiden name, okay? Perhaps Georgia would be easier for you to remember?'

Iris's head appeared abruptly at the kitchen door. 'Are you trying to imply I'm not capable of remembering a simple thing like a name? I'm not senile, young lady, if that's what you think.'

'Not at all, Mrs Braithwaite,' Georgia said, amused.

'Then I suggest you sit down in the sitting room and I'll join you there in a moment.'

Georgia went where she was told but prowled round the tidy room. It was almost as bare and clinical as the front garden, devoid of all the personal mementoes that usually cluttered up one's life. The thought occurred to Georgia that maybe this was deliberate. Perhaps Mrs Braithwaite didn't want the waters of the present muddied with reminders of the past because, as Georgia herself had come to know, retrospection of any kind led only to regret.

She sat in a high-backed winged chair and warmed her feet by the coal fire. It was two thirty on a Tuesday afternoon and here she was, lazing in an armchair feeling absurdly decadent, as if she was bunking off school. She almost wanted to laugh, but then her mood changed and she found herself feeling sorry for herself, that such a simple thing was now a complete luxury to her. She sat up straight and snatched her feet away from the fireside. Self-pity was such a wasted emotion and she couldn't afford to waste anything.

'I dare say you could manage a slice of Genoa cake,' Iris said, coming in with a tea-tray complete with a paper doily. 'You look like you could do with feeding up.'

'Please don't go spoiling me,' Georgia said briskly. A little too briskly. Iris's eyes shot up from the tea-tray.

'I've never spoilt anyone in my life,' she said firmly, handing Georgia a cup and saucer. 'I was merely making an observation,' she continued. 'In my opinion you look no more than two-penn'orth of copper. You clearly work too hard and give yourself little or no time at all in which to eat. Though I dare say you would disagree with me and tell me to mind my own business.' She passed a large slice of cake to Georgia, along with a napkin, and in a less strident tone added, 'It can't be easy for you, though, doing all that you do, alone.'

'Thank you,' Georgia muttered awkwardly. This was an area of her life on which she preferred not to dwell. There was nothing, absolutely nothing, to be gained in self-pitying explorations of the soul. If she did that she might lose the motivation to get out of bed in the morning. As it was, it was struggle enough summoning up the energy to face each day.

'So, what is it you want to discuss with me?' Iris asked, filling in the silence. 'I suppose you've come here to tell me not to be such a stupid interfering old woman. Is that it?'

'Quite the reverse, Mrs Braithwaite,' Georgia said, glad to be moving the conversation onto less personal ground. 'I've come to congratulate you and to offer my services.'

It was Iris's turn to be taken aback. 'You want to offer your help in ridding Hulme Welford of the likes of Ted Cooper? Go on.'

Georgia leaned forward in her seat. 'Yes,' she said, nodding, her long ear-rings swinging precariously 'There's no room for disgusting old men like him in this world.'

'How right you are Mrs ... Ms D'Arcy. And how refreshing to hear such a plainly spoken view on this contemptible issue. I had thought that people like yourself were full of rampant liberalism, promoting the ethos that anything goes.'

'I believe in absolute equality, Mrs Braithwaite, which means the exploitation of women has to be stopped. Do you see what I mean?'

'Good Lord, young lady. Please don't lecture me.'

'I'm sorry,' Georgia said, biting into her slice of cake. When she'd finished her mouthful she said, 'So what's the next step in your campaign?'

'I'm hoping that this newspaper article will shame the grubby little man into disbanding his ghastly scheme.'

Georgia shook her head, her ear-rings swinging again. 'No chance!' she said, with such vehemence that Iris clattered her cup on its saucer. 'I don't believe that will happen. The newspaper story will just antagonise the man. We're going to have to come up with further retaliation. We've got to produce a barrage of disapproval at what he's doing.'

'You've obviously given this some thought. And just what do you have in mind exactly?'

A slow smile spread over Georgia's face. 'Another cup of tea, Mrs Braithwaite, and I'll gladly tell you.'

Iris filled Georgia's cup, but when she handed it back Georgia nearly dropped the green Beryl-ware china as she heard the unexpected words, 'Perhaps you'd like to call me Iris.'

The three thirty school-gate gathering was buzzing with the news.

Patricia Longton pulled Hilary into the fold with evangelical zeal. 'I'm thinking of putting an opposing petition together,' she said. 'It's all perfectly innocent what Ted's selling. You'll sign of course, won't you, Hilary?'

Hilary shivered inside her coat and wondered why Patricia

never did up the zip on her smelly old waxed jacket.

'I'm sure we can rely on Hilary's support,' Kate Hampton chimed in. 'After all, she's always been one of the girls.'

'*Les girls*, that's us.' Patricia laughed.

Hilary didn't feel at all one of the girls, not after Patricia's comments this morning at the gate. She'd spent a good fifteen minutes tearing apart the organisation of the school bonfire party. 'Fancy not having enough hot dogs,' she'd opened up with. 'Not a hint of a relish to be had and as for having sparklers for all the children, well, let's just say it was a miracle we didn't have any serious casualties. *She* won't last long, take my word for it. And you know what people are saying about *her*, don't you?'

Out of habit Hilary had given the necessary tilt of the head thereby giving Patricia the green light to continue with her axegrinding.

'They say that Rory had other women because ...' here Patricia had paused for dramatic emphasis, turning her head from left to right, 'because she's a lesbian. I should keep your distance, if I were you. Just think what David would say if there were rumours that you, well, you know what I mean. People might not want to buy their home from a man whose wife ... I'm sure I don't have to spell it out for you, Hilary.'

It was all right, of course, for an estate agent to be bonking his secretary, Hilary had muttered all the way home, after managing to escape Patricia's vile tongue, but heaven forbid that his wife should have a friendship with another woman whose sexuality was in question. And how dare Patricia say such awful things about Georgia, especially when Georgia had been so kind to her? Stupid, smug Patricia was probably just jealous that she had found a new friend.

'French class tonight, Hilary,' Patricia said, bringing Hilary back to that afternoon's gossip session. 'Done your homework?'

Damn! She hadn't. 'Plenty of time yet,' she said airily.

'Hope you're not going to keep that nice Nick Bradshaw

all to yourself this evening. I'd rather like to do some con-versational work with him myself.' She gave Kate Hampton a wink.

'You're welcome to him,' Hilary replied.

'A lover's tiff already?' Kate chirped. 'How much to keep it quiet from David?'

Oh, the irony, thought Hilary. With relief she saw Patricia's infamously uncontrollable sons coming across the play-ground.

'See you all,' Patricia called as she led away the two small boys, who lagged behind her throwing leaves at the passing cars.

Kate Hampton's pony-mad daughter Victoria was next to appear in the throng of children, and when she left Hilary felt herself relax. *Les girls*, indeed. *Les bitches*, more like it. And to think she used to consider them friends.

'Hello, Hilary.'

'Georgia,' Hilary said brightly.

'I don't know what I've done to deserve a smile like that, but thanks all the same.'

'Would you like to come back for a cup of tea and some cake?' Hilary asked, not sure whether she was responding to Georgia's undernourished appearance – she was wrapped in a duffel coat and looking even more urchin-like today – or more to spite Patricia.

'Must be my lucky day for tea and cake. Are you sure? Don't you have Philip to pick up?'

'He's got a play rehearsal tonight. I don't have to collect him until six.'

'Okay, then, but only for a short while. I've left Gordon in charge. And I ought to warn you about Chloe. No time, here she comes.'

A girl in a bulky duffel coat not much smaller than Georgia's was striding across the playground. And, also like Georgia, her hair was cut short framing a small pixie face. All that was missing to complete the similarity was a pair of dangling ear-rings.

In the distance was Becky, skipping happily along in a world of her own, her plaited hair bouncing on her shoulders, her pink lunch-box swinging in her hand.

'Okay, chuck?' Georgia said to her daughter.

'Another day of the same old female repression,' Chloe announced mournfully. 'Mrs Arnold is insisting I play Mary in the nativity play. I told her I wanted to be Joseph, that I know my way round a hammer and saw better than a baby's bum.'

Georgia smiled. 'Hilary's invited us for a cup of tea, that all right with you?'

'Fine.'

'Mummy, Mummy! Guess what?' Becky said breathlessly as she joined them. 'I'm going to be an angel in the nativity play. You'll need to get me loads of tinsel for my halo and wings, some white tights and a huge white sheet.'

Chloe gave a contemptuous grunt.

Hilary set the tea-things on the pine table in the kitchen. She was fussing, she knew, over-compensating for ten-year-old Chloe's disapproval of everything Becky said and did. But Becky couldn't help being a typical girl, it was just the way she was. She had always wanted long hair and to play with dolls.

'You've had your hair done,' Georgia said, helping to pass plates of cake around the table.

Hilary sensed yet more disapproval. 'I fancied something different,' she said defensively, convinced that Georgia had guessed at the reason behind the sudden change in her appearance. 'Do you want Ribena or orange squash, Chloe?'

Chloe pulled a face. 'I'd prefer tea, please. Black, no sugar.'

Becky was impressed. She sometimes had tea but it was always milky with a tiny bit of sugar, if she was lucky. Black without sugar was dead grown-up. 'I'll have the same,' she said, looking at her mother.

Eyebrows raised, Hilary fetched two more mugs and exchanged a knowing look with Georgia.

When tea was over Chloe reluctantly agreed to go upstairs to see Becky's bedroom.

'Poor Chloe,' Hilary said, after the girls had left the kitchen, 'she's so very grown-up and modern, Becky's the complete opposite.'

'No worries. Chloe will soon have her whipped into shape. Now tell me about this new look of yours. Has it worked?'

Embarrassed, Hilary started to clear away the mugs and plates.

'Leave all that,' Georgia said, sharply. 'Sit down, stop fidgeting and talk to me. Did the rat even notice the trouble you'd gone to?'

'Oh, he noticed all right,' Hilary said. She slipped into her chair. 'I think for the first time in his life he was stuck for words.' She chewed on her lower lip. 'Then he laughed ... Oh, Georgia, he laughed at me. He's probably been having a good laugh with her as well.'

'Best not think of that,' Georgia said softly.

'I only did it because I know how much he likes Anthea Turner on the telly. It's pathetic, isn't it? I got Cindy to do it for me ... She didn't want to, but I made her do it, so that I ...'

'So that you could please David?'

'Yes.'

Georgia leaned back in her chair and shook her head. 'Believe me, it doesn't work. I tried it for years with Rory. Whatever you offer to some men, it's just not enough.'

Neither spoke for a few minutes, the ticking of the clock above the Aga the only sound between the two women, that and the occasional thud from Becky's room above them.

At last Hilary looked up. She was shocked to find Georgia staring straight at her, as if she had been doing so for some time. Something in her face reminded Hilary of being back at school with Naomi Scott. How she had wanted Naomi to look at her in the way Georgia—

Suddenly she recalled Patricia's whispered words at the school gate: '*They say she's a . . .*'

Hilary swallowed hard, horrified. What was she doing? What kind of situation was developing between her and Georgia?

'Poor you,' she heard Georgia say. Then a hand reached out across the table towards her.

Panic-stricken she leapt to her feet. 'I've got to prepare the vegetables for supper,' she squeaked. 'And then I'll have to collect Philip.'

Georgia frowned. 'I thought you said he didn't finish until six. It's not even half past four.'

'I lied . . . I mean I forgot the play rehearsal isn't tonight, it's tomorrow.' She started clattering the plates into a pile and making for the dishwasher. 'I'm like that these days. Forget things all the time, must be hormones or something. Senile, even. Yes, that's it. I'm probably going senile. Not at all the kind of person you'd like as a friend.'

Georgia laughed and got up from her chair. She walked towards Hilary, her hands outstretched.

Oh my God, Hilary thought. She's going to kiss me. Help! Somebody help me.

Help came at once in the form of two loud rings on the doorbell.

Chapter Sixteen

Never in all her life had Hilary been so pleased to see a man. And Nick Bradshaw, all six foot of him, corduroys and plum-coloured wool jacket and scarf tied loosely round his neck standing on the doorstep, was a gift from heaven.

'Come in, come in,' she said, pulling him over the threshold. 'Tea! I'm sure you'd love a cup, wouldn't you?'

Nick was bemused. He had called on the off-chance of apologising to Hilary for what he'd said to David at the bonfire party last week and had expected little more than a frosty welcome. 'Thank you,' he said, 'so long as you're sure it's no trouble.'

'No trouble at all,' Hilary burbled, leading the way to the kitchen.

'I thought you were in a hurry to collect Philip?' Georgia said coldly, staring straight at Hilary. She was leaning against the Aga, her legs crossed at the ankles and her arms folded over her small breasts.

Nick looked from one woman to the other. He sensed he had come in on the middle of something. He also sensed hostility emanating from the woman by the Aga. 'Hi,' he said, offering a smile and a handshake. Just as he had expected, both were treated to a dismissive shrug by a pair of fragile-looking shoulders.

'I'll be off, then,' Georgia said, picking up her duffel coat from the back of a chair. 'I'll call Chloe down while you see to your *guest*.'

'Don't go,' Hilary said.

Alert to the falseness in Hilary's voice, Nick watched her closely. Relief was written all over her face. Intrigued, he turned to the other woman. 'Please don't leave on my account.'

'I wouldn't do anything on your account,' came the quick-fire put-down.

He listened to the politely said goodbyes in the hall and the sound of the front door shutting.

'Sorry about that,' Hilary said, coming back into the kitchen. 'Georgia's on the PTA with me. I barely know her, really, in fact I'd go so far as to say—'

'It's okay, you don't have to explain your friends to me. I was over the road with Derek and Cindy and thought I'd call by to apologise for the other night.'

'Oh,' she said, surprised.

'Any chance of that cup of tea?' He removed his scarf and took Georgia's place against the Aga. 'Or was that just a ruse to get rid of your unwanted visitor?'

Hilary was beginning to feel tired of having to keep up with so many different conversations. Her life never used to be like this. The most taxing word game she'd ever played before was second-guessing Becky. Fed up, she filled the kettle.

'I'm sorry I pushed your husband the way I did. Some might say I was behaving in an unprofessional manner, but I'm afraid I don't go in for the conventional tried and tested views a lot of the time. Do you forgive me?'

'If it makes you feel better, yes,' she answered wearily, staring out at the back garden. It was dark outside and something must have set off the security light: the lawn and flower-beds were brilliantly illuminated – she could see a cat disappearing into the laurel bushes at the far end of the garden.

'I would rather it made you feel better.'

'Sorry?'

'You look tired, Hilary.'

'I am,' she said flatly. She made him a mug of tea and wondered why she felt so uncomfortable when he called her by her name.

'Do you think your husband will accept my apology?'

Hilary thought how defensively aggressive David had suddenly become and of his many prejudices; his condemnation of the two and a half million unemployed in the country, his dislike of change and his reluctance to part with any money, and now his obvious cynicism towards the world of therapy, something she'd been unaware of until now. 'I shouldn't think so for one minute,' she said.

When Nick didn't say anything but watched her over the top of his mug, she felt even more uncomfortable and compelled to say something herself. 'Do you counsel people on their marriages?'

'I have done in the past,' he said slowly, 'but that won't be what I'll be doing at All in the Mind.'

'But you could offer help, for instance, to a friend of mine who was having difficulties?' What on earth was she doing? Of course he'd see through what she was saying. Why couldn't she just shut up, let him drink his tea then get him out of the house?

'I'd like to think that if anyone needed advice they would feel able to ask me straight out for help. You included, Hilary.'

There he went again. Why did he have to keep calling her by her name? She decided not to say anything further. She'd let him do all the talking.

'Are you and David—'

The door opened and banged noisily against a cupboard. Becky appeared with her arms full of Barbie dolls and accessories. 'Chloe says I must chuck these out. Oh, who are you?' She gave Nick an accusing stare.

'Oh, he's just a man,' Hilary said quickly, grateful for once for her daughter's habit of barging into conversations.

Becky gave a shrill laugh and squeezed her eyes tightly

shut. She looked constipated, but Hilary knew better: some newly learned piece of knowledge was about to be given an airing.

'Chloe says that when God made man she was only joking.'

It was pitch black and Philip was alone. All the others had gone, picked up by their mothers or fathers. He peered into the darkness of the badly lit school driveway, hoping to see his mother's Renault Clio. Some of the mothers drove to school in sports cars, most drove estates or Shoguns. It would be nice if Mum had a flashier car. In the mornings he came to school by bus, which was okay, but because there were so many activities to do after school it usually meant that he was picked up by Mum in the afternoon.

Most of his friends from junior school had gone on to the High, but he'd won a scholarship to the same school that Tiffany went to. He could remember the look on his dad's face when the letter had come in the post. Yeah, that had been great. He and Mum had bought him a computer for doing so well in his exam. It was hard being at St Hugh's, though, more difficult than he'd thought it was going to be. Some of the masters seemed to enjoy making him get upset when he couldn't do the work. He cringed at how he'd wet himself on his first day. Bloody hell! Eleven years old and he'd wet himself. Bloody, bloody hell!

He looked at his watch. Where was she? He hoped she was okay. He'd heard her crying last week and just the other day. Why? What did she have to be sad about?

Batesy said his mother was like that last year. But, then, she'd had something to cry about. Batesy's dad had left home last year just before Christmas; brought them all presents, Batesy said, then disappeared off with another woman on Boxing Day.

Philip chewed what was left of his bitten thumbnail. His dad wasn't going to leave, so Mum wouldn't be crying for that reason, would she? Stuff Batesy! Batesy's dad probably left home because Batesy was such an idiot. He wasn't an idiot, he'd won a scholarship. So that was okay then.

But where was Mum?

'Still here, Philip?'

'Yes, sir.'

'Why don't you come into the warm and wait?'

'I'm all right, sir. I'm sure my mother will be here soon.'

'Suit yourself.'

He watched Mr Wells, the Latin master, disappear into the school building. Mr Wells was okay. He was one of the nicer teachers. It was Mr Wells who had caught those boys the other day. Tiffany had warned him that there were bullies in the school. She'd even said that she'd sort them out if he needed help. Flipping heck, no girl was ever going to sort out his problems. Anyway, if those boys tried it on again, he'd be ready for them.

He looked at his watch. In the distance he heard the sound of a car and saw two headlights coming towards him. He held his breath. Please let it be Mum. The car drew level and he caught sight of Becky sticking her tongue out at him. He let out his breath in one long deep sigh.

'How are you getting on with *Emma*?' Hilary asked Tiffany, watching her drop her large bag of schoolwork onto the floor in the sitting room.

'That geek Mr Elton has just tried it on with her. He's really got the hots for her, hasn't he? Serves her right, if you ask me. I can't understand what George Knightley sees in Emma – you'd think he could do better for himself.'

'Well, I'd better leave you to it,' Hilary said, gathering up her own schoolwork. 'Becky's in her room having a sort-out and Philip's on his computer. I've left some cake for you and there's plenty of biscuits in the cupboard.'

'Thanks, have fun with your French.'

Hilary banged the door shut after her and turned up her

coat against the wind as she walked the short distance to school. Have fun, Tiffany had said. How could she? Not only was that wretched Nick Bradshaw going to be there but she hadn't done her homework. A sudden gust of wind cut through her coat and she shivered. And on top of that Patricia would be gloating like mad that she'd done hers.

The day had rushed past her in such a flurry of activity that she'd barely had time to think of David. Even when he'd got in from work she'd been so preoccupied thinking about Georgia and Nick that she hadn't thought twice about what David may nor may not have been up to at the office, or, indeed, whether he would be going anywhere near the squash club that evening. Thinking about it now, he had seemed distracted at the supper table and hadn't even said anything when the children had started bickering. Philip had started to tell one of his jokes and Becky had looked him in the eye and said, '*You're* just a boy.'

''Course I am. So?' he had answered.

'My new friend Chloe says that boys don't grow as fast as girls, so you know what that means, don't you? It means I'm probably more intelligent than you.'

'Let's see *you* get a scholarship, then!'

Even when Becky had flounced out of the kitchen with her nose high in the air like Miss Piggy and had then bumped into the door and started wailing like a siren, David had seemed oblivious to it all and had got up from the table saying he'd better hurry or he'd be late for his game of squash.

It started to rain just as Hilary crossed the main road opposite St John's. She quickened her pace and shuddered as a drop of water trickled down her neck. By the time she reached the school gate the rain had turned to hail. She bolted across the playground, head down, at the same time trying to shelter her textbook by tucking it close to her chest. At the main entrance door she stepped inside and gasped for air, shaking her wet and bedraggled hair. As she walked along the echoing corridor she could hear Martina's voice giving out instructions for the lesson.

Damn! She was late.

Then behind her she heard the sound of the door crashing shut, followed by hurried footsteps.

'Glad I'm not the only one who's late.'

Without turning round she knew who it was. Subconsciously she slowed her step. Some mad part of her wanted to be able to enter the classroom with Nick – That'd show Patricia, she thought.

Nick held the door open for her and she went in. 'Hello, Martina,' she said brightly, 'sorry I'm late.'

'Me too,' Nick said.

'Make them stand in the corner,' Patricia said, 'but not together.'

'Shame,' laughed Nick, making his way to the back of the classroom where he'd sat previously. Hilary immediately started for a free chair next to an elderly woman who had never once, in Hilary's knowledge, opened her mouth during any of the lessons.

'Hilary, would you mind sharing with Nick again?' Martina asked. 'I haven't managed to get a book for him yet. We're on page thirty-one: "Dans la Chambre à Coucher".'

Hilary heard a snigger from the front row – Patricia. Reluctantly she sat next to Nick.

'Sorry to get you lumbered with me again,' he said. Then, in a quieter voice, he added, 'Thanks for the tea earlier, by the way.'

After Becky had made her dramatic entrance into the kitchen, Hilary had been surprised at how Nick had treated Becky. He'd bent down to her and thoughtfully examined one of the Barbie dolls destined for the bin. He'd shaken his head and tutted loudly. 'Dolls, instruments of oppression without a doubt. I'd get rid of the whole lot of them if I were you.' Then he'd stood up and, with his back to Becky, he'd winked at Hilary and smiled. 'Time I was going. Looks like you've a revolution on your hands, I'll leave you to it.'

'Hilary. Qu'est-ce qu'il y a dans l'armoire?'

Hilary studied the picture. *Armoire*. What on earth was an *armoire*? 'Um ... *le lit*?' she said hopefully.

Patricia laughed. 'It'd be a pretty big wardrobe!'

'Quelle chatte!' Nick whispered at Hilary's side. 'Me-ow!'

'Non, Hilary, le lit est sur le plancher. Qu'est-ce qu'il y a dans l'armoire?'

Hilary hesitated. What was the wretched word for clothes?

'Vêtements,' whispered Nick.

'I knew that,' she hissed at him. 'I don't need any help. Vêtements,' she said out loud.

'Bien, et maintenant vos devoirs. Patricia?'

'Oui, Martina. Mes vacances en Florida.'

Hilary closed her eyes and groaned quietly to herself. She'd heard it all before at the school gate. Patricia and family at Manchester airport. Patricia and family miraculously upgraded. Patricia and family at Kennedy Space Center. Patricia and family at Universal Studios. She felt a nudge at her elbow and opened her eyes to see a scrap of paper on the desk in front of her. On it was written, *You thinking what I'm thinking?*

She nearly laughed – nearly risked one of Patricia's disapproving looks. She turned the piece of paper over and wrote, *I doubt it.*

He passed her another note: *Do you think you could chance just one drink with me when we've finished here tonight?*

Certainly not. I'm married! she scribbled in large letters.

'Does that mean you never get thirsty?' he whispered.

She laughed. Patricia huffed in her direction. 'Quand nous sommes arrivés ...' she repeated for Hilary's benefit.

Good grief, thought Hilary, we haven't even got to the bit where the hotel porter got the brand-new Samsonite luggage mixed up with some inferior cases.

At this rate maybe she'd need a drink by the end of the class.

Chapter Seventeen

'Come on, stop fussing. They'll be fine.'

Hilary heard David leave the room and go downstairs. She thought how easy it was for men to switch off their emotions, even when it came to their children.

Very carefully, Hilary sat on the edge of Becky's bed – she was fast asleep and looking her most benign. Hilary kissed her lightly on the cheek and breathed in the smell of her newly washed hair. It made her want to take off her coat and nestle down beside Becky. She didn't want to go out. She didn't want an evening with David, pretending to all those at Derek and Cindy's launch party that their life was just fine. Her life was far from fine and she felt like shouting it out to everyone that night that David was an adulterous, selfish swine.

She kissed Becky once more as if for luck, then went across the landing to Philip's room where she could hear the low throb-throb of Oasis's latest CD. Philip was bent over his desk staring at a book.

'How's the homework going?' she asked.

'The Crusades,' he answered, without looking up. 'It says here they boiled babies alive and then ate them. You don't suppose we could do the same with Becky, do you?'

'Philip!'

'Only joking.'

'And I only came in to say goodbye. You're sure you'll be all right?'

'I'll be fine, Mum, honestly.'

'I'll keep popping back every thirty minutes.'

'You're only going over the road. I'll be okay.'

'You won't go watching anything unsuitable on the television, will you?'

'Mum!'

She gave him a quick kiss on the top of his head, so quick he didn't have time to duck out of the way.

Philip waited for the sound of the front door to shut. Then, reaching across his desk, he parted the bedroom curtains with the end of his pencil and peered through the inch gap. He watched his parents cross the road but flicked away his pencil when he saw his mother glance back up at the house. Had she seen him? He hoped not. He didn't want her thinking he was scared of being on his own.

He wasn't scared.

Like he wasn't scared of those idiots in the changing rooms at school. Batesy was pathetic to have given in to them. He shouldn't have done that, not when they'd promised each other they'd stick together.

He chewed his little finger and returned his attention to the gruesome pictures of severed heads and blood-tipped spears in his history book, convinced that what the Crusaders had experienced was nothing compared to what he was going through.

When at last there was nothing left of his finger-nail he slapped the book shut, threw himself on his bed and buried his head under the pillow to block out the thought of Batesy's betrayal and how alone he felt.

It was almost freezing, just as the weather forecast had predicted, and their breath formed gauzy clouds in the still night air. Alex wrapped his arm round Charlotte. 'Shall we make a run for it?' he asked, as they set off down the drive of Ivy Cottage.

'What, in these heels?'

'Well, I'm not carrying you. I'm saving all my energy for

the honeymoon. There are certain obligations a man's got to fulfil on his wedding night.'

Charlotte laughed. 'You've still not told me where we're going.'

'And nor shall I.'

As they turned into Derek and Cindy's drive Charlotte stopped and faced Alex. 'What, not even if ...' She buried her face in his neck and whispered in his ear. He laughed out loud and kissed her.

'Well really!' reprimanded Iris Braithwaite, appearing from nowhere in the darkness with a puff of dragon-like steam coming out of her mouth.

Ignoring the ticking off and taking in Iris's voluminous fur coat Alex said, 'You're looking very fetching tonight, Mrs Braithwaite.'

'Don't waste your flattery on me, young man. Save it for Mrs Lawrence. It might help you to get her to the altar quicker.'

'Hadn't you heard, Mrs Braithwaite? We've already set a date for the wedding,' Charlotte said, as they fell in step up the floodlit driveway of All in the Mind.

Iris gave her a reproachful glance. 'Yes, I had heard talk, but not having seen hide nor hair of an invitation I dismissed it as nothing more than idle gossip.'

'Alex, you surely didn't forget Mrs Braithwaite's invitation?'

'Silly me,' he said, squeezing Charlotte's hand. 'I must say, I'm surprised to see you here tonight,' he said to Iris. 'You're not exactly one of Derek's greatest fans, are you?'

'I'm here in an official capacity. In a small community such as ours it pays to keep one's finger on the pulse.' And coming to Derek and Cindy's front door she raised her hand and gave the bell a long, hard prod.

Tiffany greeted them.

'Love the dress,' Charlotte said, kissing Tiffany. 'Very vampish.'

Tiffany smiled, one hand fiddling with a wispy tendril of hair hanging in front of her right ear and the other playing with a black velvet choker at her throat.

'You'll catch your death of cold, young lady,' declared Iris, casting a disapproving eye over Tiffany's *décolletage*. It was encouragement enough for Tiffany to lower both her hands and push out her chest.

'Attagirl,' whispered Alex, coming forward to kiss her. 'Take no notice, you look great – especially without the Doc Martens.'

'I'm into glamour these days,' she purred provocatively, and kicked him with an elegant black suede shoe with a three-inch heel. 'Give me your coats and I'll throw them on the bed upstairs.'

'You'll do no such thing with mine,' Iris said. 'I've had this coat since nineteen fifty-seven.'

'Too late to give it back to the poor animal who lost it in the first place, then.'

'I beg your pardon, young lady. I'll have it—'

'Stuffed?' said Tiffany, under her breath.

'Hung up, if you don't mind.'

'Go through and help yourselves to a drink,' Tiffany said to Charlotte and Alex. 'Barry's here somewhere. He's come home for the weekend specially for Dad's big night.'

The sitting room was packed and guests had spilled out into the conservatory. Both rooms were decorated with navy blue and gold swags with matching balloons with the words All in the Mind printed on them. Music was playing but was only just discernible above the noisy hubbub of voices.

'There's Dad,' Charlotte said straight away, seeing her father standing alone. He was giving all his interest to a large ornately framed photographic portrait of the Rogers family. She and Alex grabbed a couple of glasses of champagne from a passing waiter and headed over towards Neville.

'Charlotte. You've rescued me at last. What took you so

long? I've been waiting ages for you. You know how I hate parties.'

'I'm partly to blame,' Alex said. 'Mrs Braithwaite caught us kissing.'

'Not enough of it going on, in my opinion.' Neville laughed.

'Not enough of what going on?'

'Kissing,' Charlotte said with a wink, making room for Derek to join them. He was dressed in cream trousers with a dark navy-blue T-shirt with the words All in the Mind scrolled across his chest in gold letters.

'You really must stop all this sexual harassment, Charlotte. After all, I am a married man.'

'And since when has that ever stopped you?' Cindy said, coming over with a tray of bite-sized vol-au-vents. She, too, was wearing cream trousers and a top just like Derek's.

'So how are all the alterations going?' Alex asked.

'Fine, just fine,' Derek answered. 'The only job pending is to repaint the outside of the house. I know you'll all be disappointed, but I'm afraid it's time to say goodbye to Windolene Cottage. Anyway, how do you like the T-shirts? Good bit of advertising, eh? I'm thinking of selling them to the punters ... I mean, clients.'

'I feel like having one with Losing my Mind on it,' Cindy muttered.

'Hey! I like that.' Derek laughed. 'Catchy slogan, "Losing your mind? Then come to All in the Mind". You're a genius, Cindy. Perhaps we could get it put to music and have it as a jingle on local radio.'

Cindy groaned – he was probably serious.

'Well, I think we ought to drink to your new venture,' Charlotte said, raising her glass. 'To All in the Mind. May it be all in the bank as well.'

'Oh, Charlotte,' Derek said, shaking his head. 'No, no, no. This isn't about making money. This is a window of opportunity to save lost souls.'

'I thought that was my department,' Malcolm Jackson called over, from where he was talking to Louise.

Derek grinned. 'The ones we can't help I promise to send on to you.'

'Very generous of you,' Malcolm said. 'Any chance of a repeat performance of Barry's confirmation party tonight? Music's a bit on the dull side so far.'

Cindy looked away guiltily. As a precautionary measure she had hidden some of Derek's favourite CDs, knowing what the outcome of the evening would be if he and Malcolm got together over Meatloaf's *Bat Out of Hell*. She had never forgotten the sight of Derek and Barry singing together at his confirmation party over a year ago. She had been moved to tears that it had taken eighteen years for father and son to reach a point where they could enjoy each other's company.

'Hey up, Cindy's off in a dream,' Derek quipped.

'I'm sorry,' she said quickly, 'I was thinking of Barry.'

'Where is he?' Charlotte asked. 'Tiffany said he was home for the weekend.'

'He was just finishing off some work the last time I saw him,' Cindy answered.

'Nothing changes, then,' Alex said.

'*Au contraire*,' Derek said enigmatically. He pointed to his chest. '*Au contraire*.'

Hilary wanted to go home. She'd had enough of listening to David talking about the state of the property market. But, most of all, she'd had enough of watching David lie his great big fat head off. He was a liar, a cheat, a betrayer of trust, a complete and utter double-crosser – all the right credentials, some might say, for a good estate agent.

Disconsolately she wandered away from David, who didn't even notice she'd gone – he merely closed up the gap she'd created by moving one step to the right within the circle and waving his arms about more expansively as he spoke.

'You look glum.'

Automatically she forced a smile to her lips, even before she'd registered who was talking to her. It was Nick Bradshaw and, like Derek and Cindy, he was wearing one of the specially designed T-shirts. She decided, though, that she liked him better in a polo-neck sweater and jacket.

'How did you enjoy hearing about Florida in such detail the other night?' she asked, finding herself slipping into conversation with him more easily than she had previously.

'I feel like I've been there,' he answered.

'Me too. Many times.'

'Tell me, Hilary, you were almost tempted, weren't you, to have a drink with me after the class?'

How arrogant of him. 'Not for a single moment,' she replied.

As she'd walked home afterwards she'd asked herself the question over and over again: Why not? Why not go to the pub with him for a drink? If he'd been a woman she wouldn't have thought twice about going home to David and saying she'd been for a drink with one of the girls from the group.

'I wouldn't have tried anything, if that's what you were worried about.'

'Well, of course, you wouldn't,' she said quickly, 'I know that.'

He stared at her. 'Why?'

'Why what?'

He smiled. 'Why are you so sure I wouldn't make a pass at you?'

'Because ... because you just wouldn't, not with somebody like me. Men make passes at women like my sister Charlotte. Look, there she is, over by the fireplace talking to Derek, and that's Alex next to her. They're getting married next month.'

'She's an attractive woman,' Nick said, glancing across the room. He turned his attention back to Hilary. 'And would I be right in thinking that you're the younger sister?'

Hilary frowned. 'Yes, but what's that got to do with anything?'

'Quite a lot I should think. When was the last time you read *The Ugly Duckling* to Becky?'

She opened her mouth to reply, then snapped it shut.

'Think about it, Hilary.'

'Stop teasing me,' she said, in a small voice.

'I'm not, I assure you.'

A loud laugh coming from David made Hilary frown again. Anger flared within her.

'Your husband's enjoying himself tonight,' Nick said, watching her closely.

'And why shouldn't he?' she said crossly.

'More to the point, why aren't you?'

'Says who?'

'Hilary, how long do you think you can live like this?'

She stared at him, suddenly scared. 'Like what?' she asked, hesitantly.

'Pretending. Pretending that whatever it is in your life causing you pain isn't happening.'

'Heavens, Mr Bradshaw. Whatever makes you say something as ridiculous as that?'

'Don't Mr Bradshaw me, Hilary. Just stop lying, not only to other people but to yourself. Face up to what David is doing to you.'

Hilary felt sick. The noise of so many voices, together with the sound of the Gypsy Kings, began to pound inside her head. In front of her Nick's face filled her vision and she swayed slightly. She felt his hand on her arm. She jerked away. 'I need to check on my children,' she said, pushing past him.

When she was outside she breathed in deeply, wanting the icy air to cut through her, wanting everything that was hurting inside her to be cut clean away.

'You okay?'

Damn. It was him. 'Yes,' she lied, and started to walk away from the house. But she heard his footsteps coming up behind her. She had no idea what to say, so she said nothing and let him follow her across the road to The Gables.

The children were both fast asleep and when she came downstairs she found Nick in the kitchen. He handed her a glass of water. She took it gratefully and sat down. 'Must have been all that champagne,' she said, avoiding his eyes. 'It suddenly made me feel sick.'

'How long has this been going on?'

She gripped the glass in her hands, unable to speak.

He sat down opposite her. 'Hilary, I'm pushing you, I know. Something tells me that things are not right between you and David and it won't be long before everyone else starts noticing it. And what will you do then?'

She ignored his question.

'Look,' he carried on, 'people don't have to go around in pain, and that includes you. If you had a broken arm and I was a doctor you'd let me help you, wouldn't you?'

She nodded.

'You've potentially got a broken marriage on your hands, so why not let me help you?'

'I have nothing of the sort,' she said adamantly. Broken marriage – how awful that sounded, how statistical! 'And how dare you suggest David doesn't love me? Why on earth wouldn't he? Now please—'

'I didn't say that, Hilary.'

'Oh, stop it, stop it! You're too clever for me. You're trying to trip me up. All these ghastly word games I keep getting caught up in. If you want to help, just leave me alone and stop trying to make me say things I don't mean.'

A few minutes later she heard the front door close quietly.

'Oh, come off it. What harm is he doing?'

'Muffin 'ell, Dad! You've got to be joking.' Tiffany looked

around the group for support. Charlotte was the first to speak.

'Tiffany's right,' she said. 'Ted's gone too far.'

Derek laughed. 'Didn't have you down as a prude, Charlotte.'

'Far from it,' added David, tottering towards Charlotte.

She pushed him away in disgust, thinking how pathetic he was at that moment, her drunk, adulterous brother-in-law.

'And you, Mr Hamilton,' Iris said, poking Alex's shoulder with her finger. 'Where do you stand on this issue? Should we, in your opinion, be subjected to this filth Mr Cooper seems intent on peddling right here under our noses?'

Alex took a long, deliberate sip of his wine. 'No,' he said at last, 'no, I don't believe we should, I think—'

'Thank you, Mr Hamilton,' Iris said, pleased, and turning her attention to Derek, she said, 'I think you'll find yourself outnumbered, Mr Rogers.'

'How about we widen the net?' Derek said.

'Certainly,' Iris replied, sure of her ground.

Derek went out to the conservatory and asked Nick and Rosie to join them.

'Now, Nick,' he said genially, his hand on Nick's shoulder, 'you're a man of the world, liberal and broad-minded, wouldn't you say?'

'I'd like to think so, yes.'

'Now I know you don't live here in Hulme Welford, but I'm sure you're aware of some ill-feeling in the village regarding our local newsagent selling something a little more exotic than the usual newspapers and sweets.' He gave his nose a tap and added, 'And I'm not talking mangoes, Nick.'

Nick ran his hand over his chin and looked at the expectant faces all around him. 'All things considered, I don't think it's appropriate for a village newsagent to be selling the things Ted Cooper is.' Then, shrugging his shoulders, he went on, 'Call me old-fashioned, but if I wanted to go and buy some seductive lingerie for a special person, then I'd rather go to a shop which specialises in such things, not a paper shop run by a man who doesn't know a camisole top from a filter-tip cigarette.'

'I've heard all I need to hear,' Iris announced, allowing herself a small triumphant smile. 'I congratulate you, Mr Rogers, on your choice of personnel. Mr Bradshaw has a refined quality about him which I admire and I would strongly recommend you to take note of it.' She acknowledged Nick with a nod, then turned away and went in search of something to eat.

'Hear, hear!' laughed Tiffany. She was delighted with Nick's response to her father and offered Nick one of her most beguiling smiles. Charlotte nudged Alex and whispered, 'I think you've just been usurped.'

'I don't agree with you, Nick,' Rosie Williams said serenely, her long fingers steepled together in front of her, just below her nose, as though deep in an act of worship. 'What are you all afraid of?' she asked, facing them all, one by one. 'Why are you so hung up about sex, because that's what this is about, isn't it?'

'I agree,' said Derek. 'Our old friend sex, once again, pulling back its foreskin and penetrating the bashful.' Everyone cringed at this graphic metaphor, but undeterred, Derek carried on. 'Sex,' he said loudly, 'the Englishman's—'

'Achilles' heel?' suggested Rosie, helpfully.

'Cock-up!' finished Derek.

They laughed but all fell silent when Iris rejoined the group with a plate of food. In the ensuing quiet a voice said, 'Hilary likes underwear.'

Surprised, they all looked at David, who seemed to stagger under the sudden focus of attention.

'She's got drawers full of the stuff. She thinks I don't know. She buys it and then hides it. What do you make of that?' His eyes swept round the hushed and embarrassed group. When he saw Nick Bradshaw he repeated the question. 'What do you make of that, then?'

'I think you've had too much to drink,' Nick said politely.

'No, I haven't,' David answered, his voice slightly raised. 'Now answer my question, Mr Damn-Know-It-All-Psycho . . . Psycho-bloody-Expert.'

'Come on, David,' Charlotte urged. 'Leave it be and go home before you make a fool of yourself.'

He shrugged her hand away from his arm and moved nearer to Nick.

Derek tried to intervene. 'Let me get you another drink, old mate. Come out to the kitchen.'

'Another drink, I should think *not*!' declared Iris. 'He should be horsewhipped for his appalling behaviour, besmirching his wife's good name in public.'

'I want an answer,' David demanded, continuing to hold his ground.

'Okay,' Nick said calmly. 'Perhaps your wife feels the need to fill a void created by someone she loves.' He met David's angry gaze and didn't flinch, not until David landed a fist in his jaw and sent him sprawling across the room.

Chapter Eighteen

Hilary gave the visiting curate from Knutsford a cursory glance then ran her tongue over the top row of her teeth. She had been up early this morning after waking from one of her recurring dreams – the teeth dream. Ever since she'd sat her O-level exams and in subsequent periods of stress she'd had the same dream of her teeth crumbling and falling out. Apparently it was a sure sign of anxiety.

Last night she hadn't bothered going back to the party after Nick had left The Gables, and, convinced that David wouldn't even miss her, she had gone upstairs to bed. He'd come home just over an hour later and when he'd flopped onto the bed fully dressed she had pretended to be asleep. He had fallen into a heavy stupor almost immediately, leaving her wide awake and thinking what nonsense the phrase 'no peace for the wicked' was.

She had left him half an hour ago, still asleep but now under the duvet. The children had been in one of their lazy moods and, feeling the need to be alone, she had willingly left them with a video to watch and made her escape to St John's.

'And now let us confess our sins to Almighty God,' the visiting curate said, his arms outstretched and his voice resonating with a touch too much of the dramatics. Hilary lowered her head along with the rest of the congregation. But I haven't sinned, she thought, lifting her head. I haven't done anything wrong. It's David who's sinning like mad. Indignation bit deep as she stared at the robed man in front of her. How dare this silly young curate with his newly acquired theological-school piety tell her how bad she was. If he wanted a real sinner he should go and knock David up and make him confess. Why was it always the innocent who were called to ask for forgiveness?

To the right of the curate in the choir stalls, Hilary noticed Iris Braithwaite. She had one beady eye open and it was directed at Hilary. Hilary bent her head and snapped her own eyes shut, blocking out that dreadful face; not so much the beady eye but the shocking and improbable smile the woman had just given her – shocking because Hilary recognised it as a smile of sympathy. Did it mean ... that Mrs Braithwaite knew about David's affair?

Had Charlotte told her? Surely not. Cindy, then? Even more unlikely. Perhaps David and Catherine had been seen together and the pot of gossip was already beginning to bubble.

Oh, God! she started to pray, don't let everyone start talking about me. I'm sorry if I've ever gossiped in the past. Sorry that I might have said the odd unkind word about anyone. I'll never do it again. Just please don't let people talk about me – give them somebody else to gossip about.

Audience participation had never gone down well at St John's and this morning was no exception. The inexperienced curate had now taken up residence in the pulpit and was on to his sermon, and it was falling flat. Hilary felt almost sorry for the man. Perhaps over in Knutsford this kind of thing went down well, but here in Hulme Welford they didn't take kindly to being asked daft questions. One or two rebel members of the congregation were deliberately calling out the wrong answers. What awful stories would go back to Knutsford, she wondered. That they were all as thick as two short planks in Hulme Welford? Undaunted, he continued to take them by the hand through Isaiah's condemnation of sin, fully determined to get his message across.

'Would anyone care to share with us,' the curate offered

up, his eyes scanning the congregation, 'what they think the great prophet would have said if he had been approached by one of his contemporaries and asked, "What's the matter, Isaiah?"'

'That's obvious,' somebody called out from the back.

The curate's relief was obvious too, that somebody was actually listening to him. 'Yes?' he said eagerly.

'He'd say, one eye's higher than the other! Boom, boom!'

Guffaws of laughter reverberated around the church and even the young man in the pulpit had the grace to concede a small smile. If he had started out that morning believing himself to be of the Laurence Olivier school of liturgy he was now heading for the club circuit, where he'd be lucky to finish his act.

But, true to his profession, he carried on valiantly. 'Don't think for one moment that I'm scaremongering,' he said, beginning to raise his voice and alerting everyone to the fact that that was exactly his intention, 'but there's real evil going on out there. We live in a fallen world. Society is falling apart. Businesses are falling apart. Marriages are—'

Stop! Hilary wanted to shout back. Stop it. I don't want to hear any of this. Don't you understand, you silly fool of a man, we don't want to hear this kind of thing. Hulme Welford's a nice place in which to live. We lead nice, comfortable lives where not very much happens. We don't want people like you coming here and telling us how awful the rest of the world is. Leave us alone. I want to be happy. I don't want to be miserable and dream of my teeth falling out.

'I sense real pain here in this church,' the curate said, theatrically, at the same time pointing his finger round the congregation.

'Yes, and I'm looking at it right now,' someone muttered behind Hilary.

Over coffee it seemed that part of Hilary's prayers had been answered. Almost everybody was talking about the sermon they'd just been forced to endure and agreeing that Malcolm Jackson had had no business going away to visit his elderly mother in Lincolnshire without checking the suitability of his locum.

Reluctant to go home, Hilary busied herself with collecting stray pew bibles.

'There you are, Hilary,' her mother said, handing her a bible. 'Wasn't that just the most banal sermon you've ever heard? How's David after last night?'

'What do you mean?' Hilary said warily.

Louise smiled. 'Exactly what I said.'

'He was asleep when I left him.'

'I bet he was. Sleeping it off, more like it.'

'Are you trying to tell me something, Mother?'

'I hope you gave him hell and didn't fuss over him with any sympathy.'

'Sympathy?' she repeated. 'Whatever for?' There were times when Hilary felt sure that Louise lived in a different world.

'Come on, Hilary, loyalty only needs to go so far. It's very admirable that you should want to stand by your husband, especially after the things he said about you, but so many people heard and saw what he did last night that you're going to have to face up to what happened.'

'Mother, I have no idea what you're talking about. I left the party early. Just what did David—'

'Don't start bleating, Hilary,' Louise said, deciding that her daughter really didn't have a clue what she was referring to. 'David hit somebody last night. To the ground, in fact.'

'I don't believe you,' Hilary said, astonished.

'Close your mouth, Hilary, or we'll all fall in. If you don't believe me, ask your sister. She'll tell you exactly what we all saw with our very own eyes. David punched a man to the floor, right there in front of everyone.'

'Who?'

'That new fellow, just started at Derek and Cindy's—'

'Nick Bradshaw?'

'Yes. That's right. You know him, then?'

Something in Louise's voice made Hilary feel guilty. Ridiculous. She had nothing to feel guilty about. 'He's in my French class,' she said. 'But why did David hit him?'

'I rather think David had enjoyed too much of Derek and Cindy's champagne and started talking. Well, more like shooting his mouth off, really. You know the way he is when he's had too much to drink.'

'Can you get to the point, Mother?'

'Okay, seeing as you've asked. But I'm warning you, you won't like it. David said something about you of rather an intimate nature and then asked Nick whatever-his-name-is to comment. He wouldn't – obviously more of a gentleman than your David – and that seemed to make David fly off the handle and he forced Nick to answer his question. When Nick did, David punched him in the face.' Louise laughed. 'You've got to hand it to Derek. Whenever he's at a party something always happens. Remember at your welcome home party for Charlotte and how drunk—'

'What did he say?' Hilary demanded, more concerned with what David had said about her than her mother's admiration for Derek's effect on any social gathering.

'What? When Nick was lying on the floor?'

'No. About me?'

Louise tried her best to keep a straight face. 'Something about you having a penchant for drawers full of lingerie.'

Hilary's face coloured. How could he! 'So what did Nick say that made David hit him?'

'David wanted this penchant of yours psychoanalysed by Nick. He refused at first. Then, when pushed, and you know how pushy David can be at the end of a good evening, he said that maybe you were filling a void created by someone you loved.'

'What rubbish!'

'If you say so, Hilary. By the way, is it possible David's

suffering from some sort of stress? It might explain his bizarre behaviour. Maybe you should book him into All in the Mind. Leave that little thought with you. Must dash. See you.'

Stress! What a joke, thought Hilary, watching her mother hurry away to shake hands with the curate.

'Mother looks as if she'd like to take him by the scruff of the neck, doesn't she?'

'Charlotte!' Hilary exclaimed, seeing her sister at her side. 'Don't say anything to me, just take me back to Ivy Cottage, please. I don't want to go home today. I've had enough.'

Outside St John's the cold air hit them full in the face and, buttoning their coats, Charlotte, Alex and Hilary walked in silence down the gravel path, through the lychgate and out onto the main road. There they caught up with Iris Braithwaite, who was staring straight ahead of her and clutching her handbag as though it were a shield.

Charlotte followed her gaze. 'What on earth's going on?'

The main street of the village was lined on both sides with cars parked bumper to bumper, and outside Ted the Toup's was a queue of men waiting to go in.

'Armageddon,' replied Iris, her face like thunder. 'I warned you.'

They crossed the road, Iris leading the way. She accosted a youth just getting out of a rust-pocked Ford Fiesta. He wore a cap back to front and a thick unbuttoned check shirt over a T-shirt with the words *Stay Cool* written on it. He gave Iris a scornful look and said, 'You'll catch myxomatosis in that fur coat.'

'I beg—'

'Forget it,' he answered, and sauntered away to join the queue outside Ted's.

Hilary and Alex went over and peered inside the shop. It was full and Ted was up to his armpits in red and black lace. Hilary thought of what her mother had just told her and turned away.

'Come on, Mrs Braithwaite,' Charlotte said, when Alex and Hilary came back. 'Let's go home.'

'Outrageous. Outrageous. I shall personally see that that disgusting Ted Cooper is hounded out of the village.'

They left Iris marching up her own drive and walked on to Ivy Cottage, where they were greeted by Mabel as Charlotte let them in through the conservatory.

'Go into the sitting room, Hilary,' Charlotte said. 'We banked the fire up before we went out and it should be nice and warm in there for you.'

When they were alone Alex turned to Charlotte. 'What's wrong with Hilary?' he whispered. 'She's not herself at all.'

'It's nothing,' she said, remembering her promise to Hilary.

'Charlotte?'

Oh, what was the point? The way things were going it wouldn't be long before others found out what was happening. And who knows, Alex might be able to help.

'It's David,' she replied. 'He's having an affair with his secretary.'

'Bloody hell! Since when?'

'I haven't a clue,' she said, shaking her head. 'And I doubt whether Hilary has either. So far David doesn't know that Hilary has sussed him. She thinks if she stays quiet she'll ride out the storm while David comes to his senses and gets over his mid-life crisis, or whatever it is that makes a man jeopardise everything he once held precious.'

'But that takes all the coolness and determination of . . .'

'Of somebody like Cindy,' Charlotte said, reaching into the fridge for a bottle of wine. 'That's why Hilary's in the mess she is. She's too impulsive to play the hard, confident wife willing to preserve her marriage.' She took three glasses from the cupboard and handed Alex the bottle of wine. 'Come on,' she said, 'I'm going to get my sister to loosen up and then hopefully talk some sense into her.'

'What about David? Won't he wonder where Hilary is?'

'Stuff David! Let him wonder.'

Chapter Nineteen

As Georgia drove along Acacia Lane she thought how it was that a good cause never failed to bond a group of people together, even the most diverse characters. In her experience it was usually a transient yoke of loyalty but one that was guaranteed to bring out the gung-ho spirit in all concerned.

'You sure we've got enough stuff?'

'Plenty,' Georgia answered, looking at Tiffany in the mirror. Next to Tiffany was Chloe, her small face hidden by a balaclava and on whose lap was a large cardboard box with the lid firmly down. Georgia hadn't questioned her daughter on the contents of the box as they'd rushed out of the house after Iris's call, but she'd noticed when locking the back door that the cat-litter tray was suspiciously empty. Tiffany's box, on the other hand, had a far less sinister look about it and contained an innocent collection of hair products.

In the front passenger seat, as rigid as a corpse, and about as white, was Iris Braithwaite, nursing a box of the remains of a Chinese takeaway from Georgia and Chloe's supper last night, half a dozen eggs, some overripe tomatoes along with what Iris had personally contributed, a quantity of rotting vegetable peelings. It was to be real chemical warfare.

They hadn't had much time to put together their weapons – Iris had only called her fifteen minutes ago.

'Ms D'Arcy,' she'd commanded down the phone, 'I would greatly value your assistance. Now!'

Chloe had jumped at the chance to join in with the action.

'Time to nuke the oppressors!' she'd shouted, climbing into the Jeep. They'd left Gordon holding the fort with a bemused look on his face.

It was while they were parked outside Iris's house that Tiffany had appeared. Tiffany had babysat once or twice for Georgia on the few occasions Winnie had been busy and, seeing her coming out of the drive of All in the Mind, Chloe had leaned out of the window and waved to her, shouting, 'We're going to have some fun down at Ted the Toup's. Want to come?'

They turned right at the end of Acacia Lane and drove along the main street of the village. Georgia could see a small line of parked cars and a tall thin man standing outside the newsagent's. She felt a rush of adrenaline.

'There's one!' shrieked Chloe. 'Open the sun roof, Mum, quick.'

Georgia slid back the glass panel. 'Ready everybody?' she said, smiling. 'How about you, Iris?'

'Ready,' the older woman replied. 'Let's not defer a moment longer.'

Both Tiffany and Chloe were already preparing to take aim, and as Georgia slowed the Jeep, the first dollop of grey, clinging ammunition was fired through the air. It caught a man full in the face just as he was coming out of the shop. His stunned pebble-dashed expression was only clearly revealed when he wiped away the sticky stones. He looked upwards, as if expecting to see a bird of enormous proportions flying overhead. The tall thin man next to him started to laugh until he caught a chest-load of shrapnel. In disbelief he, too, lifted his head skywards.

Chloe squealed excitedly, exposing her ten-year-old self in a rare moment of giddy delight.

'Talk about thick,' Tiffany shouted, aiming a plastic bottle of shampoo and firing out globs of orange gunk. Even she was surprised at what an effective cannon she had in her hands. She squeezed again on the bottle and a large jelly-like blob landed exquisitely on the crown of a bald-headed victim also standing in the doorway of the shop.

Seeing that Ted's customers had now found the source of the missiles, Georgia pushed her foot down hard on the accelerator and sped off to the other end of the village. They hovered outside Patricia Longton's double-fronted cottage.

'Close that box, Chloe!' shouted Georgia. 'The smell's disgusting.'

'An inspired idea, though,' Iris said in congratulation, turning round to Chloe, whose eyes were shining brilliantly through the holes in her balaclava.

'It's your turn now, Mrs Braithwaite,' Chloe said. 'You'll get them from your side of the car as we go past.'

'Ready for round two?' asked Georgia, revving the engine.

'Drive on,' instructed Iris, pulling on a pair of rubber gloves and delving into the box on her lap.

Still dusting themselves down, the three men didn't hear the sound of the approaching Jeep, not until it was once again alongside them, broadside fashion, with what looked like Queen Boadicea leaning out of the passenger window firing off a round of beansprouts and chewed spare ribs. Slimy, curled-up potato peelings that had taken on the appearance of slugs followed, hotly pursued by eggs which Tiffany hurled, yelling, 'Surface-to-air missiles.'

'Myxomatosis, indeed,' Iris called, taking aim with a tomato.

Georgia reckoned that the onslaught had by now girded the collective loins of their victims, so she pressed on the accelerator pedal again, but the engine stalled. 'Shit!' She turned the key. Nothing. She caught the expression on Iris's face beside her and the sound of angry voices from the pavement. She tried the key again, promising the Jeep unswerving loyalty in the future if only it would start. It did, and as the engine roared into life, she gripped the steering wheel and pushed her foot to the floor. They rocketed away, just as the group of men began to move towards them.

Georgia gave them a glance in her mirror and grinned at the sight of the man – the one who had been the first on the receiving end of the ballistic cat litter – losing his balance on the mucus-like mixture of shampoo and raw eggs. She watched him land on his backside with a bump.

The bald man with the skullcap of protein-enriched shampoo was now also sporting a medal of beansprouts on his right shoulder. He threw his hands in the air. 'Sodding hell! I only came here for a present for my wife.' Bewildered, he wiped away the beansprouts and wandered back to the safety of his car. He'd stick to catalogues in the future, he decided, less bother that way.

At the nursery, Georgia brought the Jeep to an exhilarating halt, sending up a cloud of dust behind them.

'Mission accomplished,' she said, snatching on the hand-brake.

'I'll say it is,' agreed Tiffany, grinning broadly and pulling off one of her father's skiing hats.

'Iris?' Georgia asked cautiously. 'You okay?'

The older woman was staring straight ahead through the windscreen. She was motionless and still bearing the same cadaverous pallor she had worn earlier. The only colour in her face came from her eyes, which were as dark and as shiny as those of a bird.

'Iris?'

She turned to face Georgia. 'I heard you the first time,' she said, carefully peeling off her rubber gloves as though they were expensive kid leather.

'I need to wash my hands,' Chloe said, opening the door and getting out.

'I bet you do,' Georgia said, cuffing her daughter lightly round the ears. 'Take Mrs Braithwaite and Tiffany over to the house while I check that Gordon's okay. I'll be with you in a minute.'

Chloe led the way, and once she'd washed her hands, she went outside leaving Tiffany and Iris alone.

Tiffany threw herself onto the sofa and fiddled with the fringe of the throw-over on it. She watched Iris Braithwaite, who was standing perfectly still at the window, and began to wonder how she had ended up spending part of her Sunday afternoon lobbing rubbish out of a sun-roof with, of all people, old Ma Braithwaite. She herself was a known trouble-maker in the village, but what the hell would people start saying about Mrs Braithwaite when they found out that she had been part of the attack on Ted the Toup's shop?

'Gordon seems to have managed pretty well without me,' Georgia said, joining them. 'Won't you sit down, Iris?'

Iris threw a disdainful look at the only free chair with its threadbare arms and collection of brightly coloured cushions. She remained standing. She was still deathly pale.

'You okay?' Georgia asked, concerned. Since her afternoon-tea session with Iris some days ago she had surprised herself at how often she had thought of her, surprised, too, that she found herself caring about Iris. Sure, she was nosy, bossy, interfering and as dogmatic as hell, but the old girl had spirit in spades, which was more than you could say for most of the people in Hulme Welford. It amused her to know that she felt a curious sense of empathy with Iris. She hadn't yet worked out why. 'No regrets, I hope?'

The loose skin under Iris's chin wobbled, reminding Georgia of a turkey, and suddenly laughter filled the room. 'Good Lord, why on earth would I regret anything? I've just had the time of my life!'

'I wondered if you thought we'd gone too far,' Georgia replied, relieved. How could she have doubted Iris's nerve?

'Too far? We've barely begun. Our cause has a long way to go yet, young lady, if we're to beat our old enemy Beelzebub. St Paul himself told Timothy that they had to fight the good fight.'

'Good for you,' Georgia said, not sure that she wanted the

likes of St Paul brought into it – he'd had some pretty weird ideas about the role of women. 'I can see you would have been one of the first to have been tied to the railings.'

'That's as may be, but I certainly would not have been so stupid as to throw myself under a galloping horse.'

'I wouldn't half mind pushing Ted the Toup under one, though,' Tiffany said, with a giggle.

Ted pulled at the blind on the shop door. He was knackered, like he'd just been knocked flat and run over by a steamroller. The shop had never been so busy. Stroke of luck, that publicity in the paper – it had attracted no end of people. A shame he hadn't had enough stock. Thongs were obviously the thing and he'd looked bloody stupid turning all those customers away empty-handed.

And as for that trouble outside, well, he knew who was behind that. Stupid old woman. Just what was wrong in selling some saucy kit anyway? Plenty of the usual customers had been in and made a few purchases during the week, like that Mr Longton. He'd come in yesterday to pay his paper bill and had left with a nice pair of knickers for his wife.

Providing a service, that was what he was doing.

He opened the till and began to count that day's takings.

Chapter Twenty

Charlotte was surprised at the depth of contempt she felt for David as he stood at the door. She had always got on well with her brother-in-law. In fact, there had been times in the past when they had turned to each other for help, especially when Hilary had what David would call 'one on her'.

'I'm sorry,' she said, standing two steps higher than David, her arms folded in front of her – an assertiveness technique Peter had learned on one of his many management courses and had come home and tried on her. 'Hilary's lying down. She's probably asleep by now.'

'But why?'

'I told you, she's got a headache.'

'Yes, but why here? Why didn't she come home and go to bed?'

Charlotte gave an exaggerated roll of her eyes. 'Come off it, David. You know jolly well you and the children wouldn't have given her a moment's peace. As soon as she'd walked through the door it would have been, "What time's lunch?" "Where are my football boots?" '

'Odd,' he grunted. 'Bloody odd I call it when a wife doesn't come home from church and goes to bed in another person's house. How do I know she's even here? She's been acting pretty strangely these past few weeks.'

Charlotte tried to lighten the mood with a laugh. 'So I'm just another person, am I?'

He scraped at some loose paint on the door frame with his fingernail. 'I should have known you moving back here would mean trouble.'

Again she laughed. 'You know what sisters are like.' She started to close the door. 'I'll let her home when I'm convinced she's fully rested. In the meantime, why not make some lunch for you and the children? I expect they're hungry by now.' She closed the door and listened to the sound of David's angry footsteps fading away.

'Was he very annoyed?' Hilary asked, when Charlotte returned to the sitting room.

'Not really, just confused. I told him to go home and make some lunch.'

'Talking of which,' Alex said, 'I'll do us some omelettes, shall I?'

'I couldn't eat a thing,' Hilary said morosely, staring into the fire.

'Nonsense,' Charlotte threw back, knowing at once how like her sister she was sounding – not the poor confused version sitting before her now but the strident, bossy Hilary, who had always turned any monumental crisis into an everyday occurrence with a hearty let's-roll-up-our-sleeves attitude. She would have been great in the war.

Alex laid a gentle hand on Hilary's arm. 'You'll feel better for some food inside you.'

They watched him leave the room. With tears in her eyes, Hilary said, 'You *will* marry him, won't you, Charlotte?'

Charlotte came and sat on the floor in front of Hilary's chair. 'Of course I will. You know as well as I do, the wheels are already in motion for our big day.'

'But you might get cold feet between now and then.'

Charlotte thought back to her wedding day with Peter, remembering how she had stood at the altar fighting against the nagging doubt that she shouldn't have been there. She shook her head. 'No cold feet this time.'

Hilary lifted her eyes. 'This time,' she repeated. 'What do you mean?'

'Oh, Hilary, it's a long story, and one I'll save for another day. Talk to me about David.'

148

'How's the dress coming on?'

Charlotte could have shouted at her sister for her persistent prevarication, but she knew it would get her nowhere. Right now, bullying was not the answer. She would have to cajole her. She reached for the bottle of wine and refilled Hilary's glass, inwardly cringing at the thought of Becky following her up the aisle on Christmas Eve. She must have been mad to have given in to her niece's pleading a few weeks ago. 'I've never been asked to be a bridesmaid before,' she'd said, 'please let me do it.' I'm not surprised, Charlotte had wanted to say. Who, in their right mind, would want to court disaster in such a deliberate fashion on such an important day? Goodness knows why, but she had finally said yes.

'It was good of Dad to suggest having the reception at their place,' Hilary said. 'I had no idea he was becoming such an expert in the kitchen.'

Charlotte frowned. And that was another act of reckless foolishness on her part. Who knows what on earth they'd get to eat? Dad might have developed a new hobby out of watching cookery programmes on the telly, but doing the buffet for her wedding reception was surely way beyond his capabilities. She suddenly smiled to herself – he'd never yet let her down, had he?

'David's not much cop in the kitchen,' Hilary said quietly. In the background they could hear Alex whistling to himself as he prepared their lunch. 'In fact, I don't think he's much cop at anything any more.'

'Oh, Hilary. This is all such a mess. What can we do to help you?'

'We?' Hilary repeated.

'I ... I told Alex just now when we were in the kitchen,' Charlotte confessed.

Hilary covered her face with her hands. She started to sob. 'Not *another* person who knows what a failure I am. I can't bear it. Oh, Charlotte, how could you?'

Charlotte let her sister cry.

'How could you? How could you?' Hilary repeated over and over, rocking herself backwards and forwards in the armchair. 'I don't want anyone to know. I feel so disloyal towards David. It's as though I'm telling tales out of school.'

'And where's David's loyalty in all of this?' Alex asked, coming back into the room with a large tray.

Charlotte stood up and took one of the plates and handed it to Hilary. 'Alex is right,' she said. 'Why should you be so hung up on being loyal when David clearly doesn't give a damn?'

Hilary gave a loud sniff and looked down at the omelette on her lap. She should have been at home cooking roast pork, roast potatoes, sage and onion stuffing, apple sauce, parsnip chips – David always had to have parsnips – she shouldn't be here at all. What were they doing over the road? How were they managing without her? Just what kind of a mother was she to let her family go without their Sunday lunch? And who was Charlotte to say whether David gave a damn or not? 'He does love me,' she said defiantly. 'I know he does.'

'You may well be right,' Alex said, sitting down next to Charlotte on the sofa, 'but the problem still remains. How are you going to cope with David loving you and perhaps thinking he loves another?'

She prodded uninterestedly at her omelette. 'I don't know, but if Cindy's managed it all her marriage, then so can I.'

'But you're not Cindy,' Charlotte said.

'Then maybe I should become more like her.'

'That,' Alex said softly, 'would be a great shame. For what would happen to the real Hilary?'

'Is he always like this?' Hilary asked Charlotte.

Her sister smiled. 'From the moment I met him. Don't you remember him bullying me round your dinner table that night?'

Hilary managed a smile, remembering vividly the time to which her sister was referring. 'I was so very proud and sure of myself that night ... Now look at me.'

'You like to be in control, Hilary, don't you?' Alex said, unexpectedly.

'Yes,' she answered, not looking at him. 'I like to know what's happening, when and how. There's nothing wrong in that, is there?'

'Not at all. So, who at the moment would you say is in control? You or David?'

Hilary pushed her untouched meal away from her. She reached for the box of tissues. 'I ... I don't know. And I don't know why that question should upset me so much.'

I do, thought Charlotte. All those years in her own empty marriage with Peter she had kidded herself that she was in control of her life. She had convinced herself that as long as she was in charge she could control the amount of pain she was experiencing. But it was all a lie. Peter had been the one in charge of her emotions. She had been at his mercy, waiting for him to pull on the strings of her heart – today would be an okay day, or today would be a day of despair. She had even stopped trusting her own judgement because she'd been so busy trying to control her surroundings in the belief that that would prevent anything from hurting her. She had lived like that for too long – lying to Peter, but worst of all, lying to herself. Just as Hilary was now doing and was prepared to go on doing for as long as it would take. 'Answer Alex's question, Hilary,' she said. 'Think hard and answer truthfully. Which one of you is in control?'

Hilary shook her head. 'David,' she said. 'Bloody David is and I hate him for it.' She bit her lip. 'No!' she cried out. 'I don't hate him. I love him. I do honestly. Oh, God, I sound quite mad.'

'Not mad,' Alex said, 'but hurt and confused.'

In the silence that followed, Charlotte got up and threw another log on the fire. The light outside was already fading. She switched on the lamps, casting the room in a gentle roseate glow, then drew the curtains.

Hilary watched her sister moving about. She felt like a young, cosseted child, sitting here in Charlotte's warm and comfortable sitting room. Compared to The Gables it was a sanctuary of peace and quiet. Lucky Charlotte, she thought with envy, conscious that, for the first time in her married life, she wanted something her sister had.

Ever since she'd met David her world had revolved around his and while Charlotte had bounced from one precarious relationship to another, in her late teens and early twenties, she and David had lived in each other's pockets, planning with meticulous care each stage of their lives – careers, marriage and children. Everything had been so straightforward, so well controlled ... until now. The rigid timetable that had given her such security and comfort had suddenly been taken away from her, and in contrast it was Charlotte who was now cocooned by love and the stability of a settled existence.

That's what I want, she whined to herself, in the voice Becky usually used when she wanted something her brother had.

Just after six o'clock there was a knock at the back door. It was Philip.

'I'm afraid your mum's still asleep,' Charlotte said, quite truthfully, for Hilary was indeed now asleep by the fire.

'Oh,' he said, disappointed.

'Did your father send you over?' she asked suspiciously.

Philip shook his head.

Charlotte was no expert when it came to children, but this one looked upset. 'You okay?'

He wobbled his head in no particular direction.

She wasn't sure how to proceed with her unsmiling nephew – a nephew with whom she had never really had much contact. And now here he was in her kitchen, a picture of misery. What was she to do? 'How's school?' she tried.

'Okay.' Philip knew the score. All grown-ups asked about school.

'Made many friends?'

'A few. There's Batesy. He's okay . . .' But he didn't want to think of Batesy. 'Is Mum all right?'

'She's fine. She's just worn out,' Charlotte replied, genuinely surprised at the concern in Philip's voice. It showed in his eyes as well. 'She'll be home soon. Don't worry.'

He shrugged and turned away, his head bent and his feet dragging disconsolately.

Charlotte watched him go out into the dark. Poor Philip, she thought. She had never seen a more miserable-looking child.

Chapter Twenty-one

Cindy missed the smell of In the Pink – shampoo and hair spray in the salon, water-treatment chemicals in the Jacuzzi, the combination of perspiration and deodorant in the gym, even the smell of towels in the tumble-dryer.

All in the Mind smelled of new carpets and barely dry paint, with the occasional waft of essential oils. Cindy had insisted they kept on their aromatherapist, and with Hazel now reinstalled in her newly decorated room, the familiar smell of lavender oil and rosemary acted as a welcome balm against the insanity of Derek's latest idea on this their opening day.

So far they had got off to a good start. The classes were fully booked, just as Derek had predicted. Even when Cindy had helped to fill out the booking forms for people to sign up for their chosen seminars she had refused to believe that All in the Mind could possibly work – now, of course, she consoled herself with the thought that it couldn't possibly last.

For the life of her she couldn't understand what made anyone want to sit in a room full of strangers and bare their souls. Why couldn't they simply learn to keep their mouths shut and be quiet about their problems? Constantly talking about the problem served no purpose, in her opinion. Worse still, she had come across those who had merely exploited the role of a counsellor and got their wrong-doings sanctioned by continuous rationalisation of their appalling behaviour.

Just as well she'd never found the need to go running off

to some counsellor every time Derek had hurt her. If she'd done that she wouldn't have had time in her life to do anything else. Though what any counsellor would make of Derek was anybody's guess.

Sitting in the office, she started writing out a cheque for the exorbitant decorator's bill. She slipped the cheque into an envelope and sealed it up, then drummed her long fingernails on the desk and sighed.

She was bored. In the days of In the Pink her time had been crammed with appointments with her regular customers. Now she had nothing to do. So much for finding a niche, as Derek had claimed she would.

She got up from the desk and opened the door on to the corridor. All was quiet. Not a sound of a hair-dryer or the local radio station, not even the whirr of the washing machine. The place felt dead. She breathed in deeply, catching the smell of gloss paint. It reminded her of she and Derek decorating their first salon. It was over in Northwich, a tiny box of a place squeezed in between a down-at-heel ironmonger's and a flower shop – Derek had always been next door buying her flowers from the old woman, who he had said looked like the flower-seller in Trumpton. Their first day, all those years ago, had given them both such a thrill. Derek, with his Kevin Keegan hairstyle, had rushed about the salon chatting up the clients, seeking customer loyalty, while she, too, had enjoyed herself, achieving her ambition of running her own business. But she had been happy enough just seeing Derek so pleased with life.

So why wasn't she happy today, then? It was obvious to everyone that Derek was over the moon with their new venture, as Tiffany had pointed out at breakfast before she'd set off for school. 'Dad looks like he's died and gone to heaven,' she'd said.

'A man needs to be fulfilled to really know himself in order to be happy,' he'd said, his mouth poised over a croissant.

Typically Tiffany had laughed at her father and taken the

croissant from his hand. But not so typically she'd squeezed Cindy's arm and said, 'Best of luck, I think you're going to need it.'

Cindy went back into the office. It wasn't luck she needed, it was something to do. And what was frightening her most was that she suspected she was no longer required. Had Derek done this deliberately? Had he planned to squeeze her out of the business . . . and his life?

She went over to the bookcase beside the filing cabinet and idly read some of the titles of Derek's recently purchased books – *The Search for Self-Awareness*, *Journey into the Unknown* and lastly *Are You in Control?*. She picked this one off the shelf and started to flick through it.

'Hope you don't mind, Nick, old mate,' Derek said, coming into the largest of the seminar rooms. 'Just thought I'd sit in at the back and see how it all hangs together.'

The group of women looked up eagerly. They had been sufficiently encouraged with Nick to think the two-day course their managing director had sent them on wasn't going to be a total waste of time, and now they had the added bonus of a Phil Collins lookalike.

'I don't normally allow onlookers,' Nick said firmly. He was sitting in a chair in the gap of the horseshoe of occupied chairs around him, one leg crossed over the other, his hands clasped behind his head – he knew better than anyone how important body language was, and watching Derek stroll to the back of the room he could see quite plainly that his employer gave off an undisguised air of confidence.

'Shan't make a noise,' Derek said, smiling round at the group. 'Forget I ever came in.'

'We'd rather not,' one of the women said provocatively, and then laughed coarsely. Her personnel department colleagues joined in with her and instantly the atmosphere of the room turned into a girls' night out.

Derek smiled back at the ringleader, enjoying being the

focus of attention at the same time as wanting to get his hands on her hair and tone down all those over-bleached highlights – he realised too late that he should have been looking for the woman within.

'So,' Nick said loudly, leaning forward and clapping his hands together sharply. Instantly the group was back with him. 'Reaching your full potential is what we're about this afternoon, as indeed we will be tomorrow. What I hope to show you is the unlearning of unconscious responses which you learned as children. By unlocking this particular door you'll discover just how much potential there is deep inside each and every one of you. This will be the first step to freeing yourselves of the mental as well as the physical stress we are all likely to experience at various stages in not only our working life but our private life. Everyone with me so far?'

The woman with the highlights looked over to Derek. 'Certainly am,' she said.

The phrase 'money for old rope' was dangerously close to the tip of Derek's tongue as he left Nick to wind up his mid-afternoon session, but the new Derek made him swallow this unworthy thought clean away.

He pushed open the office door, hoping to find Cindy, but there was no sign of her. He felt disappointed. He wanted to talk to her about how well the day was going. This therapy game was going to be easier than he'd thought. All those years he'd been messing about with the outside of people's heads when all the time the inside was a whole lot more straightforward. Why he hadn't cottoned on to the therapy industry before he didn't know.

He sat back in his chair and put his feet up on the desk. He had Bas to thank for this, of course. Good old Bas. A rush of fatherly pride crept over him. God, he was proud of Bas. Medical school. Just think of it, a son of his a doctor one day, maybe even a surgeon. And wasn't he practically in the medical world himself now? He smiled. No more feeling inferior to his son. Those days were gone. At last he was on an equal footing with Bas.

He looked at the diary planner on the wall and saw that Rosie was about to start her six-week seminar on 'Marriage, Sex and Happiness – They Needn't Be Incompatible'. He decided to go and have a nosy.

Rosie welcomed him with a broad smile, unlike Nick, Derek reflected. 'Mind if I sit in on this?' he asked.

'No free-wheelers,' she answered, crisply.

Derek wondered if she was as brusque in bed. 'Now, darling,' he mimicked in his head, 'left a bit ... right a bit ... Here, let me do it!'

'Mr Rogers?'

'Sorry,' he said. Not only was Rosie looking at him but so were her clients – a lacklustre group of two couples. 'Miles away,' he apologised again.

'If you stay, Mr Rogers, you'll have to join in with the session.'

'Oh ... perhaps not, then.' He moved towards the door.

'Not frightened, are you?'

He recognised the challenge in her voice. 'Group sex? Nothing like it!' he shot back, and promptly sat next to a poker-thin woman in a flowery pinafore dress with eyes like gobstoppers. Her husband, the other side of her, was a Mr Comb-Over wearing a jumper that was home-made and looked far too small – to the point of asphyxiation. The old Derek thought they would both be better off for a damn good shop in Wilmslow to smarten themselves up and if that failed they should shoot each other and put everyone else out of their misery at having to look at them. But the new Derek considered how many sessions of positive stroking it would take to lick them into shape and give them both a new lease of life.

'Can we get on?' asked a large burly woman with nipples protruding like shuttlecocks through her turtle-neck sweater – she had more facial hair than Derek had ever seen in his entire career. 'Take the Braun to her!' Derek wanted to shout across the room. 'Somebody hold her down and I'll do it.' He tried hard to see her as a whole and complete person but all he could think of were those two enormous nipples and a beard which would have given ZZ Top a scare. 'We've already lost five minutes,' she continued, 'and I've come here expecting value for money because, since poor Alan's depression, we don't get out much.'

I'd have depression if Cindy had whiskers like that, thought Derek, contemplating *poor Alan* beside the incredible bearded woman. *Poor Alan* was wearing what looked suspiciously like Crimplene trousers, which were hitched up almost to his knees as he sat, straight-backed and embarrassed, trying to lose himself in the mind-bending business of pushing back his cuticles.

'Marriage,' struck up Rosie, her hands steepled in front of her, 'designed in heaven but lived out in hell. Does that mean anything to anyone?'

Nobody spoke, but the man in Crimplene hitched up his trousers a notch.

Tiffany saw Nick before he saw her. She flicked her hair back from her face, except for one tendril which she twisted round her finger. Despite the cold wind she unbuttoned her school-regulation duffel coat and walked nonchalantly up the drive. 'Hi,' she said, as he opened his car door.

'Hello,' he called back. 'Good day at school?'

She tried to think of something clever to say. 'It's a means to an end,' she said, with a long, bored sigh.

Nick smiled. She reminded him of his youngest daughter, who had recently left home to go off to university – all that reluctant enthusiasm for life stored up in such a delightful package.

'So how was your first day?' she asked, coming round to his side of the car and leaning against it.

'Your father's pleased with the way it went.'

Tiffany flicked at her hair. 'You mean nobody accused him of being a bungling quack?'

'No,' Nick answered, with a laugh.

'What about a bonehead? Somebody must have said that?'

He shook his head.

'A bogus—'

'Now why exactly would you think anyone would want to say those things about your father?'

'Because he is all those things! Therapy indeed!' She suddenly saw her mistake. 'I mean, he doesn't know the first thing about what makes people tick.' She tilted her head and smiled. 'But I'm sure you know what you're doing.'

'Quick on your feet, aren't you, Tiffany?' he said good humouredly.

Glad to have recovered the situation so easily, but cross with herself for having wasted valuable talking time discussing her father, she said, 'How's your jaw?'

'Not a mark on me,' he answered, giving his chin a rub.

'Do you always go around making such provocative comments?'

He laughed. 'It never fails to invoke the right response.'

'And getting David Parker to thump you, was what you wanted?'

'Ah. As you said a few moments ago, it was a means to an end.' He threw his briefcase onto the back seat of his car and stooped to get inside.

'I'll see you, then,' Tiffany said.

He heard the expectant tone in her voice. 'I should think so,' he replied, putting the key in the ignition.

As he indicated to turn left at the end of the drive – conscious that Tiffany was still watching him – he saw Hilary's car coming towards him. He flashed his lights at her in the dark, she came alongside him, and as they both wound down their windows he heard her young daughter say clearly, 'Here's Mummy's boyfriend,' followed by a loud ssh.

'How's things?' he asked.

Awful, Hilary wanted to say, I've had about as much as I can take. But instead she said, 'Busy. I've got a hundred and one things to start doing for the PTA Christmas Fayre.'

He looked thoughtfully at her. It never ceased to amaze him how adept human beings were at pretending.

'I heard about you and David . . .' she started to say.

But sensing that she didn't want to say anything more with the children in the car he shook his head and said, 'No worries. He's obviously got a lot on his mind at the moment.' He saw her grip the steering wheel, her knuckles turn white and, reaching inside his jacket pocket, he took out a card with his name and telephone number on it. He handed it to her. 'Ring me if you need to.'

'I'm never going to get married,' Becky declared, when Nick had driven off.

'Why's that, dear?' Hilary asked, as she parked outside The Gables. She brushed away an unchecked tear rolling down her cheek.

'I'm going to live on the moon with lots of other women and we'll talk about important things like making the men stay at home to look after the babies. Chloe says that way there won't be any wars because the men will all be too busy and exhausted to fight one another.'

'It's a commune, you idiot,' Philip said scornfully.

'Okay, then, a commune. But, Mummy, do you think Daddy's busy enough?'

Nick stopped his car one more time on Acacia Lane or, rather, Iris Braithwaite brought him to an abrupt halt by staging what looked like a stick-up in the dark alongside the entrance to the White Cottage. He quickly wound down his window. 'What's the problem?' he called out.

She lowered her arms and came round to his side of the

car. 'I wonder, Mr Bradshaw, if you could possibly help me.'

'Of course. What can I do? You've not locked yourself out, have you?'

'I may be many things, Mr Bradshaw, but careless is not one of them. Now if you'd just wait there for a few moments, I've got something which I'd like you to deliver to a friend for me. Not being able to drive can be such a nuisance at times.'

Nick watched Iris march back up her driveway and disappear into her cottage. Within seconds she reappeared carrying two large biscuit tins.

'I'm so pleased to have caught you,' she said, passing him the tins through the car window and offering him a smile. 'I had meant to call round and see you during the day at All in the Mind, but then who knows what I may have burst in on. So very kind of you to do this for me. I knew you were a decent and honourable man when I met you at the Rogers's party and you showed yourself to be a willing supporter of my campaign here in Hulme Welford. I'm most grateful to you. Good night.'

'But, Mrs Braithwaite,' Nick replied, nonplussed, 'where exactly am I taking these?'

She let out an unexpected laugh. 'Oh, didn't I say? I am sorry. If you could just see your way to dropping them off at Ms D'Arcy's. I believe you live only a short distance from her.'

'Do I?'

'She runs Hulme View Nursery, just off—'

He nodded. 'Yes, I know where it is. I had no idea it was her place and, to be honest, I'm not so sure she'll be all that delighted at seeing me.'

'Nonsense, Mr Bradshaw. She must get very lonely stuck out there with only her young daughter. She'll enjoy your company. Now hurry along, I've kept you long enough. Tell Ms D'Arcy those scones are best eaten tonight but the cake will last a few days.'

*

Driving out of the village Nick smiled to himself. He had the distinct feeling he was being manipulated. But from what he knew of Iris Braithwaite and from what Derek had told him of the woman, she was the last person in the world to try her hand at matchmaking. More likely she possessed a perverse sense of humour.

The main entrance to Hulme View Nursery was barred by a large, padlocked metal gate and Nick was forced to leave his car on the road and walk across the gravel car park, which he entered through a small wooden gate hanging off its hinges. His shoes crunched noisily in the dark and twice he nearly stumbled into the bushes, tripping over goodness knows what.

'Hell!' He righted himself a third time, only just managing to keep a hold of Iris's tins. He pushed on a few more steps, finding himself on what he hoped was a path. A security light flashed in his eyes, momentarily blinding him, then ahead of him a door opened spilling out yet more light from a small squat building.

'I can't afford double glazing or a time-share ... Oh, it's *you*, what do you want?'

'Mrs Braithwaite asked me to drop these off for you,' he answered, when he reached Georgia D'Arcy, who was leaning against the door frame.

She looked at him suspiciously, then at the tins in his hands. 'What's in them?'

'Testicles. Mashed up and trodden underfoot.'

She tried hard not to smile. 'Are you trying to tell me something?'

'No, I'm simply the errand boy trying to make a delivery.' He pushed the tins at her. 'And I've been told to tell you to eat the cake tonight and ... No, wait a minute, that's not right. You've to eat the scones tonight and keep the cake.'

Georgia laughed. 'The sly old bird.'

'Sorry?'

'Don't worry about it. And don't worry about me being

polite and asking you in and you having to put up with thirty minutes of deadly conversation.'

'I wouldn't dream of putting you to all that trouble,' he answered smoothly, already turning to go. 'Good night.'

'Who was that, Mum?' asked Chloe, as she came out of the bathroom and into the hall.

Georgia closed the front door. 'Just somebody Mrs Braithwaite conned into acting as a delivery boy.' She opened one of the tins and smiled. 'Silly old woman thinks I don't eat enough.'

Chloe picked out a scone. 'Mmm, yum. Have we got any jam?'

'Not sure. Have a look while I ring and thank her.'

Georgia left Chloe rummaging in the kitchen cupboards and went into the sitting room to look for the telephone book. She then picked up her mobile phone.

'Iris?'

'This is Mrs Braithwaite speaking.'

'It's Georgia, just ringing to say—'

'Ah, so Mr Bradshaw found you all right. He's a pleasant enough man, wouldn't you say?'

So she was right.

As improbable an idea as it was, Georgia was left in no doubt that it wasn't just her weight that Iris was concerned about. So why not tell her to mind her own business? Iris had no right to go poking her nose into her life. She was fine just as she was. The last thing she needed right now was a stupid man mucking up her life again.

'Ms D'Arcy, are you still there, I was just saying what a pleasant—'

'I heard you, Iris, and I wish you'd stop ...'

'Yes?'

'I wish you'd stop ...' She took a deep breath. 'You really must stop calling me Ms D'Arcy all the time. I told you before, call me Georgia, okay?'

Soft! She was going bloody soft in the head! Heaven help her.

Chapter Twenty-two

'Dinner?' repeated David. He lowered his *National Geographic* magazine. 'Why?'

'Does there have to be a why?' asked Hilary. 'I thought it would be nice to eat out tomorrow night. We haven't for ages.'

'I suppose so, if you really want to.'

'I do,' Hilary said firmly. The book she'd got out of the library said it was essential to keep a marriage alive by finding time to be alone with one's partner – *just the two of you*, the author of the book had stressed, *to enable each to focus on the other.*

It was a week now since Derek and Cindy's party, and while David had played down the Nick Bradshaw incident, laughing it off by attributing his loss of temper to high spirits and a misunderstanding between him and Nick, Hilary was aware that others were not so keen to accept this explanation.

At the school gate Patricia had given Hilary one of her notorious reassuring squeezes of the arm. 'Is he under a lot of pressure, your David? He's not being violent at home, is he?'

And as if it wasn't bad enough knowing that everybody knew that David had punched someone to the ground there was the small matter of his having made it public knowledge that she ... that she liked to buy underwear and save it for a special occasion. It was only an innocent treat she allowed herself now and again and David had somehow managed to turn it into something vulgar and shamefully sordid. She hadn't had the nerve to confront him over it, for fear of her anger and humiliation being unleashed at what he'd done, which would quite likely lead to her revealing that she knew about his affair.

But at least the Ted the Toup fracas of last Sunday afternoon had taken the heat off her and provided a diversion for the likes of Patricia. A picture in the *Chronicle* of Ted, standing outside his shop with the caption 'Ted Terrorised by Tomato-throwing Tearaways', had gone a long way to fuel the argument in the village as to whether Ted Cooper was right in what he was doing. There was no disagreement as to who was responsible for the attack, though. It was generally accepted that Georgia D'Arcy and her Jeep had been involved, but as to her accomplices, no one could come up with any names.

'She was outside my house for a bit,' Patricia had told Hilary, again at the school gate. 'I saw her face quite clearly, but the others were dressed up like bandits. Probably a load of her *friends*. They do things like that, you know. I'm just so grateful we haven't got any trees in the village that need knocking down or she and her friends would be up them like a shot! But I'm sure that on my evidence alone Ted Cooper could prosecute. Only I won't say anything, because what would happen to poor little Chloe if her mother went to prison?'

It seemed strange to Hilary that the whole point of what Georgia had done, if indeed Georgia had been responsible for taking up a stance against Ted the Toup, was being lost. The actual protest was being buried beneath the trivia of whether or not the protesters had any right to do what they had done.

Personally Hilary thought Ted deserved what he got, but David had read the local paper on Wednesday evening and said, 'They want a damn good sorting out!'

'I suppose you mean by having a decent man in their lives?' she had thrown back at him.

He hadn't caught the irony in her voice. 'Yes,' he'd said, 'I suppose I do mean that. After all, look at you, Hilary. You don't go around indiscriminately throwing eggs and tomatoes at strange men, do you? And why not? Because you've always had me in your life.'

'I think they were most discriminate,' she'd replied in a low voice, appalled at David's arrogance. 'But haven't you forgotten how I poured whisky over you a couple of weeks ago, or doesn't that count?'

His answer had been lost in the kerfuffle of Becky crashing into the kitchen with yet more toys destined for the dustbin.

'I think it would be a good idea for us to go out,' Hilary pursued, as she watched David pick up the remote control for the television.

'Okay,' he said, tuning into Trevor McDonald and *News at Ten*. 'How about we go to Tony Farrand's place over at Knutsford? The children like it there.'

'The children?' Hilary repeated, crestfallen. 'I thought we'd go alone.'

'No. Let's take them – that way we don't have to bother with a babysitter.'

No, we don't, thought Hilary. And you can hide behind Philip and Becky all evening and not speak to me. She got up from the sofa and went out to the kitchen where she had a pile of ironing to get through. She switched on the iron and picked up one of Philip's school shirts from the wicker laundry basket. The phone rang. She waited for David to answer it. After six rings she went through to the hall herself.

'Hello, is that Hilary – Hilary Archer as was?'

'Yes,' she answered, cautiously.

'Hi, this is Lesley Blake, or you might remember me more as Skinny Lesley or Lesley the Rake. I found your parents in the phone book, gave them a ring just now and your mother gave me your number.'

The voice at the other end of the phone rattled on while Hilary collected her thoughts. Lesley Blake, she said to herself several times before she heard the words *school reunion* mentioned.

'I thought it was time for a reunion,' Skinny Lesley was saying, 'especially when I heard how poor old Richard was killed in that plane crash in Scotland. Definitely time to gather everyone together before any more of us snuff it. I've had such a job tracking everyone down. You'll come, won't you?'

Hilary gripped the receiver in her hand. A school reunion was the last thing she needed right now. All those clever people brought together to outdo one another and what did she have to boast? A failing marriage. That was all. 'It's lovely to hear from you,' she said briskly, trying to imagine Skinny Lesley as an adult, 'but no, I shan't be able to make it. I'm so busy these days.'

'But I haven't even told you when it is.'

'Oh.'

'You always did jump to conclusions, Hilary. Remember how you caught me at school with my hands full of Wagon Wheels and you thought I'd stolen them from the tuck shop and reported me?' Skinny Lesley laughed.

Hilary squeezed her eyes shut. 'When is the reunion?' she asked politely.

'The eighth of December. Say you'll come. Everyone else will be there. Even Johnboy Malone has said he'll turn up. You'll never guess who he married. That stuck-up Naomi Scott! Can you believe it? And he was so sweet on you, Hilary.'

No. Hilary couldn't believe it. And neither could she believe this conversation.

'I'll send you a letter with all the details of the hows, whys and whens. I shan't ask you now what you've been up to these past eighteen years, you can tell me on the eighth. See you.'

The phone clicked and Hilary went back to the kitchen to stand over the ironing board and Philip's school shirt.

Skinny Lesley, Johnboy Malone and Naomi Scott all appeared in front of her. She slammed the iron down on top of them.

Star Struck was packed. It always was, and not just because the restaurant had such a good reputation for its menu. It was also renowned for its entertaining owner, Tony Farrand, who behaved like an eccentric showman – because that was what he was or, at least, what he had once been back in the seventies when, for a few short years, he had been very much the current flavour and had hosted not only his own comedy show, but *Star Struck*, a celebrity-quiz panel show. His act had been ostentatious and exuberant and had gone down well in the glittering seventies but the eighties audience had required something a little more succinct and sophisticated. His popularity had waned and brought him to the north-west of England, where house prices were lower than in the south and his style could be put to good use in the restaurant trade.

When he greeted Hilary and David at the door he was dressed in a flamboyant suit that had more than a touch of the Liberaces about it. Sparkling like a Christmas tree, he took Becky by the hand and led them to a central aisle table. He offered her a kiss and Hilary was amused to see how readily Becky accepted this, for all her recently acquired feminist tendencies. Philip was given a cigar, which was immediately snatched away, and when Tony blew into it a daisy popped out of the end.

Next Tony kissed Hilary's hand but thumbed his nose at David. Watch yourself, Hilary thought, as she sat down, or he might punch you in the face.

Menus were handed round the table, along with a bottle of Calpol for the children. 'Oh, so you're not ill?' he said, seeing the bemused look on Becky's face. 'Okay, then, I'll bring you something else.' He returned with two glasses of lemonade and said, 'These are on the house ... my house.

You're paying my mortgage!' He laughed and left them alone.

Hilary suddenly felt scared. Having Tony around had offered her a kind of protection. In his crazy way he made life seem sane and infinitely more bearable. She peeped over the top of her menu at David and caught him pushing back the cuff on his jacket to look at his watch.

'In a hurry?' she asked.

He ignored her, or perhaps he hadn't heard her above the loud music – she still wanted to give him the benefit of the doubt.

Next to David Becky was crumbling a breadstick into her mouth, while Philip was swinging on the back two legs of his chair, reading his menu.

'What do you fancy?' she asked him.

'The ravioli with ricotta cheese, please,' he answered, tossing the menu onto the table and bringing his chair down with a sudden bump.

'Not the Bolognese? You usually have that when we come here,' Hilary said.

'I had it at school for lunch yesterday.'

'How is school?' David asked, finally joining in with the conversation.

Philip looked at his father. 'I hate it!' he wanted to shout at him. 'And it's all your bloody fault I'm there!' It was true, it had been Dad who'd suggested he sat the scholarship exam and Dad who'd promised him a computer if he passed. Well, he had passed and he had got a computer but he was getting hell kicked out of him into the bargain. He reached under the table and rubbed his bruised shin. Yesterday he'd been pushed over. Then he'd had his briefcase taken and his work thrown around the classroom and all because he wouldn't give in and hand over any money. But at least Batesy had helped to pick everything up. 'Just do as they say and they'll leave you alone. It's easier that way,' he'd whispered. The hell he would!

'It's okay,' Philip said at last.

'What about Latin and classical studies? You didn't think you'd enjoy those, did you?'

Philip stared at his father again and shrugged his shoulders. 'It's not so bad. Yesterday was a bit tedious – we were learning about love.'

'Yuck,' Becky said, pulling a face. Hilary reached for a packet of breadsticks and started fumbling with the wrapper.

'Oh, yes,' David said. 'And what earth-shattering conclusions did you learned youngsters reach? Not to have anything to do with it, I expect.' He gave a short laugh which, to Hilary's ears, sounded pompous. Had he always laughed like that? Did other people find him pompous?

Philip ignored his father's question. 'There are three types of love,' he said, 'eros, agape and one other that I can't remember. Sir says that eros is the kind of love that makes you do stupid things like Romeo and Juliet did, and agape is the unconditional love, which according to sir goes on for ever. How do you love Mum, Dad, in the eros way or agape?'

David shifted awkwardly in his chair. 'The most I learned in Latin at school about love was amo, amas, amat, never mind all this guppy stuff.'

'Agape,' Philip corrected.

'I want a pizza,' Becky announced, banging her menu down on the table and knocking over a tiny vase with its single red carnation. Water flooded across the paper tablecloth.

'Ah!' shouted Tony, appearing from nowhere to mop up the damage. 'An extra ten pounds on the bill. That was holy water I brought back from the Vatican after cooking dinner for the Papa. You don't believe me, eh? I'll ring him up and ask him to tell you it's the truth.' He grabbed a large pepper-mill from a passing waiter. 'Hello,' he said, talking into it as though it was a telephone. 'Hey, Papa, you tell the girl here about the holy water.' He passed the pepper-mill to Becky, who slowly raised it to her left ear but when she saw the look on Philip's face she flung it back at Tony.

'Silly man,' she said, embarrassed.

He took their order and, once again, Hilary felt the strain of being left to their own devices.

'I want the loo,' Becky said loudly above the sound of Wet Wet Wet – her boredom threshold nearing zero.

'You only want to play with the soap dispenser,' Philip accused her.

'I do not. I'm bursting and I'll prove it if—'

'Hurry up and go,' interrupted Hilary, who knew better than anyone to call her daughter's bluff.

'I'll go as well,' Philip said.

Just you and me, then, David, Hilary thought, watching David's turned-away face as Becky and Philip left the table. Speak to me! Say something nice. Give me some hope ... just a hint of hope that you do still love me.

He said nothing to her unspoken questions and his silence made her want to run away and cry. She felt unimaginably sorry for herself and blew her nose in an effort to hold back the tears. Oh, God, don't let me fall apart now, not in front of all these people. 'I think I'd better go and check on Becky,' she said, getting to her feet and stumbling away.

She met Philip and Becky coming down the narrow staircase on their way back to their table. Inside the ladies' there was soap everywhere. Without thinking she started to clear up the washbasins, throwing paper towels – which she suspected Becky had been using as water bombs – into the bin.

While Wet Wet Wet sang 'Put the Light On' through the restaurant sound system she tried to stem the flow of tears threatening to stream down her cheeks. Why doesn't he love me? she asked herself, looking in the mirror as she wiped away yet more soap. What's wrong with me? Why am I not enough for him? Nick obviously thinks I'm all right.

Horrified, she stared at her reflection in the mirror. Where had that thought come from? And why had Nick Bradshaw appeared in her life the moment she had discovered David's unfaithfulness? Thoughts of guardian angels crept into her mind. Had he come into her life to help her? *Ring me if you need to.* His echoing words seemed to join forces with those of Marti Pellow. '... put a little light in her darkest day ... ring me.'

Her meal was waiting for her when she got back to the table.

'We didn't wait,' David said, forking up a pasta bow and staring at a young waitress with a skirt no bigger than a napkin at the top of her long, slender legs.

When had he started doing that, Hilary wondered. He never used to eye up other women, let alone a girl young enough to be his daughter. So when had he got so bored with her and changed? Or was it she who had changed? Had he always been like this and she was only now waking up to him and his irritating habits?

'I need the loo again,' Becky said, having picked over her pizza and lined the edge of her plate with little bits of onion.

Oh, if life was as easy as playing around with a soap dispenser every time you got bored, thought Hilary, watching Becky disappear once more.

Playing around – she glanced across the table to David. He met her stare.

'You're not eating,' he said, pointing with his knife at her untouched plate.

'I'm not hungry,' she said faintly.

He rolled his eyes. 'A waste of an evening and more money down the drain!'

'More money?' she repeated. 'What do you mean?'

'New hairdo, new clothes, a meal out, and all for what, I ask you?'

That was it! He'd gone too far now. Her mind was made up.

Ring me if you need to.

She would! She would ring Nick. That would show David!

'Does that mean another lemonade's out of the question?' Philip asked, awkwardly.

'You'd better ask Scrooge here,' Hilary replied, unable to keep the anger and sarcasm out of her voice. Obviously running a mistress as well as a family was proving a more expensive proposition for David than he had thought.

Chapter Twenty-three

Hilary was up before anyone else. It was still pitch black outside and in the light cast from a couple of underlighters in the Aga alcove she stirred a pot of porridge.

She hadn't eaten a thing at the restaurant last night and had woken up at five o'clock almost sick with hunger. Knowing that she couldn't lie there a moment longer next to David's restless body, tossing and turning, she'd come downstairs in search of something to eat.

As she stirred the bubbling pan she found the smell of warm milk comforting and reassuring. In those first few days after finding out about David and Catherine she had cooked mechanically and without enjoyment. It had all taken too much effort. Then last week she had thrown herself into spending hours filling the freezer and cake tins with what she had felt sure would lure David back to the safety of The Gables, tempting him with his favourite Delia Smith sticky toffee puddings and gingerbread. She had done it because she recalled that earlier in the year David had said that Catherine was a lousy cook. At the time it had never occurred to Hilary to ask him how he knew this. Had she simply told him in the office one day or had he discovered for himself that she was disastrous in the kitchen but dynamite in bed?

Now, though, as she scooped out some porridge into a bowl she didn't give a fig about finding the way back to David's heart through his stomach. She made herself a pot of tea, opened the fridge for a bottle of milk and found a half-empty pot of double cream. She poured it over the bowl and then added a sprinkling of brown sugar, followed by some more and then a dollop of honey. She contemplated some maple syrup, but decided against it. That was going too far.

To hell with that, she thought, this was no time for propriety. She squeezed the plastic bottle over the bowl and it fired off a loud raspberry.

And with years of everything-in-moderation out of the window, Hilary raised the first wicked spoonful to her lips and wondered if this was how Eve had felt. Had she got up early one morning and wandered into the garden and done the unthinkable because Adam had pushed her beyond what she could bear – just as David was doing with her? She swallowed another spoonful of porridge and pushed this thought aside, preferring instead to equate herself with Goldilocks – Goldilocks hadn't meant any harm, had she? She helped herself to some more cream and thought of her resolution, made last night at the restaurant – the moment when she had decided to take control.

As she'd lain awake in the early hours listening to David's unsteady breathing and occasional bursts of muttered words in his sleep she had thought not just of Nick Bradshaw but of Johnboy Malone.

Skinny Lesley had been right: Johnboy had been sweet on her all those years ago. And at teacher-training there had been that rugby player with arms like bolsters who had always been knocking on her door wanting to have coffee with her – much to David's annoyance. She had been attractive once, hadn't she? So when had that all changed? When had she become so sexless? Was it during pregnancy? Or had it happened during those matter-of-fact years of leaky breasts, disgusting nappies, prize-winning moments of potty training and heroic sleepless nights? She had no idea. She got up from the table, went over to the dishwasher and placed her empty bowl on the top rack. In pursuit of yet more self-indulgence she opened one of the high cupboards where she kept a secret supply of goodies – deliberately stored there out of Becky's reach. She pulled down a packet of chocolate biscuits, sat at the table again and started flicking through her latest copy of *Hello!* Chocolate and the rich and famous with their beautiful designer homes and clothes – was there ever a better combination for inspiring and encouraging a search for something more exciting in one's own drab life?

When she had finished reading about the latest society goings-on in London she moved on to *Cheshire Life* and this month's feature article on the north-west's most wealthy and eligible men. 'Thirty-nine and how many millions?' she said out loud, looking at a photo of the handsome owner of a well-known chain of sportswear shops. She wondered whether the magazine would ever do an article on Derek and Cindy's latest enterprise. In her mind's eye she pictured the two of them smiling into the camera lens and appearing, to all intents and purposes, the perfect couple, with their long marriage and business partnership behind them and their new venture launching them into the future.

How many lies did they all cover up? Was everyone out there pretending to live lives that in truth they found unbearable at times? Was the answer simply to make the best of a bad job and get what satisfaction one could?

She picked up another chocolate biscuit and chewed it thoughtfully.

'Nick?' she whispered into the phone five minutes later.

'Yes ... Hilary?'

'I'm sorry it's so early, but you said if I needed help you'd—'

'I can be ready in ten minutes. Where do you want to meet?'

'I don't know,' she said, suddenly unsure.

'Come here, then, and we'll talk. That is what you want, isn't it, Hilary?'

She nodded dumbly into the phone and listened to him giving her directions to where he lived.

'Who were you on the phone to?' David asked, when she went upstairs to get dressed and found him awake in bed.

'Georgia D'Arcy,' she lied.

'What on earth do you want with that man-hater at this time of day?' He yawned.

'PTA stuff,' she answered, from the depths of the wardrobe. 'I need to go through a few of the arrangements for the end-of-term Christmas Fayre. I'm going to see her now.'

'What, this early? And, anyway, won't she be sharpening her claws in that nursery of hers?'

'She's capable of doing more than one thing at a time. Perhaps you could haul yourself out of bed and take the children to church this morning.'

David groaned. 'God won't miss them just one Sunday.'

'They missed last week so they really should go today,' she said, wanting her children to be in the safe hands of God for the next few hours. She selected one of the outfits Cindy had helped her buy in Manchester and sped off to the bathroom to get dressed. The thought of dressing for duplicity in front of David was too much. She slipped into the softly pleated trousers Cindy had chosen in preference to the crisp navy ones she had wanted, then pulled the pale pink angora sweater over her head. She brushed her hair away from her face and tried to apply some make-up. She managed some blusher and lipstick but her hands were trembling so much she had to give up on the mascara. She didn't look at all like Anthea Turner any more but she gave herself six out of ten for effort.

She closed the front door, climbed into her car and reversed out of the drive. She didn't look back at the house for fear of catching sight of the children peering out of a window at her. This, she told herself sternly, had nothing to do with the children. This was between her and David.

At the end of Acacia Lane she stopped the car and reached into her handbag for her small bottle of Anaïs Anaïs. She sprayed her neck and wrists liberally, then had to wind down the window for air. She coughed and spluttered, trying to catch her breath, and nearly jumped out of her skin at the sound of tapping and Iris Braithwaite's face appearing through the open window.

'You're surely not driving to early-morning communion, Mrs Parker.'

'Heavens, no,' squeaked Hilary.

'So where are you off to at this time of day, and all dressed up?'

Only Mrs Braithwaite could be so direct. Nerves and guilt rendered Hilary's reply almost inaudible.

'I beg your pardon, Mrs Parker.'

'PTA ... Georgia D'Arcy,' she managed more intelligibly.

Mrs Braithwaite's powdery face broke into an unexpected smile. 'Hulme Welford would be a far better place if we had more people like that young woman living here. And how's that ill-mannered husband of yours? Brawling in public and over what, one asks oneself? Where was his sense of decency and respect when he took it upon himself to besmirch your name?'

'I really must be getting on,' Hilary said boldly, and, ignoring the other woman's questions, she pressed lightly on the accelerator pedal and tweaked the engine.

As she turned the corner onto the main street of the village Hilary had the uncomfortable feeling that Mrs Braithwaite was still standing in the middle of Acacia Lane staring suspiciously after her and putting two and two together. The older woman's appearance had acted like a spectre at the feast, intruding in an area where Hilary wanted no reminders of everyday life. As she drove out of the village she struggled to reinstate the picture of the world she had created in her mind while reading about the Earl of Whatsit and his beautiful new girlfriend on holiday in the Maldives.

Nick's house was not far from Philip's new school, and as the fields and recently cut hedges of the familiar lanes slipped by she watched the sky on the horizon release its hold on the last remnants of night, finally giving way to morning strands of pink and gentian blue.

She saw the sign for the trout farm Nick had described and slowed down to third gear on the bend in the road as he'd instructed. His small end-of-terrace cottage was set back from the road and a plume of smoke was rising from the chimney. She felt her body go taut with nervous expectation.

She parked the car on the verge, switched off the engine, gathered up her bag, locked the car door and breathed in deeply. High up in the oak trees she heard the loud cawing of crows – or were they rooks? Dear God! She could think of things like that when she was about to embark on ... She cleared her throat, tucked her bag under her arm and went up to the door, which was at the side of the cottage. It opened before she had even raised her hand to the knocker.

'I've made us some coffee,' he said, as she stepped inside. He took her coat and hung it on the back of the kitchen door alongside an overcoat she recognised from bonfire night. 'Have you eaten?'

She nodded and looked awkwardly about the tiny kitchen; there was an empty wine bottle on the floor along with a brown carrier bag of foil cartons with the remains of some pilau rice clinging to the edges. 'You're not very tidy, are you?'

He passed her a mug of coffee. 'And you're making small-talk.'

She turned away and stared out of the leaded window which overlooked the road. She wondered if anyone would recognise her car.

'We all do it,' he said.

'Do what?' she said, facing him again.

'Avoid saying what we really want to say. Come through

to the other room. It's just as untidy but at least it's warm. I lit a fire as soon as I put the phone down.'

'I'm sorry to have put you to all this trouble. Oh,' she said, standing in the middle of the sitting room, 'you're right, this is as untidy.'

He laughed, gathered up a pile of books and files from an armchair by the fire, and flung the heap onto the floor where another stack of books teetered with intent. 'I'm disappointing you, aren't I?'

'How long have you lived here?' she asked, sitting cautiously in the chair he'd cleared. She half expected it to collapse beneath her. The fabric was wearing through on the arms and she played with a loose thread that stood proud from a faded dianthus.

'About three years. And if you want a life résumé before you're going to talk properly to me I'll give it to you.'

'I didn't mean to sound—'

'Relax and listen for a change. I get the impression you don't do a lot of listening, Hilary. You make a lot of assumptions, don't you?'

She said nothing. It wasn't turning out exactly how she'd imagined it would. Surely this wasn't how the Earl had wooed the lovely Annabel.

'I'm forty-eight years old. I used to be a lecturer in organisational behaviour, then when my second marriage hit the skids five years ago I took a long hard look at myself and found I didn't much like what was there. I decided to make the switch from always talking to occasionally listening, which is what I want to do with you.' He moved away from his position by the fire and sat in the chair opposite her. 'Are you ready to talk to me now?'

Would tears work? she thought. If she started to cry, would he take her in his arms and ...?

'David doesn't love me,' she said. 'He barely looks at me these days, let alone talks to me. He's ... he's having an affair and I feel ...'

She heard him move towards her, then felt his hand on hers.

'You feel hurt,' he said, taking her untouched mug of coffee away from her. 'You feel betrayed and rejected. You feel spread all over the floor and about as worthless as you can get ... and you want someone to put you back together again and make everything better.'

'Yes,' she whispered. Now hurry up and kiss me.

He did.

Chapter Twenty-four

Nick was surprisingly gentle with her, unlike David who had always treated her as though she were a rag doll. 'Don't push me about,' she had told him on their second date, when he had pressed her against the door of her room in the college hall of residence.

As Nick tilted his head to one side she wondered if she was going about things the right way – it was so long ago since she'd been in this situation. Would it be better if she was to open her mouth wider? And what about her hands? Should she be doing something with them?

One of Nick's hands was stroking the nape of her neck. She felt wobbly inside and even more conscious of his lips, so warm and soft against her own.

Just as she closed her eyes Nick pulled away. 'Tell me, Hilary,' he said, 'has that made you feel better? Did it stop you thinking of David for a few moments?'

'Yes,' she lied, 'completely.'

He gazed at her steadily and she sat waiting for him to say or do something else – she wanted him to stroke her neck again. He stood up abruptly and went and stood by the mantelpiece in front of the fire.

'It's only a short-term answer, Hilary,' he said firmly, his arms crossed in front of him. Suddenly he looked like a stern headmaster. 'And how about the guilt? Could you cope with that?'

Kiss me again and I'll see, she wanted to say flippantly, high on the thrill of having kissed another man – she had actually kissed another man! 'David's managing pretty well,' she said.

'But is he? He's obviously under an enormous strain at the moment, living his double life. How much longer do you think he can go on as he is?'

'Why is everyone so concerned about the strain David's under? What about the strain he's put on my life? This is no picnic for me I can assure you.'

He smiled, and came and sat next to her again. 'I know,' he said gently, no longer a stern headmaster. 'But having an affair with the first available man is not the answer.'

'So why did you kiss me?' she asked. 'Were you making fun of me?'

'I kissed you because I knew that was what you wanted.'

'I ... I didn't,' she stammered.

'And I wanted to prove to you that it's not the answer. Tell me, Hilary, has your marriage made you happy?'

'I—'

'Or have you assumed you were happy – have marriage, have happiness? Can you remember the last time you were heart-stoppingly tickled pink with the love you feel towards David?'

She lowered her eyes and fiddled with her sapphire engagement ring. 'It's not like that,' she said at last. 'You just muddle along. Nobody can be expected to dance around the supermarket on a Monday morning in a state of euphoria after more than a decade of marriage. Life simply has a habit of getting in the way.'

'What a sad world we live in where our expectations become so dulled by routine. Hilary, when will you, and everyone like you, understand that this is not a dress rehearsal? This is it. You have to live life to the full.'

'I suppose that's what David's doing,' she said in a small voice, pulling absentmindedly at the thread on the arm of the chair.

'It could be. Though ask yourself this. Does he seem

happier because of what he's doing?'

Hilary thought of David's miserable face, his thin lips drawn in a tight line and his apparent ambivalence to their life together. 'No,' she said, 'he doesn't look like a man who's enjoying himself.'

'Because he's feeling guilty. He knows what he's doing is going to hurt you and the children, if he's found out. Like so many seeking a quick fix he's not thought this through. He should have looked carefully at his life to find the reason he felt the urge to stray.'

'Perhaps it's all my fault. Maybe because of the way I am I've made him have an affair. If I had been more—'

'It's a possibility. But in reality quite often it's not what's happening around the home that causes a partner to be unfaithful. I'm not making excuses or trying to justify what David's done but I guarantee that the reason for his infidelity lies deep within his own make-up, not yours. As Thoreau said, "The mass of men lead quiet lives of desperation." '

Hilary looked up sharply. 'Why's it always the men having such a hard time?'

He smiled. 'Don't take things so literally. And, as I just said, I'm not making excuses for David but what I am trying to say is that we all react to a given situation and our response determines the consequences.' He stared hard at her. 'David chose to have an affair ... just as you chose to come here today.'

She turned away.

'Did you really expect me to whisk you upstairs and bed you?'

She continued to stare into the fire, watching the flames lick at the loose bark on a log in the grate. 'You make it sound so sordid.'

He laughed lightly. 'The state of my sheets, it would have been.'

She tried to laugh as well but it came out more like a whimper. 'I've made a complete fool of myself, haven't I?'

'Not at all. You've done what so many people do in your situation.'

'Predictable as well as foolish. I'm sorry to be so boring.'

'Stop giving yourself such a hard time, Hilary. You're an attractive, intelligent woman with everything going for you—'

'Please, don't say any more or you'll start me crying.'

He put his arm round her shoulders and kissed her forehead. 'Go ahead. Feel free. But go easy on that armchair or it'll be shredded by the time you leave.'

She looked down at the thread of cotton in her fingers: it was twice its original length and there was now a hole in the middle of the dianthus. 'I'm sorry—'

'Would you stop apologising and listen to what else I've got to say? You've got some very difficult decisions ahead of you and only you can make them. You can talk it through with me, if you like, or any amount of your friends and family, but ultimately you're the one who is going to have to live with whatever is decided, so it's only right it should be you who reaches a decision. Remember, nothing is by chance. We each make a choice to determine our future. And the priority in your immediate future is telling David that you know about his affair. When are you going to tell him?'

'Not yet. Not with my sister's wedding and Christmas coming up so soon. I'll talk to him in the New Year.'

'And will you be ready for his response if he says he wants to leave you?'

'I feel like he's left me already. At least then the awful pretending will be over.'

On her way home Hilary called at Hulme View Nursery, so at least her alibi would have some weight should David have any suspicions that she hadn't been telling the truth. She hadn't seen Georgia since that dreadful scene in the kitchen when she'd invited her back for tea and Nick had turned up unexpectedly. How horribly complicated her life had become. Would it ever be the way it used to be?

The nursery was busy with Sunday browsers selecting trays of winter-flowering pansies and heathers. Hilary found Georgia pushing a large muddy trolley of potted five-foot-high conifers.

'Hello, stranger,' Georgia said, coming to a stop. She started to unload the trolley. 'I'd ask you to help,' she said, as she lifted the first of the tall conifers, 'only you're done up like a lardy cake. I suppose you've been to church, have you?'

Hilary nodded.

'I didn't think the devout still thought God loved them more when they were decked out in their finery.'

'They don't!' Hilary retorted. Dear God, she was fed up with all these sharp-witted people around her.

'I'm sorry,' Georgia said, settling the conifer next to a row of small laurel bushes. 'That was rude of me. The unconverted don't have the right to knock the few who do believe. What can I do you for?'

Hilary hesitated. She was doing a lot of that, these days. She never used to. She'd always known exactly what she wanted to do and say. 'PTA,' she blurted out. 'I thought we could go through some of the Christmas Fayre arrangements.'

Georgia frowned. She reached for another conifer but then changed her mind. She pushed back the sleeve of her donkey jacket. A quarter to eleven. She returned her attention to Hilary. 'Have I got this right? I'm making the assumption that you've been to church this morning and that you've left early to come here and talk to me about the fayre. How am I doing?'

Hilary looked awkwardly at her feet. 'It just crossed my mind—'

'To dip out of the Eucharist and dash along here. Well, that seems eminently feasible. I wish all the members of the PTA were as diligent as you. Just fancy, there you were, down on your knees, and suddenly you thought of me, or perhaps it was the hand of God intervening, "P-T-A," his sepulchral voice boomed through the vaulted ceiling.'

'Hardly anybody gets down on their knees at St John's,' Hilary said, petulantly.

'You speak for yourself,' Georgia said, struggling with another conifer. 'I'm frequently on mine.'

Hilary felt tired and out of her depth.

Georgia looked at Hilary's miserable and confused face. 'Oh, shit,' she said, 'I'm sorry. I'm premenstrual and feeling as bloated as the *Hindenburg* and about as volatile. Forgive me?'

Hilary nodded. 'And I'm sorry I lied to you.'

Georgia smiled. 'You mean, no PTA talk? You do surprise me. Come on, let's go over to the caravan and you can tell me what you've really come for.'

'But what about your customers?'

'Gordon's here today. He's taking care of them, leaving me to clear a space ready for the order of rooted Christmas trees coming in tomorrow.'

'I don't want to keep you from your work, I can easily—'

'Give it a rest, Hilary.'

The caravan felt only marginally warmer than it was outside. Georgia switched on a small heater, which whirred noisily. 'Fancy a coffee? I've got some in a Thermos here.'

Hilary shook her head.

'Suit yourself,' Georgia poured some for herself. She cradled her half-mittened fingers around the plastic cup. 'So what's been going on at The Gables since I saw you last? Which reminds me, you were acting very strangely that day. I could have sworn you were suddenly frightened of me.'

Hilary picked up a packet of lupin seeds and tipped it upside down. She listened to the seeds trickling from one end to the other.

Georgia laughed. 'And if I didn't know better I'd say that witch Patricia Longton put some silly idea into your head.'

'Goodness, of course not,' Hilary said, too quickly.

'Stupid bitch has always thought I was gay ever since I kicked Rory out. Well, to put the record straight, I'm not. Look at me when I'm talking to you, Hilary. I'm not some sex-starved lesbian about to take advantage of a vulnerable woman. Okay?'

'Okay,' Hilary repeated quickly. Heavens, what a morning it was turning into!

'Not that there's anything wrong in being gay, some of my closest friends are. But that's beside the point. Get on and tell me what you came here for.'

Hilary had had no intention of telling Georgia about Nick Bradshaw when she'd driven through the nursery gates, but now that their friendship was back on a more reassuring level she decided she wanted to confide in her. She explained about wanting to use Georgia as an alibi and why, then went on to tell her partly what had happened at Nick's.

'Bloody hell, Hilary! You mean you let that wily bastard get his tongue down your throat?'

Hilary frowned. 'I only let him kiss me,' she said defensively.

'Crap! *You* kissed him.'

The two women looked at each other in silence. Hilary was disappointed. She had made Georgia angry and she didn't want that. Then she saw her friend's face soften with a smile. 'Well, you've learned two important things this morning, Hilary. One is that you don't have to worry about me leaping on you and the other is that you've proved to yourself that if you wanted to dip your toes into the shark-infested waters of catching yourself a man, you could. So where exactly does that leave you?'

'Lord only knows. Probably going clean round the bend.'

Chapter Twenty-five

She was mad. Stark raving bonkers mad. She looked again at the clock on the dashboard. Five to eight – nearly half an hour late. What had made her agree to Skinny Lesley's invitation? Worse still, what had actually made her stick to it when she could have so easily backed out at the last minute claiming a headache? Nobody would have been the wiser.

It had been Charlotte who had insisted she go. 'It'll be a laugh, Hilary,' she'd said that afternoon at the shop.

'And how would you know?' she had thrown back at her sister. 'You've never been to one of these dos.'

'Only because nobody's bothered to go to the trouble to organise one for my year.'

'Well, I wish Skinny Lesley hadn't bothered. What on earth am I supposed to say to all those people I haven't seen for nearly twenty years?'

'I'm sure you'll think of something,' Charlotte had said, adding, 'strange, isn't it, that we haven't seen much of anyone from our schooldays?'

As Hilary flicked her headlights to full beam on the unlit stretch of dual carriageway she wondered about what her sister had said. Charlotte was right, it was strange. Their old school wasn't exactly a million miles from Hulme Welford but it was in a different county, chosen specifically by their mother for its vigorous hard-work ethic and long hours – it had been the only day school within a twenty-mile radius that had insisted on compulsory Saturday-morning attendance, something that had fitted in perfectly with Louise's work commitments at her antique shop and their father's surgery hours and house calls in the village.

But, then, perhaps it wasn't so much the geography of the school's location that had meant there had been no contact between the classmates once they'd left. Maybe it was simply that most people had moved away at the first possible opportunity and that it was only she who had unimaginatively moved back after going away to teacher-training. After a moment's reflection, she consoled herself with the thought that, years later, Charlotte was equally dull.

She turned left at the roundabout and there it was. School. Not that there was anything about the Victorian Gothic edifice in front of her that filled her with dread: she had enjoyed the period in her life that the building represented. School had been fun. All that structure and work to get on with, it had suited her just fine. But what *did* fill her with dread was facing everybody tonight, and them all guessing, one by one, that her marriage was on the rocks.

The car park – which had once been the netball courts – was almost full of sleekly moulded cars: Mercedes, BMWs, Audis, Volvos, a couple of Jaguars and every conceivable variety of four-wheel-drive vehicle, shining examples of success and affluence. Hadn't they all done well? she thought cynically.

She parked her Clio alongside a smart little midnight blue BMW Coupé. She had planned to drive David's Volvo, but only that afternoon he'd booked it in for a service. The garage had telephoned later, saying they'd found a fault on one of the wheel-bearings and that it would be at least Tuesday before they'd be able to fix it. So much for turning up in style.

She pulled on the handbrake, released her seat-belt and jerked the mirror towards her to examine her make-up. She bared her teeth, checking for any wayward smears of lipstick.

The main entrance door was decorated with a couple of balloons, one of which was already showing signs of deflating and wrinkling – not unlike herself, Hilary thought, as she pushed against the glass-panelled door. The foyer was empty, save for a massive Christmas tree covered with art-department-generated decorations and flickering lights. The door to the main hall, which had been used for gym and morning assemblies, was wide open and through it she could see a crowd of animated faces. Automatically she put on her best smile, hoping it would conceal the look of failure on her own face.

'Not so fast. You need a badge before you can go a step further.'

Standing to attention behind a table and holding a clip-board and a pen was ... Skinny Lesley?

'Hilary, it's you!' whooped an amazingly large Skinny Lesley.

'Lesley!'

'You look great, Hilary, and you've not changed a bit.'

'Neither have you.'

'Oh, come on! I've put on four stone since those days – gained one for each child I've produced and one for luck.' She let out a loud laugh and smacked a name badge on Hilary's shoulder. Hilary staggered slightly under the force of Skinny Lesley's hand. 'Now the procedure is this. First question is, do you still live in the area, followed by, are you married and how many children have you got? Bar's over there in the corner. I'll catch up with you later when I'm off duty.'

Hilary turned from Skinny Lesley's bristling efficiency and straight away saw Carrie Maxwell standing alone, an empty wine-glass in her hand – heavens, she'd been a terror with a hockey-stick in her hands. She went over to her. 'Hello, Carrie.'

'Hilary!' Carrie's delight was obvious. 'Just look at you! Apart from the colour of your hair, you're exactly the same.'

'Except I don't wear tank tops any more,' Hilary said, with a smile, finding some of her nervousness beginning to slip away.

'My eldest daughter does, though. You should see her, flares and platforms, the whole performance all over again.'

Hilary laughed and took a quick glance round the hall. 'Isn't this whole thing bizarre? How many have you stayed in touch with?'

'Nobody. I moved away after A-levels and never came back. I live in Kent now.'

'Married?' Hilary ventured.

'Hell, no! The rat deserted years ago.'

'Oh, I'm sorry.'

'And you?'

'Hilary Archer! I don't believe it!'

They both turned to see Johnboy Malone advancing towards them. 'I don't believe it!' he repeated, *à la* Victor Meldrew – he even had the same cropped thinning hair.

'Hello, Johnboy,' Hilary said, quietly.

'No, no, no. That won't do at all. You've got to get into the part, Hilary. The men slap and punch one another and you girls are supposed to throw your heads back and squeal loudly with your arms either side of you waving like a mad thing. Here, hold my glass and I'll show you.'

'You're such an exhibitionist, John,' came a deep, sexy voice from behind him. It was Naomi Scott.

Hilary gulped unthinkingly from Johnboy's wine-glass – Naomi Scott, dark-haired, dark-eyed and looking as fabulous as a model, dressed in an Audrey Hepburn tailored black suit with a small shiny handbag, no bigger than a handkerchief, hanging from her wrist. She was utterly gorgeous – and didn't she know it? Hilary watched, fascinated, as Naomi placed a hand of red-painted nails on Johnboy's shoulder.

'Introduce me,' Naomi purred in Johnboy's ear, then, looking at Hilary and Carrie beneath her long lashes, she said, 'I shouldn't really even be here, not being in your year group, but John never goes anywhere without me, these days.'

'I vaguely remember you,' Hilary said crisply. She was furious that this smouldering beauty couldn't even remember who she was. 'You're four years older than the rest of us, aren't you?' she carried on and, fired up with resentment, she pointed to the name badge on her left shoulder and added, 'You must have forgotten your glasses.'

'I'm dying for a drink,' Naomi said uninterestedly, after giving Hilary a vacant stare. She unwrapped herself from Johnboy and walked away.

'I don't remember you being such a tiger, Hilary,' Johnboy said, with a laugh. 'How about a kiss for old times' sake?' He leaned towards her and kissed her cheek. 'Can I have my glass back now?'

Hilary handed it to him. She suddenly felt very bold. There had been more than a hint of malice in the words she had just spoken to Naomi Scott and she knew that not only had she meant every ounce of it but that the poignant humiliation she had recently recalled over that wretched box of chocolates and what she had once felt for Naomi Scott had magically vanished.

'I'll get you a glass of wine while I leave Johnboy to chat you up like in the old days,' Carrie said, already moving off.

'You look well,' Hilary said awkwardly, when they were alone and she had the opportunity to take in Johnboy's expensive wool blazer and silk tie.

'Thank you. Though I can't say that stockbroking has done anything for my hair.' He ran his hand through what little he had. 'I like your hair short, by the way. You always wore it long, though I don't remember you being so fair.'

She smiled self-consciously. 'A bottle job.'

'Aha. To cover up the grey?'

'Certainly not!'

'Naomi does it all the time. But she'd bloody kill me if she knew I'd told you.'

Hilary wanted to hug Johnboy. What other spectres from

her past would he put to rest for her tonight, she wondered.

'So how about you, Hilary? What have you been up to since 'seventy-eight?'

'Nothing very exciting, I'm afraid. Teaching, marriage and children.'

'I always had you down as a career girl. When the rest of us were larking about you were there handing in the longest essays known to mankind. I dread to think how many times you saved my skin by letting me read through your work so that I could at least have a clue what the teachers were expecting me to write about. God, but you were sweet.'

'How long have you been married to Naomi?' Hilary asked, revelling in Johnboy's flattery. He hadn't changed.

'Only a year.'

'Is that all?'

'I kept putting marriage off then, purely by chance, along came Naomi. We met on a skiing holiday last year in Wengen.'

Hilary was just imagining the beautiful Naomi on skis – as quick and as sleek as a snake – when Johnboy said, 'We're not suited, I know it. I can see it in people's eyes every time they look at us. I'm her third husband.'

Hilary gawped. 'Third?' she murmured. She felt extra-ordinarily sorry for Johnboy. And was there nobody here tonight who had experienced a normal happy marriage?

'What's your husband like, Hilary?'

'He's an estate agent—'

Johnboy threw back his head and laughed. 'Are you telling me he's a dishonest, underhanded so-and-so?'

Hilary bit her lip, then remembered her lipstick.

But Johnboy had caught the change of expression on her face. 'I'm sorry,' he said. 'In poor taste, I assume.'

She didn't know what to say but was glad to see Carrie coming towards them with two glasses of wine.

'Sorry I've been so long, I've been talking to Craig Montana – just discovered he only lives a short distance away from me. Not married either.' She handed Hilary her glass. 'Mind if I get back to him?'

They watched Carrie disappear.

'Children?'

Hilary turned back to Johnboy. 'Sorry?'

'You said you had children. How many?'

'Two. Philip and Becky.'

'That's nice. And is Becky like her mother?'

'Lord, I hope not. Or, rather, I hope no one thinks she takes after me. She can be very difficult at times.'

'Substitute challenging for difficult,' Johnboy said, quietly. He leaned into Hilary. 'That's what I say to myself about Naomi at times.'

'I hope you're not trying out the my-wife-doesn't-under-stand-me routine,' Hilary said with a giggle, enjoying the close proximity of Johnboy and the expensive smell of him.

'As if I would,' he said, with a twinkle in his eye. 'But, then, you always were an expert at keeping me at arm's length.'

Hilary blushed. Right now she'd switch that particular skill for any other, given the opportunity. 'Where are you living?'

'Haslemere. Bloody great barn of a place and nothing to fill it.'

For the first time in their conversation Hilary sensed traces of anger in Johnboy's words, or was it regret?

'Kids,' he said flatly. 'I love 'em, but can't have any.'

'You could adopt,' Hilary said, beginning to feel uncomfortable with the way the conversation was going. Should they be talking about such personal things? Wasn't this whole evening supposed to be superficial and on the level of merely comparing notes on what they had all achieved?

'Can you see Naomi with her hands anywhere near a nappy?'

'She might if given the chance,' Hilary said brightly.

'She only married me because she knew I wouldn't be able

to get her pregnant and spoil that lovely body of hers.'

'I'm sure she didn't.'

He shook his head. 'You really haven't changed, have you, Hilary? You always did look on the bright side of things and see life through rose-tinted spectacles. What a wonderful way to be.'

The party broke up just after eleven. A few were heading off into town to a club but after Hilary had said her goodbyes she drove home, pondering on the evening. What had threatened to be a nightmare had actually turned out to be an enjoyable evening out. It had been fun catching up with all those people she hadn't thought of in years. What had surprised her most was that there had been no one-upmanship. Life had dealt each one of them a hand of cards which they had simply got on and played. It didn't seem to matter whether they had achieved incredible wealth, notoriety, or had been made redundant, got married or divorced, had children or not, they were simply living their lives as best they could – failure didn't come into it. What was it Johnboy had said when they'd been looking at the school photographs together? 'We're all monumental successes just to have got this far.'

He was right. And had he been right when he'd suggested it was time for her to start thinking about herself, now that the children were both at school? 'Go back to teaching,' he'd said, 'if that's what you're good at.'

Half an hour later, and still reflecting on the evening, it struck Hilary with force, as she drove along the main street of the village, that from now on David's affair was not going to make a failure of her. No longer would she allow her breaking heart to make her think her life was completely worthless. Skinny Lesley, Carrie Maxwell and Johnboy – especially Johnboy – had unwittingly helped her to see things more clearly.

She turned into Acacia Lane and, as the street-light on the

corner lit up the interior of the car, she caught sight of her handbag on the passenger seat. She smiled as she thought of Johnboy's business card tucked inside her purse. He had insisted they exchange addresses. 'We must stay in touch,' he'd said. 'Who knows what might happen to us from this night on?'

'Who knows indeed?' Hilary said out loud, as she looked thoughtfully up at The Gables.

Chapter Twenty-six

It was less than a week until Christmas and Hilary was rolling out a ragged oval of pastry to the sound of Johnny Mathis singing 'When a Child is Born'. For the first time ever, she was way behind with her festive preparations: the marzipan wasn't on the cake, the crackers weren't bought and she hadn't given a thought to the brandy butter.

She sprinkled more flour onto the worktop, glad at least that she'd ordered all the cards and wrapping-paper through one of those charity catalogues at school and that the children's presents were carefully hidden at the top of the airing cupboard – they'd been there since before ... before she'd found out about David.

She'd lost count of how many weeks it was since her life had undergone such a dramatic change, but somewhere along the line, during the time that autumn had given way to winter, the impossible had happened: she had become accustomed to this new way of life. Only yesterday one of those current flavour-of the-month clerics on the radio had been saying that when people accept that their lives are about to change they are more able to cope with what lies ahead.

Hilary started pressing out small circles of pastry, knowing that it was all well and good acknowledging the changes being forced onto her by David but she was still struggling to accept the consequences.

She looked up from the cutter in her hand, remembering what Nick had said, that awful day at his cottage: '... our response determines the consequences'.

Her response, for the time being, was to stay quiet and put her mind to thinking about a new course of direction for her own life as Johnboy had said a few weeks ago: 'Go back to teaching.' Well, come the new year, she would make enquiries. If nothing else, a job would give her independence ... independence she might well need.

The egg-shaped timer on the window-sill gave a loud shrill ring and, shaking the flour from her hands, she pulled on a pair of oven gloves and reached into the Aga for the fourth batch of mince pies she'd made that afternoon. She placed the hot tray on the draining board and wondered what David would buy her for Christmas. Probably the *Which? Guide to Divorce*. He'd want a quick economical divorce, wouldn't he?

Last year he'd bought her a daring négligé in a large box with a ribbon, and he'd been so embarrassed after the Queen's speech when everyone had insisted she open her present there and then in front of them all.

'Go on,' her mother had urged. 'Let's see what David's got for you.'

David's face had been a picture as he'd tried to deflect Louise with another glass of port. His own mother had tried to hide her shock at the transparency of the garment when, finally, the box had been opened. 'Very nice,' she had muttered, pretending to be more interested in the *Batman* film the children were watching on television.

Hilary placed the last of the hot mince pies on a cooling rack and was about to dust them with icing sugar when the doorbell rang.

It was Charlotte with Mabel. 'It's Tuesday, my day off from the shop, so how about a walk?'

'That sounds more like an ultimatum than an invitation,' Hilary said.

'You're right, it does. So get your coat and lock up.'

'But it's been raining all day, it'll be wet and—'

'It's stopped, now get a move on.'

They set off for the mere along the narrow footpath between All in the Mind and the White Cottage. Iris Braithwaite was in her back garden. She was wearing an old mac and a plastic rain-hood tied with a large bow under her chin. She was prodding at a reluctant bonfire with a long stick. 'Can't seem to get the wretched thing going,' she said, through the privet hedge. 'The leaves are too wet after all this rain.'

As Hilary and Charlotte carried on down the sheltered muddy path, a low pale sun burst through the parting clouds catching the drips of rain on the wet black branches of the trees either side of them and turning each droplet of water into a sparkling pearl. But when they reached the more exposed area overlooking the mere, where there was a large gap in the trees, an icy blast of wind swept across the water, rippling small waves as it did so.

Hilary buttoned her coat, right up to her chin. She watched Charlotte bend down to let Mabel off the lead. 'I feel like our roles have reversed,' she said unexpectedly.

Charlotte had never before credited Hilary with much intuition. Her sister had always blundered her way through any thought-provoking situation with as much mental agility and sensitivity as a charging bull. 'I know what you mean,' she said, slipping her arm through Hilary's. 'For once I do actually feel like I'm the eldest.'

'Ever since I can remember, I've always wanted to be the older sister. As a child I was maddened by our mother's ineffectualness and decided from an early age that if she didn't want to play the part of mother hen, then I would. And now—'

'And now you can't cope with supervising me because your well-ordered life has come to an end ... just as mine did.'

They walked down the sloping bank to the water's edge. Hilary picked up a flat stone and sent it skimming across the water. 'One ... two ... three ...' she counted, before the stone disappeared from view. She turned and faced Charlotte. 'Do you think Peter would have ever had an affair?'

Charlotte suddenly laughed. 'Oh, Hilary, Peter had been having an affair almost from the day I met him, probably before as well.'

Hilary was shocked. 'But you never said anything. Who was it? Anyone you knew?'

Charlotte bent and picked up a stone. She angled her arm low and spun the stone away from her. It disappeared into the water at once. 'It was work with Peter. His career was his all-consuming mistress.'

'Well, that doesn't count,' Hilary said off-handedly. She reached for another stone.

'Oh yes it does. When a man implies to his wife that his job means more to him than his marriage, believe me, it counts. An affair with a career is just as damaging as a sexual one. So much so, on the morning Peter died, I ... I had just asked him for a divorce.'

The stone in Hilary's hand dropped to the ground. 'Charlotte ... I don't know what to say. Why didn't you tell me? Does Mother know about this?'

Charlotte shook her head. 'No, but I told Dad a few months ago.'

'I had no idea you were so unhappy. I wish I'd known – I could have helped in some way.'

'I didn't tell anyone ... I didn't want people to know I'd failed.'

'Oh, God, that's just how I feel and Mother's the last person I'd want to know that I'd failed in my marriage.'

Charlotte went over to Hilary and hugged her. 'I can hear Mother's words now – "You girls are so careless with your husbands!"'

Hilary managed a laugh and they rejoined the path and began the circuit of the mere. In the distance they could see Mabel's furry white body moving in and out of the trees.

'What would you have done if you had discovered Peter

was having an affair – I mean, a conventional bed-hopping type of affair?'

Charlotte thought for a moment. She tried to imagine Peter in bed with another woman but found it difficult even to picture his face. Unable to come up with a suitable image, she said, 'With hindsight I'd like to think I'd have wished him a small amount of happiness in his miserable existence. But that's with hindsight and with the safety of Alex in my life.'

'But what about before Alex? Say, two years ago.'

'I probably would have gone berserk and done the same as that woman in the paper last summer.'

Hilary almost smiled. 'What – cut off all the arms and legs from your husband's expensive suits?'

'Exactly, and probably a lot worse.'

'I smashed all David's expensive glasses from his mother,' Hilary admitted.

Charlotte laughed. 'Brilliant! And how very out of character.'

'I tried something even worse,' Hilary said, quietly. She pushed her cold hands into her jacket pockets, remembering with annoyance that she'd left her gloves on the oak chest in the hall.

'Go on,' Charlotte urged. 'What did you try?'

'I . . . I wanted to prove – Oh, Lord, I don't know how to say it.'

'It can't be all that bad.'

'I threw myself at another man,' she said, coming to a stop by a wooden bench that gave an uninterrupted view of the mere. She ran her fingers over the back of the seat. 'And not by chance. I planned it to happen.'

Charlotte raised her eyebrows.

'You see, you *are* shocked. I knew—'

'Calm down. Of course I'm shocked, but that's not to say I don't understand why.'

'Did you ever . . . well, you know . . . Were you ever unfaithful when you were so unhappy in Brussels?'

'No, I wasn't. Though who's to know what might have happened if I'd met Alex before Peter's death? But never mind me. What do you really feel about David? Do you love him or is it the tick-tock of your anniversary clock that keeps your marriage going?'

'I'm not sure of anything now. I thought I loved David and then, oh, I don't know, I just seem to be conscious of all his faults right now. Because of his affair I can't see anything good or attractive in him.'

The wind was bitingly cold as they stood still. Charlotte indicated that they should carry on walking and said, 'And what does Nick Bradshaw mean to you?'

Hilary looked up sharply. 'How do you know it was him?'

'A lucky guess. Probably it was his behaviour towards David at Derek and Cindy's party, and I'd also seen the two of you talking together earlier on in the evening.'

Hilary was shocked. 'You don't suppose anyone else will have thought the same, do you?'

'I doubt it.'

'Honestly, Charlotte, nothing's actually happened between us, I swear.' Hilary's face was earnest. 'I planned to make him seduce me, but he refused to play along. It was all rather humiliating.'

'Horrible man,' Charlotte said sympathetically. 'But why did you ... why did you turn to him?'

Hilary thought back to the night at the restaurant with David and the moment when she'd made up her mind to ring Nick. She quickly swallowed back the hurt and anger that were rising in her throat. 'I wanted reassurance, I suppose.'

'Hardly surprising, given the circumstances.'

'And now I keep asking myself the same question: Is my marriage worth saving?' She gazed into the distance across to Bosley Cloud, looming high on the horizon, then turned back to her sister. 'I've decided to confront David after Christmas.'

Charlotte put her arm round Hilary's shoulders. 'I'm so proud of you. You're handling this far better than I would have done.'

'Common sense, I suppose. You always said I was the practical one.'

As the light began to fade and a hazy twilight blurred the water's edge, they completed the circuit of the mere and returned to the clearing in the pine trees. While Charlotte put Mabel on the lead, she reflected on how much closer she and Hilary had grown in the past few months. She hoped that when Hilary's life was back on an even keel they would never lose this new-found deeper level of understanding.

'We haven't even discussed your wedding on Saturday,' Hilary said, cutting into Charlotte's thoughts. 'I'm sure I should be doing more.'

'Rubbish!' Charlotte said, recognising that the time for shared disclosures and intimacy was over. 'You've got enough on your plate. But you are coming to the rehearsal tomorrow night, aren't you? Seven o'clock. Is that okay?'

'It's fine. Becky and I'll be there.' Suddenly Hilary's face broke into a frown.

'What's wrong?' Charlotte asked, concerned.

'The children,' Hilary said in a tightly controlled voice. 'What about the children? It's all very well us having this sophisticated grown-up talk about whether or not my marriage is worth keeping, but the bottom line is that a wrong decision on my part could destroy their lives.'

'That won't happen,' Charlotte said firmly, and with more assurance than she felt. 'Now, tell me how Becky looks in her bridesmaid's dress.'

'She looks beautiful,' Hilary said, accepting Charlotte's distraction, 'but she's refusing to wear it on Saturday.' Then, looking at her watch, she said, 'Goodness, we must hurry or I'll be late for Becky coming out of school.'

As Charlotte followed her sister along the footpath she had the terrible feeling that her big day wasn't going to go exactly as she and Alex had planned. She let Hilary's words go, preferring instead to live a little longer in hope and ignorance.

Chapter Twenty-seven

'Heureux anniversaire, Martina!'

Martina smiled round at the group. 'Merci,' she said.

'Maintenant, les bougies,' Patricia instructed, glancing up from the scrap of paper in her hand with its selection of carefully thought-out phrases.

'Yes, blow them out so that we can get on and have something to eat, I'm starving,' Nick whispered in Hilary's ear.

Hilary had hoped that Nick might have missed this, their final French class of the term and small party to celebrate Martina's birthday. He hadn't turned up for the previous two lessons, since the embarrassing incident at his cottage, and now here he was standing next to her and reminding her only too well what a fool she'd made of herself.

She watched Martina cut the birthday cake which Patricia had made specially – the fondant icing was even coloured the same as the French tricolour. What a monumental creep, thought Hilary, as she stabbed a stick of celery into the Stilton and *crème fraîche* dip she'd made that afternoon after her walk with Charlotte.

Nick squeezed past her and helped himself to a stick of celery. She felt she ought to say something to him. But what? What on earth could she say to a man who, in a moment of madness, she had kissed in the hope of getting him to ...?

'I hope you're not going to ignore me.'

She crunched on her celery.

'I should be very disappointed in you, Hilary, if that's to be the case.'

She crunched some more.

'We can still be friends,' he persevered.

At the front of the classroom Patricia was fiddling with a ghetto-blaster and suddenly the room was filled with Edith Piaf's husky voice singing 'Non, Je Ne Regrette Rien'. 'Just to get us in the right mood for our little *soirée*,' Patricia called out.

Nick looked at Hilary and smiled. 'Come on, Hilary, we can't pretend it didn't happen, so let's not regret it either.'

'But I do,' she murmured.

'What embarrasses you most? The fact that we kissed or that we didn't make love?'

'Please,' she said desperately, 'keep your voice down.'

'Only if you answer the question.'

Hilary tried to think straight. Just what exactly was her honest answer? There was no doubt in her mind that she had enjoyed kissing Nick, just as she'd enjoyed Johnboy's attention at the school reunion a couple of weeks ago. Thinking of that night she saw that what she'd hoped to get from Nick in a moment of madness she had, in fact, gained from Johnboy – and without making a fool of herself. In just a few short hours, her old classmate had sufficiently raised her self-esteem so that she could imagine herself coping with the future.

'You two are very cosy together, aren't you?' Patricia interrupted, handing them each a slice of birthday cake on paper napkins. 'Quite the Romeo and Juliet of the group with your regular hushed *tête-à-têtes*.'

'Always willing to make it a threesome,' Nick said lightly.

Patricia eyed him. 'A *ménage à trois*, you mean?'

'No,' he said firmly. 'Technically that would mean that Hilary and I would have to be married.'

Patricia laughed. 'Now I think David might just have something to say about that.'

'And to think I used to like that awful woman,' Hilary said quietly, as they watched Patricia move on to dole out more of Martina's tricolour birthday cake.

'Perhaps you're becoming more discerning these days.'

She looked up at Nick and met his eyes. 'You know, I do believe I am. Since I discovered David's affair I've started thinking and acting quite differently. What used to matter to me no longer does. You're the expert, is that normal?'

'Whether it's normal or not, is irrelevant, it's what—'

'I wish you'd answer my questions with a simple yes or no.'

He took a bite of birthday cake and chewed it. 'Yes,' he said at last. 'Hilary, I pronounce you quite normal.'

'Thank goodness,' she said, biting into her piece of cake. 'Ugh! Cheap margarine and too much sugar.' She looked about her for a suitable hiding place for the rest of Patricia's baking disaster.

'Here, let me finish it for you,' Nick said, taking it from her. 'I'm obviously not as fussy as you, and while I eat you can tell me why you're learning French – I've never asked you that before.'

'No,' she said, handing him her slice of cake, 'you've been too busy prying into everything else in my life.'

He smiled. 'Sharper as well as more discerning. Go on, tell me why you're here.'

She helped herself to a handful of crisps. 'Just a boring case of the annual pilgrimage to France being backed up with the ability to do more than navigate one's way around a menu.' She shook her head and sighed. 'Ironic, isn't it? At the rate things are going, a camping holiday in France *en famille* is the last thing I'll be doing next summer.'

'Who knows where we'll all be in a year's time?'

'Who knows?' she repeated, thoughtfully.

'Penny for them?'

She told him about the school reunion and what Johnboy had said to her.

'He's right, of course,' Nick said. 'This Johnboy character, he's not going to become a complication, is he?'

She shook her head. 'I shouldn't think so for one minute. So, why are you learning French?'

'Same reason as you. I love Brittany and go there each summer and last year I decided to put a stop to looking such an idiot every time I opened my mouth.'

'I don't think you could ever look an idiot.'

Nick laughed. 'Are you flirting with me?'

Hilary laughed, too, seeing for the first time that even in the depths of wretchedness there was always a degree of humour to be found.

From the other side of the room Patricia gave them both a long, hard stare.

Later that night Georgia's Jeep crept quietly along the deserted main street of the village. It stopped just outside Ted the Toup's, its engine still running. Three silent figures got out and went and huddled around the glass door of the shop. The smallest of the figures pushed open the letter-box; it made a loud grating noise.

'Ssh,' the tallest of the trio said.

The third person then inserted a polythene bag through the opening, turned the bag upside down and began to shake it.

Georgia smiled as the trio climbed back inside the Jeep. Once word got round, Ted would be lucky to sell a news-paper, never mind anything else he kept hidden under wraps at the back of his shop.

The shop was still in darkness when Ted came downstairs the next morning. He hated the winter months and having to get up in the cold to organise those militant newspaper boys and girls. They were always asking for more money or complaining that the bags were too heavy for them. Kids! Wimps, the whole lot of them. Nosy too. He'd caught that lad with the whiskers just showing through on his top lip having a good old rummage in the boxes of new gear he'd got out the back. It was expensive stuff, and he didn't need the likes of that lad's grubby hands fingering any of it.

He yawned, then pulled out a cigarette from the box in his cardigan pocket. He flicked at his lighter and walked over to the door to bring in the papers left there on the doorstep. He was looking forward to reading about that politician who was supposed to be doing it five times a night with his research assistant. No wonder the Government was making such a bloody mess of running the country, they were all too exhausted.

As he walked towards the door his shoes made a strange crunching sound. He looked down at the floor.

'Shit!' he yelled, jumping back in horror and knocking into one of the rotating racks of novels. Bonk-buster novels crashed to the floor, scattering a thousand wriggling white bodies yet further.

'Shit!' he shouted again, seeing his wig lying amongst what looked suspiciously like maggots.

A bang at the door made him jump again. It was the nosy lad with the whiskers. Ted let him in.

'Yuck,' the lad said, looking about him. 'Where've all these maggots come from?' He tried hard not to look at his employer's bald head.

'Bloody good question,' Ted said. He bent down, picked up his wig and waved it vigorously at arm's length. 'Well, don't just stand there. Get a broom and sweep up this mess.'

The lad shook his head. 'I'm a paper boy not a cleaner.'

Ted sucked so hard on his cigarette he almost bit it in two.

Within half an hour most of the village had heard from the paper boys and girls that Ted's shop was crawling with maggots. Within an hour, Iris Braithwaite had appeared and declared the shop a health hazard. And within two hours, a sharp-faced woman from the Environmental Health

Department had arrived. While Ted tried to conceal his recently bought merchandise, the woman filled in a form, slapped it on the counter and announced that unless the shop was cleaner than an operating theatre by five o'clock that day it would be officially closed.

'I've been set up,' he said, 'this is all to try and prevent me—'

'Prevent you from what, Mr Cooper?' the sharp-faced woman asked, knowing full well of the raging debate currently going on in Hulme Welford.

'Nothing,' Ted muttered. He knew disapproval when he saw it and he was looking at it right now in the face of the representative from the Environmental Health Department.

'Either I or a colleague will be back later,' she said, her hand already pulling open the door. 'Oh, and by the way,' she added, 'I think you'll find you have a maggot crawling out from under your – I mean, crawling in your hair.'

As she closed the door behind her Ted snatched off his wig and hurled it across the shop.

Chapter Twenty-eight

While Ted the Toup grappled with a mop and a bucket of Jeyes fluid, the school gym, decorated in paper chains and depictions of the Three Wise Men, erupted with enthusiastic and relieved parental applause.

Flashbulbs sparked and video cameras rolled as the school nativity play came to the end of its one and only performance of the year to a packed house, and right in the front row of a cast of a dozen or more curtsying angels, Becky, with her lopsided wings and tinsel halo, waved energetically at her mother next to Georgia. Hilary discreetly waved back. Chloe, holding an upside-down plastic Jesus and dressed in expiation blue, was sulking in the back row along with a multitude of cotton-wool-bearded shepherds. She caught sight of her mother and scowled. Georgia stuck her fingers in her mouth and let out a piercing whistle.

'A way to go!' she yelled. She nudged Hilary and whispered, 'I'm only doing that to annoy Mesdames Longton and Hampton. That, and Chloe bet me I wouldn't have the nerve. That's a week's pocket money she owes me and just look at the smile on her face now.'

When the clapping finally subsided and Mr Atkinson, the headmaster, made his way to the front of the stage and stood alongside the stable, which looked more like an exotic poolside bar than a ramshackle Judaean outbuilding, Hilary and Georgia got to their feet and crept along the row of applauding parents and associated grandparents. A few other mothers joined them. As members of the PTA, they knew from experience that the headmaster's vote of thanks would be sufficiently long-winded to give them ample time for any last-minute finishing touches required for the Christmas Fayre.

During lunch-break the PTA had decorated the classrooms in which the stalls were to be set up. The room where Hilary had her French lessons each week was to be home to 'Pin the Red Nose on Rudolf', while the surrounding classrooms were to have home-baked goods, refreshments, a bottle tombola, 'Throw the Angel's Halo Over the Crib' and the white elephant stall – where last year's unwanted Christmas presents were to be recycled.

Unable to get away from the nursery any earlier, Georgia had turned up at the last minute with her Jeep full of green foliage to decorate the classrooms, along with an armful of mistletoe. 'A wind-up for Chloe's benefit,' she'd said to Hilary as they unloaded the back of the Jeep.

While the headmaster got on with thanking his excellent and overworked staff, Georgia assembled the PTA in the largest of the classrooms, where alcoholic refreshments were to be served. 'Right,' she said briskly. 'Patricia, here's the money for each stall-holder's float, it's clearly marked, so go round all the classrooms and—'

'Yes, I'm well aware of the procedure,' Patricia said, reaching for the money-bags and snatching them out of Georgia's hands. 'I *have* done this before.'

'Look, chuck,' Georgia said, placing a hand on Patricia's arm, 'try making it easier on yourself. Okay?'

Patricia was horrified and shrugged away from Georgia's hand. 'Don't you ever, ever touch me again, you—'

Georgia laughed. 'Oh, you're beautiful when you're angry, Pattie babes!'

'Why do you do it?' Hilary asked, when they were left alone after Patricia had flounced off in a panic of potential defilement.

'I can't help myself,' Georgia replied, taking the lid off a large saucepan on a hot plate and giving the contents a stir. She popped in a few more slices of orange. 'She's such a sitting target. All that prejudice and middle-class crap all rolled up into one almighty time-bomb just waiting to go off.' She put the lid back on the mulled wine. 'Why are you looking at me like that?'

Hilary shook her head and sighed. She draped a garland of green tinsel along the front of a table covered in red crêpe paper. 'You're so sure of yourself, aren't you?'

'Arrogant, you mean?'

'No, not arrogant. I always get the feeling that you don't care what anyone thinks of you.'

'And you'd be right. Now stop jabbering on like this. Lost-His-Way Atkinson will be winding up any moment now and we've got all these cups to set out, and you know how everyone makes a bee-line for anything alcoholic after suffering one of his interminable speeches.'

Georgia was right. A flood of eye-rolling parents soon descended upon them, hands outstretched for a sedative cup of mulled wine. But the mood soon changed and with what sounded like Pinky and Perky singing 'O Come All Ye Faithful' on Patricia's ghetto-blaster, mothers who had stayed up late the night before running to earth a checked tea-towel for a shepherd's headdress, or who had knocked up a last-minute pair of wings, began to relax while their husbands, who were all playing hookey from work, stood around in groups jangling coins in their trouser pockets and comparing notes on the latest mileage allowances on their company cars.

As she took in the familiar scene Hilary felt angry that David wasn't there. At breakfast that morning he'd told her that he'd be unable to make it in time for the nativity play, something about a meeting with his accountant. Accountant, my foot, she'd thought afterwards as she'd stripped the children's beds and stuffed the sheets and duvet covers into the washing machine. Now he can't even spare an hour or so to see his own daughter on stage. Fired up with anger she had raced around the house with the vacuum cleaner, deliberately bashing into David's armchair in the sitting room, then the desk in his study. But when she'd taken the washing outside to hang on the line, her anger had miraculously vanished. Sunlight was filtering through the naked branches of the cherry trees at the end of the garden, throwing long spindly shadows across the lawn, and she found herself smiling. As she pegged the first of the sheets on the line and breathed in the pleasant smell of washing powder, she wondered at the absurdity of her situation; that even in a moment of extreme anger and bewilderment she could derive enjoyment from something as simple as sunlight streaking across the lawn. Perhaps it was true, after all, that the ordinary could always outweigh the unexpected and traumatic.

'You're looking serious, Hilary.'

'Dad, what are you doing here?' she asked, surprised to see her father on the other side of the table holding out his hand for a cup of mulled wine.

'You didn't think I'd miss Becky's big performance, did you?'

She was touched. 'Oh, how sweet of you. Is Mother with you?'

He shook his head.

'Of course not,' Hilary said, her voice matter-of-fact as she handed him his drink. 'Busy at the shop.'

'Can't stop long myself.'

'Oh?'

'Things to do in the kitchen,' he replied. 'I've got the cake to ice.'

'I haven't done mine yet either.'

'I don't mean the Christmas cake, I'm talking about Charlotte and Alex's cake.'

Hilary felt a stab of jealousy. Charlotte's wedding cake. Just as she'd set about playing Cupid last year with Charlotte and Alex, so, too, she had fully intended to take care of the catering for her sister's big day. Now that pleasure was to be denied her. She had been usurped by – of all people – her father, who up until six months ago had done little more in the kitchen than stir his own low-calorie cocoa. Now here he was preparing a finger-food buffet for an army of guests, who were going to expect a darn sight more than a few pickled onions and bowls of crisps to pick over. She knew it was nasty of her but she couldn't help but wish that Neville had stuck to his lifelong hobby of gooseberry-growing. Why the sudden change?

But it wasn't only that she'd been upstaged by her father that was causing her to feel jealous. For years she'd known and accepted that she didn't mean as much to her father as Charlotte did; there was a closeness between them that she herself had never experienced. As a young child she'd been conscious of a gap between her and her father; a gap she'd never been able to bridge. It hadn't bothered her at the time – like all children, she had simply filled her life with the busyness of growing up. The intricacies of relationships are nothing to a ten-year-old girl intent on a life given over to choir practice and ballet lessons. That Charlotte had preferred their father's company to perfecting a *grand battement* had seemed slightly bizarre to Hilary, all those years ago. Often she had come home after an arduous ballet class and found Charlotte and Neville together in the garden bent over a gooseberry bush, each convincing the other that this was the bush which would yield a prize-winning berry.

Hilary watched her father take a sip of his wine as he cast his eyes about the room. Rarely did she take the time to regard him with anything more than a passing look of interest. She did so now and, to her surprise, was taken aback by what she saw and felt. There was a reassuring benignity to his face that made her throat tighten. She felt cheated. Why had he not bestowed more of that kindliness on her? Anger and hurt merged together inside her. She felt almost as badly betrayed by her father as she did by David – the two men in her life who should have loved her most had let her down. Why?

'See you,' Neville said, as he moved away from her.

'Yes,' she replied, filled with a sudden need to rush over to him and ask what terrible thing she had done. What crime had she committed to be on the receiving end of so little love?

'Mum!' It was Becky, now out of her angel costume and wearing her school uniform. In her hands was a large jar of Smarties. Chloe was by her side and she was holding a note-pad and pen. 'We're doing "Guess How Many Smarties in the Jar",' Becky said, her eyes wide as she looked down at the sweets.

'Lovely,' Hilary said, ladling out two cups of mulled wine for a customer and trying not to think of her father. 'Don't get in anyone's way, will you?'

'Fifty pence a go,' Chloe shouted above the music. 'Each Smartie represents an oppressed woman.'

'What's that, dearie?' asked one of the old ladies from the local nursing home who, each year, were treated to this extravaganza of entertainment. She was wearing a snowball of a hat and too much make-up; in one hand she held a plastic cup and in the other a half-eaten mince pie. She should have been having tea and biscuits in Class I with the rest of her group but she'd escaped, following her nose to something stronger than Typhoo.

'Fifty pence a go,' Chloe repeated, even louder. 'Each Smartie represents an oppressed woman.'

'They don't look overdressed to me, dearie,' the old woman said, giving the jar of sweets a long, hard stare.

'Oppressed!' shouted Chloe impatiently.

The old woman thought about this. Then, chucking Chloe under the chin, she said, 'And what will Santa be bringing you this year? A nice little dolly?'

Chloe looked as though she was about to bite the woman's

hand off. 'No such thing as Father Christmas,' she said tersely. 'It's a silly myth invented by men to glorify their own self-image.'

'That'll do, Chloe,' Georgia intervened, catching the shocked expression on Becky's face. 'I'm sorry, Hilary, but I think you might have some bedtime explaining to do tonight.'

They watched Chloe and Becky move off to prey on an easier target.

'You were only joking, weren't you?' Hilary heard Becky asking Chloe.

Poor Becky, Hilary thought. This Christmas she would discover that Father Christmas was a sham ... and who knew what she would discover about her own father?

As Pinky and Perky moved on to 'I Saw Mommy Kissing Santa Claus' a harassed-looking Patricia came towards them.

'We're running out of small change,' she said accusingly, a five-pound note in her hand. 'You didn't make up the floats properly. We always have—'

'No problem,' Georgia said, reaching for the petty-cash box under the table. 'What do you need?'

'Ten- and twenty-pence pieces. If you had done it the way we—'

Georgia handed over the money, and from behind her back she pulled out a sprig of mistletoe. She dangled it in front of Patricia. 'Give us a kiss, Pattie babes,' she said, with a leery grin.

'I thought I'd warned you to leave me alone,' Patricia said, in a loud, angry voice. Heads turned.

'Ah, why don't you do us all a big favour and ease up? You're up to your panty-line in repression.'

'How dare you!' shrieked Patricia. 'And while we're about it, let me tell you, I'm sick and tired of being the butt of your foul humour. In fact, I'd go as far as saying that we're all sick of your views. People like you are quite out of place in a respectable village like this. And, what's more, we all know it's you who's been terrorising poor Mr Cooper. I saw, with my own eyes, you and your Jeep outside my house when all those things were thrown at his shop.'

'Well, if I was outside your house it couldn't have been me terrorising that disgusting man, could it?'

'It *was* you!' persisted Patricia, her voice now reaching a piercing soprano pitch. She was sounding and looking for all the world like a petulant prima donna, with one hand on her hip and the other pointing a finger at Georgia.

'How dare you speak to Ms D'Arcy like that?' thundered a familiar contralto with all the force and impact of the 'Ride of the Valkyries'.

Patricia lowered her finger and began to tremble as Iris Braithwaite marched into the room.

'I've heard quite enough from you, young lady,' Iris went on. 'And I can assure you that Ms D'Arcy is not alone in her brave fight against Mr Cooper. On the morning to which you are referring I was present. I not only saw what took place, I instigated it. There, now, what do you say to that?'

A shock wave of surprise rippled around the room – and while nobody was looking, the old lady from the nursing home helped herself to another cup of mulled wine. She took a large gulp. 'Happy Christmas,' she said merrily, then spat out a small black clove.

Chapter Twenty-nine

'Now, Becky,' Malcolm Jackson said, in his extra-specially patient voice – the one he sometimes used with the more troublesome members of the PCC. 'You've got a very important job to do, haven't you?' He smiled encouragingly at Becky, hoping that now that she was centre stage of Charlotte and Alex's wedding rehearsal she would pay attention and stop banging her feet against the pew in front of her.

Becky jumped up and joined him. Malcolm carefully manoeuvred her behind Charlotte. 'There now,' he said, 'you pretend your Auntie Charlotte's got her beautiful dress—'

'I think dresses are silly,' Becky said importantly, 'I've given them up. Auntie Charlotte, can I wear jeans on Saturday?'

Wear anything you want, thought Charlotte, just so long as you're quiet long enough for Alex and I to say *we do*. 'You'll have to check with Mummy.'

'Mummy said I'd have to check with you.'

Hilary and Charlotte exchanged looks of *now what?*

'As I was saying,' Malcolm persevered, 'I'm sure Charlotte likes dresses and the one she'll be wearing for the wedding will probably have a long bit trailing the floor behind her—'

Charlotte shook her head vehemently. She had deliberately chosen a dress without a train. She had no intention of running the risk of having anything touching the ground with Becky walking behind her.

'Well, imagine there is,' Malcolm continued, thinking that Job had got off lightly, 'because you must keep your distance,

Becky. We don't want you tripping the bride up by getting too close. Do you think you can remember that?'

'Easy-peasy!'

Charlotte suspected that this was about as likely as hell freezing over, given that her niece had the attention-span of a goldfish.

'But what about Gramps?' Becky asked. 'Shouldn't he be practising this with us?'

Malcolm looked at his watch. 'We'll try it once without Gramps, then with him.'

'You in a hurry to get home to watch *Brookside* like Mum?'

Malcolm smiled stiffly.

'It might be nice to catch the *News at Ten*, though,' Louise said, from the front pew. Neville was sitting next to her, his head drooping so low that his chin was almost touching the knot in his tie.

'Are you sure about wanting to marry into my family?' Charlotte called over to Alex, who was sitting alone on the opposite pew to Louise and Neville.

'So long as we only have the one wedding,' he answered.

'I don't understand why Auntie Charlotte's got to practise. This is her second wedding, isn't it?'

'Because she didn't get it right the first time,' suggested Louise.

'What did you do wrong, Auntie Charlotte?'

'She didn't do anything wrong,' Malcolm interrupted, hoping his wife would have the presence of mind to put the video recorder on. 'Neville, perhaps you'd like to come and join us, after all. Neville?'

'*Neville!*' Louise shouted in her husband's ear. 'You're wanted.'

'Sorry, everyone,' Neville apologised, as he got to his feet and staggered towards the group. 'Sorry, Charlotte, shan't do it on the big day.'

And as the trio at last began the walk up the aisle, to the

sound of Louise singing 'Stately as a Galleon I Sail Across the Floor', Charlotte wondered whether it wasn't too late to call the whole thing off.

It was snowing when they finally got outside, with soft downy pillows of snow lying against shadowy tombstones. Becky whooped with delight and danced excitedly about the churchyard. She picked up a handful of snow and threw it at her mother. Light and powdery, the snowball disintegrated before it reached its target. Hilary laughed at her. She turned to Charlotte. 'Do you remember New Year's Eve, all those years ago, when you danced in the snow without your shoes?'

Charlotte smiled. 'I think I was showing off.'

'Fancy trying it now?' Alex said, slipping his arm through Charlotte's.

'What, and catch pneumonia just in time for Saturday? Second thoughts, maybe that's not such a stupid idea.'

'You're marrying me in three days' time and that's an end to it,' Alex said, 'or otherwise—' He bent down and scooped up a handful of snow.

'Oh no you don't!' shrieked Charlotte. She ran off along the whitened path and out through the lychgate. Alex chased after her with Becky close behind, their feet crunching the snow.

'How about everyone coming back for a drink?' asked Hilary, thinking of the wall of silence at The Gables when she and Becky returned home.

'No,' Louise answered with a shiver. 'There's another one of those court-room dramas on the telly I want to see.' She pushed her hands into her sheepskin gloves and braced herself for the walk back up the hill.

Neville was disappointed. He would have liked to join in the fun. He kissed Hilary good night and followed in Louise's trail of footsteps.

With her parents' figures already little more than blurred

outlines in the snowy darkness Hilary crossed the main street of the village alone. Ahead of her she could hear Becky's happy voice in the muffled silence of the snow-filled sky, and within the orangy glow of light cast from the lamp-post at the top of Acacia Lane snowflakes were falling in an easy, constant rhythm. It was a perfect Christmas card setting and reminded Hilary of the scene in *The Lion, the Witch and the Wardrobe* when Mr Tumnus first appears to Lucy. How perfect it had all seemed to Lucy until she found out the truth from the sad little faun.

She hurried on and soon caught up with Charlotte and Alex. It was then that Becky's scream rang out long and shrill, jarring terrifyingly with the quietness of Acacia Lane.

They rushed over to the White Cottage where Becky stood at the open gate staring down at the ground, her eyes wide and frightened. Beneath a blanket of snow lay a body, and at one end of it a small patch of snow was turning pink.

Alex knelt on the ground and quickly started brushing away at the thick covering of snow. 'My God,' he said, ripping off his coat and covering the body, 'it's Mrs Braithwaite!'

Hilary clutched at Charlotte's arm and Becky whispered, 'Is she dead?'

'She's only mildly concussed, but we'll keep her in overnight to be on the safe side,' the nurse told Charlotte and Alex. 'We've stitched and patched her up but, like most old people who are mugged, she's as mad as hell. It's their pride as much as anything that gets hurt. I'll let you see her for a few minutes, but only one of you, mind. She's had enough excitement for one night.'

Charlotte found Iris propped up in bed with several pillows behind her. Her bandaged head was sagging to one side as if she was asleep, but when Charlotte approached, her bruised and swollen eyes immediately flickered open.

'I just came to make sure you—'

'Spare me the pleasantries, Mrs Lawrence. The man who did this to me is going to be locked up.'

'Did you see who it was?'

'Of course I did. It was Ted Cooper.'

Chapter Thirty

'Hi,' Tiffany said, as she saw Alex close the post-office door and start walking towards where she stood outside the baker's.

'No school today?' he asked, when he reached her after negotiating his way through the shovelled-up piles of snow on the pavement.

'Last day of term yesterday,' she answered. 'Barry comes home tomorrow. He said on the phone last night that the snow's been really bad in Leeds. I hope he makes it – I don't much fancy Christmas without him.'

'He'll make it,' Alex said, beginning to feel the cold – minus four had been given on the weather forecast earlier that morning, along with more snow. He stamped his boots on the pavement, shaking off the clumps of ice, while marvelling at Tiffany's ability, like most of her contemporaries, to brave the elements in little more than a skimpy black denim jacket and thin silky skirt.

'He better had, or I'll come and spend Christmas with you and Charlotte.'

'You're forgetting that Charlotte and I won't be there. We're getting married on Saturday.'

'Muffin 'ell, so you are. I wish you'd reminded me yesterday. I was late-night shopping in Manchester with Mum and Dad and could have bought you your wedding present. Now you'll have to make do with something local.' She glanced up and down the row of shops. 'What do you fancy? A pound of carrots or a bag of custard tarts?'

'Louise has got some rather nice Georgian silver candle-sticks in her shop.'

'In your dreams! Either that or I'll have to go out and mug somebody.'

Alex flinched.

'What's wrong?'

'Haven't you heard about Iris Braithwaite?'

'Why, what's she done?'

Alex told Tiffany what had happened last night, how they had discovered the old lady lying unconscious in the snow and how they'd called an ambulance to take her to the hospital. 'It must have all been going on while you were coming back from Manchester.'

'Was it a burglar?'

'We're not sure yet—' but the rest of Alex's words were lost in the noise of a police car pulling up outside Ted Cooper's next to the baker's. Two uniformed officers got out and went inside.

'It's not about the maggots, is it?' Tiffany asked Alex. 'He's not prosecuting or anything daft like that, is he?'

Alex noticed the anxious look on Tiffany's face. 'I should think that's the least of his worries, right now. Mrs Braithwaite told Charlotte last night at the hospital that it was Ted who attacked her.'

'*What?*' And then it dawned on Tiffany. 'You mean revenge? He beat Mrs Braithwaite up because of the protest?'

Alex shook his head. 'I can't believe that he would do a thing like that. I know he's an old sleaze-bag, but to attack a woman he's known all these years and in a community like this . . . Well, it just seems so unlikely.'

'Bloody men! You all stick together, don't you?'

'Tiffany, I'm just trying to be objective.'

'Shit you are!' She turned away angrily and pushed open the door of the bakery. From inside the shop she watched Alex walk back down the road.

'I'd like to squeeze the jam out of that one,' the younger

227

of the two assistants said, as she arranged a tray of doughnuts in the window display and stared after Alex.

Tiffany cleared her throat noisily. 'A French stick and a large wholemeal, when you've got a moment.'

'Got one on you this morning, have you, Tiff?'

'No, I haven't,' she replied indignantly. 'But that Ted the Toup soon will have when the police have finished with him. They're next door, right now.' She leaned towards the counter. She knew that what she was doing was malicious, but she was so angry. 'He attacked Mrs Braithwaite last night. She's in hospital, in a really bad way.'

Tiffany watched their faces with satisfaction, handed over her money and left the shop, sure in the knowledge that, within the hour, practically everyone in the village would know that Ted Cooper wasn't just a pervy but a dangerous attacker of innocent women.

On her way home, she decided she'd give Georgia a ring. Perhaps they could visit Mrs Braithwaite. As she passed Charlotte's shop she saw Nick Bradshaw's car coming along the main street, his tyres churning the slush and ice on the road. He turned slowly into Daisy Bank. Immediately all thoughts of Mrs Braithwaite were put out of her mind. She tucked the French stick and wholemeal loaf under her arm and hurried home.

She arrived at All in the Mind just as Nick was reaching into the back of his car for his briefcase. 'Hi,' she said, trying to conceal that she was out of breath.

'Been running?' he asked.

Damn! 'Jogging,' she said, with an easy laugh.

'In the snow?'

'I have to keep fit, even in winter.' What was she doing? Why was it every time she wanted to talk to Nick she ended up sounding a right geek?

He slammed the car door shut and moved towards the house. 'You look fit enough to me,' he said over his shoulder.

She smiled. 'Do you think so? If you fancy a run, you could always come—'

'Never touch the stuff,' he said.

'What?'

'Exercise.' He pushed the door open. 'And something else I never touch, my employer's daughter, especially when she's young enough to be my own daughter.' He held the door and waited for her to go ahead of him.

She held back. 'Shit before the shovel,' she said. 'After you.'

Tiffany went inside and called Georgia on the mobile from her bedroom.

'You sound upset,' Georgia said. 'What's up?'

Tiffany threw a wet screwed-up tissue across the room. She told Georgia about Iris Braithwaite, which accounted for part of her anger, but she said nothing about Nick. 'Mrs Braithwaite says it was Ted Cooper who attacked her. The police are with him now.'

'The bastard!'

'You don't suppose we went too far and pushed him—'

'Look, Tiffany, shoving maggots through somebody's letter-box doesn't mean it's open season for beating up old ladies. How bad is Iris?'

'I don't know. Alex Hamilton only just told me ... Oh, God, Georgia, what have we done?'

'Hold tight, Tiffany. I'll ring the hospital.'

By the time Georgia had dialled the number for the hospital hot tears were pricking at her eyes. She rubbed them roughly with the heel of her hand, to the sound of Tiffany's words echoing accusingly in her head. *What have we done?*

'Come on, come on,' she said angrily into the mobile phone, as she paced the few available feet of space in the caravan. 'Answer the wretched thing!'

No answer came.

She pressed the off button, followed by redial. Still no

answer. 'Bloody government cut-backs!' She cursed loudly and slammed the phone down on the table. She stared out at the snow-covered greenhouses and was suddenly struck by how very alone she was. There was no Gordon today – he and Winnie were Christmas-shopping in Macclesfield – and Chloe was at a friend's. She let out a long sigh and, resting her head against the flimsy wall of the caravan, she thought of the unimaginable horror Iris must have gone through ... alone. She clenched her fists, knowing that it was all her fault, it was down to *her* that this terrible thing had happened. She should never have got involved. She should have left the silly old woman to her ineffectual posters and clipboard. What right had she had to go stirring things up?

And just what the hell had she thought she was doing, getting herself involved with a woman like Iris? Nobody liked her. She was a pain. A nosy, interfering woman who irritated the hell out of everyone and who had even had the nerve to start butting in on her life – baking her cakes and sticking up for her against the likes of that bloody Longton woman. Bloody cheek!

She didn't need help like that. She could manage on her own. Life was about coping, managing and getting on with it. It wasn't about tins of cakes being delivered to the doorstep.

She tried to keep hold of this anger, forcing herself to rail against the image of someone who had tried to impose an unwanted presence on her life but, despite her anger and despite her defiance, a solitary stinging tear escaped and slowly made its way down her cheek. She let it go, surprised at the unexpected warmth of it against her cold skin. Another followed, and then another.

When Nick couldn't find anyone to help him pick out a Christmas tree, he knocked on the caravan door.

He found Georgia slumped on the floor, her head tucked hard against her drawn-up knees. She was shaking and crying so violently he could get no sense out of her. He picked her up and carried her over to the bungalow where he set her down on the sofa in the sitting room and wrapped her in the throw-over from the back of a chair. He made no attempt to stop her tears but went to the kitchen to make a hot drink. When he took it through to her she had stopped sobbing but her frail body was still shuddering with uncontrollable spasms of what he took to be shock.

He held the mug of hot sweet tea against her chattering teeth and forced her to drink.

She took a sip, then looked at him through distant eyes and stammered, 'It's ... Iris. She really isn't the dragon everyone thinks she is.'

'If you say so,' he replied soothingly, pressing the mug against her mouth again and wondering whether he should call a doctor.

Cindy paused outside an empty seminar room, where earlier that morning Nick had given his class, 'Phone Home to Your Inner Self'. Peering through the glass panel she had watched a group of women lying on the floor. At first glance it could have been a fitness class from the days of In the Pink, except that these women hadn't formed a rainbow array of brightly coloured leotards and Lycra tights, they had been in their everyday clothes covered with a blanket and a pile of books under their heads – she kept meaning to ask Nick, why books? Why not a cushion? According to Nick, this supine position was a sure way to understanding your internal stress. Watching the women she had wondered how many of them lying there in front of Nick had anything remotely stressful going on in their lives. Most of them gave the impression of being completely at ease with life and here only to enjoy the attentions of their good-looking counsellor.

Nick had certainly turned out to be an asset to All in the Mind. Whether or not it had anything to do with his counselling skills Cindy wasn't entirely convinced. She suspected the popularity of his classes had more to do with the soft black curls at the nape of his neck; that and the tousled style of his dress caused most of the more mature women to want to take him in hand and mother him. The younger ones probably had sex on their minds as they lay there submissively on the floor with their legs slightly apart.

To her shame she had actually pressed her ear to the door and tried to hear what he was saying. She'd caught snatches about energy systems and auras and a lot of other nonsense. Then he'd gone on to say, 'Now imagine yourself floating ... Does that give you a sense of freedom ... or does it make you feel helpless and vulnerable?'

Remembering how his question had made her feel like a monumental con merchant, Cindy moved along the corridor and on to the next seminar room. Through the open door she caught the unmistakable sound of Derek's laughter. She raised her hand to push the door further open but hesitated when she heard a woman laughing. A million and one past scenarios leapt into Cindy's mind, along with the conclusion that a leopard really couldn't change his spots.

She listened at the door.

'Rosie, you've got me all wrong.'

'Have I, I wonder?'

'Yes, you really couldn't be more wrong.'

'Derek, you must stop focusing on the negative. Now, come here and let me help you channel—'

'I need to get back to the office – Cindy will be expecting—'

'What are you afraid of, Derek?'

'Nothing.'

'You're afraid of me. I've sensed it for some time now.'

'Nonsense!'

'Are you sure I don't unnerve you because of my strong sexuality?'

'Rosie, I'm well aware of your—'

'Derek, I know you want me, I can see it in your eyes, but it's fear that keeps you from touching me, isn't it?'

'I've never been frightened of anyone in my life.'

'I don't believe you.'

'Certainly not of a woman.'

'Then touch me.'

'Rosie!'

'Yes, Derek.'

'This has gone far enough. Shouldn't you be preparing for your next seminar? What is it?'

' "When Heavenly and Earthly Bodies Collide".'

'I don't remember that being in the diary.'

'A change of plan. Why don't you come along? You could help me with the practical side of the session.'

'I'd love to only . . . Rosie, what do you think you're doing? Get up!'

Cindy had heard enough. She stuffed a fist into her mouth, held her breath and ran as quickly and as quietly as she could to the office. She shut the door behind her and leaned against it. Tears began rolling down her cheeks as she laughed and laughed. Poor old Derek, he'd finally met his Waterloo.

She was still laughing when Derek, red-faced and sweating, came into the room.

'I'm not sure we chose exactly the right person when we took Rosie on.' He slumped over the desk, his head in his hands.

'Oh, do you really think so?' Cindy said, with only a trace of amusement in her voice. 'I thought you made an excellent choice.'

'She's a man-eater, Cindy!' He looked up at her and thumped his fist on the desk. 'You've got to help me!'

When Ted came back from the police station he couldn't believe his eyes. The front of his shop was daubed in graffiti. 'Vicious pervert' was scrawled across the window, and underneath in red letters were the words 'No scumbags in Hulme Welford'.

'Spot of bother?' the taxi driver asked, his hand outstretched.

Ted said nothing. He handed over his fare, then caught Jane and Brenda in the baker's staring at him. When he returned their gaze they both turned away. So did all their customers.

'I didn't do it!' he shouted at them. 'I didn't touch the silly old bag.'

Chapter Thirty-one

From her fireside armchair Iris saw a third plate of mince pies being ushered into the kitchen. 'I've been viciously assaulted, not starved,' she shouted through to Hilary and Neville.

Hilary appeared in the doorway with a pretty blue and white china bowl of fragrant hyacinths – another gift from a well-wisher. She put the flowers on the table in front of Iris.

'Not so close, I can't abide the smell.'

Hilary moved over to the window and placed the bowl on the sill, behind a small, prim, artificial Christmas tree that had all the charm of a toilet brush. 'Now, are you sure you're warm enough?' She began straightening the tartan rug on Iris's lap. Iris pushed her hands away.

'I'm quite warm enough, thank you. It's thirst I'm dying of, not hypothermia.'

'I'll go and see if Dad's made the tea.'

'How's it going?' Neville asked, when she joined him in the kitchen.

'Nursing a scorpion suddenly has its attractions. Honestly, Dad, she's so ungrateful. No wonder she was let out of hospital so soon, they probably couldn't cope a moment longer with her.'

'I'll take her tea through. You take a break out here and see what you can rustle up for lunch.'

'Mince pies, by the looks of things,' Hilary muttered as her father disappeared and she viewed the doily-lined offerings of

Mesdames Haslip and Bradley and the vicar's wife – a woman more known for her views on prisoners' rights than for parish pastry.

Hilary had had no intention of babysitting Iris Braithwaite when she came out of hospital that morning, but as the children had gone to friends for the day, and in the absence of anyone else being brave enough, she had volunteered. Then, surprisingly, Neville had stepped forward to collect the old lady from Macclesfield. Together they had brought her home and had put up with a constant barrage of orders and ill-temper, and now the task of pleasing her palate had fallen to Hilary. Oh, joy!

She opened the fridge and stared at the near-empty shelves: a packet of Lurpak, a couple of tomatoes – one that looked as swollen and as bruised as Iris's face – a plate of left-over cooked cabbage and a saucer of mashed potato, which had the beginnings of a fur coat. Two eggs in the door rack shone like beacons in a wasteland and Hilary picked them up and carried them carefully to the enamelled draining board. As she hunted for a small saucepan she found herself thinking of the cheerless contents of Iris's fridge – it was unseasonably empty, given that Christmas was only two days away. She had never before considered what Iris did over the festive period.

It was common knowledge that she never attended midnight mass on Christmas Eve – she had been quoted many times as saying that, over the years, the service had turned into nothing more than a drunken orgy of revellers, who on being tipped out of the Spinner found the warmed pews of St John's a welcome diversion from the bitter reproach they would expect to receive from their wives when they finally made it home.

As for Christmas Day itself, Hilary had no notion what Iris did. Friends, perhaps? Mrs Haslip or Mrs Bradley? Certainly Hilary couldn't recall any sightings in the village of anyone who could remotely be described as family coming to stay.

So what did she do? Did Malcolm take pity on her and invite her into his home for the day?

Hilary had the uneasy feeling that, perhaps, everyone, including herself, had refused to think too deeply how Iris amused herself over the festive period so as not to court disaster on themselves. A pricked conscience was a painful thing to have for Christmas.

As the eggs began to boil Hilary turned the timer upside down and watched the trickle of sand pass from one glass balloon to the other. Reluctantly she knew what steps she would have to take if she was to avoid any feelings of guilt over the next few days. It would be a squash, what with David's parents arriving tomorrow for five days.

Five days! She closed her eyes, not wanting to think of the terror in store for her. Five whole days of listening to her mother-in-law's incessant praise of her only son – David, the blue-eyed wonderboy who could do no wrong.

Ah! Did she have news for them!

She brought the flat of her hand down on the draining board with a loud crack. Plates and cutlery rattled noisily in the plastic rack.

'Steady on there, Hilary.'

She turned round to her father. She suddenly felt furious and wanted more than anything to take her anger out on someone. And here was her father, good-natured Neville, whom everyone liked and respected. So why couldn't he see how upset she was? Why couldn't he put his arm around her and make it all better for her? Wasn't that what fathers did? Hug me! she wanted to scream at him. I'm your daughter. I may not be as interesting as Charlotte but I'm still your daughter.

'How's lunch coming along?' he asked, awkwardly.

She couldn't speak.

He glanced about the kitchen for some sign of food. 'Hilary? This isn't like you, what's wrong?'

She gulped. 'No. You're right, it's not like me at all.' And that's the problem, she thought miserably, reaching into the bread bin. Everyone thinks of me as good old Hilary, the born organiser. Want anything doing? Then give it to Hilary. Sunday school, PTA secretary, Christmas Fayre. Well, I don't want to play that part any more. I'm tired of being a pillar of the community. I'm crumbling and can't anyone see that?

'Hilary, how long has that egg-timer been like that?'

'Hell!'

Neville was startled. He'd never seen his younger daughter like this before. He watched her whip the saucepan off the heat and douse the eggs under the cold tap. She then moved about the kitchen in a fury of activity. Something was wrong, very wrong, and he had the uncomfortable feeling that he was somehow partly to blame.

'Hilary—'

'Not now, Dad,' she said briskly, loading a tray with the eggs and slices of bread and butter. She was battling to stay in control.

Neville could see that her eyes were moist with the threat of tears. 'Let me take that to Iris,' he said.

'I can manage,' she answered flatly, trying to push past him.

'Give it to me,' he said, surprising himself at how stern he sounded. Perhaps he should try that tone with Louise some time?

'*Two* boiled eggs?' Iris said, when Neville set the tray in front of her. 'Good gracious, Dr Archer, you and Mrs Archer may be able to afford to live the high life, but a woman in my position can't possibly—' She turned away from him, distracted by something moving outside. Neville sensed her nervousness.

The sound of the door knocker made them both jump. Hilary went to answer it.

It was Ted Cooper, a heavy dusting of snow on his overcoat, a frozen dew-drop on the end of his nose and a small poinsettia in his hands. 'I want to see her,' he said.

'Whoever it is, I'm not at home,' called Iris.

'I don't think it's a good idea,' Hilary whispered to Ted.

Only a matter of minutes after Ted had arrived home from the police station, word had gone round that he had been eliminated from their enquiries. A few in the village had received the news with shamefaced expressions, but Iris had not been convinced of his innocence. 'I saw him with my own eyes,' she had said in the car coming away from the hospital. 'I assure you, I'm not going senile,' she'd added. 'I know what I saw.'

'Please, Mrs Parker. I want her to know it wasn't me.'

'Is it that dreadful man, Mr Cooper?' Iris called. 'Tell him to go away or I shall telephone the police.'

'Calm down, Mrs Braithwaite,' Neville placated. 'Why don't you see him for a couple of seconds? What harm could—'

'What harm?' Iris repeated. 'You stand there with the state of my disfigured face before you and you have the gall to—'

'Please, Mrs Braithwaite, nothing is going to happen to you while I am in the room.' Neville was beginning to wonder at himself. Twice now in one afternoon he had taken charge.

Iris stared hard at him. 'You're getting very high and mighty these days, Dr Archer, I must say.' She waved a dismissive hand at him. 'Very well, let Mr Cooper in by all means, but be assured, the responsibility is all yours. Be it on your own head.'

Neville went and joined Hilary and Ted Cooper in the hall.

'You'd better take your shoes off,' Hilary warned Ted. She led him through to the sitting room and watched Iris give him one of her notorious gimlet-eyed looks – black eyes or not, she was still capable of giving a good dressing-down.

Ted held out the sad little poinsettia. Iris made no attempt to take it from him and neither of them spoke.

There was something dreadfully pathetic about the scene –

a grown man in his stockinged feet with a peace-offering and a proud woman with a face like a war victim. Hilary couldn't bear it. She stepped forward and took the plant from Ted. 'Hurry up, Mr Cooper,' she urged, 'Mrs Braithwaite needs to have her lunch.'

Ted steeled himself. 'Mrs Braithwaite,' he began, at the same time pushing his hands deep inside his coat pockets. He could feel his packet of cigarettes, his lighter, too. Automatically he started fingering the packet open, then remembered where he was and jerked his hand out. Light up at the White Cottage and die!

'Yes, Mr Cooper?'

'You and me—'

'You and I, Mr Cooper. If you are going to apologise, you might just as well be grammatically correct.'

'I'm not bloody well apologising—'

Iris tutted. 'Ever wondered why one's fingers are the shape they are, Mr Cooper?'

Ted shook his head, baffled.

'It's so that one can plug one's ears when one hears such disgusting language.' She promptly stuck both her forefingers in her ears.

Ted turned to Hilary and Neville. 'Now what?'

Neville shook his head at Iris and she slowly removed her fingers. 'Merely making a stand,' she said stoically. Hilary was reminded of Becky.

Ted took a deep breath. 'I may not be much of a bloke to you, Mrs Braithwaite, but I can tell you I'd no more hit a woman to the ground than—'

'How do you know I was hit to the ground if you weren't there?' retorted a triumphant Iris.

'Jeeze! It's common knowledge. It'll be in the paper next week.'

Iris raised her fingers to her ears again.

'I didn't do it,' Ted said impatiently. 'I was at the Spinner. They all saw me there. I'm innocent.'

'Well, somebody did this to me,' Iris said, pointing to her battered face. 'Somebody who looked a lot like you.'

'It wasn't me. You told the police it was somebody with a hat on. So it couldn't have been me because I never wear a hat on account of—'

'On account of what?' Iris asked.

'On account of my wig,' he replied, embarrassed. 'I can't wear a wig and a hat.'

'Piffle!'

'It's true and I'm very sorry you're hurt, Mrs Braithwaite, and I'm sorry too about all the fuss at the shop, and ...'

'Go on.'

'And I want you to know that I've decided to get out of the clothing business. It's too much hassle.' He started shuffling towards the door. 'I've said my piece now so I'll show myself out.' He paused and then turned back to face Iris. 'By the way, you wouldn't happen to know anything about maggots would you, Mrs Braithwaite?'

'Nasty things, maggots, Mr Cooper.'

'Yes,' Ted said, scratching the skin under the front of his wig, recalling all too vividly just how nasty the little blighters were.

'That wasn't so bad, was it?' Hilary said, when Ted had slipped on his shoes and left the White Cottage.

Iris banged down her spoon on one of the boiled eggs. It made little impression. 'Hard and cold,' she replied, pushing the tray away from her. 'But, as you say, not too bad.'

Hilary was sure that beneath Iris's swollen lips there lurked a hint of a smile – a smile of victory.

As Ted plodded through the snow back to his shop, a smile hovered on his lips. Okay, so he'd given in to the old bat, but mail-order was the thing to get into anyway.

Georgia woke with a jolt, disoriented and heavy-headed. She caught sight of Nick reading a book in the chair opposite her and sat bolt upright. 'What the hell's going on?'

He closed the book and smiled at her. 'I was rather hoping you'd put me in the picture there.'

She pushed back the throw-over and got clumsily to her feet. This was her house, right? This was her sitting room, right? 'Where's Chloe?' she demanded, trying to make sense of a situation that was all wrong.

'Relax. Somebody called Cas phoned and said they were going to watch a film and she'd drop Chloe off just after six. Is that okay?'

Georgia rubbed her hands over her face, the fog of confusion beginning to lift. She could remember Cas coming for Chloe early in the morning, then Tiffany calling and sounding upset, and telling her something about Iris. Again she rubbed her face, forcing a further piece of the puzzle to appear. At last it did. Iris had been attacked ... Iris was in hospital. She swallowed hard and slowly sank back on to the sofa, remembering now her reaction to the news. She raised her eyes to Nick.

'When I found you,' he said, in response to her unasked question, 'you were on the floor in the caravan. You were crying, very cold and shaking, like you were in a state of shock.'

She looked away.

'Do you want to tell me what had upset you so much?'

'No!'

'Fair enough.'

They sat in silence and, to Georgia's disbelief, Nick opened the book he'd been reading and started casually flicking through to find his page.

'And just how long do you intend to sit there?' she said suddenly.

'Until you've decided to tell me what happened,' he answered, without even looking up at her.

She scowled, leaned back against the sofa and crossed her arms in front of her.

He raised an eyebrow. 'You look just like you did the first time I met you at Hilary's.'

'Oh, this is ridiculous!'

'I agree.' He put the book down and shifted forward in his seat, somehow managing to appear as if he were almost touching her. 'Tell me, Georgia – may I call you Georgia?'

She nodded.

'Do you always cry so violently?'

'Don't be absurd, of course I don't. I never cry.' She stood up and walked over to the window, but the sight of the caravan at the other side of the car park brought back the pain she had felt earlier. She moved away.

'Never?'

'Never what?'

'Cry.'

'Well, obviously not completely never, as today's débâcle testifies to.'

'So when was the last time you were upset?'

She ran her hand through her hair. 'What the hell is this? Derek Rogers not got enough customers to keep you busy? Talking of which, I need to get outside and get on with some work – there'll be punters wanting Christmas trees.'

'There won't be,' Nick said quietly. 'I turned the sign round at the gate. I thought it best.'

'You did what?' Georgia turned on him. 'How dare you? You make yourself well and truly at home in my house, you read my books and have the cheek—'

'Yes,' he said, rising slowly from the chair. 'How dare I call in during my lunch-hour for a Christmas tree and find you all alone curled up on the floor howling like a baby, and how dare I carry you into the warm and make you a mug of tea, and how dare I have the bare-faced cheek to sit here with you for over two hours to make damn sure you're all right. By God, they don't come much worse than me, do they?'

'I . . .'

243

'Yes,' he said, standing over her, his face dark with fury.

'So masterful when you're angry,' she said, with just the hint of a smile.

He stared at her, his eyes blazing and she thought, for a moment, that he was going to retaliate with a further outburst. But he didn't. Instead, he reached for his coat and scarf from the back of the chair he'd been sitting in and said, 'I'll turn the sign round on my way out.'

As he pulled on his coat, she said, 'If you still want a Christmas tree you can have one for free, if you like,' her voice was conciliatory, 'seeing as I've put you to so much trouble.'

'Thank you.'

She helped him choose a tree, then watched him drive out of the snow-covered car park, the boot of his car wedged open with the last six inches of a Norway spruce poking out. She shivered in the freezing cold and looked at her watch. It was nearly three o'clock and the light was already beginning to fade. She'd lost the best part of the day and there was still so much to get done.

But first she had to find out about Iris, which she knew would mean she'd have to face up to why, today, she'd cried for the first time in three years.

Georgia found Iris alone, having eventually got through to the hospital only to be told that Mrs Braithwaite had been discharged just before lunch-time.

'Thank goodness you haven't brought any more wretched mince pies with you,' Iris said, slowly leading the way into the sitting room after Georgia had removed her boots. She pointed to a chair for Georgia and settled herself in her own armchair, which was surrounded by a collection of small tables covered with an assortment of invalid requirements – tissues, boiled sweets, a Thermos flask, a cup and saucer, a glass of water, a bottle of aspirin, two magazines and an untouched plate of mince pies. 'Dr Archer and his daughter have spent the afternoon with me,' she said, pulling a tartan blanket over her legs, 'for which I'm very grateful, but they do fuss so.'

'What on earth happened, Iris?' Georgia asked, straight to the point, but doing her best not to stare at Iris's ghastly face. She was alert, though, to the tiredness in the older woman's voice, which made her wonder for the first time just how old she was. She had to be seventy-something, which was about how old she herself felt today. 'Tiffany said something about it being Ted Cooper who attacked you.'

'Apparently I was mistaken in thinking it was that shabby little man.'

'Oh.'

'Oh, indeed.' Iris stared back at Georgia. 'And what, may I ask, is troubling you, young lady? You look red-eyed and worn out.'

'You, you tiresome, bothersome old woman, that's what's troubling me,' Georgia answered, with a small smile. 'You've caused me no end of trouble today.'

'I have, have I? Well, perhaps you'd like to help me out with these mince pies and tell me what I'm supposed to have done.' She handed Georgia the plate. 'Go ahead, they're Hilary Parker's, so perfectly edible, not like Mrs Bradley's. I wouldn't offer you hers.'

'There you go again!' Georgia exclaimed loudly, pushing the plate away. 'You see, that's what you do to me. Nobody else tries it on. You're the only one. You're the only bloody person that's got the nerve. And don't you see what that does to me?' Suddenly she was leaning forward in her seat, her head in her hands, her shoulders shaking involuntarily just as she'd cried earlier that day. 'I don't want you being nice to me,' she sobbed. 'Be horrible or leave me alone.'

'Kindly blow your nose and stop that language. I simply won't have it, not even from you.'

And as if by magic Georgia's tears immediately stopped. Looking up she saw that Iris was holding out a box of

Kleenex. She took a handful of tissues. 'I'm sorry,' she mumbled. 'It's so long since I've cried. It's all Rory's fault. When he started messing me about I was so angry and so upset I clamped a lid on anything I felt and vowed I'd never again let anyone screw me up like he did.'

'Which meant you had to stop anyone getting near you,' Iris suggested.

'Yes. And somehow, you, you silly old woman, managed to sneak under all my carefully erected barriers. How did you do it?' She started crying again. 'It's the bloody juxtaposition of how you appear to everyone else and then how you treat me,' she bawled. 'Why do you do it?'

'Ever thought that perhaps I like you, Georgia?'

Georgia blew her nose. 'No you don't, you don't like anyone.'

'And are you going to add that nobody likes me?'

'Everybody's terrified of you, you know that.'

'But not you? You're not scared of me, are you?' Iris asked softly.

'Too right I'm not.'

'And perhaps that's why I like you, Georgia. Mince pie?'

Georgia threw her pile of soggy tissues on the fire and laughed. 'Iris, you're the strangest and strongest woman I know.' She took a mince pie. 'Other than myself, of course.'

'Of course.'

Georgia bit into the pastry, sending up a small cloud of icing sugar into the air. She munched hungrily. She'd had nothing to eat since breakfast. When she'd finished, she said, 'Iris, can I ask you something?'

The old lady nodded.

'I know you've been widowed for years, but did you have ... well, are there any Braithwaite juniors running amok somewhere?'

It was a while before Iris said anything. 'Sadly no,' she answered, her hands clasped together on her lap and her eyes staring dimly into the flickering fire. When at last she turned her attention back to Georgia, she said, 'I'm very tired now, would you mind ...?'

'Of course,' Georgia said, getting quickly to her feet. 'I shouldn't have kept you talking for so long. Is there anything I can—?'

'No, nothing.'

'I'll call you tomorrow, then.'

'Thank you, that would be kind.'

Georgia had the strongest of urges to hug Iris but instead she patted the old woman's hand. She was surprised, though, when Iris took hold of hers and squeezed it gently.

Chapter Thirty-two

'Come on, David old mate,' Derek yelled above 'I Wish It Could Be Christmas Every Day'. 'It's your round so dip your hand in that dusty old wallet you keep hidden and get the beers rolling.'

Alex noticed David's long face as he approached the crowded bar. For a man who was indulging in illicit sex he looked far from happy. From the moment Charlotte had told him that David was having an affair Alex had tried to equate his future brother-in-law – a man who had never before struck him as a risk-taker – with the concept of a man who was throwing all caution to the wind.

He watched David pull out his wallet and was shocked to see his hands shake slightly. Was that the result of his duplicity? Obviously David wasn't cut out for a life of extra-marital spice.

'What's that serious expression for, Alex? Getting doubts for tomorrow?'

'No chance.' Alex turned away from David and faced his brother sitting next to him.

James cast his eyes about the public bar of the Spinner in amusement. The place was dripping with red and silver tinsel and gaudy paper chains that criss-crossed from one wall to another; from every light-fitting clusters of green baubles sparkled with glitter and dangled like swollen grapes. Over in the corner, by the entrance to the men's toilets, an old woman stood over a fruit machine, her loose false teeth sliding backwards and forwards as she stabbed with her fingers at the electronic buttons, her eyes lighting up with each spin of the drum. 'And to think we could have had your stag night in a smart little wine bar in Sloane Square,' James said, with a wry smile.

'And been bored to death.'

'You really have gone native, haven't you?'

Alex laughed. 'Come to my senses, more like it.'

'You always were an awkward bugger.'

'And still am, hopefully.'

James drained his glass of beer, then leaned back against a fake beam. 'How you found someone like Charlotte in a place like this I'll never know. But then maybe you're not the fool I thought you were.'

'So which fool does that make him?' Derek interrupted, as he handed out another round of drinks from the tray David was carrying.

Alex noticed that David still looked miserable. He watched him go over to the dart-board where Malcolm and Nick were challenging Barry and Stephen to a game.

The evening had been totally unplanned until last night when Derek had called round, saying, 'No neighbour of mine is getting married without proper respect for tradition.' His insistence had put paid to the decision that he and Charlotte had come to, which was to ignore convention and spend the evening with James and old friends, Stephen and Sally, who were coming over from Yorkshire for the wedding with their young deaf son Mark.

'Don't worry, Charlotte,' Derek had persisted. 'I've been to more last nights of freedom than there have been Conservative scandals. He'll be in safe hands with me.' Then, of course, had come the inevitable parting shot at the door. 'By the way, how do you like your kiss-o-grams, male or female?'

Over by the dart-board Alex could see Nick approaching David. He decided to join them – the last thing he wanted on his stag night was a repeat performance of Derek and Cindy's party.

*

'Muffin 'ell,' shouted Tiffany, springing forward in her seat and scattering peanuts over the floor. 'How can she say such a bloody stupid thing?' She mimicked Mia Farrow's thin, highly strung voice, ' "... That's the best thing a girl can be in this world, a beautiful little fool." '

'Quiet,' Cindy reprimanded, 'I can't hear what they're saying.'

Charlotte looked about the sitting room and smiled. She was enjoying her 'girls' night' that Hilary had arranged. 'We must do *something*,' her sister had said, when she'd heard that Derek was organising an evening out for Alex. 'The men can't have it all their own way.'

Hilary had said more or less the same thing before her wedding with Peter and had put together a night out in Manchester. Now, nine years older, they had both decided that a night in with a good video and a meal would be preferable to an exhausting night out on the tiles. Charlotte had been touched by the polite, almost tiptoey way Hilary had gone about things – normally she would have taken charge of the whole event, steamrollering everybody into turning up at the appointed time whether they wanted to or not. But not tonight. Instead, she had been most solicitous to Charlotte's request for a fuss-free evening. But her thoughtfulness had not stopped there. Hilary had remembered that Charlotte's all-time favourite film was *The Great Gatsby* and had bought the video specially. Even now Charlotte could recall how as teenagers they had gone to the cinema together and had sat in the front row both quietly drooling over Robert Redford.

'I hope this film isn't about male dominance—'

'Ssh, Tiffany!' both Hilary and Charlotte said, each knowing that Gatsby was about to make his entrance.

'When are we eating?' Tiffany asked, in a bored voice, tilting her head back and dropping a handful of nuts into her mouth. She was sick of men, especially one in particular. Nick Bradshaw, the arrogant ratbag! As if she'd ever shown any interest in him. 'I said, when are we eating?'

'Ssh!'

Bob Evans, the landlord of the Spinner, brought out the last of the steak and chips. 'Started snowing again,' he said, setting the plates on the table. He began to collect up the empty glasses. 'Another round?'

'Same again,' repeated Derek. 'I'm spitting feathers.' He dropped a dollop of Colman's on the side of his plate and offered the jar to James. 'So what tales have you got on our Alex, then?'

James looked at his brother and laughed. 'I reckon I spent nearly all my time bailing this idiot out of trouble at school.'

Derek raised an eyebrow. 'Round here he gives the impression butter wouldn't melt. Tell us more.'

'Nothing to tell,' Alex said, quickly. He had the feeling that, despite himself, his brother was beginning to enjoy the evening.

'We'll be the judge of that,' Malcolm said. 'Go on, James, I could do with a bit more background information for the service tomorrow.'

'Butter wouldn't melt, eh? As I remember it, he hated being told what to do. He was full of all that anti-Establishment bunkum and with the right provocation he could make James Dean look like a beatific Noddy high on LSD.'

Alex stuck a chip in his mouth, let it hang like a cigarette, and squinted. 'How's my belligerence rating now?'

'About as high as Mother Teresa's!' answered Stephen, with a laugh.

'Ah, of course, the best man,' Derek said, turning to him. 'You were students together, weren't you? You must have a regular cache of titbits for us. Fire away.'

'More cheesecake, anyone?' Hilary asked, standing in front of Tiffany.

'I can't see,' Tiffany said, her head moving from side to side as she tried to keep her eyes on the television.

'Changed her tune, hasn't she?' Charlotte whispered to Cindy, who nodded and helped herself to a second portion of dessert. Charlotte had never seen Cindy eat so much. Nor had she seen her drink wine before. It was strange when people started acting out of character.

'Everything all right upstairs?' she asked Sally when she came back into the room and sat cross-legged on the floor beside her.

'Fine. Mark's fast asleep. Have they got to the bit in the film where Daisy—?'

'Ssh!' hissed Tiffany.

Charlotte smiled to herself and glanced across the room at her sister. Despite all the trauma and uncertainty in Hilary's life right now, she was looking surprisingly calm and assured. Perhaps she had always underestimated Hilary. Then, in the background of her thoughts, she heard Tom Buchanan's arrogant voice, talking about people sneering at family life. She watched Hilary turn away from the screen, her eyes instantly dark with sadness. Like a swan, Charlotte thought, serene on the surface but paddling like crazy underneath.

Alex was almost disappointed in Derek. They were being tipped out of the Spinner and still nothing had happened. Where were the practical jokes? The cooking oil and feathers? The triple vodkas in the beer? The tart in nun's clothing? Perhaps Derek's behaviour had been tempered by having Barry with them for the evening – nothing like the presence of a child, even a grown-up one, to bring out the maturity in an adult.

'I'll be off home,' Malcolm said, peering out into the darkness at the snow-covered road. 'See you all tomorrow. Mind how you go.'

Shouldering each other to stay upright, they watched

Malcolm trudge through the snow, which was coming down so fast that his footsteps were almost immediately covered up.

'I've got an idea,' Derek said suddenly.

'Dad?' warned Barry.

Derek grinned. 'Follow me.'

'What are we doing here?' David asked, when at last they'd staggered to a stop in the churchyard. He swayed slightly as though the wind had caught him.

'We're going to build a pair of snowmen,' Derek said, 'like the figures on Alex's wedding cake tomorrow.'

They laughed, then James said, 'I've got a better idea.' He was sitting on top of a tombstone dangling his legs like a small child. There was no mistaking how drunk he was. The mistake was that none of the others realised that they were equally inebriated.

Chapter Thirty-three

Hilary looked at her daughter's implacable face and knew that it was the turd-in-the-potty syndrome all over again.

When Becky was sixteen months old she had, much to Hilary's delight and motherly pride, sat on Philip's old Thomas the Tank Engine potty and performed splendidly. Then, to a round of applause, Becky had stood up, seen what was behind her and had promptly burst into tears. She was horrified with what had come out of her tiny perfect body. From that moment, toilets and potties were no-go areas and served only to remind Becky that something ghastly had once happened to her. Until the age of two and a half she had clung tenaciously to her Pampers, her mind made up that she would never undergo a repeat performance of such abject humiliation. Hilary had tried all manner of chocolate-button bribery, together with persuasive arguments along the lines of, 'But everyone does it, Becky, even the Queen.' Such comments were sometimes met with quiet contempt but usually a full-blown Oscar-winning tantrum would be the response. Either way Becky would display a grim determination that she was not going to give in, or be taken in for that matter.

Hilary was face to face with that expression now. It was Christmas Eve, the morning of Charlotte and Alex's wedding and Becky, still in her pyjamas, was holding her bridesmaid's dress in one hand and a pair of kitchen scissors in the other.

'As a member of the Sisterhood I'd rather die than wear this dress.'

Becky's words were slow and well rehearsed and sounded more than a little absurd spoken by a seven-year-old. But Hilary knew her daughter well enough to understand that her words had the equivalent of a Herculean task force behind them. It was certain that Becky had no idea what Chloe was teaching her, but the whole thing was bound to appeal, given the club-membership perks on offer – immediate supremacy over her brother and the licence to rebel at will.

Hilary watched Becky flex open the kitchen scissors and decided that it was now or never to take control. She pounced on the dress, but Becky held on tightly, and the terrible but inevitable sound of ripping filled the gap between them. They stared in astonished silence at each other – Hilary because she didn't want to let herself believe her ears, and Becky because she was just beginning to wonder how much more courage she would need to remain Chloe's friend.

'So what do you suggest we do now, Becky?' Hilary asked, frighteningly calm.

Becky remained silent.

'Any ideas?' Hilary pushed on.

Still neither of them lowered their eyes, each lacking the courage to see just how much damage they had caused.

Becky opened her mouth to speak. She wanted to say sorry but she couldn't. Instead she could feel herself about to cry, like when she'd been told off at school last week for flooding the toilets. She had only meant to see what would happen when you unravelled a roll of toilet paper and stuffed it down the loo. How was she supposed to know that water would pour all over the floor? Mrs Wilson had been furious and had made her stand up in class the next morning and apologise to everyone. Mum didn't know about that ... but she did know about the dress. Then inspiration hit her. 'You shouldn't have tried to snatch it from me,' she said, in a clear loud voice. 'It's your fault I can't wear the dress. You'll have to tell Auntie Charlotte.'

Hilary stared in disbelief. Surely she had misheard. But no. There was Becky pushing the dress away and walking over to her unmade bed. She threw herself on top of the rumpled duvet and lay on her front, elbowing Peter Rabbit and Jemima Puddleduck out of the way as she opened and shut the scissors in her hands, snipping the air as though keeping in time to a piece of music.

The performance was breathtaking.

When and how had she gone so badly wrong? Hilary thought desperately. Then, as the satin fabric slipped through her fingers and dropped to the floor, she thought, To hell with that! Why did she always assume it was *she* who had gone wrong?

'I'm not sure I even want to be Auntie Charlotte's bridesmaid any more,' Becky said, tossing away the scissors and turning over onto her back. She kicked both legs in the air above her head and did a neat roly-poly. She faced her mother once more. 'Chloe says marriage is like a verruca, the more you pick it the worse it gets, and then one day it just disappears.'

Hilary breathed in deeply. 'Perhaps,' she said slowly, 'you'd like to go over the road and share your pearls of wisdom with your aunt. Then maybe you'd like to tell her what a spoiled brat of a niece she has.'

Becky pouted. Spoiled brat? Her mother had never called her that before. Precious. Special. Clever. Brilliant. Beautiful. Lovely. Perfect. That's what she'd always called her. Indignation made her jump off the bed. 'I'm not a spoiled brat!' she screeched.

'Oh yes you are!'

It was Philip. He came into the bedroom and stood by his mother.

'How long have you been standing there, Big Ears?' Becky shouted.

'Long enough to know you've got a vending machine of a gob.'

Becky scowled and moved back to the bed. She picked up Peter Rabbit and held him to her.

'Right,' said Hilary, finding she was gaining strength from Philip standing next to her. 'You've got a couple of hours to sort yourself out, madam. You've created the problem as to what you're going to wear for my sister's wedding, so you can resolve it.' She turned to go, but then added, 'And a word of warning. If you make yourself look ridiculous everybody will laugh at you.'

When she was alone Becky rushed to the door and slammed it shut. She picked up the silky dress from the floor and looked at it reproachfully. Tears began to trickle down her cheeks and she stuffed her face into the cool fabric. It wasn't fair.

She sat on the bed and hunched herself up against the pillows. She thought about running away. That would show them. She got off the bed and went over to the window. It was misted up with condensation and a small pool of water had gathered in the mildewy corner of the frame. She wrote her name on the glass then drew a Christmas tree with a large star on the top. She placed her eye to the star and peered through it. It was snowing again. Perhaps running away wasn't such a good idea ... but she could hide for a while, couldn't she?

She quickly got dressed and wondered where nobody would think of looking for her.

Chapter Thirty-four

Alex was up first. After he'd showered and shaved he made a large cafetière of strong coffee. He took it through to the small sitting room where James and Stephen were still on the floor in sleeping bags. They looked like two gigantic comatose caterpillars.

He drew the curtains and stared out at the garden. It reminded him of a Brueghel landscape. The trunks and branches of the trees, darkened by the effect of so much snow, were set against a pewter sky. Laurel bushes and rhododendrons, almost buried in deep snowdrifts, drooped beneath the weight of last night's blizzard, and in the distance a crow landed on a branch and created its own mini snowstorm.

Alex turned his attention to the two sleeping bodies at his feet and rattled a spoon against an empty coffee mug. There was no response. He bent down on one knee, held the mug next to his brother's ear and rattled the spoon again.

'Go easy with that bell, won't you?'

'Not a bell, James, just an empty mug which I'm about to fill with coffee for you.'

Stephen slowly surfaced. 'Somebody mention coffee?' he asked with a yawn. Then with a sudden burst of movement he stretched out his arms above his head and punched James in the eye.

Sally stopped tying Mark's shoe-laces. 'Am I imagining

things, Charlotte, or did I just hear a scream from next door?'

Charlotte put her flowers down on the table and smiled. 'A scream followed by something quite rude is what I heard.'

'It didn't sound like Stephen?'

'Alex neither.'

'James, then,' Sally said, continuing with her son's shoe-laces. 'He's not at all like Alex, is he?'

The sound of crashing furniture and more outbursts of angry words made them turn towards the wall that backed onto 1a Ivy Cottage.

'Here,' Charlotte said, grabbing a glass and handing one to Sally. 'Let's have a proper listen.'

'Having fun, aren't they?' Sally said, as they jammed themselves up against the wall.

'What are you doing, Mummy?' asked a bemused Mark, who was unaware of the commotion next door.

Sally put down her glass and faced Mark so he could read her lips. 'We're listening to Daddy and Uncle Lex next door, they're having a fight.'

'A fight?' Mark looked worried.

'Not a real fight,' Charlotte said, kneeling in front of Mark, 'they're just being silly. Men are like that.'

She stood up, suddenly serious. 'Sally, you don't think it's all going to go disastrously wrong today, do you?'

Sally gave a loud laugh. 'Not disastrously wrong.' She put her glass against the wall again. 'But I have the sneaky feeling it could well be the funniest day of your life.'

As the bells rang out and the wedding guests arrived they were met by the sight of a six-foot fully erect penis against the west wall of St John's. It was quite complete in all its icy construction even down to a frozen ejaculatory spurt of semen.

'Busy last night, were you?' Malcolm greeted Alex's entourage when they made their appearance. They stared shamefaced at the sight of their handiwork – it looked bigger in daylight.

'Boys will be boys,' James said, sheepishly, from behind a pair of borrowed sunglasses.

'Hangover, or a bad case of snow blindness?' Malcolm enquired, looking at him. He also noticed that Alex was wearing a bandage on his left hand. Stephen, though, looked as if he'd come through the night unscathed. He led the way towards the front of the church. The gathering congregation were in buoyant mood, laughing over what they'd just seen outside. It struck Malcolm as odd, however, that they all looked so red in the face. Blushing? Surely not.

'I should watch yourselves,' Malcolm said, reaching out to Alex as he skidded slightly off balance. 'The floor seems a tad slippery today. Must be all this snow people are bringing in on their shoes.'

They paused at the front reserved pew just as James slid to a halt. He reached out to a long mahogany candle holder at the end of the pew and snapped it clean in two. It crashed on top of his head, knocking his sunglasses to the floor.

Malcolm flinched. 'Heck of a black eye you've got there. How—'

'Don't ask,' growled James, scrabbling on the floor for his sunglasses.

Malcolm picked up the broken candle holder. 'Right,' he said, 'seeing as you're the usher, James, I need you to come back to the porch with me.'

'Do I have to move? This aisle's like a bloody ice rink.'

Malcolm laughed. 'Come on. You can hang on to me if you like.'

'Bloody odd show you've got here,' grumbled James as he followed behind. 'Most unorthodox.'

'I assure you we're straightforward Anglican.'

'What the—!' This time there was nothing for James to reach out for. Malcolm helped him to his feet. 'I'm all right,' he said bad-humouredly. Red-faced, he dusted down his suit and inched his way towards what he hoped was the safety of the porch. 'If I'd known it was going to be like this I'd have brought snow chains,' he muttered.

Neville eased his gleaming Volvo carefully out of Charlotte's driveway. Everywhere was inches deep in snow with a treacherous layer of ice beneath, and he drove painfully slowly down Acacia Lane. At the end of the road he turned into Daisy Bank and glanced up to look in his rear-view mirror. He caught a glimpse of Charlotte in the back of the car. She looked beautiful.

'I wouldn't have minded walking,' said Becky, who was sitting next to Charlotte.

In the front passenger seat Hilary turned round. 'So that you could have worn wellington boots up the aisle, no doubt, just to finish off your attractive attire.'

'Becky looks fine,' Charlotte said, in an effort to keep the peace.

Becky took a sideways peek at her aunt. 'Do you really think so?'

'Yes,' Charlotte said, looking at Becky's wrinkled black leggings and oversized check shirt. She hadn't liked the dress Hilary had chosen in the first place.

'And is my hair okay?'

'Really suits you,' Charlotte answered truthfully. Becky had done her own hair and had tied it up into two stubby bunches either side of her head – she looked like a little devil complete with horns.

'You don't mind me not wearing—'

'I told you, you look great.'

Becky almost felt guilty about the ripped dress now. After she'd got dressed earlier in the morning she had come up with the perfect hiding-place. The only trouble was that no one had come to look for her and she'd got bored all on her own and had then gone home, only to find that nobody had missed her anyway. She'd stayed in her bedroom, then, and spent ages trying to decide what to wear and fiddling about with her hair. She was glad Auntie Charlotte liked it.

Neville slowly manoeuvred the car alongside the pavement on the north side of the church. A sudden tooting of a horn from behind made him slam his foot down hard on the brake pedal. But instead of the brake he hit the accelerator and lurched the car into the Volvo in front. 'Oh my God! Oh my God!' he panicked. 'What have I done?' His face was white with shock. He looked round to check his passengers.

'Calm down, Dad,' said Charlotte, picking up her posy of red and white carnations. 'We're all fine.'

'Hilary?'

Hilary turned to her father, and with a strange smile on her lips, said, 'That's David's car in front.'

Another toot from behind made them open the doors and start to get out. They were greeted by Barry coming towards them. 'You okay?'

'We're all fine,' Charlotte said calmly.

Barry went round to the front of the car and stopped to pick up a piece of smashed headlamp in the snow. 'I told Dad not to hit the horn.'

Tiffany came over, followed by Cindy, her face wreathed in concern. Derek, who was oblivious to what he had caused, sauntered towards them and let out a long whistle. 'Charlotte, have I ever told you how ravishing you—'

'Derek, this is certainly not the time or the place to be trying your luck.'

'Cindy, as if I would.' He faced Charlotte and grinned. 'Bit cheeky of you to go for white, don't you think?'

Charlotte laughed and pulled the fur-lined hood that formed part of the Cossack-style dress over her head. 'I'm freezing, can we get a move on?'

'Allow me,' said Derek, offering his arm.

'That's my job,' Neville said, and with his composure fully restored he pushed Derek's arm aside and, with all the grandeur he could muster, steered Charlotte towards the lychgate.

As the small party made its way up the path – their eyes to the ground as they picked their way through the snow – Charlotte let out a sudden laugh. She had just caught sight of the large penis. Her poor father stood still, his face white with shock again.

Derek stared appreciatively. 'Now that's what I call—'

'What is it, Mummy?' interrupted Becky.

'It's a . . .' Hilary looked around for help.

'Could be a bottle of champagne,' Barry suggested.

'Yes,' said Tiffany, smirking, 'it's just been opened, you can see the bubbles coming out of the end.'

'That's enough, you two,' said Cindy.

'Well, I think you're wrong,' Becky said, her voice matter-of-fact. 'It looks like an enormous willy to me.' She ran on ahead and waited for them in the porch.

Malcolm greeted Charlotte; he looked hot and flustered. 'Here at last,' he said, relieved. 'A word of warning, make sure you—'

But his words were lost as Mr Phelps, eager to get on, caught sight of Charlotte and started up with Mendelssohn's Bridal March.

'Oh, never mind,' muttered Malcolm, and he started to walk tentatively up the aisle. To Charlotte's surprise he almost fell over. Drunk? It would explain his red face. She watched him reach out to the back of the pew and saw that in front of him one of the decorative candle holders lay in pieces on the floor.

'I think we'd better sit down,' Hilary said to Cindy, 'or we'll spoil Charlotte's big entrance. Let's hope David and Philip have saved us a pew.' She turned to Becky. 'Now, you know what to do, don't you?'

'Go on,' urged Neville, 'leave her to us.'

Derek led the way and straight away found the going slippery. Miraculously they managed to reach the safety of a pew and, thinking that he was home and dry, Derek sat down and slid clean off the wooden seat, his knees firmly planted on a hassock.

'Say one for me while you're down there,' giggled Tiffany.

'I'm not bloody praying!' he hissed. 'Help me up, won't you? God, but it's hot in here, I'm sweating cobs.'

As Barry and Tiffany helped their father, Charlotte and Neville, followed by Becky, made their entrance. Someone from the congregation yelled out, 'Steady as you go, it's as slippery as hell out there.'

'And about as hot,' joined in somebody else.

By the time Charlotte stood beside Alex she was stiff with concentration and her face felt like cement with the effort of trying not to laugh. 'Okay?' he whispered.

She pushed back the hood of her dress. 'I feel like Maria Vetsera in this.'

'Just so long as I don't have to agree to a suicide pact. It's turning into a bit of a farce, isn't it?'

Charlotte looked at his bandaged hand and then at James on the other side of Stephen. 'What have you all been—'

'If you don't mind,' Malcolm interrupted, tiredly. He ran a finger round the inside of his collar, then wiped at the sweat that was beading on his forehead. 'It's Christmas tomorrow and I've still got my shopping to do, so can we get on?'

'Yes, Malcolm,' laughed Charlotte. She lifted her eyes up to the ceiling bosses and thanked God that Sally had been right – this was fast becoming the funniest day in her life.

As Malcolm started the ceremony she looked at Alex out of the corner of her eye and gave his hand a squeeze.

He winced and withdrew his bandaged hand.

Chapter Thirty-five

'Goodness! I suppose you really are quite married? It was all such a fiasco it's hard to know.'

Alex handed his mother a glass of sweet sherry. 'I think it was when the boiler blew that I really felt things were getting a bit out of hand.'

'Out of hand,' his father repeated, eschewing the sherry and helping himself to a tumbler of Famous Grouse. 'It was wonderful. The whole thing was tremendous. Never seen anything like it. Not many wedding guests leave behind them a trail of devastation like we just have. I counted at least two twisted ankles, a platoon of firemen, not to mention a rather flaccid John Thomas.'

'I thought Malcolm was drunk when I saw him,' laughed Charlotte, 'he looked so flushed and then when I saw him nearly fall over—'

'It was the heat from the boiler,' Alex said, 'it was getting to us all.'

'And to your handiwork outside,' Charlotte said, with a grin. 'The boiler backs onto the west wall.'

'Doesn't explain why the floor was like a black run, though, does it?' Alex's father said. 'By the way, how did your brother get that shiner?'

'Yes, tell us what the three of you were getting up to this morning. Sally and I heard you through the wall, but couldn't for the life of us work out what was going on.'

'It was Stephen.'

'Not maliciously so,' said Stephen, coming over and

stooping slightly to avoid one of the beams in Louise and Neville's sitting room, to where they'd all escaped for the reception, leaving poor Malcolm to sort out the mess at St John's.

'It was you who punched James in the eye then knocked the coffee all over my hand.'

Stephen shrugged his shoulders. 'Just as well I'm a doctor, then.'

'Thought I was going to need a doctor at the start of that service,' joined in Derek. He was carrying a plate piled high with cold meat and salad. 'My bum slipped off the pew that fast. What the hell do the good ladies of the parish use to polish those pews? T-Cut?' He bit into a large pickled onion and chomped noisily.

'Don't go blaming me for your inability to sit down properly,' Iris Braithwaite called from an armchair by the log fire where she was comfortably settled in her fur coat with a pot of tea by her side. A wide-brimmed hat perched on her head gave her an elegant and superior air and went a long way to disguising her disfigured face. 'I can assure you Mrs Haslip and I have not polished those pews in over three months. Have you any idea of the price of beeswax, Mr Rogers? Perhaps if you contributed more to the running costs of St John's we—'

'Got your drift, Mrs B. I'll think on it,' Derek replied, poking out a piece of onion from between his front teeth. 'It did look like fate was determined to keep you two apart,' he said to Charlotte. 'Maybe the Big Fella up in heaven doesn't approve of your earthly match. I reckon it was a wrathful thunderbolt that made the boiler blow up.'

'Ignore him, Charlotte,' Barry said, over his father's shoulder.

Charlotte noticed the badge pinned to the lapel of Barry's suit: 'Without Jesus at Christmas You're a Dead Turkey.' She smiled at him and he winked at her. How he had changed. Just over a year away at university and he'd lost all his nervousness and was now completely at ease with himself and, Charlotte suspected, at ease with his father.

'I hope you're aware, Dad,' Barry said, 'that Malcolm thinks it was you who sabotaged the church and the service.'

'Now why on earth would Malcolm think I had anything to do with it? I mean, Charlotte's like a sister to me. Why would I want to spoil her big day?'

Alex laughed, and Charlotte said, 'Seriously, though, it was you, wasn't it, who turned up the heating too high, changed the hymn numbers and did heaven knows what to the floor to make it so dangerous?'

Derek shook his head. 'Hand on heart. Not guilty. The only crime I'll admit to is my share of the artwork outside St John's.' He gave Charlotte a nudge. 'Modelled on me, of course.'

'Don't you believe it.'

'Ah, Cindy,' Derek said, draping his arm loosely round her shoulder.

'Seen Tiffany?' she asked.

'She herded the children upstairs ten minutes ago to watch a video,' Barry answered.

'That's right,' Louise said, coming among them with a tray of chicken nuggets and chips. 'I'm on my way up there now with this little lot.'

'I didn't know you had a telly upstairs, Mother.'

'Lots you don't know about me, Charlotte. When your father's fallen asleep I need something to amuse me, so I bought myself a clever television with a natty little built-in video player. I saw one of those interesting Tarantino movies the other night. One has to get one's pleasure somehow.'

'You'll have to excuse my mother,' Charlotte said to Alex's parents, when Louise had disappeared. 'She has a strange sense of humour.' She was conscious that Peter's parents had always acted like 'Horrified of Aldershot' whenever the two families had got together. She wondered how last night had gone: her parents had offered to have Angela and Toby

Hamilton to stay with them. She hoped her mother had behaved.

'She's an interesting and colourful woman,' Toby said, crinkling his eyes approvingly.

'You make her sound like a Jackson Pollock painting.'

'Language, Mrs Lawrence ... I mean, Mrs Hamilton,' Iris called once again from the fireplace.

'So, then,' Angela said, slowly and deliberately, looking first at Charlotte then at Alex. 'Grandchildren.'

'Banging on the wrong door there, I shouldn't wonder,' Derek said, waving a cold sausage in Alex's direction.

'Derek!'

'Yes, Cindy?'

'I'd like a glass of wine.'

'But you don't drink wine,' he said, incredulously.

'I do now.'

Derek sloped off.

'Now, about these grandchildren,' Angela tried again.

Alex rolled his eyes.

'And we're banking on you, Charlotte, to get Alex back into a proper job. Children need a father who's bringing in a regular salary.'

'Attaboy, Dad,' agreed James, who was over by the window talking to Hilary.

'You always could sniff out an argument, couldn't you?' Alex answered, good-humouredly.

James came over. 'Am I right in thinking, then, that Charlotte is pregnant and this is in fact a shotgun wedding?'

'No,' said Charlotte, her voice slightly raised. 'I am not pregnant.'

'Conceived out of wedlock but at least born within it,' chipped in Iris.

'No, Mrs Braithwaite,' Charlotte said, horrified, and in a loud voice she said as clearly as she could, 'I said I am *not* pregnant.'

'There there, Charlotte,' Derek said, reappearing with a

glass of wine for Cindy and putting his arm round Charlotte. 'Don't take on so. If Alex can't cut the mustard I know a man who can.'

Cindy took a sausage roll from Derek's plate, stuffed it into his mouth, then dragged him over to talk to Hilary who was now standing all alone.

It had started snowing again when everyone gathered outside in the dark to see Charlotte and Alex off.

Becky stood in front of her mother and next to Mark. They had spent most of the afternoon together and, despite all Chloe's warnings about boys being stupid and growing up into selfish men, she had found herself enjoying the company of this quiet thoughtful boy. He had told her he was deaf and that if she spoke slowly he'd be able to read her lips and understand what she was saying. He'd even told her she was very good at it. It was then that she'd decided to tell him what she'd done. He had laughed and told her he thought she was very funny.

She was bursting now to tell somebody else.

She looked at her Auntie Charlotte through the open window of the car and, seeing her so happy, she stepped forward and said, 'You didn't mind about everything at the church, did you?'

Charlotte smiled back at her. 'I wouldn't have missed it for the world.'

'Good.'

Charlotte hesitated and then laughed. 'For a moment there, Becky, I had the craziest of feelings that maybe you had something to do with it.' She then stopped laughing. 'Becky, you didn't, did you?'

Becky beamed. 'It *was* me,' she said proudly. 'I went over to the church this morning because I was so cross with Mummy. I hid there, but then nobody came to look for me and I got bored and . . .'

Everybody around the car, including Hilary, was staring

at Becky but, blissfully unaware, she carried on, '... and I went into that funny little room at the back and found some cans of polish. I started spraying one of the pews, then the floor ... I thought it looked so dirty. Then I got cold and so I fiddled with the boiler ... I've seen Mummy do it when she does the flowers ... It was funny when it exploded, wasn't it?'

Nobody spoke, but when Charlotte saw the expression on David's face, she whispered to Alex, 'Start the engine before we get caught up in another explosion.'

Becky's confessional timing was perfect. As Charlotte and Alex drove slowly away, another car appeared. It was Nanna and Grandpa Parker. They had arrived too late for the wedding, but in time for Christmas.

Chapter Thirty-six

The Parker Seniors followed the Parker Juniors back to Acacia Lane. Barbara and Jeffrey were listening to the closing moments of the afternoon play on Radio Four – a nineties inner-city interpretation of *The Little Match Girl* – and Hilary, David, Philip and Becky were listening hard to nothing in particular. Nobody seemed inclined to speak. Hilary wanted to but was terrified of laughing.

She tried to excuse herself on the grounds of too much wine and champagne that afternoon, but she knew that wasn't the real reason behind the bubble of mirth rising within her. Every time she recalled Charlotte and Alex standing at the altar and Malcolm pronouncing them man and wife she thought of the explosion that had come only seconds later from the boiler room next to the vestry. And trust old Derek to have his mobile phone with him so that they could call for the fire brigade.

The funny thing was that she didn't feel at all cross with Becky. By rights she should be punished and if David had his way she would be, but Hilary had no intention of taking her daughter to task. She couldn't remember a time when she had laughed more.

She felt her face breaking into a smile even now, and turned to look out of the window as they pulled up at The Gables. The children leapt out of the car at once, as if they were glad to escape the threatening silence, and started scooping up handfuls of snow. Inside The Gables the timer device had automatically switched on the lights, including the pretty fairy lights on the Christmas tree in the sitting room and the house beckoned welcomingly.

It wasn't by any means the smartest or most attractive property in the village but Hilary had loved the beautifully proportioned Edwardian house from the moment they had viewed it and had wanted David to make an offer to the owners there and then. Six months later they had moved in – Philip had been five at the time and in his first term at school, and Becky had been a wobbly toddler just finding her feet.

'You love this house, don't you, Hilary?' David said, unexpectedly at her side.

She froze. What was he saying? That he was leaving her and they'd have to sell it? Was that it?

'What do you mean?' she said, turning slowly to face him. She was shocked to see how tired he seemed. There were lines around his eyes, shadows even. And had he lost weight? She couldn't remember the last time she had sat this close to him and looked at his face, *really* looked at it.

To her annoyance she found herself feeling sorry for him, but this was one emotion she didn't want and immediately she stamped on it. 'What do you mean?' she repeated, her voice hardened with resolve.

'I just meant . . .' He, too, now stared up at the house. 'Oh, nothing,' he said, and got out of the car to help his parents with their luggage.

'Oh, nothing to hell and back!' Hilary muttered as she unlocked the front door and walked through to the kitchen. Hadn't Cindy warned her that she might lose the house? She covered her face with her hands and leaned against the Aga. She felt miserable. And furious. Furious that her future lay so hopelessly in the hands of a man who no longer loved her.

She reached for the kettle, knowing that at any moment Barbara would come waddling into the house bringing with her half a dozen suitcases and enough edible 'contributions' to stock an entire corner shop. She turned on the tap and felt the familiar feelings of isolation and alienation she experienced whenever David's parents stayed with them. David was their only son and between them they never missed a chance to take the credit for having treated the world to such a splendid chap.

When Hilary had first met David's parents she had assumed that their comments towards their son and about him were heavily loaded with sarcasm – in those days she knew no other kind of parental affection, having been fed all her life a continuous diet of sarcasm by her mother. But then it had slowly dawned on Hilary that Barbara and Jeffrey were in earnest: in their eyes they had quite literally produced a Christ-like super-being.

She put the kettle on the Aga and noticed Becky's cut-out nativity scene tucked behind an open packet of shortbread and a tissue box. She smiled. There they were, the Parker clan – Barbara kneeling at the manger with Jeffrey standing dutifully behind, the pair of them gazing down at the world's Saviour in among the straw.

Well, by the end of this Christmas dear old Barbara and Jeffrey were in for one hell of a shock. They'd produced a Judas, not a Jesus. And just how would they come to terms with that?

Heavy footsteps told Hilary that Barbara was heading this way.

'Hilary, there you are. I've brought you some Darjeeling, I know how much you like it. And never mind that it's almost twice the cost of PG Tips.'

'Thank you, Barbara,' Hilary said, bracing herself for the rest of her mother-in-law's offerings from the large box she was carrying into the kitchen. She hated Darjeeling. It was Earl Grey she liked. She had told Barbara that a million and one times, but the simple message had never once penetrated those ghastly grey poodle-perm curls. She watched her lower the heavy box to the floor, her wide-skirted bottom sticking up in the air revealing a large area of dough-like flesh bulging over the top of a pair of brown pop-sox.

'Dates. I've brought you some stuffed dates. Just how David likes them.'

'Lovely.' Hilary took them and plonked them on the worktop.

'A pot of damson jam. Home-made, of course.'

'Naturally.'

'Mince pies. Reduced. I simply couldn't let them go in the supermarket this morning.'

'Super.' They'll go nicely with the four dozen in the freezer and the two dozen in the pantry.

'Lime marmalade. David's always had that on his toast ever since he was a boy. I know how fond he is of it.'

'Wonderful.' These days he has orange.

'Coffee. Real coffee beans. I thought I'd treat David. That decaff you give him is all very well, but it's got no taste.'

'How thoughtful.' Yes, why don't you go ahead and just poison him for me? Save us all a lot of trouble.

'Turkish Delight. Do you remember the Christmas when David ate so much he made himself—?'

'Yes, Barbara. I remember cleaning the bathroom afterwards.'

'Poor boy. He never did know when to say no.'

Oh, how true. 'Well, Barbara, how about I put all this away while you go upstairs and sort yourself out? You must be exhausted from your journey.' Come on, Hilary, show her whose house this is!

'A cup of tea while I'm in the bath would be most agreeable.'

'Good idea. You go ahead and I'll send David up with a—'

'No, no, no. The poor boy's exhausted. Let him have a glass of whisky in the drawing room with Jeffrey. He must be so upset after Neville crashing into his car like that. How careless of your father. Don't forget the ice, will you?'

'Ice?'

'In their whisky.'

'Sure you wouldn't like one?'

Barbara let off a laugh that sounded as cheery as a fire bell. 'Hilary, I sometimes wonder about you. You know perfectly well that whisky's a man's drink.' Her foot already on the lower step of the stairs, she called back, 'Just the one sugar in my tea.'

'Man's drink indeed,' Hilary said, lifting the kettle off the Aga and filling the teapot. But, then, Barbara had always been obsessed with gender, especially one's femininity – this from a woman who had tufts of whiskers growing from a large mole on her cheek!

Hilary crept past the family bathroom where she could hear Barbara finally running the bathwater away – she'd been in there for over an hour, having consumed two cups of tea and a plate of Hobnobs.

Hilary held her breath until she was in her own bathroom and the door was firmly locked. She exhaled deeply, put the plug in the bath and ran the water.

She lay in it, cosseted by the knowledge that she was safe for at least the next twenty minutes. She had given David – the poor exhausted boy – strict instructions to keep an eye on the crown of lamb in the Aga and to put the new potatoes on in exactly twelve minutes' time. When she'd asked him to do this simple menial task she had been given the usual baleful-eye treatment by her father-in-law and had half expected him to say, 'She'd never have got away with that with me' – Hilary always awarded Jeffrey a broad Yorkshire accent when she imagined him speaking, it seemed so apt for his chauvinistic character, whereas in fact he was as clear-vowelled as any southerner she knew. What he had actually said as Hilary had handed him his second whisky was, 'Indispensable, David, that's what you are. You spoil Hilary, you really do. She's a lucky girl.'

Hilary sank deep into the water, her frilly shower hat

clamped tightly on her head. 'Indispensable. Well, we'll soon see, won't we?'

At the end of the bath, among the baskets of toiletries and bottles of shampoo, Captain Scarlet and Mr Blobby stared back at her – they had been decamped from the family bathroom to make room for Barbara's armoury of Bronnley products. Captain Scarlet was down on one knee, his head twisted round so that he was staring over his shoulder at Hilary. Mr Blobby, with both his arms raised in the air, had lost the dot from one of his eyes and he looked as if he was winking salaciously at her. Hilary didn't like the way they were both eyeing her and slapped her knees together.

Stupid thing! she told herself with a smile. They're only bottles of bubble bath – anyone would think they were Derek or Nick sitting there.

She hadn't seen much of Nick recently and she wondered what he would be doing for Christmas and why she had just thought of him. She closed her eyes and for the sheer fun of it tried to imagine him kissing her again. Disappointed, she found she couldn't. His face eluded her, as did his lips. How unfair that she couldn't even fantasise adultery, whereas David was busy doing the real thing.

She glanced at her watch, in front of Mr Blobby's left foot. In two minutes' time poor exhausted David would have to stagger along to the kitchen. She reached for the bar of soap and began washing herself. She scrubbed her neck, shoulders and breasts hurriedly and uncaringly, her eyes staring straight ahead, unable even to view her own body for fear of coming to the dreadful conclusion that, perhaps, here lay the reason for David's rejection.

She tried to think of something different as she carried on washing. Charlotte and Alex. Had they arrived at their honeymoon destination yet? Everyone had tried to prise out of Alex where he was taking Charlotte, but he had parried their questions effortlessly. Louise had joked that he was taking her back to Brussels. How typical of their mother to make a joke in such poor taste.

There was a loud rap at the door.

'Hilary, you're needed in the kitchen.' It was Barbara.

'I told David what needed doing,' Hilary answered.

'We can't find the salt for the potatoes.'

'I never put salt in . . .' Oh, what was the point? She tugged on the plug chain and reached for a towel. 'Coming.'

Later that night, when supper had passed without incident and the children had gone to bed in a state of Christmas Eve fever, Hilary left David and his parents reminiscing on his days of glory as the most perfect child ever. She put on her warmest coat, donned a hat, scarf and gloves and escaped into the snow for midnight mass.

At the top of Daisy Bank she could see the village hall. Unusually for Christmas Eve it was brightly lit and she could make out people moving about inside. As she drew nearer she noticed a piece of paper stuck to the door. She went over and read it: 'St John's out of action – midnight mass here.'

Hilary stepped inside. Rows of chairs were set out with a small central aisle. Most seats were occupied and everyone was chattering and laughing. It was more like a party than a church service.

'Over here, Hilary.'

Hilary was surprised to see Georgia waving to her from a row of seats near the back. Next to her was Chloe – she was the only child there as far as Hilary could make out.

'Hello,' Hilary said, when she'd eventually squeezed along the row of knees.

Georgia kissed her on the cheek. 'And before you pop a shot at me, this is the one and only time I ever come to church because, as everyone knows, it doesn't really count. What's up? You look exhausted.'

'In-laws. They've arrived.'

'No worries. You'll lose them when you divorce David.'

Hilary looked shocked.

'Oops. Being too blunt, am I? Tell me what you think Santa's bringing you instead.'

Hilary turned her sapphire and diamond engagement ring round on her finger. The stones caught a beam of light from a fluorescent tube overhead and sparkled brightly. 'I suppose I'd rather like Santa to bring me a ready-made solution,' she said thoughtfully.

Georgia squeezed her hand. 'I hate to put a dampener on things but he can only bring you what you've asked him for.'

They heard a loud tut from further along the row. It was Patricia, leaning forward and staring in disgust at Georgia's hand covering Hilary's. They looked at one another and laughed loudly. Enjoying the unfamiliar sensation of knowing she was misbehaving, Hilary pulled a face and mimicked Patricia's admonishment. 'Tut-tut,' she clicked with her tongue. She then wondered if this was how Becky often felt.

It was strange, but when she really thought about the shenanigans Becky had got up to earlier that day she had to admit to a curious sense of pride in her daughter. When she had been Becky's age she had never done anything naughtier than sneak the raisins from the Whitworth's packet in the larder. Small-time compared to Becky's exploits. Single-handedly, in one day, she had caused more mayhem at St John's than your average person would in a lifetime. Extraordinary. But how exciting and liberating to know that you alone had been responsible for so much. Oh, to be that rebellious, to have that freedom of self. Lucky Becky! And what if she herself was to be so cavalier? What would she do and to whom would she do it? Quick as a flash, Jeffrey and Barbara came into Hilary's mind. Odd that they should receive her first strike. Or was it? Wasn't it all their fault that David was the way he was – the sins of the father and all that?

She was just smiling to herself when the hall was plunged into darkness.

'Sorry!'

The lights immediately came back on. 'Sorry,' the voice repeated, 'caught it with my shoulder.'

Hilary looked up to see Derek by the light switches. He was holding the door open for his family. They came and sat behind Hilary and Georgia. Derek kissed Hilary and shook hands with Georgia. 'It was Bas's idea we came,' he said, by way of explanation. 'Cindy was all for an early night, but I said if my lad Bas wants us to go to midnight mass then the rumpy-pumpy will just have to go on hold.'

'A little louder, Dad.' Tiffany smirked. 'I don't think they heard at the front.'

Derek winked at his daughter, then put his arm round Cindy's shoulders.

How like Becky Derek was, Hilary reflected, as she turned to face the altar. Quite simply, the pair of them didn't give a damn.

'Good evening, everyone,' Malcolm greeted his congregation. He looked a lot less flustered than he had earlier, Hilary decided, as he stood behind his makeshift altar of two covered trestle tables. 'As you all know we had one or two surprises at St John's this afternoon, which is why we're assembled here.'

'What d'yer mean, surprises?' heckled Derek. 'We were fannying around doing more triple axels than Torvill and Dean.'

'Quite,' continued Malcolm, 'but I'd like us all to take this opportunity to pray for St John's to be back in action as soon as possible ... and for the person responsible for the chaos to stay out of my way until I've had a chance to cool down.'

Hilary lowered her head, hoping to goodness that nobody from the wedding reception had had an opportunity to talk to Malcolm. She felt Derek nudging her from behind. 'You praying extra hard, Hilary?' he whispered.

The first carol was 'Hark! the Herald Angels Sing', and as

the congregation let rip with merry gusto Hilary thought of Charlotte. It was her sister's favourite carol. Suddenly she felt sad. She wanted Charlotte here with her. It was quite likely that the next time she saw Charlotte her life would be very different. It was then that she knew with absolute certainty exactly what she wanted from Santa.

She wanted the courage to tell David that she'd had enough.

Chapter Thirty-seven

'Louise, happy Christmas!'

'You too, Barbara.'

The two women faced each other with all the warmth and enthusiasm of a pair of sumo wrestlers. Louise stepped over the threshold of The Gables and thought how fortunate she was that she and Neville had no cause to go to Peterborough and that Barbara's visits to Cheshire were limited to a minimum.

'Hilary's in the kitchen and I'm afraid to report that the turkey went in far too late.' Barbara's voice was low and confidential as if she was breaking the news that a loved one was at death's door with only minutes to live.

Here we go, Louise said to herself, rule-the-roost Babs telling tales again. But what poor, stupid Babs couldn't get into her tea-cosy of a head was that she didn't give a damn how inefficiently Hilary ran her life and The Gables. As far as Louise was concerned, Hilary could cavort naked in the kitchen partnering the turkey for a tango with a Christmas pudding shoved up its—

'David's absolutely shattered,' Barbara said, with a little wobble of her head. She took Louise's coat, then Neville's. 'I wonder whether you could have a word with Hilary,' she burbled from the depths of the under-stairs cupboard. 'Not exactly what you'd call spick and span in here,' she added.

'What do you want us to say to Hilary?' Louise asked, reaching out her hands as if to close the cupboard door on Barbara. Neville smiled and walked away.

Barbara finally emerged, a sticky cobweb clinging to a grey curl. Louise decided not to tell her it was there.

'I think Hilary expects too much from David,' Barbara said, smoothing out the creases in her new Christmas frock. She produced a neatly folded handkerchief from her sleeve and blew her nose. 'So much dust in there.' She blasted noisily a second time into the small square of embroidered linen.

'In what way, exactly?' Louise was intrigued.

'I'm sure you must have noticed how tired David's looking,' Barbara stepped closer to Louise and added, 'to say nothing of the atmosphere.'

Perhaps only since you arrived, Louise thought. 'To be honest I think it's Hilary who's worn out. Ever thought that your son might be expecting too much of his wife?' Louise had no grounds for suggesting such a thing, but why should dreary old Babs have it all her own way?

Barbara gave a dismissive laugh. 'Louise, dear. I've been here barely twenty-four hours, but grant me sufficient intelligence to detect which way the wind is blowing. Your Hilary is constantly asking David to do a never-ending number of jobs around the house. Little jobs that Hilary's quite capable of doing herself. Call me old-fashioned, but the kitchen really is the woman's domain.' She gave off another irritating laugh.

Louise wanted to grab the nearest object to hand.

'I think you've spoiled your girls,' Barbara went on. 'You taught them to expect too much.' She smiled, as though her opinion would be welcomed as an enormous act of kindness. 'Let's join the others for a glass of Christmas sherry. We've brought some of our favourite. Especially dry.'

'I'll have a gin and tonic,' Louise said, through clenched teeth. 'Especially strong, please.' Bloody queen bee, she scowled as she followed Barbara in her fluffy mules through to the kitchen. Why couldn't she just sting herself and have done with it?

'Mother,' said Hilary with a potato peeler in her hand and

a harassed expression on her face. 'Happy Christmas.'

Louise embraced her and whispered in her ear, 'How long's the witch staying this time?'

'Five days,' Hilary whispered back.

'You poor devil,' Louise said, her arms uncharacteristically still round her daughter's shoulders. She then stepped back and in a louder voice, said, 'Goodness, all these guests staying and no one to help with the vegetables. Here, let me give you a hand.'

Both Hilary and Neville stared at Louise in surprise. Louise never offered to help in the kitchen, or anywhere else for that matter. 'Where's David and the children?' Neville asked, by way of conversation.

'Dear David's upstairs with Becky and Philip,' answered Barbara. 'He's loading a new game on to the computer. I think that's the correct expression, isn't it?' She looked around the kitchen as if waiting for a burst of applause. 'Ah, there you are, Jeffrey,' she said, as her husband appeared in the doorway with a tray of filled sherry glasses. He was dressed in a smart double-breasted grey suit and his shoes gleamed as if they'd been treated to a lick of black gloss paint. Neville fiddled with the top button of his old tweed jacket and rubbed one of his Hush Puppies on the back of his trouser leg.

'I thought it was about time for a sherry,' Jeffrey announced.

Barbara beamed. 'Call me old-fashioned but I do think a man should pour out the drinks, don't you? It's like carving the turkey. It's proper etiquette for the man of the house to carve.'

'Well, let's hope David won't be too exhausted to carry out that onerous task later on this afternoon,' Louise said, attacking a potato with a small knife. 'Though doubtless Jeffrey or Neville could step into the breach if one of us poor idiotic females couldn't manage it. Personally I love nothing better than carving up an old bird, especially a dumb old bird.'

Hilary joined her mother at the sink. Normally it was she who was on the end of her mother's tongue – it was good to hear somebody else coming in for a good lashing.

'I rather think Louise has been sleeping in the cutlery drawer again,' Barbara said with a patronising little laugh. She ran her hand over her sculptured hair and found the cobweb. She pulled a face.

Go on, Mother, Hilary silently urged, say something else. In the past she had always seen herself in the role of a peacemaker. Now to her surprise she found herself wanting to encourage her mother to fight on, but not only that: she found herself wishing that she could be more like her maverick mother. She cut a potato in half and plopped it into the saucepan on the draining board, thinking that only yesterday she had been wishing she was more like her daughter. She had never before thought that Becky was anything like Louise, but it was as plain as the nose on her face that Becky was exactly like Louise. And didn't Charlotte have that same rebellious streak of not wanting to conform? So why had she always been such a Goody Two Shoes? Why had she missed out on the genes of nonconformity? Or had they always been there but she had suppressed them?

With the sound of polite conversation in the background about the quality of the amontillado they were drinking, Hilary reached in front of her mother for another potato.

'Silly old witch,' Louise muttered. 'Does David really mean that much to you that you can put up with her?'

'No,' Hilary said, without thinking.

Her mother looked at her.

Hilary stared at the potato in her hand.

'Hilary?'

She looked up and met her mother's questioning gaze. 'I didn't mean—' she started to say, then she thought of her decision made during midnight mass and what lay ahead of her. 'I meant exactly what I just said,' she said. Her voice quiet but firm.

'I see,' was all Louise said. She turned the tap on and rinsed her hands. 'I suppose you'll eventually get around to telling me what's going on here.'

Barry was wearing another of his badges. Derek wondered how many more his son had. Today's was 'Stuff the Turkey, Not Jesus!' He smiled and looked down at his plate. An enormous half-eaten turkey leg stared back at him along with a lone sprout. He didn't know about the turkey but he felt pretty stuffed himself. He leaned back in his chair, picked up his glass of Hunter Valley red and took a large mouthful. Contentment flowed through him. He was one hell of a happy man.

He noticed that Cindy was staring at him. He noticed, too, the smile on her face as she twirled her wine glass round between her fingers. Strange that she should have suddenly taken to drinking wine . . . odd, also, the way she was looking at him. Self-conscious, he turned his attention to Tiffany on his right.

There she was, gorgeous, angry Tiffany. His little girl, all but grown-up now. He thought of all those years of confrontation with her. How the hell they'd survived he didn't have a clue, especially Cindy who had borne the brunt of Tiffany's toddler to teenager tantrums. He looked over to his wife and found she was still staring at him, and there was that smile again.

Bloody hell! Was she flirting with him?

He reached for the bottle of wine, refilled his glass and tried to remember when he'd last felt this good. To hell with that! When was the last time he'd felt this turned on at the family dinner table?

He tried to think of something else and turned to his left where Bas was sitting. He was chatting across the table to Tiffany and was telling her about some medical-school prank that had involved a jar of eyeballs. What a bloody neat son he was.

And what a bloody fantastic family they were.

He risked a quick look at his wife again and found she was *still* staring at him. 'A toast,' he said, raising his glass and crossing his legs.

They turned and looked at him.

'To my bloody neat family,' he said. 'I feel like the luckiest man alive.'

'Are you drunk?' Tiffany laughed.

'And what if I am?'

'Dad's right,' Barry said, 'we are pretty neat.' He and Tiffany raised their glasses against their father's.

'Cindy?' Derek waited for her to lift her glass. It was suddenly important to him to hear his wife's agreement, as though it would be the seal of approval to all he felt and had achieved over the past years, and more recently the creation of All in the Mind. But as he waited for her response, it occurred to him that what was also important to him was not just his own happiness ... but Cindy's. Had he made Cindy happy?

Never before had Cindy felt herself to be the entire focus of her family. And right now she was. Tiffany, Barry, even Derek, they were all looking at her. She knew, too, what they wanted to hear from her. Ironic, that for what seemed for ever they had each pulled in different directions, each straining against the other.

'I've got something to say,' she said, sensing her family's disappointment. 'Barry, would you go and get me that large brown envelope with the red ribbon I showed you last night? It's at the bottom of the Christmas tree.'

'This what you want?' Barry asked, when he came back into the dining room.

Cindy nodded. 'Thank you.' She took the envelope and pulled at the satin ribbon. 'I'm afraid you'll think this totally self-indulgent. It's a Christmas present to me, from me.' She met her husband's eyes as the ribbon slipped away from the envelope.

'I don't have a problem with that,' Derek said, watching Cindy's fingers playing with the ribbon.

It reminded him of a strip-tease.

'You told me not so long ago that we've all got to find a niche in this life. Well, I've decided that you don't really need me here, Derek, so before it's too late I'm going to—'

'Mum, you're not ... you can't—'

Cindy looked at her daughter. 'What, Tiffany?'

Tiffany turned to her father. 'Dad, don't let her do this. Do something. Say something.'

Derek was silent. All the joy and contentment he'd experienced only moments ago drained out of him. Dejected, he stared down at his dinner plate. He pushed it away. The idea was unthinkable.

Barry reached over to his mother. He touched her hand lightly and smiled. 'I think you'd better finish what you were going to say, Mum, and put them both out of their misery.'

Cindy smiled, embarrassed. 'I've got Barry to thank really,' she said, pulling a brochure out of the envelope in her hands. 'He's convinced me that I should go back to school, so I'm joining what's known as an access course for a year and then I'm going to have a go at studying ... What is it?' she asked, seeing the look first on Tiffany's face and then on Derek's. 'Don't you think I can do it?'

Tiffany laughed. 'Muffin 'ell! 'Course you can do it, Mum.'

Derek slowly got to his feet. He went to Cindy and kissed her.

'What's that for?' she asked, genuinely surprised.

He swallowed hard. 'No reason,' he answered, his hand resting on her shoulder.

'Liar!' shouted Tiffany with a smile. 'You thought Mum was—'

Barry reached across the table and waved a cracker under his sister's nose. 'Pull a cracker with me and shut up, will you, Tiffany?'

'Anything I can do?' Iris asked for the third time from the quiet comfort of the sitting room.

'You've done quite enough already,' Georgia called, from the chaos of the steam-filled kitchen. 'More than enough, in fact,' she muttered under her breath, as she drained off the fat from the meat juices in the roasting tin. Inviting Iris to spend Christmas Day with her and Chloe had turned out to be nothing more than a monumental battle of wills rather than a festive act of good cheer to all men.

The day after she had made a fool of herself in front of Iris she had phoned Hilary, who'd said she was just about to call on Iris to suggest she spend Christmas at The Gables. 'No,' Georgia had said. 'You've got enough on your plate with the dreaded in-laws coming, she can come to me.' Hilary's relief had been almost palpable but when the idea had been put to Iris she had refused point-blank even to consider the invitation.

'I couldn't possibly spend Christmas Day away from the White Cottage.'

By this stage Georgia was determined that if it was the last thing she ever did, it would be to get Iris away from that depressing little sitting room for Christmas Day. By their third phone call Georgia lost her temper with the old woman and shouted down the line, 'I shall never speak to you again if you don't do this one simple thing for me.'

'What a pity,' Iris had responded, 'but so be it. Unless ...'

'Unless what?' Georgia had asked, recognising a classic negotiating opening.

'Why don't you make more of an occasion of the day? Why not invite Nick Bradshaw as well?'

'No way!' she'd roared, when she'd regained the power of speech.

'I shall see you some other time then. Goodbye.'

'Don't you dare hang up on me, you meddling snake in the grass!'

A long silence had ensued between them until Iris had said craftily, 'So what time will you be expecting me? Perhaps Mr Bradshaw would be kind enough to give me a lift?'

Georgia had conceded the battle on the basis that the war would be won with Nick turning down such a ridiculous invitation. But she had been wrong. Nick had accepted and offered immediately to act as chauffeur for Iris and now here he was back in her house once again and in the sitting room charming the thermal underwear off Iris and quoting Simone Weil to Chloe. God rest ye merry, gentlemen, indeed!

'I've set the table,' Nick announced, standing in the kitchen doorway. 'What else can I do?'

'You can pour some of that wine you brought, and quick, before I pass out.'

He filled two glasses and handed her one. 'Happy Christmas,' he said, chinking his glass against hers, 'and thanks.'

'Oh, no, you don't!' she said, taking a gulp of wine. 'Don't start on all that sincerity stuff about Christmas not being Christmas unless you're amongst friends and family. You're here because it was the only way I could get Madam in there to accept my invitation. Okay?'

'I'm flattered.'

'Yeah, well, don't let it go to your head. Now pass me that dish by your elbow – these sprouts are ready.'

As she stood by the sink and drained the vegetables, one hand holding the saucepan and the other holding the lid firmly against the pan, she felt Nick come up behind her. He kissed her neck lightly just below her ear. She was so taken aback at his sheer nerve that she almost dropped the saucepan. She put it on the draining board and then turned and faced him. 'What's that for?'

'I should think that's obvious.' He handed her the dish for the sprouts.

She stared at it for a moment and then at him. 'So why wait until my hands were full before kissing me?'

He smiled. 'It was the only way I could be sure of you not hitting me.'

Georgia laughed loudly.

'Everything under control out there?' enquired Iris.

'Oh, yes,' answered Georgia, smiling, 'everything's completely under control.'

Lunch was noisy and fun, with Chloe in high spirits insisting on pulling crackers with everybody in turn – crackers that, late last night after coming back from midnight mass, Georgia had doctored by slipping some extra novelties inside the green and gold cylinders of card and crêpe paper. And now Nick at the opposite end of the table was wearing a false nose and Poirot-style moustache, with Chloe on his left sporting a pair of Mr Spock ears, while Iris was laughing and playing with a pair of clockwork false teeth, winding them up and then sending them chattering across the table. 'Perfectly disgusting,' she chortled, reaching out for them to set them off again.

'Come on, Mum,' Chloe said, 'it's your turn now to pull your cracker with me.' She grinned. 'And I know what's inside it.'

'You do, do you? Well, here goes.'

They both tugged hard, but it was Georgia who fell back against her chair the victor. 'What's this?' she asked, when a small silver brooch decorated with tiny sparkling marcasites tumbled out of the cracker and onto the table. She was expecting a plastic bleeding finger with a nail through it, not this exquisite piece of jewellery.

'Let me see,' Chloe said. 'Cool! It's great.'

'It certainly is,' Nick agreed, leaning over to have a closer look. 'Looks expensive as well.'

'But I only put silly things inside the crackers, not anything like—' She looked up and stared round the table, her eyes finally resting on Nick.

He shook his head. 'As much as I'd like to take the credit, it's got nothing to do with me.'

Iris cleared her throat. 'It was me,' she said. 'I put it there.'

'You! But when?'

'Don't look so surprised. I had plenty of time when you and Mr Bradshaw were busy in the kitchen.' She smiled and looked across the table. 'And Chloe was a willing accomplice by keeping a look-out for me.'

'But why?'

Iris swallowed. 'It's a present, and before you start with any of your nonsense I insist that you accept it. It belonged to my mother and I'd very much like you to have the pleasure of wearing—'

'Give over and give me a hug, you silly sentimental old woman.'

With eyes wet with tears they held onto each other tightly. Nick smiled to himself. He knew little about the strange relationship between Georgia and Iris but he could see only too well that they touched each other in a way that forced themselves to acknowledge some part deep within them that they had previously kept from anyone else. He winked at Chloe, hoping that one day she, too, would know that sometimes a risk was worth taking, especially where relationships were concerned.

'Nanna Parker?'

'Yes, Becky dear.'

'Why have you got that black thing with hairs growing out of it on your cheek?'

'Because she's a witch,' muttered Louise, helping herself to a dollop of brandy butter.

'I beg your pardon?'

'I asked why you had that black—'

'Not you, dear,' Barbara said, without looking at her granddaughter. 'Louise, what did you say?'

'I was just saying what a pretty dish this is,' Louise said, making a play of examining the bowl of brandy butter. 'Alfred Meakin, excellent condition.'

Barbara viewed Louise suspiciously with her pale grey eyes. 'I could have sworn I heard you—'

'So why have you, Nanna Parker? You'd look nicer without it.'

Barbara straightened the purple paper hat which she had swapped for David's so that he could have one to match the red tie she'd given him. 'Even if I put myself through the painful experience of having the mole removed,' she said, her voice matter-of-fact, 'I'd still be the same lovely old Nanna Parker, wouldn't I? Outward beauty is nothing compared to inner beauty.'

Louise snorted into her wine.

'I wonder how poor old Mrs Braithwaite is today,' Hilary ventured, desperate to avoid any bloodshed at the table. 'I had invited her to join us for the day but—'

'Yes, David mentioned that to me last night,' Barbara interrupted, seizing her opportunity. 'And I told him how wonderfully thoughtful he was to open his home to a lonely old neighbour on Christmas Day.'

'Apparently the police have caught the man who attacked her,' Louise said to Hilary, ignoring Barbara at the other end of the table. 'He was after Royal Doulton figurines, which is ironic because he wouldn't have found anything like that in Iris's house.'

'I knew a woman who had her entire collection stolen. The burglar came right into—'

'Any more takers for Christmas pudding?' asked Hilary, who couldn't bear the thought of Barbara clacking on a minute longer.

Everyone shook their heads. 'In that case perhaps you'd like to make some coffee, David, to go with our mince pies and cheese?'

'Hilary! There you go again.' Barbara looked triumphantly at Louise. 'You see what I mean? She just never leaves him alone.' Barbara reached out to her son. He looked on as though in numb sufferance; a sad and lonely figure at the head of the table surrounded by bits of spent crackers. Barbara patted his hand. 'You sit there, my love. Hilary and I'll make the coffee.'

'Can we get down now, please?'

'Yes, Philip,' Hilary said quickly. If something awful was about to happen amongst the adults she didn't care for her children to witness her mother wrestling Barbara to the floor.

'Tell you what, I'll make the coffee,' Neville said, helpfully, when the children had gone.

'Barbara always makes the coffee in our house,' Jeffrey asserted as Neville slipped out to the kitchen. 'Damn fine coffee maker she is too.'

'You make her sound like a percolator,' Louise said, acidly.

Barbara made a warning rattling noise in her throat. 'Tell me, Hilary, was that the recipe I gave you last year for the Christmas pudding?'

'No, it's Delia's—'

'I thought not,' Barbara said smugly, pulling the string on the light-up Santa brooch she was wearing.

'Okay, Babs. I've had enough. Are you going to spend the whole of Christmas criticising my daughter's cooking, or is there any hope of you keeping that rictus mouth of yours shut?'

Everyone gaped.

'You have always shown us, Louise dear, what a way with words you have. But you have to admit that leaving the bag of giblets in the plastic bag inside the turkey is certainly a novel way to serve the lunch. I wonder how David has survived Hilary's cooking all these years.'

'Perhaps he won't have to much longer,' Hilary said quietly.

'And what's that supposed to mean?' demanded Jeffrey.

Hilary, who had always been a little scared of her father-in-law, met his hostile gaze. She then looked at David at the opposite end of the table. He stared back at her unseeingly. His indifference was the final straw. She screwed her napkin into a tight ball and threw it at his face.

'Barbara and Jeffrey, there's something you should know,' she began in a determined voice. 'Your son is a cheat, a liar, and he's been having an affair for goodness knows how long. There, what do you say to that?'

Chapter Thirty-eight

Barbara kept her pale insipid eyes on Hilary, never once letting them drop or turn towards her son. She got to her feet slowly, as though she were about to deliver an after-dinner speech.

'If you had been a better wife he wouldn't have needed to look elsewhere. If you had appreciated what a wonderful and special—'

But Barbara's words were lost in the sound of crashing crockery and glass as David, in one single movement of his arm, swept his place setting onto the floor. He looked up at everyone around the table. 'I've lost everything!' he shouted.

'That's what happens when you play with fire,' Hilary screamed back at him, on her feet now and shaking with the awful truth hammering inside her that there was no going back. This was it.

Barbara moved towards David. She put her hand on his shoulder and stared defiantly at Louise. 'You see what you've brought upon your family.'

'Oh, shut up, you old trout,' Louise fired back.

'Shut up, the lot of you,' David roared.

'Well said—'

'Be quiet, Dad, and let me speak.' David looked at Hilary. 'I don't know where you've got this idea that I'm having—'

'You are!' she shouted. 'I know you are. Don't sit there denying it. After what I've been through at least have the decency to own up to what you've been doing.'

He got to his feet and moved towards her but she backed away, tears streaming down her cheeks.

'Hilary, I don't understand—'

'And what about all those nights when you said you were working late or at some Rotary meeting? You weren't there. I know you weren't.'

David's face darkened and he turned from her. 'I can explain—'

'I bet you can. But it's too late because I've had enough. I want a ...' She clenched her fists and willed herself to say the dreaded words. 'I'm leaving you.' There! She had done it. She sobbed even louder and stumbled out of the room crashing into her father, who had been hiding outside in the hall. She grabbed her car keys and slammed the front door after her.

It was dark when she returned. Two hours of driving around on her own in the snow had left her feeling numb with exhaustion. She let herself in. The house was in darkness and behind her there was no sign of her parents' Volvo on the drive or of Barbara and Jeffrey's Rover. She stepped into the hall and reached for the light switch. She started.

David was on the bottom step of the stairs, slouched against the wall with an empty wine bottle next to him. He looked dreadful and as he blinked and tried to shield his eyes from the light he said, 'Hilary, please listen to me. I've got something to tell you.' He moved the empty bottle for her to sit next to him.

She stayed where she was. 'Where is everyone?'

'At your parents', I thought it best.'

'It's a bit late for your consideration,' she said flatly. She turned away from the sight of him and hung her keys on the hook by the telephone.

He stood up and came towards her. 'Hilary, I'm not having a bloody affair.' He took her by the shoulders and turned her round to face him. 'We're in a worse sodding mess than that!'

He sounded drunk and she recoiled from him. 'Mess?' she said angrily. 'What kind of mess?'

He stroked her hair gently, as though suddenly distracted. 'I've been seeing a new firm of accountants these past few months. The business is ... Oh, God, Hilary, I'm so sorry.' He lowered his eyes and moved back towards the stairs and leaned heavily against the banisters.

'David, what is it? Tell me.'

'I've lost it all.' He shrugged his shoulders, then covered his face with his hands, unable to speak.

She stared at him. Was he so drunk that he was saying the first thing that came into his head?

'I'm so sorry, Hilary,' he whispered, coming back to her. He held her hands. 'It's all been such a nightmare ... and the worst part was I couldn't tell you.'

Dear God, he was serious.

'I didn't want you to think I was a failure, that I couldn't ... I just didn't want you to find out, ever.'

'... *Hilary must never find out* ...' She felt sick. What had she done? 'Catherine!' she blurted out, clutching at the last remnants of what she'd thought was the truth. 'You've been seeing her. I know you have.'

He looked confused. 'My secretary? Or my new accountant? They're both called Catherine.'

Hilary swallowed. 'In your sleep ... you've been talking about Catherine ...' Her voice trailed away.

They stood in silence. Then David said, 'We might have to sell the house.'

She looked up at him, remembering his words in the car only yesterday – '*You love this house, don't you?*' 'And Philip ... his school fees?'

He shook his head. 'Hilary, I'm so sorry. It's the recession. I thought I could ride it out, I ...'

In disbelief she shook her head and then slumped down onto the bottom step of the stairs. 'How? How's all this happened? Surely this doesn't happen to people like us?'

He sat next to her. 'Hundreds of small businesses are going to the wall. Rents are so high these days. I thought I could sell the business to a chain. That's what I've been trying to set up with Catherine these past few months. But then they discovered things weren't as good as I'd tried to make out. They lowered their offer by half just this week. They've told me to take it or leave it.'

Hilary raised her eyes. 'But you could stay on as manager, couldn't you?'

He shook his head. 'They want me out.'

'Oh, David. Isn't there anything else we can do?'

'If I refuse this offer, word will get out and I'll be lucky to get even as much from anybody else.'

'Well, then, there's nothing else for it, I'll have to get a job,' she said briskly. 'I'll go back to teaching. I always said I would.'

He stared at her, but she lowered her eyes, unable to bear the suffering in his face.

The phone rang and made them both jump. Hilary went to answer it, glad of the diversion.

'Charlotte! ... Where are you? ... Lake Coniston ... Snowed in, I'm not surprised ... We're all fine ... Well, not really, David's just told me ... No, not an affair, after all ... It's the business, he's lost it ... I've no idea. Yes, well, it does explain things. Yes, I'll give him your love. 'Bye.' She put the receiver down.

'My God,' David said, 'did you really think I was having an affair?'

She walked through to the kitchen and he followed her. 'Hilary, did you?' His words were clearer now, as though he had sobered up.

She chewed her lip and nodded. 'It's always been my worst nightmare, David, that you might leave me ... I ... I just jumped to the conclusion that—'

'But how the hell did you manage to carry on as if nothing was happening?'

'I could ask you the same thing. How did you hide all your problems from me?'

'And Charlotte, did she think—?'

Hilary nodded again.

David rubbed his chin with his hand. 'I thought she was distant, that somehow she didn't approve of me.'

Hilary began to cry. 'Oh, David, I'm so sorry ... I feel dreadful that I thought the worst of you, when all the time you were going through hell and ...'

He smiled. It was the first time in months that she could remember him smiling.

'It'll be all right, won't it?' she said, as she tentatively reached out to his hands. She wasn't sure just what she was really asking him, but she knew that losing the business was nothing compared to what she had thought she was going to lose.

Chapter Thirty-nine

Star Struck was busy with people wanting to escape Boxing Day turkey remains. Tony Farrand himself was resplendent in one of his sparkly seventies game-show-host suits. He greeted Hilary and David at the door in his usual flamboyant manner and stuck out his tongue at Becky and Philip.

'I love Christmas,' he said, as he showed them to a table. He held a chair for Hilary. 'One day of being polite with the miserable old relatives and everybody's here wanting to lap up my scintillating company. What can I get you to drink? Something lavish and expensive – champagne?'

'Yes,' said David, 'why not?'

'But, David,' Hilary said, when Tony went off to fetch a bottle, 'we mustn't, we can't afford—'

'Today we'll eat and drink exactly what we want—'

'And tomorrow?'

He smiled. 'We'll see.'

'Are we going to be really poor?' Becky asked, tipping over the salt pot and making a white trail. She dipped her finger in the salt and then licked it. She looked up when nobody answered her question.

'I don't know,' Hilary replied awkwardly. She didn't know what to say. It was all so bewildering. One minute she had thought David was having an affair and the next he was about to join the ranks of the unemployed.

Last night, after David had explained everything to her, she had telephoned her parents. Her father had been wonderful and had insisted that Barbara and Jeffrey stay the night with them. 'You and David need to be alone,' he'd said. 'The children can stay as well.' But Neville's suggestion had been met with a firm refusal from Barbara. They had set off for Peterborough immediately, saying that neither of them was prepared to stay under the same roof with a woman who had been so intolerably rude. When Hilary had apologised to David for her mother's behaviour he had laughed and said that it was about time somebody had taken his mother in hand.

'We'll be a lot better off than some,' David said, meeting Hilary's gaze.

'Chloe's poor, isn't she, Mummy?'

Hilary thought of Georgia's tiny bungalow and the coldness of the caravan that she and Chloe had lived in and how she herself had viewed it all with an air of 'I couldn't possibly live like this'. But then she thought of the closeness between Georgia and her daughter. 'No,' she said at last, 'no, Chloe isn't poor.'

'You're very quiet,' David said to Philip, who was next to him, his head hidden behind the menu. 'What are you going to eat?'

'I'm not hungry,' Philip answered, his head still lowered.

David leaned into his son. 'You don't have to be that stoic,' he said. 'You can eat exactly what you want tonight.'

Philip looked up. 'Will I have to change schools?'

David frowned and Hilary's heart went out to him. 'Let's not talk about that,' he said.

'Only I'd like to.'

Hilary and David both stared at Philip. 'Why?' they said together.

'No big deal.' He shrugged. 'I just don't like it very much.'

'But you're doing so well,' Hilary said, 'your report was excellent at the end of term and Mr Wells himself told me—'

'I keep being picked on.' Philip's words were almost lost in the noise of a large party at a nearby table suddenly cheering.

'You mean you're being bullied?'

Philip looked up at his father. 'Yes,' he said, his voice still quiet, his face a picture of misery.

'Why didn't you tell us?' Hilary asked, every ounce of her wanting to protect her child. 'You should have told us. We could have helped.'

Philip shrugged again. 'You can't go running home to your parents every time something goes wrong at school.'

Hilary was appalled. All this time she'd been so pre-occupied with her own life that she'd been totally unaware of Philip's problems.

'Mum's right, you should have come to us,' David said, putting his arm round his son. 'But if you're anything like me,' he looked across the table at Hilary, 'or your mother, for that matter, you kept it to yourself because you thought you could sort it out on your own.'

Philip smiled awkwardly. 'So can I leave and go to the High where all my friends are?'

'We'll see.'

'I'll take that as a yes. Thanks, Dad.' His problems over, Philip picked up his menu and said, 'I'll have a pizza with everything on it and a large Coke.'

'I need the loo,' said Becky, who had now written her name in salt on the table in front of her.

'You'd better go with her, Philip,' laughed David.

As Philip shepherded his sister towards the toilets Tony Farrand arrived with their bottle of champagne. When he left, another waiter squeezed past their table with more customers.

Hilary felt a hand on her shoulder. 'Hello, Hilary.' It was Georgia with Chloe. 'Did Santa bring you what you wanted?' she asked, glancing at David.

'He brought a total surprise,' Hilary said. 'How about you?'

'The same, I guess,' she answered with a sly smile on her face. She turned away.

Hilary followed her gaze and saw Nick over by the door pulling off his overcoat and scarf and hanging them up. He came towards them.

'Hello,' he said, seeing Hilary and David. 'Happy Boxing Day.' He turned to Georgia. 'Have they kept our table for us?'

'Yes. You go on ahead with Chloe.' Georgia bent down and whispered in Hilary's ear, 'See you in the loos.'

'That all sounded rather cryptic,' David said, when they were alone.

Hilary laughed and, not giving any explanation, she said, 'I need the loo too. I'll have a pizza like Philip's.'

On her way to the toilets she crossed over with Becky and Philip and a couple of seconds after the door closed behind her it opened and in walked Georgia.

'Come on then, spill the beans.'

Hilary told her everything.

'Bloody hell and the stupid idiot couldn't bring himself to tell you because of his huge ego. It's the same old story, again and again.'

Hilary frowned. 'Don't be so hard on him.'

'I'm sorry. I didn't mean it quite like that. It's just that these poor fools are moulded into being super-beings and can't ever be seen to fail. I blame the parents.'

Hilary thought of David's parents. Georgia was right. She'd never thought of the pressure David must always have been under. All his life Barbara and Jeffrey had built him up to practically god-like status. She wondered now whether David in a strange way would feel relieved that he was no longer Mr Perfect, that no more would he have to stand precariously aloft the pedestal of his mother's making. She suddenly remembered what Nick had said to him the night of the bonfire when he'd asked him if he was frightened of not making the grade in some way. Poor David, no wonder he'd been so aggressive towards Nick. And no wonder there had been that scene at Derek and Cindy's.

'Aren't you going to ask me about Nick?' asked Georgia, looking at Hilary in the mirror.

Hilary smiled at the coincidence of their thoughts and delved into her handbag for her lipstick. 'Go on, then,' she said, through stretched lips. 'What have you been up to?'

'You were right about him being a good kisser. He's bloody good.'

Hilary laughed. 'Hypocrite!'

Georgia smiled. 'And, believe me, this is no meeting of the minds, this is purely physical. When I'm finished with him I'll send him on his way.'

'Will you, I wonder.'

'Oh, no, not you as well. Look, I'm having enough trouble in that department with Iris.'

'So how was Christmas with Iris?'

'Unbelievable! I've never known anyone to cheat so blat-antly at Scrabble.'

'I get the feeling she's taken a liking to you,' Hilary said, with a smile. 'I think it's rather sweet.'

'And since when has there been anything wrong in a simple case of mutual respect?'

'I think there's more to it than that.'

'You do, do you?' Georgia replied, looking in the mirror and straightening one of her ear-rings. 'And so what if she's decided I'm the daughter she never had? I don't have a problem with that. In fact, like you just said, it's rather sweet. Now get a move on, I've got a mug out there offering to buy me supper.'

When Hilary returned to David he was alone. He said, 'Tony's taken the children off with Chloe to watch the pizzas being tossed about the kitchen.' He handed her a flute of champagne. 'Do you remember the last time we came here and Philip was asking me how I loved you?'

'Yes. He was talking about different ways of loving, wasn't he?' She reached for a breadstick and broke it in two. She offered David half.

'I can't remember which way round it was,' David continued, 'whether it was *agape* or *eros*, but – and I know I'm not very good at this romantic stuff – but I love you unconditionally, Hilary.' He clinked his glass against hers. 'And I'm sorry for mucking up our lives and spoiling everything.'

She leaned across the table and pressed a finger to his lips. 'Nonsense, I think we were ready for a change anyway.' Then she kissed him, happy in the sure knowledge that whatever the future held, it could never be anything like the hell they'd both just put themselves through.

'You sound like you're already rolling up your sleeves to sort this mess out.'

She squeezed his hand. 'It's easy when you know what you're up against. It's the not knowing that turns your world upside down.'

*

'Boxing Day,' wrote Iris in her diary, sitting by the fire, 'spent quietly and alone listening to the radio. Tomorrow, though, Georgia and Chloe are coming for tea. Must remember to order an extra pint of milk and bake a cake.'

She closed the diary then flipped it open again and re-read her entry for Christmas Day: 'Quite a departure from the norm. Spent the day with Georgia and Chloe and that nice man, Mr Bradshaw. I can't recall a happier time. A change certainly does one good!'

All Orion/Phoenix titles are available at your local bookshop or from the following address:

Mail Order Department
Littlehampton Book Services
FREEPOST BR535
Worthing, West Sussex, BN13 3BR
telephone 01903 828503, *facsimile* 01903 828802
e-mail MailOrders@lbsltd.co.uk
(Please ensure that you include full postal address details)

Payment can be made either by credit/debit card (Visa, Mastercard, Access and Switch accepted) or by sending a £ Sterling cheque or postal order made payable to *Littlehampton Book Services*.
DO NOT SEND CASH OR CURRENCY.

Please add the following to cover postage and packing

UK and BFPO:
£1.50 for the first book, and 50p for each additional book to a maximum of £3.50

Overseas and Eire:
£2.50 for the first book plus £1.00 for the second book and 50p for each additional book ordered

---

BLOCK CAPITALS PLEASE

name of cardholder _____

address of cardholder _____

delivery address
(if different from cardholder)
_____
_____
_____

postcode _____   *postcode* _____

☐ I enclose my remittance for £_____

☐ please debit my Mastercard/Visa/Access/Switch (delete as appropriate)

card number ☐☐☐☐☐☐☐☐☐☐☐☐☐☐☐☐☐☐

expiry date ☐☐☐☐   Switch issue no. ☐☐

signature _____

prices and availability are subject to change without notice